Mo Hayder has written some of the most terrifying
crime thrillers you will ever read. Her first novel,
Birdman, was hailed as a '**first-class shocker**' by
the *Guardian* and her follow-up, *The Treatment*
was voted by *The Times* as one of '**the top ten
most scary thrillers ever written**'.

Mo's books are 100% authentic, drawing on her
long research association with several UK police
forces and on her personal encounters with criminals
and prostitutes. She left school at fifteen and has
worked as a barmaid, security guard, English teacher,
and even a hostess in a Tokyo club. She has an MA
in creative writing from Bath Spa University.
She now lives in England's West Country
and is a full-time writer.

www.mohayder.net

HAVE YOU READ THEM ALL?

The thrillers featuring
Detective Inspector Jack Caffery are:

BIRDMAN

Greenwich, south-east London. **DI Jack Caffery** is called
to one of the most gruesome crime scenes he has ever seen.
Five young women have been murdered – and it is only
a matter of time before the killer strikes again...

'A first class shocker'
Guardian

THE TREATMENT

Traumatic memories are wakened for **DI Jack Caffery** when
a husband and wife are discovered, imprisoned in their own
home. They are both near death. But worse is to come:
their young son is missing...

'Genuinely frightening'
Sunday Times

RITUAL

Recently arrived from London, **DI Jack Caffery** is now part of Bristol's Major Crime Investigation Unit. Soon he's looking for a missing boy – a search that leads him to a more terrifying place than anything he has known before.

'Intensely enthralling'
Observer

SKIN

When the decomposed body of a young woman is found near railway tracks just outside Bristol, all indications are that she's committed suicide. But **DI Jack Caffery** is not so sure – he is on the trail of someone predatory, and for the first time in a very long time he feels scared.

'Warped...bloodthirsty...
Hayder is brilliant at making you read on'
Daily Telegraph

GONE

A car has been stolen. On the back seat was an eleven-year-old girl, who is still missing. It should be a simple case, but **DI Jack Caffery** knows that something is badly wrong. Because the car-jacker seems to be ahead of the police – every step of the way...

'Grips her readers by the scruffs of their necks'
The Times

Have you read Mo Hayder's stand-alone thrillers?

THE DEVIL OF NANKING

Desperate and alone in an alien city, student Grey Hutchins accepts a job as a hostess in an exclusive club. There she meets an ancient gangster rumoured to rely on a strange elixir for his continued health; it is an elixir others want – at any price...

'Left me stunned and haunted. This is writing of breathtaking power and poetry'
Tess Gerritsen

PIG ISLAND

When journalist Joe Oakes visits a secretive religious community on a remote Scottish island, he is forced to question the nature of evil – and whether he might be responsible for the terrible crime about to unfold.

'The most terrifying thriller you'll read all year'
Karin Slaughter

HANGING HILL

MO HAYDER

BANTAM BOOKS

LONDON • TORONTO • SYDNEY • AUCKLAND • JOHANNESBURG

TRANSWORLD PUBLISHERS
61–63 Uxbridge Road, London W5 5SA
A Random House Group Company
www.transworldbooks.co.uk

HANGING HILL
A BANTAM BOOK: 9780553824360

First published in Great Britain
in 2011 by Bantam Press
an imprint of Transworld Publishers
Bantam edition published 2012

Addresses for Random House Group Ltd companies outside the UK
can be found at: www.randomhouse.co.uk
The Random House Group Ltd Reg. No. 954009

The Random House Group Limited supports The Forest Stewardship
Council (FSC®), the leading international forest certification
organisation. Our books carrying the FSC label are printed on FSC®
certified paper. FSC is the only forest certification scheme endorsed
by the leading environmental organisations, including Greenpeace.
Our paper procurement policy can be found at
www.randomhouse.co.uk/environment

Typeset in Sabon by Falcon Oast Graphic Art Ltd.
Printed in Great Britain by Clays Ltd, St Ives plc

2 4 6 8 10 9 7 5 3 1

HANGING HILL

The funeral was held in an Anglican church on a hill just outside the ancient spa town of Bath. Over a thousand years old, the church was no bigger than a chapel, and its driveway was too small for the reporters and photographers who jostled each other for a good vantage-point. It was a warm day, the smells of grass and honeysuckle drifting across the graveyard as the mourners arrived. Some deer, which were used to coming here in the afternoons to nibble moss from the gravestones, were startled by the activity. They bounded away, leaping the low stone walls and disappearing into the surrounding forests.

As people filed into the church two women stayed outside, sitting motionless on a bench under a white buddleia. Butterflies swatted and flitted around the blooms over their heads but the women didn't raise their eyes to look. They were united in their silence – in their numbness and disbelief at the string of events that had led them to this place. Sally and Zoë Benedict. Sisters, though no one would know it to look at them. The tall, rangy one was Zoë, the elder by a year; her sister Sally, much smaller and more contained, still had the round, uncluttered face of a child. She sat looking down at her small hands and the tissue she'd been kneading and tearing into shreds.

'It's harder than I expected,' she said. 'I mean – I don't know if I can go in. I thought I could, but now I'm not so sure.'

'Me neither,' Zoë murmured. 'Me neither.'

They sat for a while in silence. One or two people came up the steps – people they didn't recognize. Then some of Millie's friends: Peter and Nial. Awkward-looking in their formal suits, their formal expressions.

'His sister's here,' Zoë said, after a while. 'I spoke to her on the steps.'

'His sister? I didn't know he had one.'

'He does.'

'Strange to think he'd have a family. What does she look like?'

'Nothing like him, thank God. But she's asked if she can speak to you.'

'What does she want?'

Zoë shrugged. 'To apologize, I suppose.'

'What did you say?'

'What do you think I said? No. Of course the answer's no. She's gone inside.' She glanced over her shoulder at the doors to the church. The vicar was standing there, talking in a quiet voice to Steve Finder, Sally's new boyfriend. He was a good man,

Zoë thought, the sort who could hold Sally together without ever suffocating her. She needed someone like that. He glanced up, caught Zoë looking at him and nodded. He held up his wrist, tapping his watch to indicate it was time. The vicar put his hands on the doors, ready to draw them closed. Zoë got to her feet. 'Come on. We may as well get it over with.'

Sally didn't move. 'I need to ask you something, Zoë. About what happened.'

Zoë hesitated. This wasn't the right time to be talking about it. They couldn't change the past by discussing it. But she sat down again. 'OK.'

'It's going to sound strange.' Sally turned the bits of tissue over and over in her hands. 'But do you think, looking back . . . do you think you could have seen it coming?'

'Oh, Sally – no. No, I don't. Being a cop doesn't make you a psychic. Whatever the public wish.'

'I just wondered. Because . . .'

'Because what?'

'Because looking back I think *I* could have seen it. I think I got a warning about it. I know that sounds nuts, but I think I did. A warning. Or a premonition. Or some kind of foresight, whatever you call it.'

'No, Sally. That's crazy.'

'I know – and at the time that's what I thought. I thought it was stupid. But now I can't help thinking that if I'd been paying attention, if I'd foreseen all of this . . .' she opened her hands to indicate the church, the hearse pulled up at the bottom of the steps, the

11

outside-broadcast units and the photographers '. . . I could have stopped it.'

Zoë thought about this for a while. There had been a time, not so long ago, when she'd have laughed at a statement like that. But now she wasn't so sure. The world was a strange place. She glanced up at Steve and the vicar, then back at her sister. 'You never told me about a "warning". What sort of warning? When did it happen?'

'When?' Sally shook her head. 'I'm not completely sure. But I think it was the day the business with Lorne Wood started.'

Part One

Part One

1

It had been a spring afternoon in early May, the time of year when the evenings were lengthening, and the primulas and tulips under the trees had long frayed and gone blowsy. The signs of warmer weather had made everyone optimistic, and for the first time in months Sally had come to Isabelle's for lunch. The sun was still high in the sky and their teenage children were out in the garden, while the two women opened a bottle of wine and stayed in the kitchen. The windows were open, the gingham curtains fluttering lightly in the breeze, and from her place at the table Sally watched the teenagers. They'd known each other since nursery, but it wasn't until the last twelve months or so that Millie had shown any interest in coming up here to Isabelle's house. Now, however, they were a gang – a proper little group – two girls, two boys, two years apart in age, but at the same private school, Kingsmead. Sophie, Isabelle's youngest at fifteen, was doing handstands in the garden, her dark ringlets bouncing all over the place. Millie, the same age, but a head shorter, was holding her legs up. The girls were dressed in similar jeans and halter-necks, though Millie's clothes were faded and threadbare in comparison to Sophie's.

'I'll have to do something about that,' Sally said ruminatively. 'Her school uniform is falling to pieces too. I went to Matron to see if I could get a second-hand one, but she didn't have any left in Millie's size. Seems all the parents at Kingsmead want second-hand now.'

'That's a sign of the times,' said Isabelle. She was making treacle tart – weighting the pastry base with the handful of marbles she kept in a jar on top of the fridge. The butter and golden syrup were bubbling in the pan, filling the kitchen with a heavy, nutty smell. 'I've always passed on Sophie's things to Matron.' She dropped the marbles and pushed the pie dish into the oven. 'But from now on I'll save them for Millie. Sophie's a size up from her.'

She wiped her floury hands on her apron and stood for a moment, studying her friend. Sally knew what she was thinking – that Sally's face was pale and lined, that her hair wasn't clean. She was probably seeing the pink HomeMaids cleaning-agency tabard she wore over her faded jeans and floral top and feeling pity. Sally didn't mind. She was slowly, after all this time, beginning to get used to pity. It was the divorce, of course. The divorce and Julian's new wife and baby.

'I wish I could do something more to help.'

'You do help, Isabelle.' She smiled. 'You still talk to me. Which is more than some of the other mums at Kingsmead do.'

'Is it that bad? Still?'

Worse, she thought. But she smiled. 'It'll be fine.'

'Really?'

'Really. I mean – I've spoken to the bank manager and I've moved all my loans around so I'm not paying so much interest. And I'm getting more hours with the agency now.'

'I don't know how you do it, working like you do.'

Sally shrugged. 'Other people do it.'

'Yes, but other people are used to it.'

She watched Isabelle go to the hob and stir the treacle. There were bags of flour and oats opened on the side. Every article bore names like 'Waitrose', or 'Finest' or 'Goodies Delicatessen'. At Sally and Millie's cottage all the packets had 'Value' or 'Lidl' written on them and the freezer was full of the feeble, stringy vegetables she'd struggled to grow in the back garden – that was a money lesson Sally had learned in a hurry: vegetable-growing was for the idle rich. It was far cheaper to buy them in the super-market. Now she nibbled her thumbnail and watched Isabelle moving around the kitchen – her familiar, sturdy back in the sensible mud-coloured shorts and blouse. Her apron with the flower sprigs on it. They'd been friends for years, and she was the person Sally most trusted, the first person she'd go to for advice. Even so, she felt a little shy of talking about what was on her mind.

Eventually, though, she went to her bag and pulled out a blue folder. It was shabby and only held together with an elastic band. She carried it to the table, set it down next to the wine glasses, pulled off the band and emptied out the contents. Hand-painted cards, embellished with beads, ribbons and feathers, all sealed down with varnish. She placed them on the table and sat there uncertainly, half ready to snatch them up and shovel them back into the bag.

'Sally?' Isabelle lifted the pan off the heat and, still stirring, came over to look. 'You didn't do these, did you?' She peered at the top one. It showed a woman wearing a violet shawl, sprinkled with stars, that she had pulled across her face so only her eyes were showing. 'God – they're beautiful. What are they?'

'Tarot cards.'

'Tarot? You're not going all Glastonbury on us, are you? Going to tell us all our futures?'

'Of course not.'

Isabelle put down the pot and picked up the second card. It showed a tall woman holding a large, transparent star at arm's length. She seemed to be gazing through it at the clouds and the sun. Her tangly dark hair, flecked with grey, hung long down her back. Isabelle gave a small, embarrassed smile. 'That's not me, is it?'

'Yes.'

'Oh, honestly, Sally – you're a bit too flattering with the cleavage, if you don't mind.'

'If you look through them all you'll see lots of faces you know.'

Isabelle shuffled through the paintings, stopping from time to time when she recognized someone.

18

'Sophie! And Millie too. You've painted us all – the kids too. They are *beautiful*.'

'I was wondering,' Sally said tentatively, 'if I might be able to sell them. Maybe to that hippie shop in Northumberland Place. What do you think?'

Isabelle turned and gave her an odd look. Half puzzled, half amused, as if she wasn't quite sure whether Sally was joking or not.

Instantly Sally knew she'd made a mistake and began hastily pulling the cards together, a blush of embarrassment racing up her neck. 'No – I mean, of course they're not good enough. I knew they weren't.'

'No. Don't put them away. They're great. Really great. It's just that . . . Do you really think you'd get enough from them to help you with the – you know . . . the debts?'

Sally stared down at the cards. Her face was burning. She shouldn't have said anything. Isabelle was right – she'd make hardly anything from selling the cards. Certainly not enough to make a dent in her debt. She was stupid. So stupid.

'But not because they aren't good, Sally. They're brilliant! Honestly, they're great. Look at this!' Isabelle held up a painting of Millie. Little crazy Millie, always smaller than the others and surely not a product of Sally, with the choppy fringe and mad, shaggy red hair, like a little Nepalese street child. Her eyes as wild and wide as an animal's – just like her aunt Zoë's. 'It's just great. It really looks like her. And this one of Sophie – it's lovely. Lovely! And Nial,

19

and Peter!' Nial was Isabelle's shy son, her older child, Peter Cyrus his good-looking friend – the hell-raiser and the favourite of all the girls. 'And Lorne – look at her – and another of Millie. And another of Sophie, and me again. And—' She stopped suddenly, looking down at one card. 'Oh,' she said, with a shiver. 'Oh.'

'What?'

'I don't know. Something's wrong with the paint on this one.'

Sally pulled it towards her. It was the Princess of Wands – pictured in a swirling red dress, struggling to hold back a tiger that strained on a leash. Millie had been the model for this one too, except that something had happened to her face on this card. Sally ran a finger over it, pressed it. Maybe the acrylic had cracked, or somehow faded, because although the body and clothing and background were as she'd painted them, the face was blurred. Like a painting by Francis Bacon, or Lucian Freud. One of those terrifying images that seemed to see beyond the skin of the subject right through into their flesh.

'Yuk,' said Isabelle. 'Yuk. I'm glad I don't believe in this stuff. Otherwise I'd be really worried now. Like it's a warning or something.'

Sally didn't answer. She was staring at the face. It was as if a hand had been there and stirred Millie's features.

'Sally? You don't believe in stuff like that, do you?'

Sally pushed the card into the bottom of the pile.

She looked up and blinked. 'Of course not. Don't be silly.'

Isabelle scraped the chair back and carried the pot to the hob. Sally pulled the cards into an untidy pile, shoved them into her bag and took a hurried sip of wine. She'd have liked to drink it all at once, to loosen the uneasy knot that had just tied itself in her stomach. She'd have liked to get a little squiffy, then sit out in the sun on deckchairs with Isabelle the way they used to – back when she still had a husband and the time to do what she wanted. She hadn't realized how lucky she was back then. Now she couldn't drink in the sun, even on a Sunday. She couldn't afford the good sort of wine Isabelle drank. And when lunch was finished here, instead of the garden she was going to work. Maybe, she thought, rubbing the back of her neck wearily, it was just what she deserved.

'Mum? *Mum!*'

Both women turned. Millie stood in the doorway, red-faced and out of breath. Her jeans were covered with grass stains, and her phone was held up to face them both.

'Millie?' Sally straightened. 'What is it?'

'Can we switch on your computer, Mrs Sweetman? They're all tweeting about it. It's Lorne. She's gone missing.'

21

2

At the police station, just two miles away in central Bath, Lorne Wood was all anyone could talk about. A sixteen-year-old pupil of a local private school, Faulkener's, she was popular – and fairly reliable, according to her parents. From the get-go, Sally's sister, Detective Inspector Zoë Benedict, hadn't had even a speck of confidence that Lorne would be seen alive again. Maybe that was just Zoë – too pragmatic by far – but at two o'clock that afternoon, when one of the search team beating the undergrowth next to the Kennet and Avon canal found a body, she wasn't in the slightest surprised.

'Not that I'd ever say "I told you so",' she murmured to DI Ben Parris, as they walked along the towpath. She kept her hands shoved in the pockets of the black jeans the superintendent was always telling her she shouldn't wear as a warranted officer with a duty to the image of the force. 'You'd never hear those words come out of my mouth.'

'Of course not.' He didn't take his eyes off the group of people up ahead. 'It wouldn't be in your nature.'

The site had already been cordoned off, with portable screens fixed in place across the path. Hovering outside the screen were ten or twelve people – barge owners, mostly, and already a member of the press, dressed in a black waterproof. As the two DIs pushed their way through, warrant cards held up, he raised his Nikon and fired off a few shots. He was a sure sign that word was getting out faster than the police could keep up with, thought Zoë.

An area of nearly two thousand square metres had been cordoned off, away from the eyes of the public. The path was loose, chalky gravel giving way on one side to the bulrushes of the canal, on the other to a tangle of undergrowth – cow parsley, nettles and grass. Officers had left a gap of about fifty metres between the screens and the inner cordon, limited by police tape. Thirty metres or so past that, in a part of the undergrowth that formed a natural tunnel, stood a white tent.

Zoë and Ben pulled on white forensic suits, tightened the hoods, and added gloves. They ducked into the tent. The air inside was warm and packed with the scents of crushed grass and earth, the ground crisscrossed with lightweight aluminium tread plates.

'It's her.' The crime-scene manager stood a foot inside, making notes on a clipboard. He didn't look up at them. 'No doubt. Lorne Wood.'

Behind him at the end of a walkway the crime-scene photographer was circling a muddy tarpaulin, taking video.

'The tarp's the type they use to cover firewood on

the barges. But no one on this stretch of canal is missing one. The guy threw it over her. To look at her you'd think she was in bed.'

He was right. Lorne was lying on her back, as if asleep, one arm resting on top of the tarp, which was pulled up to her chest like a duvet. Her head was lolling to one side, turned up and away from the tent entrance. Zoë couldn't see her face, but she could see the T-shirt. Grey – with 'I am Banksy' across the chest. The one Lorne had been wearing when she'd left her house yesterday afternoon. 'What time was she reported missing?'

'Eight,' said Ben. 'She was supposed to be on her way home.'

'We've found her keys,' said the CSM, 'but still no phone. There's a dive team coming to search the canal later.'

In the corner of the tent a technician dropped a pair of black ballet pumps into a bag. He put a red flag in the ground, then sealed the bag and signed across the seal. 'Was that where they were found?' she asked him.

He nodded. 'Right there. Both of them.'

'Kicked off? Pulled off?'

'Taken off. They were like this.' The CSM held out his hands, straight and neatly together. 'Just placed there.'

'Is that mud on them?'

'Yes. But not from here. From the towpath somewhere.'

'And this grass – the way it's been flattened?'

24

'The struggle.'

'It's not much,' she said.

'No. Seems to have been over quickly.'

The photographer had finished videoing. He stepped back to allow Zoë and Ben to approach the body. The tread plates divided into two directions at the foot of the tarpaulin and circled the body. Zoë and Ben went carefully, taking the side that led to Lorne's face. They stood for a long time in silence, looking down at her. They'd both been working in CID for more than a decade and in that time they'd dealt with just a handful of murders. Nothing like this.

Zoë looked up at the CSM. She could feel her eyes wanting to water. 'What's made her face go like that?'

'We're not sure. We think it's a tennis ball between her teeth.'

'Christ,' said Ben. 'Christ.'

The CSM was right: a piece of duct tape had been placed across Lorne's mouth. It was holding in place a spherical object that had been jammed inside as far as it would go, luminous green tufts visible at the top and bottom. It had forced her jaw open so wide she seemed to be snarling or screaming. Her nose was squashed into a bloodied clot, her eyes were screwed up tight. There was more blood in her hair. Two distinct lines of it ran from under the duct tape down to her jaw – almost in the places the jaw of a ventriloquist's dummy would be hinged, except that they met her jaw almost under her ears. She must have been lying on her back when the bleeding had happened.

'Where's it coming from?'

'Her mouth.'

'She's bitten her tongue?'

The CSM shrugged. 'Or maybe the skin's split.'

'*Split?*'

He touched the corners of his mouth. 'A tennis ball forced into her mouth? It would put strain on the skin here.'

'Skin can't spl—' she began, but then she remembered that skin *could* split. She'd seen it on the backs and faces of suicide victims who'd jumped from high buildings. The impact often split their skin. The thought put a cold weight in her stomach.

'Have you pulled back the tarp?' Ben was leaning over, trying to peer under the tarpaulin. 'Can we see?'

'The pathologist's asked no one else to touch it – asked that you come to the PM. He – I— Both of us want her down to the mortuary just as she is. Tarp and all.'

'So, I'm guessing there's a sexual element?'

The CSM sniffed. 'Yes. You can definitely say there is. A strong sexual element.'

'Well?' Ben checked his watch and turned to Zoë. 'What do you want to do?'

She dragged her eyes away from Lorne's face and watched the officer on the other side of the tent label the bag with the shoes in it. 'I think . . .' she murmured '. . . I think I want to take a walk.'

3

For a while Lorne Wood had been part of Millie and Sophie's little group – but then, about a year ago, she had seemed to grow apart from the other girls. Maybe they hadn't had that much in common to begin with – she had been at a different school, was a year older and always struck Sally as more sophisticated. She was the prettiest of them all and she seemed to know it. A blonde with milky skin and classic blue eyes. A true beauty.

That lunchtime the teenagers gathered around the computer in Isabelle's study, trying to get all the gossip they could, trying to piece together what had happened from Facebook and Twitter. There wasn't much news – the police hadn't made any public statements since the one they'd issued this morning, confirming she was missing. It seemed Lorne had last been seen by her mother yesterday afternoon when she'd headed into town, on foot, for a shopping expedition. Her Facebook page hadn't been updated in that time and no calls had been made on her mobile: apparently, when her parents had rung, the phone was switched off.

'It could just be a tiff,' Isabelle said, when the kids had gone back outside. 'Fed up with her parents, run off with a boyfriend. I did it when I was that age – teach your parents a lesson, that sort of thing.'

'Probably,' agreed Sally. 'Maybe.'

It was nearly one thirty. Time to get going. She began to pack up her things, thinking about Lorne. She'd met her only a handful of times, but she recalled her as a determined girl, with a slightly sad air. She remembered sitting in the garden with her one day, when she and Millie were still living with Julian in Sion Road, and Lorne saying, quite out of the blue, 'Millie's so lucky. You know – for it to be just her.'

'Just her?'

'No brothers or sisters.'

That had come as a surprise to Sally. 'I thought you got on with your brother.'

'Not really.'

'Isn't he kind to you?'

'Oh, yes, he's very kind. He's kind. And he's nice. And he's clever.' She pushed her hair away from her pretty face. 'He's perfect. Does *everything* Mum and Dad want. That's what I mean. Millie's lucky.'

It had stuck in Sally's mind, that exchange, and it came back to her now as clearly as if it had happened yesterday. She'd never heard anyone say it was a dis-advantage to have a brother or a sister before. Maybe people thought it, but she'd never heard anyone actually voice it.

28

'I wish they wouldn't do that.' Sally looked up. Isabelle was standing in the window, frowning out at the garden. 'I've lost count of the number of times I've told them.'

Sally got up and joined her. The garden was long, planted with fruit trees and surrounded by huge poplars that rustled and bent when so much as a breath of wind came through. 'Where are they all?'

Isabelle pointed. 'See? At the end. Sitting on the stile. I know what they're thinking.'

'Do you?'

'Oh, yes. Pollock's Farm. They're wondering if they can get down there before we notice.'

Isabelle's house was a mile to the north of Bath on the escarpment where the steep slopes of Lansdown levelled out. To the north-west were the lowlands and the golf courses; to the east, and butting up to Isabelle's garden, was Pollock's Farm. It had been derelict for three years since the owner, old man Pollock, had gone mad and had started, so people said, drinking sheep dip. The crops stood dead in the field, weed-choked; dead brown maize heads drooped on their stems. Half-dismantled machinery rusted along the tracks, pig troughs filled with stagnant rainwater, and the decomposing pyramids of silage had been broken into by rats and gnawed until they seemed like the crumbling ruins of a forgotten civilization. The place was notoriously dangerous – not just for the hazards in the fields, but for the way the land stopped abruptly in the middle, interrupted by an ancient quarry that had cut a steep drop into the hillside. The farmhouse was at the bottom of the quarry – you could stand in the top fields and look down through the trees on to its roof. It was where old man Pollock had died – in his armchair in front of the television. He'd sat there for months, while the seasons changed, the house decayed and the electricity was turned off, until he'd been discovered by a meths addict searching for privacy.

'The boys are worse since that happened. Honestly, it's like a magnet to them. They gee each other up. They just love frightening themselves, daring each other.' Isabelle sighed, turned away from the window and went back to the cooker where the treacle tart was cooling on a rack. 'It doesn't matter what I say. They pretend they don't but I know they still go there. Or if not them, then someone. I went down there about a month ago – and it's awful. The place is littered with crisp packets, cider bottles, every disgusting thing you could imagine. It won't be long before one of them steps on a syringe. I found a beer can in Nial's bin the other day and I don't trust Peter. I've seen scabs around his mouth. Do you know what that means?'

'No.'

'I don't either. I suppose I automatically thought drugs. Maybe I should tell his mother – who knows? Anyway – that place.' She gestured at the window. 'It doesn't help at all. The sooner the probate is sorted and they've sold it the better. I've told the gardener over and over again to close the stile off – but he just won't get round to it. They're at this age and you can't help thinking . . .'

She gave a little shiver. Her eyes went briefly to Sally's bag. Perhaps thinking about Millie's face on the tarot. Or maybe Lorne Wood. Missing for sixteen hours. Then her expression cleared. 'Don't worry,' she said. 'I'll keep an eye on her. I'll run her over to Julian's at six. There's absolutely nothing for you to worry about.'

4

It had been Lorne Wood's habit that spring to go shopping in town, then walk home, taking a route through Sydney Gardens, then out on to the towpath where her house was – about half a mile to the east. Sydney Gardens was the oldest park in Bath, famous for its replica Roman temple of Minerva. It was also notorious for cottagers – you only had to step one pace off the path to see a young man, nicely dressed, standing sheepishly in the bushes, a hopeful smile on his face. Parents frog-marched their children past the vicinity of the toilets, talking loudly to distract their attention, and dog-walkers regularly came to the local vets with dogs choking on used condoms scavenged from the undergrowth. A railway line ran through the park – police teams had thoroughly searched it already, as it wasn't unknown for bodies to be pulverized and scattered by a speeding train to the point at which they seemed to have disappeared altogether. Now, however, the search teams weren't looking for a body. They were looking for clues about Lorne's journey from town to the place she'd been killed.

Zoë and Ben walked down the canal path not speaking. From time to time one of them would stop and peer into the bushes on the right, or down into the impenetrable canal water, hoping to catch sight of something significant that the teams had missed. About a quarter of a mile back into town Zoë stopped at a small gate in a wall. The woody branches of a wisteria hung over it, the pendulous purple racemes just beginning to open. The gate led into Sydney Gardens. It was probably the place Lorne had got on to the towpath. Zoë and Ben stood opposite each other, faces lowered, considering the patch of mud between their feet.

'Is it what was on her shoes?' he asked.

'It's the same colour.'

Ben raised his head and scanned the path – the puddles that straddled the gravel. It had rained yesterday, but the sun was drying it now. 'A lot of places in Bath have mud this colour. It's the limestone in the earth.'

Zoë eyed the puddles. She was thinking about the shoes. Ballet pumps. Unsuitable for walking, really, but all the girls wore them these days.

Ben put his hands in his pockets and squinted up at the sky. 'So?' he said quietly. 'What do you think's under that tarp?'

'Christ knows.'

'Boss?' DC Goods, one of the team, was coming along the path towards them, waving to attract their attention. 'I've got a woman wants to speak to you.'

'A woman?'

'One of the live-aboards. Some of the owners got a good view of the crime scene before it was cordoned. They got the lie of the land. This one saw the body – just a glimpse. She's got something she wants to tell you.'

'Great.' Zoë set off down the path at a pace, Ben a few steps behind her. Her head was buzzing. It would be really nice – *really* nice – to tuck a solved murder into her portfolio. Be able to stand up in front of the force and Lorne Wood's family and say she'd found the killer. The person who'd shoved a tennis ball into their daughter's mouth. And done God only knew what else to her.

The barge wasn't far from the park – at least a quarter of a mile from the crime scene. It was brightly painted, with flowers daubed all over the cabin, the name *Elfwood* carved across the stern. On the roof, next to the little chimney, were piled provisions – coal, wood, water bottles, a bicycle. Ben rapped twice on the roof, then jumped on to the aft deck and bent to look down into the cabin. 'Hello?'

'I'm here,' said a voice. 'Come in.'

He and Zoë went down the steps, bending their necks to avoid the low ceiling. It was like going into Aladdin's cave – every surface, the ceiling, the walls, the cupboards, had been adorned with wooden sculptures of tree nymphs. The windows were hung with glittering cheesecloth in shades of purple and pink, and everything smelt of cats and patchouli oil. Not much sunlight filtered through, just enough for them to make out a woman of about fifty, with very long curly hennaed hair, perched on one of the bulk-head seats, a roll-up cigarette in her hand. She wore a circlet of flowers in her hair and a huge velvet cape that fastened at the neck and was open to reveal a lace blouse and a skirt with tiny gold mirrors stitched on it. Her bare legs and feet, crammed into rubber-soled sandals, were very white. Like the jars of duck fat you saw lined up when the French market came to Bath in the summer.

'Good.' She took a long draw on the cigarette. 'Nice to see the police doing something worthwhile instead of busting the innocent.'

'I'm DI Benedict.' Zoë put her hand out. 'Pleased to meet you.'

The woman put the cigarette into her mouth and shook the hand. She peered at Zoë through the smoke, getting the measure of her. After a moment or two she seemed satisfied. 'Amy,' she said. 'And him? Who's he?'

'DI Ben Parris.' Ben offered his hand.

Amy shook it, eyeing him suspiciously. Then she took the cigarette out of her mouth and motioned for them to sit down. 'No tea – generator died on me two weeks ago, and you really don't want to see me doing my thing with the Primus stove.'

'That's OK. We won't be long.' Zoë pulled out her pocketbook. After all these years, with all the tech-nology available, the force still liked everything noted in handwriting. Even so, she usually backed it up by recording everything on her iPhone. Technically she shouldn't, not without asking permission, but she did it anyway. She'd developed a technique – a quick pass of the hand over her pocket, knew the keys without looking. Beep-beep with her fingers and she was recording, pretending with the notepad. 'Our constable said you had something you wanted to talk about.'

'Yes,' said Amy. Her eyes were very intense, spiralled with broken veins. 'I saw the body. Lots of us did.'

'That was unfortunate,' Ben said. 'We do our utmost to preserve scenes. Sometimes we don't manage it.'

'Did you know,' she said, 'that you can see the soul leave the body? If you watch hard enough you'll see it.'

Zoë lowered her face and pretended to write in her notepad. If Goodsy had brought them down here to hear about souls and spirits she'd kill him. 'So – Amy. Did you see a soul? Leaving her body?'

She shook her head. 'It had already gone. A long time ago.'

'How long?'

'When she died. Last night. They don't hang around. It has to be the first half an hour.'

'How do you know it was last night?'

'Because of the bracelet.'

Ben raised an eyebrow. 'The bracelet?'

'She was wearing a bracelet. I saw it. When they found her body I saw the bracelet.'

Amy was right – Lorne had been wearing a bracelet. A dangly charm bracelet with a plated silver

36

skull and miniature cutlery: a knife, fork and spoon. Also a lucky '16', which she'd got for her birthday. It had been listed by her parents in the missing-persons report.

'What about the bracelet? Why's that important?'

'Because I heard it. Last night.' She took another deep drag, held it, then let it all out in a long, bluish stream. 'You hear it all – sitting in here you hear every part of life. They all use the towpath, don't they? You get the fights and the quarrels, the parties and the lovers. Mostly it's just bike bells. Last night it was a girl with something dangling. Chink-chink, it went.' She held up her finger and thumb, opened and closed them like a little beak. 'Chink-chink.'

'OK. And anything else?'

'Apart from the chink-chink? Not much.'

'Not much?'

'No. Unless you count the conversation.'

'The conversation?' Ben said. 'There was a conversation too?'

'On the phone. You get used to knowing if it's on the phone. At first, when I moved here, I used to think they were talking to a ghost – wandering along chit-chatting, no one answering. It took me ages to work it out. I don't do technology – haven't got a mobile phone and I won't. Thank you very much.' She gave a small, polite nod – as if Ben had offered her a free mobile and she'd been forced, graciously, to turn him down.

'And you think it was Lorne?'

'I'm sure it was.'

'You didn't see her?'

'Just her feet. Wearing the same shoes as the ones that were next to her body. I saw those too, when they found her body. I take these things in.'

'What time was this?'

'A little before eight? It was quiet – the rush had finished. I'd say maybe seven thirty, seven forty-five?'

'You sure?'

'I'm sure.'

Zoë and Ben exchanged glances. When Lorne had gone missing, the OIC – the officer in charge of the missing-persons case – had got historical cell site analysis on her phone, which revealed she'd had one phone conversation yesterday evening, with her friend – a call that finished at seven forty-five. That must be what Amy had overheard. Which gave them an accurate time for when Lorne was on the path.

'Amy,' Ben said, 'did you hear what she was talking about?'

'I heard one thing. Just one. She said, "Oh, God, I've had enough . . ."'

'"Oh, God, I've had enough"?'

'Yes.'

'So she was upset?'

'A bit fed up, maybe. But not crying or anything. Sad – but not scared.'

Ben wrote something down. 'And she was definitely alone? You didn't hear anyone else with her?'

'No.' Amy was clear. 'She was alone.'

'So she said, "Oh, God, I've had enough," and then . . .'

38

'Then she just walked on. Chink-chink-chink.' Amy clenched the cigarette between her teeth, eyes screwed up against the smoke, and waved her hand back in the direction of the crime scene. 'That way. Off to where it happened. I didn't hear anything after that. Not until she turned up dead. Raped, too, I suppose. I mean, that's what it's usually about – men and the way they hate women.'

Raped, too, I suppose. Zoë glanced up out of the window, at the sun falling on the towpath, and wondered what was under the tarpaulin Lorne had been covered with. Truthfully, she'd like to find a way of wriggling out of the PM. She couldn't, of course. Something like that would get around the force in no time.

They sat a bit longer and talked to Amy, but apart from the phone conversation, she didn't have anything to add to the case. Eventually Ben got to his feet. 'You've been very helpful. Thank you.'

Zoë rose and followed him. He'd already got to the deck and she was still in the galley when a loud, meaningful cough from behind stopped her. She turned and saw Amy smiling at her, a finger to her lips. 'What?'

'Him,' Amy hissed, jabbing a finger at the deck. 'There's no point you wasting your time on him. He's gay. You can see it from the way he wears his clothes.'

Zoë looked back to the staircase. Ben was waiting on deck in the sunlight, his shadow lying a short way down the stairs. She could see his shoes, well polished, expensive. His suit – which was probably off-the-peg M&S – he managed to wear as if it was Armani. Amy was right – he looked like something from an aftershave ad. 'This isn't something we should be talking about,' she murmured. 'Not under the circumstances.'

'I know, but he is, isn't he?' Amy smiled. 'Go on. He has to be.'

'I really wouldn't know. It's not the sort of thing I've ever given any thought to. Now.' She looked at her watch. 'I'm on my way. Thank you, Amy. You've given me a lot to think about.'

5

Sally tried not to work at the weekend, but the job she had on a Sunday paid well and wasn't as lonely as the others, because the agency had teamed her with two other cleaners. Marysieńka and Danuta – two good-natured blondes from Gdańsk, who wore lots of foundation to work and had their nails done at the new Korean parlour on Westgate Street. They had the use of the agency's pink-painted Honda Jazz with the HomeMaids logo in purple vinyl stuck on the side of the car. Marysieńka always drove – her boyfriend had a job with the First Bus Company and had taught her to negotiate British traffic like a rally driver. 'The first rule,' she maintained, 'is he who hesitates gets fucked.' That would make Danuta shriek with laughter as the little HomeMaids car shot out into traffic, forcing the sedate drivers of north Bath to slam on their brakes. The two Poles were nice girls who took cigarette breaks and sometimes smelt vaguely of fish and chips, as if maybe they shared a flat above a takeaway. Sally always imagined they talked about her when the day was finished – made promises to each other never to get that desperate, that downtrodden.

Today they picked Sally up at the end of Isabelle's long driveway. They were dressed in white jeans and heels under their pink cleaning tabards and they kept the window open, arms out, smoking and banging on the side of the car in time to the radio. They were in their twenties: they wouldn't have anything to do with a schoolgirl from the nice side of town, so Sally didn't talk about Lorne being missing. She sat in the back, chewing Airwaves gum to kill the smell of wine on her breath, watching the hedgerow race past and thinking of what else she remembered about Lorne. She'd met her mother once – her name was Polly. Or Pippa or something . . . Anyway – maybe Isabelle was right: maybe she had run away because of something going on at home. But missing? Really, really missing? And from what the kids had seen on Twitter the police were taking it very seriously, as if something awful had happened to her.

The women's client that day – David Goldrab – lived out past the racecourse and along the main route out of Bath on a side road off the area called Hanging Hill, where the great Lansdown battle between the royalists and the parliamentarians had been fought nearly four hundred years ago. It was a funny place, noticeable chiefly for the landmark known locally as the Caterpillar, a line of trees on the crest of the facing hill that could be seen for miles around. But Hanging Hill was also, to Sally's mind, vaguely sinister. As if it had been infected by its history, an air of corruption seemed to hang over everything. Local rumour had it that the Brinks Mat gold had been melted down in foundry flasks somewhere around here by a Bristol gold dealer, and there was something Sally found uncomfortable about both David and his home, Lightpil House. The grounds, with their shrubberies, gravelled walks, tree plantations, ponds and outlier groves, had all been established in the last decade by landscapers with diggers and earth-movers, and looked totally out of place. The house, too, was modern and seemed to overwhelm its surroundings. Built with the buttery stone that all the buildings in Bath were made of, in a style meant to mimic a Palladian villa, it had a huge two-storey-high portico, an orangery with a row of glass arches, and was guarded at the entrance by electronic gates topped with gilt pineapples.

Marysieńka drove the Honda down the track that led around the perimeter to a small parking area at the bottom of the property. From here they carried their cleaning kit up the long path that meandered past the swimming-pool and through immaculately tended hedges of rhododendron and ceanothus. The door was open, the house silent, just the television on in the kitchen. This wasn't unusual – they quite often didn't see David. The agency had made clear that he didn't want to be bothered or spoken to. From time to time he'd wander through the kitchen in a towelling robe and FitFlops, mobile tucked under his chin, a remote control in his hand, wincing and shaking his head disappointedly when the Sky box refused to co-operate, but often he'd be locked in his office in the west wing, or over at the livery stables where he kept his show horse, Bruiser. There'd be a list of jobs for the girls and an envelope of cash in the kitchen. He didn't get many visitors, and although he wasn't the tidiest or cleanest man, sometimes it was odd to be cleaning and scrubbing floors and sinks and toilets that hadn't had any use in the week since they'd last been there. They could have closed the door of each room and sat filing their nails, squirted a dose of polish into the air and left. No one would have been any the wiser. But they were all secretly a little scared of David, with his security systems and electronic gates, his camera mounted over the front door. So they played it safe and cleaned the place whether it needed doing or not.

The women set to work. The carpets were thick, wall to wall, in shades of blue and pink. Highly polished brass candelabra fittings hung on every wall and each window was pelmeted and dressed with swagged, fringed curtains in lush blue or gold silk. Everything needed to be dusted. There were two wings, each joined by corridors to the heart of the house where the kitchen and living areas were. The Polish girls took a wing each, while Sally got started with the ironing in the utility room.

There was always a pile of the pinstriped poplin shirts David wore, in a range of pastel colours, pink and peppermint and primrose. They all had hand-stitched labels with 'Ede & Ravenscroft' written in curlicue script. Missing, she thought, as she filled the steam iron and laid out the first shirt. Missing was never good. Not if it was a teenage girl from a nice family. And then she wondered if the police would have to interview her. She wondered if a man in a uniform would be sent out to the cottage. If, perhaps, he'd notice the way Millie and Sally were living these days and report it back to Zoë. Who wouldn't be remotely surprised that her dimwit sister with the hopeful smile and the dopey stars in her eyes had at last got her comeuppance from the world and been put where she belonged.

She'd been ironing for ten minutes when David appeared outside, walking briskly across the gravel drive from the garage. He wasn't tall but he was powerful – the Polish girls called him 'the fat man' – stockily built with cropped grey hair and a year-round suntan. Today he wore a lemon-yellow Gersemi polo shirt, breeches and Italian high boots, and was tapping his short whip against his thigh as he came. He must have been up the road at the stables in Marshfield. He hadn't removed his jewellery to ride – the sun flashed off the gold chain at his neck and the single gold stud in his ear. He came in through the orangery, stopped briefly in the kitchen and slammed the fridge door. Then he appeared in the utility room.

'The only way to end a good dressage session.' He was holding in one hand a lead-crystal flute of pink champagne and in the other a bag of peanuts. 'Peanuts to replace the salts I've lost and the Heidsieck to keep the pulse rate up. The only way.

Taught me by the best dressage boys in Piemonte.'

He had an English accent that veered between Australian, East London and Bristol – his 'U' sound always came out like an 'A', so that 'hut' sounded like 'hat'. She had no idea where he was from but she was sure he hadn't been born in a huge mansion like this. She didn't break off from her ironing, but if he noticed her lack of response, it didn't faze him. He slung himself into a swivel chair that sat in the corner, giving it a half-turn so he could throw his feet up on the worktop. He smelt of aftershave and horses – there were still marks on his forehead where the riding hat had been.

'I'm a lucky man, you know that?' He used his teeth to open the bag of peanuts, tipped some into his hand and began tossing them into his mouth. 'I'm lucky because I've got a good nose for the people I can trust. Always have had. It's got me out of a lot of problems. And you, Sally? I've already got you. Got you up here.' He tapped his head. 'Already locked away. I know what you are.'

Sally had got used to his occasional sermons: she'd heard him on the phone to his mother, talking about the latest thing he'd seen on the news, how it had upset him and how his already dim view of the human race was getting worse by the day. She'd learned, above all, that she wasn't expected to respond to his monologues, that he just wanted to be able to talk. This, though, was more personal than usual. She went on with the ironing, but she was paying more attention now.

'See, I know something you won't admit to anyone.' He smiled up at her. A slow smile that showed all his teeth and made Sally think of rats and reptiles. 'I know this is killing you. A woman like you? Scraping shit off other people's toilets? You weren't raised to be doing something like this. Those Polish slappers? I look at them and I think, Cleaners – that's what they're doing now and that's what they'll be doing when they're eighty. But you? You're different, you've seen better and you hate cleaning. You hate it with a vengeance. Every floor you scrub, every stained pair of sheets you pull off a bed, it kills you.'

The colour crept across Sally's face, the way it always did when she didn't know what to say. She tried to keep her mind on the shirt – shaking it out, laying the collar flat, testing the button on the iron. It shot out a hissing jet of steam, making her jump a little.

David watched her in amusement. He used his feet on the worktop to jiggle the chair from side to side. 'See, Sally, I think a quality girl like you deserves a proper job.'

'What do you mean, "a proper job"?'

'Let me explain. Let me give you a little bite-size lesson in David Goldrab. When I go out to work – not that I do have to much, these days, *Gottze dank* – but when I *do*, I have to deal with people. And hands-on deal with them, if you get my drift. So this is my retreat, the place I come for solitude, and the last thing I want is Shangri-La crowded with people – you can understand that, can't you? I like my space.

47

But I've got ten acres, and more than four thousand square feet of living space, and I don't need to tell you a spread like that takes TLC. The outside's sorted – the pool man comes every two weeks, and there's some half-wit lives down at the cottage between this estate and the next. He deals with the pheasants, arranges a shoot for me if I've been stupid enough to invite people down from London. I leave them a list of jobs, like I do with you, pay their wages direct into their bank accounts, only have to speak to them by phone. Great. Except it's not enough – because of the house. You only have to turn your back on it for a second and before you know it the place is falling in around you. Now call me a snob,' he put a hand over his heart, a martyred look on his face, 'but I can't bear talking to the fucking yokels who come out here to do these jobs, dragging their disgusting knuckles along the floor and blinking their one fucking eye.'

He chucked more peanuts into his mouth, waved the champagne glass around.

'I don't want to have to even *look* at these monkeys. I want to sit upstairs, watching Britney Spears get her kit off on MTV, and be completely oblivious to the half-wit rodding my drains down-stairs. Now that's where you'd come in. I still want you to clean, but I also want you to go round the house every week and make a list of what needs to be done. Then I want you to organize it, monitor it, let the fuckers in, make them coffee – whatever their inbred little hearts desire, pay them and keep a record of what I'm forking out. Get my drift?'

'Basically, you're looking for a housekeeper?'

'Yeah, well, don't make it sound like "Basically, David, you're looking for a dick-sucker." I'm offering you twenty quid an hour – off the books. No tax. Six hours a week over two afternoons. Say, Tuesdays and Thursdays. After I give the agency my fifteen quid an hour for you, how much do you go home with – in your pocket?'

She lowered her eyes, embarrassed it was so little. 'Four pounds an hour. They take emergency tax from me.'

'See? You'd have to work five hours to earn what I'm offering you for one.'

Sally was silent for a moment, doing the sums. He was right. It was a lot of money. And she had free slots on both of those afternoons that she'd been wanting to fill for a long time.

'Come on, Sally. Tell the agency you're not available two afternoons a week and come to me instead.' He tipped back his head and emptied the bag of nuts into his mouth. He crunched them up, swallowed and wiped his mouth with the back of his hand. 'You can wipe that look off your face. It ain't a trick and I'm not proposing to you.'

'What about them? Danuta and Marysieńka.'

'I'll knob them off. Tell the agent I don't need a cleaner. I don't associate with common little slappers like them anyway, their tits lolling out all over the place.'

'But – they're relying on it.'

David shrugged. He pushed with his feet and sent

the chair back across the floor, making it twirl and spin. He came to a halt, gave her a grin. 'You know what, Sally? You're a good Christian woman and now you've put it like that I can see the error of my ways. The dumb Polacks are relying on the money, so I'll do the right thing.' He stood and went to the door. 'I'll call the agent, renegotiate our contract. I'll complain about your work – say I want *you* off the job, the Polish tarts can stay.' He winked. 'Tell you what, I might even double their money. That should put a smile on their faces.'

6

'I was cagey about discussing this in the field.' The pathologist stood next to Ben and Zoë at the dissecting table in the hospital mortuary, looking down at Lorne Wood's remains. The room was closed, a uniformed officer sitting outside the door, just one mortician and the photographer in attendance. 'In my experience, a case like this? You limit the spread of information. Limit the people who know the details.

The photographer moved around the body, taking it from every angle, coming in close on the tarpaulin, which was still drawn up to Lorne's chest. Just as she'd been found. Zoë watched, her lips pursed. She had been here before, in this room, with this pathologist, but they'd always been straightforward murder cases. Horrific and tragic all of them, but uncomplicated – the victims, mostly, of bar fights gone wrong. Once a shotgun victim – a farmer's wife. Of course, this wasn't going to be anything like those cases.

When the photographer had taken all the

necessary shots, the pathologist stood next to Lorne's head, using a torch to look up into her nose, lifting both eyelids and shining the light into them.

'What's the blood?' Zoë asked. 'The stuff coming from her mouth.'

The pathologist frowned. He peeled back a tiny part of the tape and stood back so Zoë could peer down at it. The skin at the edges of Lorne's mouth was stretched around the tennis ball. And the corners had indeed split – two bloodied cracks each about a centimetre long. Just as the CSM had said.

Zoë gave a small nod. 'Thank you,' she said stiffly. She straightened and took a step back.

'I think the ball's dislocated her jaw too.' The pathologist put both hands under Lorne's ears and felt it, his eyes on the ceiling. 'Yup.' He straightened. 'Dislocated.' He glanced up to get the photographer's attention. 'Do you want to get some shots of this while I'm holding the tape back a bit?'

There was silence in the room while the photographer worked. Zoë avoided looking at Ben and she guessed he wouldn't be meeting her eyes either. Neither of them had said anything on the drive over, but she was sure his head would be full of the same things hers was – like, what was going on under that tarpaulin? The pathologist seemed to take an agonizingly long time with the photographer and with taking samples from Lorne's hair and nails. It was an age before he went to the tarpaulin.

'OK?' he said, his eyes on Zoë and Ben's faces. 'Ready?'

They nodded.

He drew the tarp back slowly, and crumpled it into an evidence bag the mortician was holding out. Zoë and Ben remained motionless, staring at what was in front of them. Taking it all in.

She was dressed from the waist up in the grey Banksy T-shirt. Below that she was completely naked. Her legs had been opened and positioned in a frog shape, knees out to the sides, soles together. At first Zoë thought her abdomen and thighs were covered with red slashes. Then she saw they were marks made in a waxy reddish-orange substance. 'What is that? Lipstick?'

'You'd think so, wouldn't you?' The pathologist pushed his glasses up his nose and leaned in, frowning. 'It says something. Maybe you should – uh?'

' "All like her . . ." ' Ben inclined his head sideways, reading the letters that ran up the inner thigh. ' "All like her"? Is that what it says?'

'And this?' The pathologist indicated her abdomen. Letters running across it below her ribs, spanning her navel. 'Very clear to me.'

' "No one"?' Zoë murmured. 'No one.' She glanced up at Ben. As if he might have an answer. He shook his head. Shrugged.

'The other thing that struck me when I was in the field was this.' The pathologist bent and looked under Lorne's buttocks. 'He's rolled up all her clothes – her jeans, her socks, her underwear, put them under there. And, unless I'm very much mistaken, they're not torn, not ripped.'

'She let him take them off?'

'Depends by what you mean by "let him". Maybe she didn't have a choice. Maybe she was beyond struggling at that point.'

'You mean he raped her when . . .'

'When she was unconscious,' Ben said quietly. 'That he knocked her out and then got on with it. Which is why no one on the canal heard anything.'

'I'm not saying anything. What I'm doing here is pointing out the areas of interest we could pay attention to during this post-mortem. Which . . .' he pushed the spectacles up his nose and moved the gooseneck lamp so it was shining directly on Lorne's face '. . . is going to take a long time. I hope you don't have dinner plans.'

7

Sally stood in David Goldrab's utility room, the iron forgotten in her hand, his words going round and round in her head. *Twenty quid an hour – off the books. No tax. Six hours a week.* A hundred and twenty pounds every week to add to her pay packet? At the moment she and Millie were just squeaking by after food, utilities, council tax and interest payments. An extra four hundred and eighty a month would mean she could begin to pay off the loans. Buy Millie a new school dress, new jeans. But working for David Goldrab? Here on her own, with all his rudeness and bluster? She wasn't sure.

Since Julian had left, it seemed that every day there had been a new obstacle, a new impossible predicament. And there was never time to think it through properly. Back in the days before Sally and Zoë had been separated from each other and sent away to different boarding-schools, Mum used to watch old films on TV on Saturday. There was a character in one of her favourites who liked to say, 'Morals? We can't afford morals.' That was what happened at the bottom of the pile: you let ideals, like not stealing other people's work, sink to the bottom of the list – somewhere beneath the electricity bill and the school uniform. You learned to swallow the things you really wanted to say.

She put down the iron, slid its plastic heat-cover closed and went into the kitchen. David was standing in the breakfast room, scratching his chest, idly clicking through the channels on the big wall-mounted TV screen. Danuta was crouched next to the sink, her back to them, sorting through the cleaning equipment. When Sally came in David raised his eyebrows, as if he was surprised to see her. 'OK, Sally?'

She nodded.

'What can I do for you, darling?'

She made a face – nodded fiercely at Danuta, who was still rummaging in the cupboard.

'Sorry?' David said politely, glancing uncomprehendingly at Danuta's back. 'Beg pardon?'

Sally swallowed hard. 'Mr Goldrab, have you got a moment? There's something I need to ask you about.'

David gave a small smile. He turned away from her and went back to clicking through the channels. Sally waited. She watched as he calmly passed news channels, channels where everyone seemed to be under water or on a mountain ledge, one with a woman lying on a bed, dressed in nothing but a pair of bright orange pants and cheerleader socks, staring at the camera with her finger in her mouth. When he'd got to the end he clicked all the way back again.

Then he turned to Sally. Again, he seemed surprised to see her still there.

'OK, OK.' He sounded impatient. 'Go to the office and I'll be there in a bit. Don't give me a headache over it.'

The office was on the ground floor and was filled with computers, shelves of recording equipment, and cabinets of golfing trophies. On the walls were framed pictures of David looking proud with horses, his arm round girls in bikinis, grinning in a bow-tie next to a variety of celebrities that Sally recognized from programmes like *The X Factor*. She sat down and waited. After five minutes he appeared, closed the door and sat opposite her. 'Sally. How can I help? Something on your mind?'

'The agency will think it's strange – if suddenly I'm not available two afternoons a week and you cancel the agreement with the three of us at the same time. They look out for things like that.'

He grinned. She could smell the alcohol on his breath. 'See? What did I say? Told you you've got the smarts. It's OK. I'll call the agency, tell them I want to cut down the hours so you and the Polish tarts don't come so often – say, every ten days. We'll let that situation cruise for a couple of months, then I'll cancel with them. It's win-win for you, darling. And anyway . . .' He smiled and bent towards her. For a moment she thought he might put his finger under her chin and raise her face to his. '. . . It's not like I'm asking you to strangle someone. Is it?'

She didn't smile.

'So? Day after tomorrow, then, Princess?'

'Just one thing.'

He raised an eyebrow. 'A request? Nice.'

'Yes. Please – I don't want you to call me a tart.'

He leaned back in his chair, put his hands behind his head and chuckled. 'Know what, girl? I'll do you a special introductory offer – I won't call you a tart and I won't call you a cunt either. OK? I won't call you a cunt. Unless, of course, you act like one.'

8

Some cops disliked post-mortems. Others were fascinated by them and could talk about them for hours, reeling out lists of technical terms like a doctor. Zoë found that once you convinced yourself to look at the body as a piece of meat – as long as you saw it as nothing else – the most overwhelming thing, sometimes, about a PM was how tedious it was. It was full of recording details, taking photos, weighing even the tiniest organs, the most insignificant glands. And the human body in death wasn't pink and red, but yellow. Or grey. It was only the initial cut – the thoracic-abdominal Y cut – she found difficult. The zipper, the cops called it. Most of them would stand away from the table during 'the zipper', avoiding the release of gases. Because she hated that part, and because it was in Zoë always to push herself, it was the part when she would stand the closest to the table. No masks or mints or smelly ointment to put up her nose. The most she would allow herself was a pinch of the nose and a squint. While Lorne's body was opened Zoë stood next to her, half of her wanting to hold her hand, squeeze it while it happened, stop it hurting. Stupid, she thought, as the mortician wordlessly lined up the implements, rib spreaders and a range of cordless Stryker saws. Like she could change any of this shit.

Pathologists hated being pressed for conclusions before the examination was complete. Just hated it. Still, it was their job to resist – and the police's job to persist, so from time to time Ben or Zoë would fire out a question, which the pathologist would answer with a disapproving click of his tongue against the roof of his mouth and a few caustic comments muttered under his breath about the basic, un-scientific *impatience* of the police, and why was it people couldn't wait for a proper *report* instead of taking his words out of context and handing them on a *plate* to some jumped-up defence brief? But slowly, as the afternoon wore on, he began grudgingly to hand out small details. Lorne's vagina and anus had tears to them, he remarked, but they hadn't bled. Evidence that the rape could have happened just before or just after her death. He swabbed her, but couldn't immediately see any semen in there, so maybe a condom had been used. Or she'd been raped using an object. There was an injury to the back of her head, probably the result of a fall. He guessed she'd been attacked from the front, which was con-sistent with the damage done to her face. And there'd been a blow to the stomach – a kick maybe – that had caused internal bleeding.

'Is that what she died of?'

He shook his head, thoughtfully examining the inside wall of her abdomen. 'No,' he said after a while. 'It would have killed her eventually. But . . .' He pushed a finger into the thickened lump of blood that had gathered around her spleen. 'No. There's not as much blood as you'd expect with the artery to the spleen ruptured like this. She'd have died shortly after the injury.'

'How?'

He raised his chin and looked at Ben steadily. Then, without expression, he pointed to the silver duct tape and the tennis ball, which had now been removed and sealed in a bag on the exhibits bench. 'I'm not saying anything officially, and I need to look at her brain first, but if your nose looked like that and you had a ball jammed in your mouth, how do you think you'd breathe?'

'She *suffocated*?' said Zoë.

'I expect that's what my report will say.' He clicked off the torch and turned to face them. 'So? You want to know how it happened? He hit her like this – here across the zygomatic arch.' The pathologist raised a hand and, in slow motion, mimed hitting his own face with a fist. 'Just once. Her cheekbone's broken, her nose is broken – she falls backwards. Then, probably when she's on the floor, completely dazed, he forces the tennis ball and the duct tape over her mouth. The blood in her nose is starting to clot at this point and, before you know it, both airways are obstructed.' Using the back of his wrist, he pushed his glasses up his nose. 'Fairly horrible.'

61

'You're not saying it was an accident she died?' asked Ben.

The pathologist frowned. 'What does that mean?'

'It's important – the guy could say he didn't mean to kill her. That he was just trying to keep her quiet. I'm picturing defence briefs and manslaughter pleas is all.'

'He could have removed the tape. Even when she was unconscious her breathing response would have kicked in automatically if he'd taken the tape off and shaken her. He could have saved her.'

Zoë stood in silence, gazing down at Lorne. Now that the tape had been removed her jaw hung open in a slack grin. Her tongue was a swollen grey piece of gristle lodged among the white enamel of teeth. Earlier, walking along the canal path, Zoë had been excited, motivated and full of energy. Not any more. She glanced up, found Ben watching her and turned away quickly, fishing out her phone and pretending to be looking at something important there. She didn't want anyone to think she wasn't holding it together. Particularly not Ben.

Peppercorn Cottage was so remote. So completely isolated. It was one of the things Sally loved about it – that she didn't have any neighbours overlooking, no one to stare and judge her, no one to say, 'Look there. Look how that Sally Cassidy's gone to rack and ruin. Look how she's letting the place fall in around her ears.' A little stone-built place set down quite alone amid miles of practical, unfussy farmland less than a mile from Isabelle's house. It had a rambling garden and a view that went on for ever and it was called Peppercorn because, years ago, it had attracted a peppercorn rent. It was the most higgledy-piggledy cottage Sally had ever seen: everything went in steps – the floors, the roof, even the bricks were askew. Not a straight line in sight. In the last year and a half she and Millie had crammed it full of the craft they did in their spare time. The kitchen was stacked with things – the eggcups glazed and studded with paste gems, the little portraits of the pets they'd owned over the years pinned crazily to the walls, the boiled-sweet Christmas stars still hanging in the windows like stained glass, filtering the sunlight in coloured topaz dots. So unlike the house in Sion Road that they'd lived in with Julian.

The living room was at the back, looking out over flat fields, not another building as far as the eye could see. That night Sally left the curtains open to the night and sat curled on the sofa with Steve, sipping wine and staring in disbelief at the TV. Lorne Wood's death was on the national news and the top story on the local news.

'I can't believe it,' Sally murmured, her lips on the rim of her glass. 'Lorne. Look at her – she can't be dead. She was so pretty.'

'Nice-looking girl,' Steve said. 'It'll get more coverage than if she wasn't.'

'All the boys were crazy about her. Crazy. And on the *towpath* of all places. Millie and I used to go there all the time.'

'It's still a towpath. You still can.'

Sally shivered. She ran her hands up and down the goosebumps on her arms and inched closer to Steve, trying to steal some of his body warmth. She and Steve had been together for four months now. On nights like tonight, when Millie was at Julian's, Sally would go to Steve's or he would come over to the cottage, bringing armfuls of treats, cases of wine and nice cheeses from the delis in the town centre. Tonight, though, she wished Millie was with them and not down at Sion Road. After a while, when she couldn't relax, couldn't stop the shivering, she swung her legs off the sofa, found her phone and dialled Millie's mobile. It was answered after just two rings.

'Mum.' She sounded half scared, half excited. 'Have you seen it? On the news? They *murdered* her.'

'That's why I'm calling. Are you OK?'

'It's Lorne they murdered. Not me.'

Sally paused, a little thrown off by Millie's dismissiveness. 'I'm sorry. It's just I thought with the way you used to be so close to Lorne you'd—'

'We weren't close, Mum.'

'She seemed to be with you all the time.'

'No – you just think she was. But really she preferred her mates at Faulkener's and, anyway, I like Sophie better.'

'Even so, it must be upsetting.'

'No – really, I mean I'm shocked but I'm not crying my eyes out. It was *ages* ago. I haven't seen her for *ages*.'

Sally looked up at the window, at the lonely moon

lifting itself from the horizon. Bloated and red. Millie was a proper teenager now. To her a year really was an age. 'OK,' she said, after a while. 'Just one thing – if you want to go out tonight will you speak to me first? Let me know where you're going?'

'I'm not going out. I'm staying in. With *them*.' She meant Julian and his new wife, Melissa. 'Worse luck. And it's the Glasto meeting tonight.'

'The Glasto meeting?'

'I told you about this, Mum. Peter and Nial are going to pick up their camper-vans the day after tomorrow. They're going to meet tonight to talk about it. Didn't Isabelle tell you?'

Sally nibbled at the side of her thumbnail. She'd forgotten it was all so close. The boys were going to Glastonbury with Peter's older brother and his friends. Peter and Nial had passed their driving tests and had been working like slaves for months, saving up money to buy two beaten-up old VW camper-vans they'd discovered rotting on a farm in Yate. Their parents, impressed by their determination, had chipped in to make up the shortfall and the insurance premiums. Millie hadn't stopped talking about going with them to the festival, but the tickets were nearly two hundred pounds. There was no way. Absolutely no way.

'Mum? Didn't Isabelle say?'

'No. And, anyway, I don't suppose there'll be any meetings tonight. Not with this news.'

'There is. They're going ahead – I asked Nial.'

'Well, there's no point in you going to a meeting if

you're not going to Glastonbury, is there? I'm sorry – but we've talked about this already.'

There was a long silence at the end of the phone.

'Millie? Is there any point in you going?'

She gave a long-suffering sigh. 'I suppose not.'

'OK. Now, you get an early night. School in the morning.'

'All right.' Sally hung up and sat for a while with the phone face down on her lap.

Steve leaned across the sofa and put his hand on her shoulder. 'You OK?'

'Yes.'

'Said something you didn't like?'

She didn't answer. On screen the stuff about Lorne had stopped and the newscaster was talking about more spending cuts. Factories closing. The country going down the drain. Jobs disappearing every second.

'Sally? It's natural to be upset. It's so close to home.'

She looked up at the moon again, a longing tugging at her. It would be nice to be able to tell him the truth – that it wasn't just Lorne, that it wasn't just Millie. That it was everything. That it was David Goldrab saying, *I promise not to call you a cunt*, and the thatch falling in, and the stain on the kitchen ceiling, and Isabelle's look of dismay when Sally had said she was planning to sell the tarot. That it was having no one to turn to. Basically it was because of reality. She wished she could tell him that.

9

Bath was nestled, like Rome, in a pocket between seven hills. There were hot springs deep in the earth that kept the old spa baths supplied, kept the people warm and stopped snow settling in the streets. The Romans were the first to build on it, but successive generations had kept up the determination to live there in the warm – whole cities had crumbled and been rebuilt. The past existed in multicoloured strata below the citizens of Bath: like walking on layer cake, every footstep crossed whole lifetimes.

Zoë had grown up in the city. Even though she and Sally had been sent away as children, to separate boarding-schools, even though her parents had moved long ago to Spain, Bath was still her home. Now she lived high on one of the surrounding hills, where the city had spread in the eighteenth and nineteenth centuries. A Victorian terraced house, all her own. The back garden was tiny, with just enough room for a few plant pots and a shed, but the inside was spacious for a person living alone, with three large, high-ceilinged bedrooms on the first floor, and at ground level a single room she'd made by knocking down the interior walls. It stretched thirty-five feet from front to back door and was arranged into two living areas – the kitchen-diner at the front, with a scrubbed wooden table in the bay window, and a TV-watching area at the back, with sofas and her DVDs and CDs. In the middle, where the dividing wall would have been, sat Zoë's hog.

The bike was a classic – a black 1980 Harley Superglide Shovelhead – and had been her only friend on the year she toured the world. It had cost her two and a half thousand pounds and some long, sleepless nights when a drive belt gave up or the carburettor jets blocked in the middle of an Asian mountain range. But she still treasured it and rode it to work now and then. That night, at half past eleven, when the city outside the bay window was lit up like a carpet of lights, the bike was still cooling off, its engine making little noises. Ben Parris turned from Zoë's fridge and came to crouch in front of it. He was carrying a saucer of milk, which he put at the front wheel. 'There you go, favoured object.' He patted the tyre. 'Fill your boots. And never forget how loved you are.'

'It's not a bloody affectation, you know.' Sitting at the table next to the window, Zoë upended the bottle of wine into her glass. 'I don't have anywhere else to put it. It's as simple as that.'

'There's a back garden.'

'But no way into it except through the house.

I'd have to wheel the bike across the floor every day anyway so I may as well park it there.'

'How about out the front on the road?'

'Oh, stop. Now you're really talking madness.'

'It's nice to see something so loved.'

'Treasured,' she corrected. 'Treasured.'

He straightened and came to the table. 'Mind you . . .' he picked up his own glass and turned to look around the room '. . . you in a house at all is a bit of a revelation. Before we got together I sort of pictured you living in the back of a jeep or something. But look.' He opened his hands, spun around as if he was amazed. 'You've got curtains. And heating. And real live electric lights.'

'I know. It's so cool, isn't it?' She leaned across to the wall and flicked the kitchen light on and off. 'I mean, look at that. Magic. Sometimes I even flush the toilet. Just for fun.'

Ben carried his glass around the room, idly turning over pots and glasses and books, studying the photo collage on her wall, which had never been planned but had started as a couple of photos Blu-tacked there to keep them out of the way and grown to cover the entire wall. Talking of first impressions, Amy in the barge had been right, Zoë thought. Ben really was hysterically good-looking. Almost ridiculous that anyone could look that good. And his appearance, she had to admit, did make you wonder about him. She'd worked with him for years and it had come as a total shock to find that, not only was he heterosexual, he was full-throttle heterosexual. When he'd first kissed her, in the car park at a colleague's drunken retirement party, her response had been to blurt out, 'Oh, Ben, don't tit around. What're we going to do if you come home with me? Share waxing secrets?'

He'd taken a step back, nonplussed. 'What?'

'Oh, come on.' She'd given him a playful poke in the chest. 'You're gay.'

'I am not.'

'Bet you are.'

'Bet I'm not.'

'OK. I bet there's not a single body hair on you. Bet you go to the barber's and get a weekly BSC.'

'A *what*?'

'Back, sack and cr . . .' She'd trailed off. 'Ben – come on,' she said lamely. 'Don't mess around.'

'What? You head case – I'm not *gay*. Je-*susssss*.' He undid his shirt and showed her his chest. 'And I've got body hair. See?'

Zoë glanced down at his chest and clamped her hand over her mouth. '*Good God*.'

'And more down here too. Hang on.' He was tugging at his zip. 'I'll show you.'

And that had been Zoë and Ben spoken for, stuck into a twenty-four-hour mission for Ben to prove to her how ungay he was. She'd emerged from it screaming and giggling and doing a naked jig at the open window, like a rain dance, singing a victorious whoop-whoop-whoop out across the city. That had been five months ago and they were still sleeping together. He wasn't intimidated by her height, or her messy thatch of red hair, or her never-ending legs,

70

which should have been in a kick-boxing movie. He didn't care about her drinking and her tempers or the fact she couldn't cook. He was addicted to her.

Or, rather, he had been. But lately, she thought, something was different. Recently a serious note had crept into the equation. That resilient, good-humoured man, the one who'd come back at Zoë in a blink, had transformed into someone quieter. It wasn't a change she could put her finger on, just something about the length of silences between sentences. The way his eyes sometimes strayed in the middle of conversations.

Now, while Zoë pulled another bottle from the rack and shoved in the corkscrew, Ben went to the little pantry to get a bag of crisps. He stood for a while, considering what was on the shelves. 'You've got stacks and stacks of food in here.'

She didn't glance up. 'Yeah – in case I get ill and can't go out.'

'You couldn't just ask someone to go out and shop for you?'

Zoë stopped struggling with the corkscrew and raised her eyes to him. Just *ask* someone? Who the hell was she supposed to ask? Her parents weren't here – she spoke to them sometimes on the phone, visited them in Spain every now and then, when she felt she ought to, but they were thousands of miles away and, honestly, things had always been strained with them. She hadn't seen Sally in eighteen years – at least, not properly to speak to, just briefly in the street – and that was all the family she had locally. As

71

for friends, well, they were all cops and bikers. Not exactly born nursemaids, any of them.

'I mean, you'd do it for someone if they needed it, wouldn't you?'

'That's not the point.'

'What is the point, then?'

She went back to opening the cork. 'Being prepared for the unexpected. Didn't they do a module on that in training? I'm sure I remember it.' She topped up her glass and set it to one side. Then she reached into her bike satchel and pulled out the file on Lorne. She spread the photos of the post-mortem on the table. Ben emptied the crisps into a bowl, brought it over to the table and looked down at the images.

' "All like her"?' Zoë used her forefinger to trace the words on Lorne's leg. 'What does that mean?'

'I don't know.'

'There are letters missing. Before and after. They're smudged.'

'That's just part of the message. I guess it's up to us to fill in the rest. If it's important.'

She picked up the photo of Lorne's abdomen. The words 'no one'. 'What the hell?' she murmured. 'I mean, really – he's nuts, isn't he? What's he talking about – "no one"?'

'I don't know.'

'That she's no one to him? That she's nothing. Dispensable? Or that no one understands *him*?'

Ben sat down. 'God knows. Bloody nightmare, isn't it? And I keep going back to what she said

72

outside the barge: "I've had enough." I spoke to the OIC when she was missing, and there was nothing unusual about the chat she was having, according to her mate at the other end of the line.'

'Alice.'

'Alice. So when Lorne said, "I've had enough," what was she talking about? And why didn't Alice say anything about it?' He gazed wearily into his drink, sloshed it from side to side. 'Someone's going to have to speak to her parents in the morning.'

'The family liaison's with them overnight.'

'I don't even want to think what they're going through.'

'Exactly. Another good reason not to have children. Someone should have read them the warnings on the pack before they got into the procreation thing.'

Ben stopped sloshing his wine and raised his eyes to her. 'Another good reason not to have children? Is that what you said?'

'Yes. Why?'

'Sounds a bit flippant.'

She shrugged. 'Not flippant – rational. I just don't see why people do it. When you look around yourself at the world – see how overcrowded it is – and then you see people having to go through what the Woods are going through, I mean, why do it?'

'But you don't not have children because you're afraid of losing them. That's crazy.'

Zoë stared at him, a little pulse beating at the back of her head, irrationally annoyed by that comment.

He'd made it sound pitying. As if not wanting children meant she was ill, or defective. 'Crazy or not, you won't ever catch me with a football up my sweater.'

Ben gave her a long, puzzled look. A car went by on the street outside and a cloud covered the moon. After a while he stood. He put a hand on her shoulder. 'I think I'll go to bed now. Got a big day tomorrow.'

She raised her chin, surprised by his tone. His hand on her shoulder was friendly, but it wasn't the touch of a lover. 'OK,' she said uncertainly. 'I won't disturb you when I come up.'

He left the room and she sat for a long time, gazing at the place on the stairs his feet had disappeared, wondering what on earth she'd said. Wondering if the natural evolution of her life was always going to be the same – always saying the wrong thing at the wrong time.

Sally had always been the baby of the family. Dolly Daydream. Wide blue eyes and blonde ringlets. Everyone's favourite – and completely lost now that the family was gone and there was no one left to look after her. Once, she'd been close to her parents, but with the divorce something had changed. Maybe it was embarrassment, shame, a deep sense that she'd let them down somehow, but she'd found herself making excuses not to visit them in Spain, and slowly, over the months, their contact had dwindled to a phone call a week – sometimes Millie would answer and speak to them and Sally wouldn't even know about it until later. As for Zoë . . . well, Zoë was never going to come into the equation. She was something high up in the police now, and wouldn't want anything to do with Sally – the spoiled, idiot doll, propped up in the corner with her vacant grin, always looking in the wrong direction and missing what was important in life.

Missing things like Melissa, happening right under her nose.

Big, tanned, leggy Melissa, with her fat frizz of blonde hair, her tennis player's shoulders and loud Australian accent. She'd crept into their lives through those fatal gaps in Sally's attention and, before anyone could draw breath, she was the next Mrs Julian Cassidy, starting a whole new chapter of Cassidys. According to Millie, the baby, Adelayde, had taken over the house at Sion Road with her playpens and bouncy chairs in every doorway. Melissa had dug up the lawn and replaced it with gravel-filled beds, huge desert plants and walkways for Adelayde. Sally didn't mind, though. She had decided there was only one way to approach the divorce – amiably. To accept it and welcome it as a new start. She didn't miss Sion Road. The house seemed, in her memory, to be murky and distant, always cloaked in cloud or orange electric light. And anyway, she told herself, Peppercorn Cottage was beautiful, with its views and clear, natural light that just fell out of the sky and landed flat on the house and garden.

Peppercorn was hers. The terms of the divorce were that Julian would pay Millie's school fees until she was eighteen and buy the cottage for her and Sally to live in. The solicitor said Sally could have got more, but she didn't like the thought of clawing for things. It just seemed wrong. Julian had set up a special kind of mortgage on Peppercorn. Called an offset, he explained, it meant she could borrow against the house should she need to. Sally didn't understand the nuts and bolts of it, but she did grasp that Peppercorn was acting as a kind of a cushion for her. She and Millie had moved out of Sion Road one November weekend, carrying their suitcases and boxes of art equipment through drifts of fallen leaves and into Peppercorn. They'd turned the heating up high and bought boxes of pastries from the deli on George Street for the removals men. Sally hadn't given a thought to the overdraft she kept dipping into. Not until the following year, when the warning letters from the bank began to fall on the doormat.

'What on earth have you spent it all on? Just because the overdraft is there it doesn't mean you've got to use it. They'll take Peppercorn away from you if you're not careful.'

That winter, Julian had met her in a coffee shop on George Street. It was sleeting outside and the floor in the café was soaking from all the people who'd come off the street and dropped snow on it. Julian and Sally had sat at the back of the shop so Melissa couldn't walk by and catch sight of them.

'I don't know anyone who could go through that

much money in a year. Honestly, Sally, what have you been doing?'

'I don't know,' she said lamely, completely at a loss. 'Truly I don't.'

'Well, I bet it hasn't gone on maintaining the house. That thatch'll need redoing before next winter. Buying things for people, I suppose. You're like a child when it comes to giving presents.'

Sally put her fingers on her temples and concentrated on not crying. It was probably true. She didn't like to turn up at someone's house without something for them. Probably it came from when she was a little girl. From the time she'd do anything to make Zoë smile. Anything at all. She'd save up her pocket money and, instead of spending it on herself, she'd wait until she overheard Zoë talking about something she wanted in one of Bath's shops, then sneak out and buy it. Zoë never seemed to know what to do with the gift. She'd stand with it in her hand and look at it awkwardly, as if she suspected it might explode in her face. As if she didn't quite know what expression to arrange her features into. Sally wished she could talk to her sister now. She wished there wasn't this awful cold distance between them.

'I've never had to think about money,' she told Julian now. 'You always took care of it. It's not a very good excuse, I know. And you're right – the thatch has got a hole in it. Something about course fixings. There are squirrels and rats in it, looking for food. Someone's told me it's going to be ten thousand to fix.'

77

Julian sighed. 'I can't keep propping you up, Sally. I'm under a lot of pressure at work and things are very fraught at home with the baby not far away. Melissa's finding it hard not to get tense about money. She wouldn't be happy at all to hear I was helping you still.' He screwed up his napkin and felt in his pocket for his wallet. It was a new leather affair with his initials embossed in gold. From it he flipped out a cheque book. 'Two thousand pounds.' He began scribbling. 'After that my hands are tied. You'll have to find other ways of supporting yourself.'

If a change in life could be marked with a point in time, the way a signpost marks a fork in the road, or an island divides a river, Sally looked back at her life and saw two markers: the first, when, during a childhood squabble with Zoë, Sally had fallen off a bed on her hand, an event their parents had treated with unexpected seriousness, behaving suddenly as if an unspeakable darkness had descended on the family, and, the second, that day with Julian – the day when she had, at last, grown up. Sitting hunched over her cup of hot chocolate, her feet wet and cold, her propped-up umbrella leaking a pitiful puddle on the floor, she saw the world in its plainest colours. Saw it was serious. It was real. The divorce was real and the overdraft was real. There really existed things like bankruptcy and repossessed houses and children living on sink estates. They didn't happen Out There. They happened In Here. In her life.

The six months that had followed were some of the hardest of her life. She got herself a job, she traded in her car for a smaller Ford Ka, she learned how to work out interest rates and how to write letters to banks. She heated only the kitchen and Millie's bedroom all winter, and never used the tumble-drier. There always seemed to be bird dirt on at least one of Millie's school shirts when it came in from the line – that, or when it was really cold, frost making the clothes as stiff as boards. But she persevered. It was an uphill struggle and even now it was like running to keep still. She didn't turn to her parents for help – they'd have been devastated to know the state she was in and, besides, it would get back to Zoë eventually. Zoë would never have got herself into a predicament like this. Zoë had always been the clever one. Amazing. She'd never have ended up accepting jobs from people like David Goldrab. She'd judo-kick him over the nearest hedge before she did that.

Still, it had to be done, she thought, as she got up the morning after Lorne had been found, and padded barefoot into the kitchen to make breakfast. There weren't any choices in this new world of hers. She switched on the kettle, set a pan of milk on the hob, arranged cups and plates on the table. Steve was still asleep so she didn't put the radio on. Anyway, it would all be about Lorne Wood and she didn't know if she could face listening to any more of that. She put some croissants into the oven. The tarot cards were still sitting in an untidy pile on the table where she'd dumped them last night. Now she paused and studied the one of Millie. It wasn't that the paint was fading, she saw. It was that something corrosive had blistered the surface, worming and chewing at Millie's face. Feeling suddenly cold, she raised her eyes and looked out of the window at the fields that strained limitlessly to the bottom of the sky. The canal where Lorne had died was miles away. Miles and miles and miles.

You don't believe in stuff like that, do you?
Of course not.

She turned the card face down and went to switch off the kettle. Millie was safe. She was fifteen. She knew how to look after herself. And, anyway, sooner or later you had to learn to take a step back.

10

On the other side of town, in her living room, Zoë stood with a cup of coffee in her hand and studied the photos on her wall. Most of them came from the trip she'd taken eighteen years ago. Just her and the bike. She'd been everywhere. Mongolia, Australia, China, Egypt, South America. Getting the money together for the adventure had been one of the toughest things she'd ever done – it had just about ripped the skin from her back. Had taken her places, made her do things she never wanted to think about again. But the trip itself turned out to be the most important time in her life. It had taught her all she knew about self-sufficiency, survival, determination. It had sprung her from the trap she'd lived in since childhood.

Lorne Wood would never have the chance to learn any of those things, she thought now, as the sun powered into her kitchen through the bay windows. That was a whole chapter of Lorne's life that would never be opened.

She put down the coffee and wandered around the

room, opening cupboards and drawers until she found a tube of Slazenger tennis balls. They'd been there for two or three summers, since she'd got it into her head she was going to beat every woman in the constabulary tennis club at Portishead. She'd done it within six months. Then she turned her attention to the men. But none of the men would play with her after that, so she'd got bored and dropped it.

Ben was still in bed, still asleep. Zoë sat on the sofa arm with her back to the stairs and popped open the tin. The balls smelt of rubber and old summer grass. She tipped one out and bounced it once on the floor, then blew on it to clean off the fluff and grit. She rubbed it on her sleeve, opened her mouth wide, and pushed the ball in as far as it would go.

It went in surprisingly easily, lodging at its widest point between her teeth – half in, half out of her mouth. The dry, chemical-tasting nap pushed her tongue to the back of her mouth, kicking in the gag reflex. The impulse was to rip the ball out – she really believed she could hear the gristle in her jaw joint popping – but she dug her fingers into the arm of the sofa, closed her eyes and tried to breathe through it, forcing herself to picture the ball being taped into her mouth. Her body shook, sweat popped under her arms, little black and white stars burst against her retinas. And then, when she thought the skin at the edges of her mouth would split open, like Lorne's had, she tugged the ball out and let it tumble to the floor, taking with it thick bands of saliva.

She sat back against the sofa, shaking, sucking in

breath after breath, while on the floor the ball bounced and bounced. It hit the curtains and came to a juddering halt.

11

'Hey. I found you.' Steve stood in the kitchen door-way. He was naked, rubbing his eyes and stretching his arms above his head. 'God, I slept well. I love it here.'

'Sit down.' Sally got an elastic band out of a drawer, bound Millie's card to the outside of the pack and pushed it into the back of one of the drawers. She turned to check the milk that was heating on the stove. 'I've got to get going. Got to be at work at nine.'

'No time for hanky-panky, then?'

'I've got to be at work.'

He smiled and stretched some more. His hands found the low ceiling and he used it to press himself down, bending his knees, lengthening his body and cracking the sleep out of his muscles. He was differ-ent in every way from Julian, who had been pale and hairless with soft arms and womanly hips. Steve was big, with dark hair and a solid, suntanned neck. His legs were hard and hairy, like a centaur's. Looking at him now, stretching, was like watching one of

Leonardo da Vinci's anatomy studies come to life.

She stood at the hob, whisking the milk into froth, shooting him surreptitious looks as he wandered around, yawning and checking inside the fridge. It had been four months since they'd got together and she still couldn't quite believe he was here. Steve had given her sex on the brain: if she had even half an hour between cleaning jobs, she'd scurry over to his house and they'd end up naked on the kitchen floor. Or on the stairs, halfway up to the bedroom. It was totally different from being with Julian. Maybe she was having a mid-life crisis. At thirty-five.

Steve was in 'corporate espionage'. Sally wasn't entirely sure what that meant – but he always seemed to be dealing with people who lived in remote and glamorous places. His address book, which she'd seen lying open at his house one day, was crammed with addresses in countries like the Emirates, Liberia and South Africa, and more than once he'd had to set his alarm for the middle of the night so he could get up and take a conference call with someone in Peru or Bolivia. He wore a suit when he left the house in the morning, but in her imagination he wore a black polo-neck and jeans and had secret knives fitted in his soles. She had no idea why he wanted to be with someone as stupid as she was. Maybe it was because she was so easy. He only had to look at her and she'd roll backwards on to the bed, her legs open, a blank, grateful smile on her face.

'So.' He linked his fingers and cracked the knuckles. Rolled his head. 'Where're you working today?'

'North.'

'Not Goldrab again?'

'No. Not today.' She spooned frothy milk on to two cups of coffee, shook cocoa powder on to them from a metal flour-shaker and put a cup in front of him. She went back to the oven and busied herself with laying croissants on a tray. 'Yesterday he offered me another job. Cleaning still, but doing the admin for his house too.'

'Are you going to take it?'

'It's a lot of money.'

Steve stirred his coffee, thinking about this. 'Look,' he said, after a while, 'I've never said anything, but the truth is I kind of worry about you when you're there.'

'Worry? Why?'

'Put it this way – I know a lot about him. A lot I'd rather not know.'

She slammed the oven door, straightened and turned to him, pushing her hair from her forehead. 'How?'

He laughed. 'How long have you lived in Bath? You know that Disneyland ride, Small World, with the little kids singing, "It's a world of laughter, a world of tears"? That's Bath for you – a small, small world. Everyone knows everyone else's business.'

She got jam and butter from the fridge, collected knives and napkins, thinking about this. He was right. They all sort of knew each other, or of each other – and people talked and gossiped so you never

86

felt entirely disconnected from others, no matter if you hadn't seen them for years. It was the way she got information about what Zoë was doing, for example (she didn't dare ask Mum and Dad – for years she'd never spoken a word about Zoë to them, knowing the spectres it might raise if she did). The grapevine was also the way she'd first become aware of Steve – in the vague, amorphous way you got to know about the other parents at a school, even though his two children were much older than Millie and now at university. He and his ex had got divorced, it turned out, on the same day as Sally and Julian. Steve had heard vaguely about her separation through the grapevine and one day, months later, he'd seen her sitting in traffic in the pink HomeMaids Smart car. He'd called the number on its side and got the manager to put a call through to her. That was the thing about Bath. Really, it was just a big village. Sometimes it was a bit creepy. As if she couldn't move without everyone knowing.

But, looking at Steve now, she didn't quite believe the small-village scenario explained how he knew about David.

'He's not one of your . . .' She searched for the word. What would he call him? A customer? A client? She knew so little about his job. 'He hasn't employed you, has he?'

'No.'

'But you still know a lot about him?'

Steve frowned. 'Yeah . . . well,' he said vaguely. 'Maybe this is a bad time to talk about it. You know, first thing in the morning.' He drew a newspaper nearer and began to read.

But Sally persisted. 'I don't know anything about your job. I feel a bit in the dark sometimes.'

He looked up at her. He had very clear grey eyes. 'Sally, that's the big drawback. If you know a bit about my job you know the lot.'

'And then you'd have to kill me.'

'And then I'd have to kill you.' He gave an apologetic smile.

'I do have to be careful. That's all.'

'But I work for him. And he is a bit . . . weird. Maybe you know something I should. Something important.'

He pursed his lips and tapped the rim of his cup thoughtfully with his nail, as if he was wondering what he could risk saying. After a while he pushed the cup away. 'OK – I can tell you this much. Goldrab's not paying me, it's the other way round. *I'm* being paid to investigate *him*.'

'Investigate *him*? Why?'

'That's where the soul baring stops. I'm sorry. If you have to work for him, I can't stop you. All I ask is you keep your wits about you.'

'Oh,' she said, feeling a little naïve not to have cottoned on to this before. 'How long have you been doing it?'

'A while now. Months. That's pretty normal – a lot of my subjects sit on my books for years. But if you want the truth, the pressure on Goldrab's been upping lately. In the last couple of weeks my clients are getting a bit pushier about him.'

'Do you mean Mooney?'

Steve put down his cup and stared at her. 'How do you know that name?'

'I think I must have heard you talking to him on the phone.'

'Then forget it. Please. Forget it.'

She gave a nervous little laugh. 'You're scaring me now.'

'Well, maybe you should be scared. Or cautious, at least. Goldrab is a nasty man, Sally. Very nasty. And the fact he's walking around free and not banged up on some life sentence is only a matter of fluke. Seriously, forget you ever heard that name. Please. For both our sakes.'

12

'There are cats at your back door.'

Zoë was sitting at the table looking at the post-mortem photos of Lorne, distractedly rubbing her aching jaw, when Ben came into the living room, fully dressed, doing up the cuffs on his shirt. She hadn't heard him get up, hadn't heard him come down the stairs. He'd had less than five hours' sleep but he was immaculate. He put his forehead to the glass door and peered down at the cats. 'They're eating.'

Zoë packed the photos into her courier's satchel and put it next to the front door. She switched the kettle on. 'Coffee?'

'You've fed them,' he said curiously. 'They've got saucers out there.'

'So?'

'It's kind of you. A secret kind habit.'

'It's not *kind*, Ben. I'm not being *kind* to them. I feed them so they don't wake the neighbourhood up. Let's not have an awards ceremony over it, eh?'

He turned and gave her a long look. As if she disappointed him and was solely responsible for driving all the fun and light out of his life. She shook her head, half cross with herself. Last night when she'd gone to bed he'd been asleep. Or pretending to sleep – she hadn't been able to tell. But their conversation about children had allowed something thin and cold and cunning to come in from the dark and slide silently between them. She knew it, he knew it. She made the coffee, banging around, spooning instant granules into mugs and slopping a little milk in.

'There,' she said, handing him one of them. 'Do you want anything else?'

Ben was silent for a while. He looked at the mug, then at her.

'What?' she said. 'What is it?'

'Zoë, I've been thinking . . .'

Christ. She sat down at the table, her heart sinking. *Here we go.* 'Thinking? About what?'

There was a pause. He started to say something, then changed his mind.

'What, Ben? Spit it out – you've been thinking about what?'

Something in his eyes dimmed a little. He shrugged, half turned towards the window. 'About the phone call.'

'The *phone call*? What phone call?'

'The one Lorne had with Alice. There's something in it that's important. Something that didn't come out when Lorne was reported missing.'

Zoë didn't move. He'd sidestepped. He'd ducked saying it, whatever 'it' was. She stood, tipped her coffee into the sink, found her car keys in her pocket. 'I'm taking the car today,' she said. 'Do you want a lift in or are you going to drive yourself?'

13

The superintendent at Bath was in his late fifties. He had curly blond hair kept very short and the sort of skin that burned easily. He'd started life in Firearms, then come over to CID and regretted the move to this day. He still wore a blue and yellow National Rifle Association pin in his lapel, had a wall covered with photos of himself in the firing range and seemed to hold every member of his team responsible for his big life-mistake. That morning he looked as if he'd far rather be at the club shooting the crap out of some 'advancing Hun' than standing at the helm of the biggest murder case that had hit the city in years.

'This is a nasty, nasty crime. Very, very serious. I don't need to tell you that – you've all seen the post-mortem pictures, you know what's going on here. But I want to remind you to keep clear heads on this. Concentrate. There are lots of things to cover. Most of them you probably know, but let's put them in a bundle so nothing's missed.' He held up his coffee cup to indicate the points outlined on the whiteboard behind him. 'To summarize. Lorne – popular girl, very pretty, as you can see. Big circle of friends – though so far no one's saying anything about boyfriends. First thing I want to run through is the list of items to flag up for the search teams. Bits and pieces here, but mostly things missing from Lorne's personal effects.'

He pointed to the picture from the mortuary of Lorne's bloodied left ear. The killer had ripped her earring out, leaving the lobe sliced from midway to bottom. A photo of her other ear showed the remaining earring intact. 'Number one, an earring. Quite an unusual design. Apparently it had been bought for her in Tangiers by her father. See this filigree? So . . .' He nodded in the direction of the DCs ranked at the back of the room, arms folded across their chests. They had been taken partly from the ranks at Bath station and partly from the Major Crime Investigation Unit. 'One of you. Get that added to the search list.'

Zoë stood near the front, her hands in the pockets of her black jeans. Her tongue was thick with last night's wine, her muscles twitchy with all the coffee she'd drunk this morning to jump-start the day, and her jaw was still hurting from having the tennis ball in her mouth. Ben was leaning against the desk next to her, his arms folded. Usually on the way in to work she'd keep up with his car on her bike, sidewinder him in traffic. Today, as she drove in to work, she'd kept her distance behind his car, feeling she suddenly didn't have the right to fun and games and flirtation.

'Her phone's missing. Switched off. But I'm comforted to know that Telephony at the bureau has got a watch on it. Am I right?'

The sergeant who headed the team's intelligence cell nodded. 'Vodafone are a nice network,' he said, 'the only one in the UK that do live cell site analysis. The moment that phone is switched on they'll get a ping on it and we'll know.'

'Except,' said the superintendent, 'chances that'll happen are, let's be realistic, zero. More likely he's slung it, so I hope it's been added to the search-team briefings. It's an iPhone, white.'

He set his cup down and picked up a girl's fleecy pink gilet. With his finger stuck through the loop at the neck he dangled it in front of the officers. 'Mum is adamant she was wearing something like this when she left home. It wasn't among what we recovered from the crime scene, so put an asterisk next to that for the search teams. And, last, there's a tarpaulin, which you've seen in the photos – we've trawled around the barge owners down there and they're all saying the same thing. It's standard stuff for a barge, a tarp to cover the wood and coal and what-have-you – but still no one's missing one. They get a lot of overnight moorings in that stretch of the canal, casual since you don't pay for the first twenty-four hours, so bear that in mind. Have a word with all the boathouses and someone speak to British Waterways to find out what the water bailiff saw moored there overnight. Someone get photos of the tarp distributed – and the fleece. Either get Exhibits to have another photo of the earring done or get the PM one Photoshopped so it hasn't got the dead ear attached. Then get it to the press office – the media can have both of these. Ben? Zoë? Can I leave it to you to decide how best to divvy that up?'

Zoë nodded. Ben held up his thumb.

'Good. Now . . .' The superintendent rubbed his hands together, as if he was about to announce an unexpected treat. 'You can see we've got a lot of meat to chew on, a lot of standard routes to walk up, but there's something else I want you to put into your pipes. We've got a visitor today.'

Everyone in the room automatically turned their eyes to the young woman who'd been sitting patiently in the corner throughout the meeting. With long, well-groomed dark hair, she was very neat and quiet, dressed in a white blouse and very tight bottle-green trousers with high-heeled sandals just peeping out under the hems. Her skin was lightly tanned, her nails polished and well kept. Zoë had noticed a lot of the men looking at her.

'This is Debbie Harry. Not, I am reliably informed, related to the other Debbie Harry.'

'Sadly.' Debbie shook her head ruefully. 'In my dreams, you know.'

One or two of the men laughed. Goodsy, standing in the back row, whispered in his neighbour's ear. Zoë could guess what he was saying.

'Now, you're from Bristol University, it says here, and you're a forensic psychiatrist.'

'Psychologist.'

'Psychologist, sorry. A bit like Cracker?'

'That's right.'

'Funny.' The superintendent put a hand up to his mouth and said, in a stage whisper, to the team, 'Doesn't look much like Robbie Coltrane to me.'

This time almost everyone laughed. Not Zoë, though. She clearly recalled the superintendent saying over and over again that he'd never, ever, let a 'fucking head doctor' within a mile of his incident room. That they were all quacks and poofs and had their heads up their arses. Evidently he'd never met a 'head doctor' who looked like this. To see her, you'd think honey would ooze out of her mouth the moment it opened. She got up and came to the front, leaning back on the desk casually, as if this was her own lecture room, half crossing one leg over the other. Just enough to be flirtatious without being totally provocative. Clever girl, Zoë thought. She knew the effect it would have on a roomful of men.

'Look,' said Debbie, a bright, open expression on her face. 'This is going to be a big leap of faith for some of you if I ask you to approach this not from an evidentiary perspective but from a psychoanalytical perspective, to ask you to think in terms of profiling the offender. Probably sounds like voodoo to a lot of you.' She smiled. 'But if you're prepared to make that leap of faith then, I can assure you, I'll be right along-side you.'

Zoë took a long, patient breath. She'd been here before, heard psychologists talking the talk. Spiels about anger excitation, power reassurance, long

97

analyses of why the bastard had done what he did, what he was thinking when he did it, what his eye colour was, what underpants he wore, what he'd had for breakfast the day he did it. In her experience they weren't worth much as investigative tools, and sometimes they were positively destructive. Still, some investigators swore by them and she could see from the glowy light in the superintendent's eyes that he was a new convert. Amazing what a nice pair of legs and a smile could do.

'First,' Debbie said clearly, 'I suppose the question that's in the front of everyone's minds, the biggest one, is, what's the writing all about?' She turned her eyes to the whiteboard where the blown-up photos of Lorne's abdomen had been pinned. Next to them, in a round, cursive hand, the words had been written out.

No one.

'I wonder,' Debbie said ruminatively, 'I wonder – is that a message to us? Could be. Or to Lorne? Or a statement to the killer himself? Let's think carefully about that wording: "*no one*". Does that mean Lorne is no one to him? A nothing? Worthless? Or is it something else? Does it mean that *he*'s a no one? That no one cares. *No one understands me.* I'm inclined to think it's something like that – which would mean we have someone here with very low self-esteem. He could be the type to form unnaturally intense relationships with people – the type to become jealous or aggrieved easily. Now that he's killed Lorne he could enter a period of self-recrimination. There may be a suicide attempt. There may already have been a suicide attempt, so I'd suggest that would be something you could check on – suicides and admissions since the time of her death.' Debbie turned back to the board. She was enjoying this. Like a reception teacher with a class full of bright-faced children gazing up at her raptly. 'Let's move on to the next sentence. He's written something on her thigh that looks like "all like her". Any ideas on that?' She scratched her head, a subtle suggestion to the team that they were thinking *with* her, that she wasn't just cramming her theories down their throats. 'Any thoughts?'

The men shrugged, waiting for her to provide the answer.

'OK.' She linked her hands round her knees and tipped her head shyly. 'Let me be a bit bold. Let me take you by the hand and lead you out on a limb. Let me say that, in my opinion, Lorne knew her killer.'

There was a ripple of attention. People murmuring among themselves. Zoë glanced at Ben to see his re-action. His head was lowered and he was busily scribbling notes to himself on his customary yellow legal pad, probably to stop himself laughing out loud, she thought.

Debbie held up her hand to quieten the muttering. 'I know – a leap of faith, but let me just work with it for a moment. What do we know about Lorne?'

'That she was popular,' said the intelligence cell sergeant. 'Had lots of friends, lots of male admirers. So that sentence could be "they all like her".'

'Exactly,' Debbie said triumphantly, beaming at

him. 'Exactly. This is a direct comment about Lorne. And, in case you think I'm grasping at straws to support a flimsy theory, let me say something else. I've analysed Lorne's tragic injuries, and those just confirm my conclusions about who attacked her that night. He definitely approached her from the front. The pathologist said it was a single blow that incapacitated her, and caused the bleeding to the nose. There are no signs she tried to run – no screams heard. Her attacker had got really close to her, really close, and she'd allowed it. Now, would she have done that if she didn't know him? No, is the answer. She wouldn't. In fact . . .' she did a little mime of a tightrope walker – arms out, trying to keep her balance '. . . now I'm out on my limb – *whoa!* – I may as well go all the way and say *I* wouldn't rule out that the offender may have had, or at least believed he was having, a relationship with Lorne. I also think he could be quite near Lorne's age. Maybe a year or two older – and probably the same ethnic and socio-political background. Could even be a member of her peer group.'

The superintendent held up his hand. 'A question.'

Oh, please, Zoë thought, ask her why she's talking such crap. Go on, ask her.

'You say he's about her age?'

'Within a year or so, yes.'

'And what makes you think he's known to her?'

'She had a blow to the face. That's a classic sign. Depersonalization, we call it. But before I go any further . . .' Debbie gave them a million-dollar smile, with the expensive dentistry on show '. . . I'm going to come back off my limb. See? I'm nice and safe in the tree now, and I want to make one thing very, very clear. OK?'

'OK,' one or two voices said.

'I want it clear that my thoughts are only for *guidance*. Only for guidance and only *my* opinion. You're all adults, and I don't want to be patronizing, but you should always keep an open mind. Please.' She sighed as if this was the one drawback in her job – the way everyone took her word as gospel. 'I reiterate: *you must keep an open mind.*'

'*Christ Christ Christ.*' After the meeting Zoë swung into Ben's office without knocking. She was the only one in the building allowed to do that. She dropped into a chair and folded her arms, her legs pushed out, heels dug into the carpet. 'Can you fucking believe it? The superintendent is being led by his dick. Known to her killer? The same age? All this from her injuries? "This blow to her face is a classic sign of depersonal-ization"? I mean, shit, Ben, it's the same injury you see in about eighty per cent of the muggings we go to and most of those victims had never met their attacker before. Don't you remember those photos of depersonalization they showed us on that course – that was de-bloody-personalization. Eyeballs out. Things carved into the forehead. Noses cut off. Twenty-seven wounds to the face. But Debbie "not *the* Debbie" Harry is saying a single blow to the . . .' She trailed off. Ben wasn't shaking his head ruefully, regretting the appalling situation. Instead he was sitting in silence. Watching her without expression.

'What?' she said. 'What's that look for? You don't agree with her, do you?'

'Of course not – she treated us like two-year-olds.'

'But?'

'What she said about the wording wasn't totally off piste. Some of it kind of had merit.'

'Kind of had merit?' Zoë stared at him open-mouthed. She couldn't believe this, just couldn't believe it. 'No. You're just getting your own back because of whatever I said last night that you didn't like.'

'I'm saying it because it sounds feasible.'

'*Feasible?* Try *irresponsible*. Have you thought how dangerous it is, screwing down our target to someone in his teens? All those Neanderthals in the incident room with their tongues on the floor at the sight of a girl in tight trousers who can use big words are going to set off with such narrow parameters that the killer could walk straight past them, and if he's not the white middle-class public-school boy Debbie said he should be they'll let him go. It's wrong on so many different levels. And it doesn't even *feel* right. It doesn't feel like someone that young would have the confidence to do what Lorne's killer did.'

'I disagree.'

'It's a free world, Ben. And it's good we disagree. As long as you remember to keep an open mind. Even Tracey Sunshine said that.'

'Of course. Of course I will.' He pushed back his

immaculate cuff and checked his watch. 'So, nine o'clock now. What're you going to take?'

'Well, I'm not going to be interviewing schoolboys, I can promise you that. I might do something really radical – like try to establish an investigation based on the evidence. You know – like we were trained? I might try to find out which barge that tarp came from.' She pushed her chair back, got to her feet. 'Or, even better, I'll meet up with the liaison officer. Go and speak to the Wood family. You?'

'Alice Morecombe, the friend on the phone. I've got to find out about that last conversation. And then . . .'

She raised her eyebrows at him. 'And then?'

'I'll take some of MCIU up to Faulkener's. Speak to all the boys in Lorne's year – and everyone in the year above her too.'

She shook her head resignedly. 'Does this mean we're at war?'

'Don't be silly. We're grown-ups. Aren't we?'

She held his eyes. 'I hope so, Ben. I really do.' She looked at him for a bit longer, then checked her watch. 'A drink tonight? Depending on how the day pans out?'

'Sure.' He gave a brief smile, then swivelled his computer screen round and began entering his password.

'I'll see you later, then?' She watched his fingers on the keys. 'About seven?'

'Seven.' He didn't take his eyes off the computer. 'Sounds perfect.'

14

Zoë would have driven the Harley anywhere – but the superintendent just hated the thought of her rolling up to interviews in her leathers, so for police business she used the car: the ancient Mondeo she'd got cheaply when the force had offloaded some of its fleet. The Woods lived out near Batheaston and to get there she had to drive past the exclusive Faulkener's School where Ben had sent his team to interview the schoolkids. She slowed the Mondeo, peered up the rhododendron-lined driveway and saw all the marked and unmarked cars parked up. Ranks of them. Already she knew where this case was going: the superintendent was going to throw all the resources after Debbie Harry's theories. Zoë could see all the swimming-against-the-tide that lay in her future.

She speeded up, passing the school, then almost as quickly slowed again. About a hundred yards ahead, pulled on to the kerb, there was a purple Mitsubishi Shogun jeep. It was a real number, tricked out like a pimp-mobile with clamped-on running-boards, angel-eye headlights and a bush snorkel. Sitting in it was a notorious piece of local pond life – Jake Drago, otherwise known as Jake the Peg, for some reason that eluded her. Skinny and always fidgeting, Jake the Peg had spent almost half his adult life inside, mostly for stupid brawls and drug-dealing. But for the last two years, people said, he'd got his act together, had found some way of staying on the straight. Zoë doubted it. She pulled the car over and got out, tucking her shirt into her jeans as she walked back along the pavement to him.

'Hey.' Jake got out of the car as she approached. He slammed the door, leaned back against it, folded his arms and gave her a long look up and down, taking in the high-heeled cowboy boots and the black shirt with the sleeves rolled up.

'Hey, Jake.' She stopped a pace away, smiled nicely. It was true what they said: he looked different. He'd cleaned up, had put on weight and muscle. He wore a tight white vest that his pumped-up pecs pushed against. His dark hair was cut short at the sides with the top gelled up. He was very tanned and oiled and, frankly, to her eyes, looked like he was on his way to a disco. 'I see you haven't learned much over the years. In the States you get out of a car like that when a cop comes along and you're liable to get yourself shot. Here, you're just liable to make me wonder if you're hiding something in there. And then I'd have to search the car, or breathalyse you, and at that point it all gets really tedious.'

'How do I know you're a cop?'

'Oh, please.' She gave a laugh – a low, forced laugh – and looked around herself as if there might be someone to share the joke with. 'Please. Don't even go there. Let's not demean ourselves.'

'What do you want?'

'What do I want? I want to look at your muscle car.' She put a hand on the bonnet. 'It's totally mint, Peg. Suits you.'

'I'm in a hurry.'

'I saw. Sitting there in the morning sun. Saw you were in a hurry.'

He scowled. 'This is starting to piss me off.'

She looked across at the entrance to the school with its big ornate gates and the unmarked police cars. You wouldn't know what they were unless you were police yourself. 'What're you doing outside the school? Why'd you pick here to sit?'

He gave her a tight, twitchy look. Then he smiled, showing the glint of a diamond set in his front tooth. 'I'm a perv. Didn't you know? Watching all the girls in their little short skirts?' He rubbed his thighs. 'Fuck, but they make me hot. Make me think about things my probation officer says I didn't ought to think about.'

'Yeah, yeah, yeah – still taking me for an idiot after all these years. You're not a nonce, Peggers. You're a lowlife piece of turd that one day, God willing, the good citizens of Bath will scrape off the bottom of their shoes for ever – but you're not a nonce. So what is it? You dealing to the spoiled little girls and boys in there?'

'I told you – I was resting. Closing my eyes.'

'You heard about the murder? That's the sort of thing that gets around.'

'Course I heard.'

'You know when it happened?'

'Yes. The night before last.'

'And you know where?'

'Over there.' He nodded in the direction of the canal. 'They found her down there, didn't they?'

'And you didn't see anything?'

'Me? Me? Nothing. Never saw a thing.'

'You sure? I mean, I could have a rummage around in that disgusting pimped-up heap of shit you're driving, you sad bastard, and take you in. Now, are you sure?'

'I'm sure.' He tucked his hands into his armpits and fixed his eyes on her chin. 'A hundred per cent.'

'It's just, you know, I'm a woman so I've got a memory like an elephant, can never wipe that slate clean. Know what I'm saying? And the thing I will *never* forget about you, Peggie, is you lying to the police. Every time you get your arse hauled in you tell lies. Now – tell me. Did you see anything?'

He blinked at her. A line of sweat had started on his lip. He lowered his head and kicked at the dirt a little. 'Dunno. I might've done. Might've seen her with one of the boys. Walking down there, near the canal.'

'One of the *boys*? What do you mean, "one of the boys"?'

'Schoolkid. They went into that wood over there.'

107

For a moment Zoë genuinely didn't know what to say. She stared at the top of his head, gleaming and gelled, thinking that Debbie Harry would have loved to hear that come out of his mouth. To confirm her theory. But then Jake shifted and kicked the dirt some more and twitched and avoided her eyes, and suddenly she got it. He hadn't seen Lorne with anyone – he hadn't seen a thing. He'd been sitting out here all day, dealing to the pupils of Faulkener's, and probably some of them had already told him that the police were questioning all the boys. He wanted her off his case, so he was just parroting back what he thought she wanted to hear.

She sighed. Swung her keys round on her index finger. Another unmarked car had just pulled into the driveway of the school. Swimming against the tide.

'Pleasant though it always is to pass the time of day with you, Peggie,' she said nicely, 'I'll let you get back to work now. I mean, you're going to need the money, what with those rear indicators being illegal and the fines I'm going to slap on you if I see you hanging around here again.'

15

The Woods' house was set in gardens that rambled for almost an acre up from the canal towpath. The narrow driveway led through an imposing grove of redwood trees, with well-tended lawns stretching away on either side, then clusters of outbuildings and greenhouses. A ride-on mower sat in the sun and a wheelbarrow full of dead bindweed had been abandoned on the hard-standing. The house itself was comparatively small and unprepossessing – a thirties pebble-dashed box, neat and well maintained but unimaginative. A uPVC conservatory had been added at the back, inside which sat floral armchairs and a dining table covered with a white linen tablecloth.

Zoë parked and walked around the side of the house. The liaison officer the family had been assigned had warned the Woods of Zoë's visit. He'd told them she had no news, that she was coming to ask questions, so they wouldn't all gather to stare expectantly at her. Lorne's father was in the garden and didn't even look up when she passed. He wore a swagman's hat, complete with dangling corks, a Singha beer T-shirt, and shorts. He was using a chainsaw to cut a felled birch into logs, and although he must have seen her, he kept his back turned to the house. According to the paperwork he was a project manager in the construction business. Zoë guessed he wasn't of the right social stratum to be down the boozer mounting posses to lynch whoever it was who'd killed his daughter. But he'd be picturing it nevertheless. He'd be having intellectual arguments with himself, huge battles of reason, about the role and logic of the justice system. About forgiveness and humanity. He'd be cutting the log and imagining it was Lorne's killer he was hacking into.

From the patio bench a tall, sorrowful-looking lad watched her approach. He sat with his elbows on his knees and was jiggling slightly, as if he was ready to jump up at any moment. He had a shock of sandy hair, and the chinos and sweatshirt he wore seemed to have been slept in. This must be Lorne's brother, driven home overnight from his university in Durham. He gave her an embarrassed nod, held up his hand to indicate the front door, then went back to his nervous jiggling.

The door was open a crack. Zoë pushed it further and found herself in a hallway filled with framed photos. Horse photos: gymkhanas, ponies clearing jumps, difficult ones – triple oxers and cross-country walls. A young Lorne grinning from under a riding hat, arms round the neck of a black pony, its browband bristling with rosettes.

'Hello?'

'In here,' came a voice from the end of the corridor. Zoë continued on and found, in the kitchen, the liaison officer sitting hunched over a computer, and Mrs Wood, standing at the worktop, scratching furiously in a small notebook. She was dressed in corduroy trousers and a Joules Elephant Polo T-shirt, a mass of curly hair tied back from her face. The moment she turned to face her Zoë noted two things. The first was that Mrs Philippa Wood had once been Miss Philippa Snow and had been at Zoë's boarding-school nearly twenty years ago. The second was that Mrs Wood really hadn't accepted her daughter was dead. She was smiling grimly, a pragmatic expression on her face, as if she was determined to get through this visit from the police as soon as possible.

'Pippa Wood.' She gave Zoë's hand a firm shake. If she recognized her she didn't say anything. 'Coffee? It'll take just a moment.'

Zoë exchanged a glance with the liaison officer, who gave a slow nod, as if to say, 'I told you so. It hasn't reached her yet.'

'Please. Black, with two sugars.' She folded her arms and leaned against the counter top, watching her switch on the kettle and get down mugs from the cupboards. 'I know you spoke to the police yesterday, Mrs Wood, and the day before that when Lorne went missing. I don't want you to think we're hassling you. I just wanted to see if anything had come up for you overnight. Anything you recalled – anything in your statement you wanted to change or add to.'

'Not really.' She held out an opened biscuit tin containing brownies and sponge fingers. Zoë hadn't seen sponge fingers in years. She took one. Pippa snapped the lid back on. 'She got home from school at one – they do a half-day on Saturday. She got changed and went into town. Completely normal.'

'She did that often?'

'Yes. She liked to go shopping. Some of the places in the centre stay open till six, even later.'

'And she didn't say she was meeting anyone?'

'No.' She got milk from the fridge. 'She liked to be on her own.'

'What was she shopping for?'

'The usual. Clothes. Window-shopping, of course, because I don't let her have money just to waste. She thought she was going to London to be a model – any money I'd given her she'd have squandered on that pipedream. We're trying to teach her the value of money, what's a sensible spend and what isn't, but with Lorne, it's in one ear and out the other. Her brother, on the other hand . . .' She shook her head, as if life was a mystery to her. 'Isn't it amazing how two children, the same genes, can turn out so differently?'

'What's a "sensible" spend?'

Pippa scrutinized Zoë, as if she was wondering whether this was a trick question. 'Well, not clothes, of course. At least, not the sort of clothes she wants. Something practical, maybe.' She gave the leg of her own trousers a shake as an illustration. 'But not these things she goes for, covered in glitter – they fall apart after one wash.'

112

At school Zoë and Pippa had been in different years, but now Zoë was remembering something of her reputation. Super sporty, captain of the hockey team, crazy about horses. And as hard as nails.

'Did she have a horse?'

'Not any longer. She did have, but she wouldn't look after him. I'd have kept him, but I didn't send him out to be broken in, did it myself, so he was never going to be happy with me on his back and he was too small, anyway. Now it's just the mare and the five-year-old.'

Zoë nibbled thoughtfully at the sponge finger, her hand cupped under it so as not to drop the sugar crusting on the kitchen floor. There had been a time years ago when she'd done a routine enquiry on a twelve-year-old girl who'd been thrown and trampled by her horse, and was lying in a coma in Intensive Care. The mother had been in tears during the interview. But in tears for what might happen to the horse, not to her daughter. All that came out of her mouth was: 'It wasn't his fault. He got scared – she shouldn't have had him on the road. It wasn't his fault.' Zoë licked her fingers carefully, then leaned a little way out of the kitchen door and peered at the staircase. 'Is her room up there?'

'There've been some teams in it already. They took her computer. They left about an hour ago.'

'Could I have a look?'

'Of course you can. You'll forgive me if I don't come with you.'

Zoë carried the coffee into the hallway and went

slowly up the stairs, past all the gymkhana photos. It stuck in her head, that line: *Any money I'd given her she'd have squandered on that pipedream.* It was years since she'd been living at home with her parents, and all the pain that had entailed, but the memory came back to her as sharp as cold air. Never quite measuring up. Wanting nothing more than to escape.

Lorne's room – with a poster of the Sugababes Blu-tacked on the door – was opposite the top of the stairs, next to the family bathroom. The persistent buzz of Mr Wood's chainsaw was more muffled here. Zoë pushed opened the door, went inside and stood for a while, taking in the room.

Lorne had been privileged – Faulkener's would have set the Woods back twelve to fifteen grand a year, probably, and here there were little giveaways of her lifestyle that pinned her as a cut above the ordinary: a framed photo of her in front of the Sydney Opera House, another of her dressed in a strapless ballgown, débutante smile on her face, age all of thirteen, Zoë guessed. Aside from that, what was most distressing about the room was its sheer normality. Exactly the sort of teenage girl's bedroom that would be replicated in hundreds of other homes across Bath. No pictures of horses; instead it was posters of girl bands dressed in what looked like lingerie. On the wall next to the window a corkboard was covered with photos – Lorne pictured on a climbing wall, tongue out to the camera, delighted grin on her face; Lorne with three other girls crammed into a photo booth; Lorne in a floaty white dress, a flower circlet on her ankle; Lorne in a strawberry-design swimsuit – the epitome of every teenage boy's fantasy. Her hair changed too, from one shot to the next, from bright blonde, cut in a fringe, to Goth, sullen black, complete with a magenta streak in the fringe. Zoë wondered how that had gone down at Faulkener's School. At her boarding-school hair dye would have been an expellable offence, but that school's speciality had been turning out no-nonsense girls. Like her. And like Pippa Wood downstairs.

She put down her cup, pulled a pair of gloves out of her pocket, put them on and opened a drawer. Underwear, in a bundle, perhaps from Lorne's own untidiness or perhaps because the police team had been untidy – knickers to one side, bras to the other. Another drawer had school socks and tights, another hair accessories, hundreds of them bursting out. She went to a small multicoloured chest of drawers and peered into the top drawer. More underwear. A stack of red gymkhana rosettes. Perhaps Lorne hadn't been allowed to throw them away so she'd done the next best thing and kept them well out of sight.

Out of sight . . .

She straightened and scanned the room. When Lorne had gone missing the OIC had come in here with a Support Group team looking for clues to her disappearance. Zoë had read through his notes and there hadn't been anything much. But a girl like

Lorne? Tension between her and her mother? There had to be something the OIC had missed. She sat on the bed, her hands resting on her lap, and concentrated on summoning up the feeling she'd had earlier. The sudden, shuddering connection to her own teenage self. If this had been *her* room, where would *she* have hidden things?

At boarding-school the dorms had been small – just four to a room. There had been a cupboard stretching the length of one wall and each girl had been allocated a section in it for her clothes. They had also been given a small bedside table each. Not much scope for hiding things you didn't want others to see. Zoë had found a way, though. Her eyes trailed to Lorne's bedside table, which was piled with magazines. She pushed herself off the bed, lay down on the floor, and reached a hand up under the table. She found just the smooth wood of the base. She got up, moved to the desk and did the same. Nothing. She went to the wardrobe. This time when she pushed her fingers underneath she found, taped to the base, a solid, block-shaped object encased in a plastic bag.

She peeled away the tape, removed the package and sat on the bed with it on her lap. Inside the plastic bag she found a small book, complete with a lock in the shape of a heart, a key in it. On the front of it were scrawled the words: 'Mum, if you've found this then I can't stop you reading it. But don't forget that you will have betrayed my trust.' Zoë smiled for the little human part of Lorne that had just peeped out. More human than Pippa downstairs, still fretting that her daughter wasn't remotely interested in horses.

Zoë opened the book, and leafed through the pages. Lorne had pasted the pages with paper cut-out flowers, and little stickers in the shape of eyes that blinked and jiggled when you moved them. Most of the earlier dates had no entry, but for the last few weeks it seemed Lorne had become an inveterate scribbler. Every page was crammed to the margins with notes in a tiny, barely legible scrawl. Zoë took her reading glasses from the breast pocket of her shirt, carried the book to the window, where the light was good, and read.

Most of the stuff was predictable teenage angst. Every day Lorne had recorded her weight and the number of calories she'd eaten, then a long, some-times desperate commentary on how her hair looked awful, how fat she was getting. She made plans for how much she would eat at weekends. Zoë had read surveys that said at least seventy per cent of teenage girls were always on a diet. She'd spent her own teens worrying about the streak-of-piss insults her gangly frame got her – but to be always worrying about what food you put in your mouth, what kind of a hell prison was that?

More than once the initials 'RH' came up.

April fourteenth. Saw RH. He's mega with the fat-tie thing. Christina says he likes me. I don't know.
Wore my Hard Candy blue eyeshadow. Totally lush!

117

RH was talking to that girl in the sixth form that's supposed to have a flat in New York. Nela says her name is Mathilda but I thought Tillie though maybe that's short for it. Quite pretty with blonde hair but she's got really fat calves. She shouldn't wear leggings. Yuk.

Went to Katinka's after school. And got some hair colour – going to do it when Alice comes over at the weekend. Mum's going to FREEEEEEEEEEAKKKK!!!!! EEEEEKKK!!!

Read about this girl who was on holiday in Goa with her family. She was just sitting on the beach and a scout from Storm in London saw her. Her first job she got £1,000 and the editor of Vogue saw her and put her on the front page. Now she lives in New York, New York!!!! And she's from Weston bloody super Mare! I look at her and I think – if you can do it . . .

The next page was taken up with nothing but the initials 'LW' entwined with 'RH'. On the page after that, on 20 April, a note said:

Kissed him!!!!! I am officially in LOVE!!!!!! Can't tell anyone. He said his mum would kill him if she knew. She's a complete witch. He says he's going to apply to University College and Imperial, so when I've got my totally lush flat in Chelsea (ha ha!) he can come and see me anytime we feel like it and his batshit crazy mother can't get us.

Zoë turned the page. If Debbie Harry saw this and the comments on his dominating mother, she'd hang, draw and quarter RH. Whoever he was.

Zeb Juice are going to see me!!! Can't believe it. That's given me a boost I can't believe. I'm going to call some of the others too. I'm going to wear my pink heels and blue jeans. Shopping list, get Noodlehead Curl Boost, St Tropez Bronzing Mist – Marie Claire says it's legend. £30. But, doh, brain freeze about where I'm going to get that money from. If I walk home every day and save all my bus fares and all my tuck money I still won't have enough . . .

After that the pages hadn't been written on. Instead they'd been filled with flowers and hearts and sketches of a girl – Lorne herself, presumably – dressed in bikinis and high-heeled boots. Zoë flicked through the remaining pages. There was nothing else of any interest. She closed the diary, and as she did, she noticed a small pocket on the back. When she inserted her nail she found a tiny object in there. An eight-gigabyte camera card.

She sorted around on the desk until she found the camera it belonged to, plugged in the chip and began clicking through the photos. Lorne was pictured here, right in this bedroom. From the awkward position it looked as though she'd taken them herself using an automatic timer. In the first three she was dressed in a bikini – standing full length. But it was the fourth and subsequent shots that made Zoë sit down on the bed, dismayed. Lorne appeared dressed in suspenders, stockings and a basque, poised coquettishly on the floor, legs crossed. In the last two she had taken the basque off and was looking provocatively into the camera, her tongue held lightly at her glossed lips.

Zoë clicked through them twice, a huge wave of sadness coming over her. Why would a nice middle-class girl like Lorne do something like that? Lots of reasons, of course – maybe it was nothing more sinister than an impressionable schoolgirl trying to ease herself into her own sexuality. Or maybe to impress a boyfriend. But it could also be nastier than that. An old ghost came to Zoë then, going pitter-patter around the corners of her mind – thinking that it could be because Lorne had learned to dislike herself early. Maybe when she realized her brother was the star in their mother's eyes she'd begun struggling to find a way to escape. Zoë knew what that felt like. Maybe that was what these photos were about.

Outside, the noise of Mr Wood's chainsaw cut through the silence. She took the card out of the camera and held it in the palm of her hand, trying to decide if the photos were important – the portal to a whole separate side of Lorne that no one was mentioning. Whether they were connected to her modelling dream and just how desperate she had been to make that dream come true. No, she told her-self, probably lots of teenage girls had photos of themselves like this, hidden somewhere from Mum and Dad. It would be better just to leave them in the diary, taped out of sight, never to be seen again. Or destroy the chip.

Or treat it as an investigative lead.

She raised her eyes to the window, saw the frondy leaves of a silver birch moving gently against the blue sky. Some time passed. Thirty seconds. A minute. Then she got to her feet and shoved the card into her back jeans pocket. 'Sorry, Lorne,' she murmured. 'But I'm not sure. Not yet.'

16

Downstairs in the conservatory, Pippa was sitting with the liaison officer. She had a diary open on her lap and seemed to be going through her plans for the next month or so. Maybe they were discussing funerals, press conferences. Outside, Mr Wood was still thrashing the life out of the tree. When Pippa heard Zoë come down she stopped talking. She closed the book and came through into the hallway. 'All finished?'

'Just one or two questions.'

'That's OK. I want to help.'

'Lorne had a big circle of friends?'

'A big circle? Oh, God, yes. I couldn't keep up with it. From the moment she hit fifteen and I gave her a phone and keys to the house I only ever saw her when she brought people back here. They're a nightmare, teenagers, absolute nightmare. Sometimes you just want to crawl under a . . .' She trailed off. As if it had just dawned on her that there'd never be another teenager to make her life a misery. 'Yes, well . . .' She rubbed her arms convulsively and glanced back at the kitchen. 'Yes. Anyway, did you want some more coffee?'

'That's OK,' Zoë said gently. 'I've had enough to send me to the moon and back. Can I ask you, though, about her friends? Were they mostly from the school?'

'No.' Pippa shook her head. 'No, not really. They were from all over. She was always talking to people. And I think with the way she looked she – she had lots of boys who recognized her. I don't know where she gets it from – not me, that's for sure.'

'But not one special boyfriend?'

'No.'

'Can I ask you the million-dollar question?'

'What? Was she a virgin? Is that it?'

'Someone's going to have to ask it eventually. It's not that she's in the defence stand here. It's just that we need to build a better picture.'

'Yes, I know. I've already been told by the—' She glanced back to where the liaison officer was sitting, studying his laptop. 'I know it's an important question. He said it would be, said it could be relevant.' She put her finger to her forehead and kept it there, as if she was concentrating very hard on something. Like keeping her balance. 'I don't know, is the honest truth. If you wanted me to put money on it I'd say no. But please don't tell other people that. I don't want it gossiped about.'

'You don't remember anyone with the initials "RH", do you?'

'No. Doesn't ring any bells. Why?'

'Just wondering. What about the name Zeb Juice? Does that mean anything to you?'

Pippa gave an exasperated sigh. 'Yes, I'm afraid so. Zebedee Juice. It's an agency in George Street.'

'An agency?'

'Modelling. I told you – Lorne was under the impression she'd be the next Kate Moss, so when the agency agreed to see her I was worried – very worried. As you can imagine.'

'What sort of modelling do they deal with?'

'What sort? Well – I don't know. The usual, of course. Fashiony stuff. Catwalk.'

So not the kind of modelling in the pictures. Zoë felt better to hear that. 'What happened – when she went to the agency?'

'They told her she wasn't tall enough. They weren't interested, thank God.'

'You were pleased?'

'Of course I was pleased.' Pippa sounded faintly annoyed. 'What mother wouldn't be? It was a ridiculous dream.'

Zoë didn't answer that. Outside the conservatory four magpies had appeared on the lawn and were hopping around, making feints at each other. *One for sorrow, two for joy. Three for a girl, four for a boy.* She could still see the big brother outside, sitting awkwardly on the bench. The one who'd got it all right in his mother's eyes.

'Is that all? Is that all you need?'

'For the time being. Yes, it is. Thank you.'

She felt in her pocket for her car keys and was

halfway out of the door when Pippa said suddenly, 'I was at school with you, wasn't I?'

Zoë turned back slowly. 'I didn't like to point it out.'

'You were good at games and you were clever. Really clever. You used to win all the quizzes. Did you go to university? Everyone said you would.'

'University? No. I dropped out. Travelled the world and ended up back here. Broke my father's back financially, putting me and my sister through school, and look what I did to repay him.' She gave a rueful smile. 'Went into the cops.'

'I didn't know you had a sister.'

'No,' she said slowly. 'She went to a different school – softer than the one we were at. The sort that turns out good wives.'

'How come you went to different schools?'

'Oh, you know,' she said evasively. 'We couldn't get on somehow. Like you said – amazing how you combine the same genes and get two totally different people.'

'And you?' Pippa said. 'How about you? Did you have children?'

'No.'

Pippa took a breath to reply – and in that second, in the slight pause, Zoë saw the cracks. The human being in there. As if the terrified Pippa Wood, the one who wouldn't know where to begin or end dealing with this horror, had peeped out of her eyes. It was a flash, just a fleeting moment, a panicked, screaming Picasso face, a terror that Zoë was going to answer,

125

Oh, yes. I have a beautiful daughter. Just like Lorne. Except mine's alive. It was basic human envy – the envy that the sick, the grieving and the old have for the young and the healthy. And the living. Then the look was gone, and the calm mask was back.

'Goodbye,' she said, and turned away abruptly, closing the door behind her.

Zoë was left standing in the sunlight with the sound of Mr Wood's saw, and the low chug-chug-chug of a barge going past on the canal.

17

All day at work people talked about Lorne Wood. Every place Sally cleaned someone would mention it, would shake their head and say how terrible it was – as if she was one of their own children. Sally didn't much want to talk about it, she didn't want to think about how easily it could have been Millie. This morning she'd taken the spoiled tarot card out of the pack and hidden it in a drawer. The remainder were wrapped in a cloth inside her tote bag because today she was working near the hippie shop, and there might be an opportunity to go in and show the cards to the owner. But in the end she couldn't summon up the courage. Instead she locked them in the boot of the car and tried to stop thinking about them.

It was the day she sometimes picked up Millie from school, rather than let her take the bus. She parked in a street opposite, along with all the other mothers, their windows open to watch the gates. Nial and Peter came out and passed, holding up a hand to say hi to her, then, after a short interval, Sophie on her own. The moment she saw Sally she hurried over to the car. 'Mrs Benedict, Millie's still in the class-room. She wants you to go and get her.'

'Why?'

'I don't know. She's upset.'

Sally locked the car and went inside quickly, hurrying down the vaulted-stone corridors. The classroom was at the other side of the school – it was very old-fashioned, lined with bookshelves, stuffed with books and learning aids. Light came through the tall mullioned windows. At one of the individual desks that faced the windows, Millie sat with her head drooping forward. When she heard the door open she turned. Her face was tight, as if a hand was holding it from behind and forcing her head to move.

'Mum.'

She came and stood at the desk. 'Are you OK? I saw Sophie.'

'I don't feel well, Mum. Can you bring the car in through the back entrance and pick me up next to the sports hall?'

'What's wrong? You should have called.'

'Nothing. I mean – it's my stomach. It's just a bit—'

'Your stomach?'

'It's crampy.'

'Your period?'

'No – just – I don't know. It feels a bit squirmy.'

Sally examined Millie's face. She'd never been good at knowing when her daughter was lying. But right now she suspected that whatever was wrong with Millie it had nothing to do with her stomach.

128

She looked as if she was hiding something. 'Did you speak to Matron?'

She shook her head, moved her eyes from Sally's scrutiny and stared out of the window. 'Please, Mum, can you just get the car?'

'Is this about Lorne? Are you upset?'

'No.'

'Then is it Glastonbury? Because, Millie, I can't change my mind, darling.'

'*No*. It's *not*. I just feel ill. I *swear*.'

Sally sighed. 'OK. I'll be waiting round the side in five minutes.'

She picked up the car from the street and stopped it in the courtyard that faced the modern buildings of the new sports hall. Millie came out, her school blazer draped over her shoulders, her face down, and got quickly into the car. 'Can we go straight home?'

'You'll have to tell me what's happening.'

'Please.' She curled into the seat and pulled her knees up. 'Please, Mum.'

'Either you tell me what's going on or we're going to the doctor's.'

'No, Mum, I feel better now. I just want to go home.'

Sally put the car in gear and drove to the end of the tarmac drive, stopping at the intersection. She indicated left. Millie jerked sideways in her seat, her hand shooting out to grab the steering-wheel. 'No! Wait – wait, Mum, please wait. Don't.'

'What is it?'

129

Millie was trembling. Her face was white, but Sally knew it wasn't pain. If she had to put a finger on it she'd have said it was fear. 'Millie?'

'Go right. *Right.*'

'But left is the way home.'

'We can go the back way. All my friends are out there. They'll do the L on the forehead thing if they see me taken off by Mummy. Loser.'

'No one's there. They've gone.'

'Can we just go the back way, Mum? Please go right.'

Sally took the car out of gear. 'I'm sorry, Millie, but it's left. Unless you tell me what's going on.'

'Oh, *God!*' She screwed up her fists. 'OK, OK. Just let me – give me a moment to . . .' She shuffled down the seat so she was crushed in the footwell.

'What are you doing?'

'There's someone out there. In a purple jeep. I've got to avoid him.'

'Who?'

'Just someone.'

Down on the floor Millie's face was white, her pupils dilated, She wasn't just afraid – she was terrified. As if there was a monster out in the street. Sally eyed the phone in its holster on the dashboard and wondered who she could call. Isabelle? Steve?

'Please, Mum! Can we go?'

Sally swallowed and put the car in gear. She inched it out over the junction and peered up and down the street. Her palms were sweating on the vinyl steering-wheel. The street was quieter now – the schoolkids

130

had indeed gone, but, on the far side of the road, its nose facing the school gates, was parked a strange-looking purple four-wheel drive. It had bull-bars, a snorkel, and what looked like daggers embedded in the wheels.

Sally pulled the Ka out into the road.

'Is he there?' Millie dragged the blazer over her head and shrank further into the footwell, her hands over her head. 'Is he? Oh, my God, I'm *so* dead.'

Sally pulled up alongside the purple car. She let the car stop in the middle of the road, and turned woodenly to look at the man. He was mixed race, with a little pencil moustache and very shiny gelled hair. He wore a tight white T-shirt and a thick gold necklace. At first he didn't notice her. He was watching the gates of the school. Then he sensed her presence. He turned, met her eyes and gave her a slow smile, revealing a single diamond mounted in one of his front teeth. 'What?' he mouthed. 'What?'

She floored the accelerator and the little car shot down the hill, screeching, making pedestrians stop and stare.

'*Mum?* What's happening? Was he there?'

At the bottom of the hill she glanced into the rear-view mirror and saw that he hadn't attempted to follow. She swung the car left past the big nineteenth-century church on the fork, then to the right, then left again, putting as much distance as she could between themselves and the man. She didn't stop until she'd reached Peppercorn, way out in the deserted country-side. She got out and stood on the lawn, breathing

131

the sulphury smell of the engine and the organic waft of cow manure and grass – scanning the valley where the line of commuters wound its sluggish way towards the motorway. When she was sure nothing had followed them she went back to the car and opened the door. Millie ventured out from under the blazer, her hair mussed and sticking out all over the place, a bleary, lost look on her face. She crawled out, limp and exhausted, her head hanging.

'Can we go inside now?'

Sally carried all her work gear into the cottage and put it in a pile in the corner. Then she went into the bedroom, Millie following. Sally kicked off her shoes and pulled back the covers.

'What?'

'Get in.'

'But it's only five o'—'

'Please.'

Millie obediently kicked off her shoes and crawled on to the bed. Sally checked the curtains were drawn tight, then switched off the light and got in next to her daughter, embracing her from behind, her head resting on her back. She didn't speak. She lay there, listening to Millie breathing, her eyes on the slit of light between the curtains. She counted in her head, slowly and rhythmically moving herself through the minutes, through the silence.

It was almost a quarter of an hour before Millie spoke. 'I'm sorry.'

Sally nodded. She was sure it was true.

'He's involved in drugs.'

'Oh, God,' she said wearily. 'Oh, God.'

'He sells drugs in the school, and at Faulkener's too. He goes back and forth between the two. I don't take them, Mum. I don't. I tried it once with Nial and Soph. Please, please, don't tell Isabelle – please. We hated it. It made my heart race and I thought I was going to die, but everyone at school's done it, honestly – you'd be so shocked, Mum, at who's done it. The prefects have, some of the ones in the hockey teams. They do it before they have a match. It's like it's totally normal.'

Sally pressed her head tighter into her daughter's back. This was what the tarot card had been trying to warn her about, this happening behind her back. God, she really was as dumb as Julian had always said. 'Is that why you're avoiding him, that man? Because of the drugs?'

'No. I don't take drugs, Mum. I swear. I swear on everything.'

'Is it something to do with Lorne Wood? With what happened to her?'

Millie turned round and gave her mother an odd look. 'No. Of course not. Why do you think it would have anything to do with that?'

'Then what?'

'Money.'

'What money?'

'He lent me some money.' She hitched in a breath, started to cry quietly. 'Oh, Mum, I honestly thought it would be OK, I honestly did. I never thought it was going to turn out like this.'

Sally blinked dry-eyed in the darkness. Millie borrowing money? From someone like that? This was a dream. 'It can't be much.' She paused, then added tentatively, 'Can it?'

Millie curled herself into a ball, her shoulders shaking, saying over and over, 'Oh shit oh shit oh shit. Mum, if you and Dad hadn't split up it would never have happened. I'd have the money if you were still together.'

'Is this about Glastonbury?'

'No – it's about Malta. If you and Dad were still together I could have gone on that school trip to Malta.'

'You *did* go to Malta.'

'Yes, but I could have gone without having to—' She began to sob loudly. 'This is such a mess. I'm such an idiot.'

Sally lifted her head. 'Dad paid for the trip to Malta.'

'He *didn't*. In the end Melissa said he couldn't. I couldn't tell you – I thought you'd stop me going.'

'So how on earth did you . . . ? Oh, Millie. You're telling me you got the money from *him*. From that man? But it must have been a *lot*. A lot of money.'

'You're making it sound awful. You don't *understand* – you haven't got a *clue* what it's like. Everyone else's parents are together. The whole class is going skiing in the autumn except Thomas and he doesn't count, and Selma is going to New York at half-term. She'll probably get loads of clothes while she's there too and that's before you even *get* to who's going to

Glasto. It's *horrible* being me, Mum. You've got no idea, it's horrible.'

'How much do you owe him?'

'He's saying because I didn't pay it back when I should have he's got to charge me interest.'

'That's completely illegal. We'll have to go to the police. We can drive there now.'

'*No*. No, Mum. You can't.' Millie twisted around, stared over her shoulder at her mother. 'You can't go to the police – you just can't. I'll get expelled and everyone'll find out – none of the parents'll let me hang out with my friends. Dad'll find out – Peter and Nial and Sophie'll all find out. And he'll hurt me next time. Really. If he finds out I went to the police I'll be dead, Mum. *Please* – please. I'll do anything. I'll stop school and go to one of the state schools, then Dad can give the money he's giving Kingsmead to me. I'll do *anything*. Just *please* don't go to the police – I can't bear it if you tell anyone.'

'How much do you owe him, Millie?'

Millie went quiet and still, as if she was crawling inside herself, rooting around to find a place where she was safe. 'Four . . .' she murmured after a while '. . . thousand. He kept adding interest, Mum, he kept making it more.'

Sally closed her eyes, rested her forehead against Millie's hot back. She pictured Isabelle's kitchen littered with expensive food and drink; she saw Melissa planting exotic shrubs in the garden at Sion Road; she saw David Goldrab swinging himself into his giant car. She saw all the mothers and fathers

135

outside Kingsmead and knew that she was looking into a different world. That in the year and a half since she'd been divorced from Julian, she and Millie had slipped noiselessly and uncomplainingly over an invisible barrier into a place they'd never come back from. And it was all because of money.

18

For the first time since Zoë had known him, Ben's appearance was less than perfect at that evening's team meeting. Last night's wine and lack of sleep were starting to show. He had the beginning of a five o'clock shadow on his jaw and his shirt was creased at the back. To her annoyance she found that creased shirt slightly endearing.

'It's all a bit disappointing,' he said, addressing the assembled team. 'I admit it hasn't been a good day. First of all we're still waiting for a single sighting. Unbelievable, I know, considering how usually a case with this much media will pop up scores of sightings all over the place. And Lorne, a striking girl, known to people, walking all that way home and not one person claiming they saw her. Nothing on any of the shops' CCTV equipment, and none of the shop assistants remember anything either – though, according to her family, she did have a habit of browsing and not buying. So, nothing very encouraging on that.'

He rolled up his sleeves. It had been hot today. Hot

enough to make those creases and so hot that summer seemed to have arrived already. Out in the streets almond blossom, blown in from the gardens and the parks, lay in drifts in the gutters. Zoë hadn't said anything to Ben about the camera chip. She wasn't sure how and when she'd do it. Whether she'd do it at all. The chip was still in her back pocket.

'Our witness at the canal reported a conversation with Lorne that really didn't tally with the conversation the OIC was told about when she went missing. So I spent an hour talking to Alice, the friend Lorne was on the phone to, and although she admitted Lorne was more upset than she'd originally said, she was evasive when I pushed her on *why* she was upset.' He took a sip of coffee, set the cup down carefully. 'So, let me just make an intuitive comment here. She was protecting someone.'

The superintendent, who had been at the back of the room, his arms folded, waiting to be impressed, now leaned forward. 'Protecting someone?'

'Yes. Alice was Lorne's best friend, I mean real to-the-death friends, inseparable. And now she's covering something up for her, even though she's dead. Something important.'

Debbie Harry, who had been sitting in silence in the corner, got up and came to the front. She stood shoulder to shoulder with Ben and addressed the team, as if this was an investigation they were running together. 'That's right. You see, from this, and from other comments some of her schoolfriends have made, we're pretty sure there's probably a boyfriend. Someone Lorne wanted to keep secret.'

Zoë stared at her. *We*'re pretty sure? Who the hell did she think she was? An investigator? Ben's partner? She was a psychologist. What was she doing still hanging around? The last Zoë remembered, these people got paid for on an hourly basis; obviously Debbie didn't get that. Obviously she thought she was part of the team. And Zoë could see from the team's faces that they were all, to a man, every one of them, sucking up her psychology-for-dummies stuff because it was coming out of the mouth of a pretty girl with some letters after her name.

'Yes. There is almost certainly a boyfriend. It accounts for Alice's evasiveness. We think Lorne may have been keeping it secret for a while – and now, of course, he's afraid to come forward. Why, we don't know, but he's out there. Whether he was responsible for her death or not . . . well, that's an unknowable. But those words, "I've had enough . . ."' Debbie gave the team her patronizing smile, the one that said, *Come along – I'm interested in what you think. Let's work together on this* '. . . does it sound to you like she and the secret boyfriend had been having trouble?'

'RH,' Zoë said. Everyone turned to her in surprise. 'His initials will be "RH".'

'How did you reach that conclusion?' said the superintendent.

She gave him a withering look. 'I've had my palm read. This morning. The psychics are great at this stuff – this investigatory shit. They said someone with the initials "RH" is going to come into my life.'

There was a brief embarrassed silence at the deliberate poke at Debbie. Ben frowned at Zoë. Then Debbie spoke. 'I'm sorry,' she said archly. 'What's your point?'

'In Lorne's diary she talks about RH. I've spent the afternoon chasing it. So far nothing. If you're looking for a secret boyfriend, look for someone with those initials.'

There was a long pause. Then Debbie let out her breath and smiled. Her inclusive, welcoming smile, as if to say: *I am so glad you've finally seen our way of thinking. Welcome aboard the Great Ship Debbie Harry. We know you're going to love your time here.* 'Thank you, Detective Benedict. Thank you. It's great to be moving forward now. And I think you'll all agree that finding "RH" . . .' she opened her hands, delighted with the way things were progressing '. . . will be absolutely crucial to cracking this case.'

19

A lot of families in Bath chose Victorian homes over Georgian – the Victorians tended to have more rooms on each floor, not so many flights of stairs to run up chasing kids or pets. They were easier to heat and easier to make alterations to because most of them weren't listed. The house Sally had lived in with Julian was a detached Victorian villa, with an extension and a conservatory at the rear, set well back from the road in large gardens that Millie used to enjoy running around. Now, though, there were paths where there never had been, a whole complex system of low lavender bushes cut severely into squares. Millie's tree-house had been repainted with purple crocodiles and elephants for little Adelayde, the new Cassidy.

Millie hated Melissa. She only came here once a week on sufferance to see her dad. Now when Sally pulled up outside, she refused to go in, or even have her presence acknowledged. She sat in the car with her nose pressed to the window and stared out as Sally walked up the path, lit by the solar-powered garden lights that were stuck in the ground every few feet.

She hadn't phoned in advance – Julian would find a way of not answering the call – she went straight to the front door and knocked loudly. From inside came a voice, Melissa, calling, 'Julian. The door.' A moment or two later he appeared, wine glass in hand.

'Oh.' His face fell when he saw her. 'Sally.'

'Can I come in?'

He glanced uneasily over his shoulder. She could see an expensively engineered pram sitting there, a row of rattles suspended above it. 'What's it about?'

'Millie.'

'Julian?' Melissa called from inside. 'Who is it, baby?'

'It's . . . Sally.'

There was a silence. Then the living-room door opened and Melissa appeared. She was a landscape gardener by trade, and when Sally had first met her she seemed to be dressed for a rodeo, with a suede cowboy hat, walking boots with thick socks folded over the tops and tweed shorts that never changed colour from day to day. She laughed like a pony and the cord of the hat would bounce around under her chin. Sometimes in the cold weather a clear drip would form at the end of Melissa's nose and tremble there unnoticed for long minutes while she talked. She was the last person Sally would have expected Julian to go for. Today she was dressed in her customary shorts, but over them she wore an enormous oatmeal cardigan with Adelayde strapped to her chest in a scarlet cloth papoose. She automatically jiggled up and down to keep the baby asleep while she eyed her husband's ex-wife.

'Sally!' she said after a moment or two, 'You look lovely. Come in.' She stepped back to let her into the living room, smiling expansively. 'Lovely to see you.'

Sally went in and stood for a while in silence. The room was unrecognizable – redecorated in deep primary colours, with sharp, uncomfortable furniture. A black and white silk curtain was pulled across half of the bay windows, the baby's playpen placed in front of them.

Melissa switched off the television, which was playing quietly in the corner, and settled on the edge of the large sofa, shifting the baby's legs in the sling so they lay on either side of her stomach. Sally glanced around for her comfy old armchair where she had fed Millie as a baby. Instead she saw a leather love seat decorated in purple and white hexagons. She sat on it awkwardly.

'How's Millie?' said Melissa, with a smile. 'Lively as ever?'

'No. She's terrible.'

Melissa's smile faded. 'Really? Is it because of that girl? Lorne Wood?'

'That's not helping.'

'One of the boys who did work experience with me knew her. He had a crush on her. I was surprised. She didn't seem his type. Terrible – cheap-looking, you know.'

'What's troubling Millie?' asked Julian. 'She seemed all right the other day.'

143

'It's been a long time, but I think she's still finding the divorce very difficult.'

'Sally,' Julian murmured, 'maybe if you want to talk about the divorce it'd be better if—'

'She's having a hard time.' Her voice came out more firmly than she'd expected it to. 'She's just a little girl and she's finding it difficult.'

Julian frowned. He'd never seen this from Sally. Looking a little nervous, he closed the door and crossed the room. He sat down next to Melissa, pulling his trousers up his thin legs so that he didn't stretch the knees. Looking at him now, Sally wondered what on earth she'd ever seen in him, except that he'd always been there somehow, paying for things and answering questions for her like a father. Until the day he wasn't, and he was doing it all for Melissa instead. 'OK. I hear you. You want a discussion. And what do you want out of that discussion? From us – me and Melissa?'

She blinked. 'Uh – money.'

Melissa took a deep breath. She sat back on the sofa and crossed one long tanned leg over the other, fixing her eyes on the ceiling. Julian closed his eyes as if he'd had a momentary sharp pain in his head. He opened them, put his elbows on his knees and placed his palms together. 'Can I just say that this is something we did talk about before? And, if you remember, I said—'

'Four thousand pounds.'

'*Jesus!*' Melissa hissed. She bounced Adelayde even

more vigorously, her eyes still locked on the ceiling. *'Jesus Christ.'*

Julian sat back in the chair, folded his arms and regarded Sally carefully. It was the sort of look she'd seen him use in business, sizing up a deal, trying to decide if a client was to be trusted. He was scrutinizing her as if, for the first time, he saw her as someone the same age as he was, and not his inferior – his little child bride. 'You're not joking, I take it.'

'I'm not.'

'What's the money for?'

'The trip to Malta. You said you were going to pay for it.'

'OK. If there's going to be aggression introduced at this point this might be the time to call a halt and say let's chat to the solicitors first and then—'

'You told her you were going to pay for her to go to Malta. You made her that promise – I was there when you did it. It would have been something quite different if you'd said no, but that's not what happened. You made the promise and broke it. She thought you were going to pay for her. She ended up having to borrow the money.'

'I suppose,' Melissa said, in a level tone, 'she *could* have cancelled it when she knew Julian and I *really* couldn't afford it.'

'All her friends were going.'

'No one mentioned four thousand to me,' Julian said. 'Four thousand! What sort of trip to Malta costs four thousand pounds? They're teenagers, for heaven's sake. They're supposed to sleep on the floor

145

of the train, not take suites in the new Airbus A380.'

'This is genuine. Millie needs the money. I wouldn't be here otherwise.'

'Millie needs it or you need it?' Melissa said. Then she closed her eyes. 'Sorry – I didn't mean that. Ignore me.'

'Who did she borrow the money from? Not Nial's parents, please, God. They've already got me on their shit list with whatever you've told them over the divorce.'

'Julian, look – I can't make you, I can't force you to do anything. I signed my rights away with the divorce, and even if I could afford legal advice I know what they'd say. All I can do is ask you, politely, to help her. She's in trouble, Julian, really in trouble. She's only fifteen and there's nothing I can do in this situation.'

He licked his lips, glanced at his wife. 'Melissa?'

She shrugged. She hadn't taken her eyes off the ceiling and was still jiggling the baby up and down. She had the look of someone humming loudly in their head to block out what was happening around them. 'You do whatever you think is the right thing.' She placed her hand protectively over Adelayde's small head, as if suddenly it was her and the baby against Sally and Julian. 'Whatever your conscience tells you is right is what you should do.'

Julian gave a hard cough. He looked from Sally to Melissa and back again. Sally had never seen him so uncomfortable. 'I'm sorry, Sally. All the maintenance I was going to give Millie went into Peppercorn.

146

I'll give you a hundred but that'll have to be all.'

Melissa made a small, disgusted noise in her throat.

'You OK about that, Melissa?'

'Fine,' she said, in a high, tense voice. 'Absolutely fine.'

He got to his feet, left the room and could be heard after a moment in his office at the end of the corridor. Sally and Melissa were left in the room on their own, Melissa breathing in and out loudly, as if she was trying to calm herself. Eventually it seemed she couldn't hold it in any longer. Her head snapped towards Sally.

'You said you weren't going to ask for anything else. You told Julian you wouldn't ask for any more. He's paid for your house – he's had to take out a massive mortgage on this place to do it – and he's already paid Millie's school for the next three years. *Three years*. He couldn't afford that but he did it anyway.'

Sally said nothing. On the way up the path she'd noticed several empty bottles of Bollinger in the re-cycling bin. When she'd been with Julian he'd drunk Bollinger on special occasions, not every night. And the oatmeal cardigan Melissa was wearing had cost three hundred pounds. She'd seen it in the window of Square earlier this week. He still had an apartment in Madeira that he rented out, and a cottage in Devon.

'I mean, is she even enjoying the school? Is she doing well? Obviously I hope so because it's a lot of money to pay out if she's not. I very much doubt

Julian will be able to put two children through private education. Adelayde probably doesn't stand a chance with what Millie is costing.' Melissa looked as if she might start crying at any moment. 'So I very much hope for Julian's sake that the one child he's poured everything into will do well.'

Sally got to her feet and went to the door.

'Don't threaten us, Sally.'

She turned back. Melissa had got to her feet and was staring at her with pure hatred. 'Don't be nasty. No need to be nasty – because as nasty as you are I can be nastier.'

Sally opened her mouth to speak, then closed it. Without a word she went into the hallway, shut the door behind her and stood next to the expensive pram, fiddling anxiously with her car keys. A moment later Julian emerged from his study. He was holding a cheque and a printed sheet. It said simply, 'I acknowledge the receipt of the sum of one hundred pounds from Mr J. Cassidy.'

'Sign, please.'

She signed, not meeting his eyes. 'Thank you,' she said quietly. She took the cheque in its good-quality white envelope, and turned for the door.

'Sally?'

She paused, one hand on the lock.

'Please . . .' Julian stepped up close to her and whispered, so Melissa couldn't hear, 'please – will you tell Millie I love her? Will you?'

20

Zoë sat in the back garden of her terraced house, one hand on her knee, the other cupped for the stray cats to shyly nibble biscuits from it. The lights were on inside, the curtains open. She could picture herself as a sad illustration: 'The lonely old spinster with her cats. The only companions she has . . .' When, after the meeting, she'd found Ben in his office he'd been distracted, busily typing up notes. She'd wanted to talk about the meeting – perhaps tell him about the photos. But she was tired of arguing, tired of her lonely position on the opposite side of the ring from the team, so she simply said, 'I'm thinking of knocking off now. See you at mine?'

There had been a pause. Then he'd glanced up at her, a little frazzled. 'I'm sorry, Zoë. I really need to get on with this.'

Afterwards she wondered why it bothered her – it wasn't as if they spent every night together. She didn't care. She really didn't care. Even so, she'd half hoped when she got back to the empty house that he'd be magically standing on the doorstep. He wasn't, though. She trudged up the path and let herself in. The saucer of milk was still in front of the bike.

It was her default to be alone, she thought, pouring more cat biscuits into her cupped hand. It was no big deal. Some people needed people, others just didn't. She thought about what Pippa Wood had said about siblings turning out so differently, of her disappointment at what Lorne had become – and, without warning, her mind opened in a place she hadn't planned, and she was looking through a doorway, seeing a room.

It was the living room from her childhood – the lights on, the fire playing merrily in the grate. Sally, aged about three, was sitting on Mum's lap, Mum smiling at her, stroking her yellow hair. And in the shadowed corner of the room – Zoë, dark-eyed and silent. Sitting on the floor in the corner, playing with building bricks, glancing up surreptitiously from time to time, wondering when Mum would look over or smile at her. Two such different children – the one a beautiful, corn-fed child from a dream, the other a broken-up fox. Spiteful and clever and obstinate.

The 'accident' with Sally's hand had been, truthfully, anything but an accident. The reality was that Zoë had had a fit of temper when what had been building for years was sparked off by something trivial. Zoë had been eight, Sally seven, and from that moment on the sisters were kept apart by their parents, and Zoë had learned for sure who she was and on which side of life she had to exist. She understood now that she was capable of 'evil' and of 'doing the unthinkable'. It was a lesson she'd never be allowed to unlearn.

She glanced up now through the open back door into the lighted room, to the pictures on the wall. Some showed the motorbike trip and some showed her at boarding-school – always grinning and resilient. Great at games and maths, always in trouble with the teachers. Everyone who met her, even Ben, thought that being enrolled, aged just eight, at boarding-school meant she was privileged. No one outside the Benedict family knew it was nothing to do with privilege and pony parties and everything to do with keeping her separate from Sally. Who was kind and sweet and adored by Mum and Dad. So lovely that they had to protect her from her cruel and uncontrollable sister.

Zoë hadn't thought about any of this for years. It was Lorne who'd put it back in her thoughts – Lorne, her perfect brother, and the places she may have gone, like Zoë herself, thinking she could escape the feelings. The photos. That was what chilled Zoë most. Because it was the same way she'd escaped. Eighteen years ago. Not a soul knew about it, but when she had first left boarding-school she'd taken a job for six months in a Bristol nightclub: a teenager still, undressing in front of men twelve times a day. At the time she'd deliberately not given too much thought to what she was doing – she'd laughed about it, insisted it was a great joke, and kept herself focused on the motorbike trip she was going to pay for at the end of it. But on the occasions she heard people talking about the sex-club industry and how it cheapened a person, her brave face would slip. She'd turn away, thinking privately that they didn't recognize that to cheapen something it had to have had worth to start with, that to devalue something it had to have had value. Which was something she, and maybe Lorne, had long lost.

Maybe it was just the natural course for the broken child to veer off into places like that night-club. Places where their own darkness was outmatched by those around them.

Zoë fed the last of the biscuits to the cats. It had begun to rain, pattering on the bike cover, which she had thrown untidily against the garden shed. Something caught her eye. She got up and peered at the cover, at the small puddle that was developing there.

'Well, holy shit and Jesus on a bike,' she muttered to the cats. 'That's what I've been missing. That's it.'

21

Sally called Steve at nine thirty, and within twenty minutes his car headlights came in through the kitchen window and travelled up the wall. On the table in front of her was a pile of papers: mortgage statements, the utilities bills, her wage slips and the estimates for the work that needed doing on the house. She'd been poring over them for the last hour, struggling to see where she could eke out an extra four thousand pounds. Now she gathered them up hurriedly and shoved them behind some books before he appeared in the doorway. He was dressed in mid-length chino shorts, sandals and a faded T-shirt with a little rain sprinkled on the shoulders. He was unshaven and looked tired.

'Hey,' he whispered, closing the door. 'You all right, beautiful?'

Sally beckoned him in. 'It's OK – she's asleep. She's like the dead when she goes.'

He came in, throwing his keys on to the table. 'So? What's going on?'

She went to the fridge and got out the bottle of

wine they'd opened the night before. 'Sorry – but I think I need a drink.' She poured one for him, one for herself, put them on the table and sat, looking into the wine, her shoulders drooping.

'What is it?'

'Nothing. I just wanted a friendly face.'

'It's more than that.'

She took a gulp of the wine.

'Come on. What's on your mind?'

'I'm sorry – I just – it's been a bad day. With Millie, with work.' She shook her head despairingly. How could this keep happening? How could she go on being so stupid? *All* the time. All the time. It just wasn't getting any better. 'The house is falling down around my ears, Steve. The downpipe at the back has fallen off and there's damp everywhere. The thatch is rotting, there are rats in the ceiling and they've eaten through the plasterboard. I found squirrel droppings in the utility room on Monday. It'd cost me ten thousand pounds to put it all back – and me? Idiot me? I don't even know if I'm going to pay my council tax this month. And then . . . then today . . .'

'Today?'

She dropped her hands from her face and looked at him seriously. 'Can you keep a secret?'

'Funny – no one's ever asked me to do that before.'

She gave a watery smile. 'Seriously. It's about Millie. I've promised her not to say anything, but I can't help it. It's all so bizarre – I can't keep it a secret. I've got to talk about it.'

He pulled up a chair and sat. 'Go on. I'm listening.'

154

'She . . . needed some money. She knew she couldn't come to me, so she went to someone she shouldn't have. Someone who wants the money back. And he's not the sort of person I know how to deal with – he's a drug-dealer.'

'Oh, Christ.'

'I know. I'm just so *dense*.' She knocked her knuckles against her forehead, wishing she could wake up the dumb, sleepy mass in there. 'I just never *get* it. I didn't see any of this coming, just like I didn't see the divorce coming, and now my only chance of making a decent living is to work for a criminal, and he's rude and you say he's dangerous, but I haven't got any choice because my daughter still thinks she can live like all her rich friends do and will make any stupid decisions because of it and now I'm—'

'Hey hey hey.' Steve reached across and caught her hand in his. '*Hey*. Take it slowly. We can work it out. I mean— Do you want me to speak to this character? Do you know how to get in touch with him?'

'You can't. If you do, Millie will find out. I've promised her not to say a word. Anyway – God knows what he'll do to her if he thinks he's not getting the money. I've thought about it. The only way is for me to pay back what she's borrowed.'

'Then I'll lend you the money. The divorce wasn't kind on me, you know that, but I can find the money. It's not a problem.'

She bit her lip and raised her eyes to his. In his open face, his straightforward smile, she saw a sweet and welcoming slope. A slope that she could step on to with ease. Fall on to and be carried along. It would be comfortable: the fear would go away. But it would lead her nowhere. Eventually she'd come back to the same numbness she'd reached with Julian.

'No,' she said, with an effort. 'No. Thank you, but no. I've got to work this out on my own. David will pay me an extra four hundred and eighty a month so it'll take a while, but I'll do it. And I borrowed a DIY book from the library – maybe I can fix some of the house myself. There are some tools in the garage that the last owners left and I can borrow some more from Isabelle.'

'OK.' He smiled. 'And what you can't get from her I'll lend you. Whatever you need.'

She smiled back weakly. 'Thank you,' she said. 'Thank you.'

Steve rose and went to the fridge for the wine bottle, but she couldn't draw the line that easily. She sat, her head on one side, turning her glass round and round on the table, watching the wet rings cross and recross.

'Steve?' she said, when he sat down again.

'What?'

'You know this morning, what you were saying about David Goldrab?'

His face darkened. He rubbed his chin thoughtfully with a knuckle. 'Yeah,' he said. 'I remember.'

'What did you mean when you said it was just fluke he hadn't been banged up years ago? If he had been put in prison, what would it have been for?'

'Oh, Sally. Are you sure you want to know all this?'

'Yes. I've got my first day at his tomorrow and, honestly, I'm nervous. I can't go on any more with my head in the clouds, always missing the plain bloody obvious, always being the last to know anything. Please . . .'

Steve shook his head. 'OK. Well, chiefly Goldrab's a pornographer.'

'A pornographer? What does that mean? He sells magazines?'

'Mostly videos. Downloads on the Internet.'

'A pornographer? Are you sure?'

'I'm afraid so. A hundred per cent sure.'

She was surprised to find she wasn't more shocked. 'Gosh – all day I've been thinking you meant he was a real criminal.'

Steve gave a dry laugh. 'He is a real criminal, a real, live criminal. One of the richest pornographers in the country – and that's saying something because we're one of the few nations in the world that doesn't have a thriving porn production industry. He makes his living from persuading young women – not even women some of them, girls, more like – to do things they'll regret for ever. Before the Internet took off he spent a long time in Kosovo making illegal porn that he smuggled into the country. And I mean nasty stuff – animals, bondage. You name it. People have suffered, I can guarantee that. I'm not going to get all Mr Morals on you, for God's sake – I'm a red-blooded man and I'm not saying I haven't watched a bit of porn in my time – but, trust me, a lot of the women he's used didn't have a choice in the matter.

157

They didn't have the freedom. Especially the ones in the Balkans.'

Sally sat in silence, digesting this. She could see the reality and all the subtle equations that came out of it – if she was working for someone like that, it kind of made her equal to him, complicit, even. But after all her consideration she knew she wouldn't back out. She needed the money. 'I suppose that makes me pretty desperate, if I'm working for him.'

Steve reached over and pushed her hair behind her ear. 'Sweetheart, we're *all* desperate. We all have to do things we're not proud of. That's just the way the world goes round.'

22

It was raining so Zoë took the Mondeo. She parked near the locked gates to Sydney Gardens and prised her way through the bushes. The park was officially closed, but unofficially it was open to business. Everywhere she looked she saw young men loitering, standing casually, hands in pockets, or leaning against trees. One or two were actually sitting on the ground, lounging as if it was midday in August and not a rainy night. As she passed most of them melted away into the bushes.

The gate in the wall was set to open out on to the canal but not to allow anyone in at night. A police sign had been placed next to it, warning people that the towpath to the east was blocked due to an incident and advising them to find a different route. Zoë flicked out her torch and shone it at the ground. The rain had eased but earlier it had been heavy enough to fill to the brim the holes left by footsteps in the mud. The little pools glinted back at her in the light. She negotiated round the mud, squeezing through the bushes along the edge, and opened the gate. On the other side of the wall a single Victorian-style streetlamp threw down a yellow glow in a circle on the gravel and the canal water. Zoë ran the torch along the ground and found what she'd expected to find about ten feet away.

A slight depression spanned the path. Maybe some pipe-laying underneath had caused a dip, or a fault in the material. Whatever the cause, it had only taken the smallest amount of rain to join the scattering of puddles into one large lake. There was no way round it. You'd either have to splosh through it or take a running jump. And, she thought, looking back at the gate, if you'd just come through that gate and you were wearing shoes that had got muddy, you would probably use the opportunity to rinse off the mud.

If Lorne had come on to the towpath here she could have cleaned her shoes, and yet there'd still been mud on them when she died. Maybe there was another entrance to the canal, another place she'd stepped in the mud nearer the crime scene. Zoë set off down the path, her hood pulled up, keeping the beam on the ground, sweeping it from side to side. The temperature had dropped and smoke was coming from one or two of the barges, which had shut their doors and lit their wood-burning stoves. The chatter of TVs and the flickering blue light came through the windows.

She'd gone about three hundred yards when a small break in the trees to her left made her stop. It was a tiny space, no more than a badger run. It rose up, away from the path, then fell into darkness on the

160

other side. Pushing aside the brambles and trees that crowded into the opening, she shone the light down. She smiled. Mud. And in it there were two clear shoe prints. They looked at a glance to be an almost exact match to Lorne's muddied ballet pumps.

'Oh, Lorne,' she murmured. 'You weren't shopping on Saturday at all. You've been lying to us.'

23

The next morning Millie refused point blank to go to school. She said it was going to be crazy, anyway, with everyone talking about Lorne, and all the speculation, but Sally knew it was more to do with the guy in the purple jeep sitting outside Kingsmead. She wasn't going to force her, but she wasn't going to leave her at Peppercorn alone, not after last night. She called Isabelle, but she was going to be in meetings all day, so, in spite of herself, she called Julian. He too was working all day.

'Please, Mum,' Millie begged. '*Please*. Just don't make me go to school.'

She looked at Millie for a long time. This was impossible. Either take her fifteen-year-old daughter to the house of a pornographer or let her take her chances with the drug-dealing loan shark. God, what a tangled web. Still, she had to make a decision.

'You'll spend four hours sitting in the back of the car.'

'I don't care. I'll take a book. I won't be in the way.'

Sally sighed. 'Go and make a sandwich. Then get dressed – and I mean *dressed*. No short skirts and a proper blouse, no skimpy T-shirts. Something *sensible*. And you'd better bring some of that English homework too – four hours is a lot of time to kill.'

It was another fine day, the sun already high in the sky, last night's rain just a memory, but all the way to Lightpil House Sally worried. She kept thinking about what Steve had said – about the girls in Kosovo, some of them not even women yet. And then, conversely, she started worrying that David wouldn't let Millie stay, that they'd have to get straight back in the car and turn round, that she'd lose the extra four hundred and eighty pounds a month she'd factored into her sums.

When they pulled into the parking area Millie opened the window and leaned out, blinking in the sun and gazing up at Lightpil House as if she was driving on to a movie set. David Goldrab must have been waiting because before Sally could park he was coming down the long path to meet them. He was wearing his towelling robe and FitFlops, a glass of green tea in his hand, and a digital heart monitor on his wrist, as if he'd just come off one of the treadmills in the gym on the first floor. Sally pulled on the handbrake and watched him, wondering what he'd do when he saw Millie. Sure enough, when he caught sight of her in the front seat he frowned. 'Who's that?'

'Millie,' she said, bracing herself for an argument. 'My daughter. She won't get in the way.'

David bent down at the driver's window, hands on his thighs, and gave Millie a long, appraising look. 'You staying with us, are you?'

'She'll be out here in the car. She won't bother us.'

'Like pheasants, do you, Princess?'

Millie glanced at her mother.

'It's all right,' said David. 'It's not a trick question. Got to learn to answer questions with honesty. If a person asks you a trick question the only person it shows up is them. So – do you like baby pheasants or not?'

'She's staying in the car.'

'Sally, please. She's not a two-year-old. She needs something to occupy herself. Won't come to any harm – better than being cooped up in this . . .' He paused and gazed at the little Ka, trying to find words to describe its lowliness. 'Yeah. Anyway – better you run around in the sunshine, Princess. Now, answer the question. Do you like pheasants?'

'Yes.'

'Good. Then I'll show you where to go and have a look.'

'Don't go out of the grounds,' Sally said. 'And take your phone.'

Millie rolled her eyes. 'I heard you,' she hissed. 'OK?'

Sally took a few deep breaths. She unbuckled her belt and got out of the car. Millie climbed out of the passenger seat and flattened her blouse with her palms, looking around, clearly impressed by everything she saw and amazed that her mother

164

could somehow, in whatever context, be part of it.

'See that path down there at the side of the house?' David came round the front of the car and pointed down to the edge of the property. 'You follow that and you'll find a gate. There's a padlock. Code's 1983. My date of birth.' He gave a laugh. Neither Sally nor Millie joined in. 'Go through and there's a shed. Full of the little buggers. When you're done, come and sit on the terrace. Mum'll make you a lemonade. Won't you, Sally?'

Millie glanced at her mother. Sally hesitated, feeling sick. But she jerked her head to tell Millie to go. To get on with it. 'Phone,' she mouthed at her. 'Keep your *phone* switched *on*.'

With another uncertain look at David, Millie set off down the path. He folded his arms and watched her go. She was very thin in her jeans, which were big in the leg but tight on the hips, and her hair bounced and gleamed in the sunlight. Sally watched the way he was eyeing her daughter. She slammed the car door, louder than she needed to, and he turned to her with a lazy smile.

'What? Oh, Sally, I'm disappointed. You think I'm checking her out, don't you? What do you take me for?' He looked back at Millie, who was just disappearing behind the flower borders. 'Do you think I'm some kind of pervert? A man of my age? A girl of that age? She's far, far too old for me.'

Sally stiffened and he roared with laughter, nudging her arm. 'I'm *joking*, girl. Joking. It was just a leetle joke. Go on – crack a fucking smile, can't you?

165

Christ.' He sighed. 'Did you have to pay extra for that stick you've got up your arse or did it come free with the convent education?'

Sally swallowed. Her mouth was dry. But she didn't let it show. She went to the car boot and began to get out her cleaning equipment.

'I'm only pulling your leg, girl.'

She took out the black attaché case she kept her notepads and pencils in and, without waiting, set off up the path, followed by David, who huffed and puffed and muttered darkly about people with no sense of humour. Inside the house was filled with the smell of bread. He must have been cooking, using the three hundred pounds' worth of automatic bread-maker that sat next to the coffee machine in the kitchen. Sally sucked at the air, pulling it down into her lungs, willing it to calm her. The smell of food always made her nerves go away.

'Know what, Sally?' David said, when they got to the office. 'Don't take this the wrong way, but I have the feeling Sally Benedict doesn't hold David Goldrab in very high esteem. Because that's the way the world works, ain't it? Now, you probably grew up in some place with turrets and stables. Me? Well, there were towers and drawbridges in my past too – a tower block with a fucking great iron security door to stop the junkies off the Isle of Dogs breaking in and shitting in the lift. Which never worked anyway, whether it got used as a toilet or not. Seventeenth floor and no hot water, no heating.'

He sat on his swivel chair, unstrapped the heart

monitor, plugged it into the back of a white Sony laptop and began downloading his day's workout readings. Then he used his heels to kick himself across the room to a larger desktop computer and switched it on.

'1957 – that was when I was really born, not 1983, in case I had you fooled there. Youngest of three boys – it was two to a bed in those days, a mattress on the floor, and count yourself lucky if you got one scabby little square inch of peeling wallpaper to stick your posters on. Always getting your dick groped – had to sleep like this.' He put his hands over his crotch and bent at the waist as if he'd just taken a cricket ball in the groin. 'Oldest brother turned into a drunk at thirteen. Mum never even noticed, she was that taken up with herself and her own bloody misery. He'd come home shit-faced and crash on top of us. Can still smell him, the miserable cunt. One morning I wake up and the bed's wet. He's wet the fucking bed, and the moment I sit up in bed, see him lying there all covered in puke and blood and his own piss but still breathing, still snoring, I know for sure that if it takes every inch of my energy, every drop of my sweat, if I have to eat shit, kill for it, I'm going to get out of there – find my own space. My *Lebensraum*.'

He opened his hands to indicate the grounds outside the window. From there the hills rolled away. There was hardly anything, just a few telegraph poles in the far distance, to indicate that there were any other human beings on the planet. The gate Millie had gone through was surrounded by trees throwing giant shadows on to the grass below. She was nowhere to be seen.

'*Lebensraum*,' he repeated. 'What Hitler wanted. Sometimes, you know, you have to wonder if Hitler didn't have a point. And there's me, Jewish name, and plenty of Jew blood in me, though not as pure as my arse of a father would've liked it – and I'm thinking Hitler had a point! My ancestors, God rest your souls, put your fingers in your ears, but Hitler *was* a vegetarian. And he *did* like animals. And most of all he liked *space*. Space to breathe, space to live, space to sleep. Space not to be groped and pissed on by your *slag* of a brother. And that's what you're here for, Sally, to run my *Lebensraum*. And to keep it like that. Peaceful. Lacking in human clutter.'

The heart monitor had finished downloading its data. David spent some time studying it. Then, seeming satisfied, he switched off the computer.

'Course,' he said, with a half-glance up at her, 'if I had my druthers I'd have a woman in my life, little golden-haired thing with big knockers, a good head for figures, and a problem in the nymphomaniac department. But I know women – most of you've only got one thing on your mind, and it doesn't begin with S. So, Sally, come and sit here.' He drew another chair up next to him in front of the computer. 'Come here and let me show you what I want you to do.'

Sally sat next to him. He smelt vaguely of sweat and aftershave. She couldn't stop thinking about the women in the Balkans, about whether he'd told *them* his life story.

'Now . . .' he waved a hand around the office '. . . this is Tracy Island – the nerve centre of Goldrab Enterprises. We're sitting in the personal section. That, over there, that's the money-making part.'

He was pointing to where a desk sat piled high with files and another computer. There was a filing cabinet next to the desk and, mounted above that, a huge monitor showing the view of the driveway from the security camera in the front. Once she'd been cleaning here and had noticed a pile of paperwork on top of that cabinet. She hadn't looked too closely but she recalled invoices in a foreign language. The name Priština had jumped out. At the time she'd thought it was the name of a city in Russia. Now, thinking about what Steve had said, she guessed it must be Kosovo.

'Sally, I don't want you going home with the idea I don't trust you, because of course I do. But you won't mind me pointing out that my work is confidential. I prefer to keep it that way. In other words, if I catch you snooping around there I'll shoot you in the fucking eye.' He gave a fat, pleased smile when he saw her reaction. 'A joke. Another *joke*. Jesus, the sense-of-humour fairy is definitely AWOL this morning, ain't she? Now, on *this* computer I keep the database for the house. See? So this is where you work. You enter the invoices here, and the receipts *here*. It's not rocket science. You make the calls, get the estimates, organize the workers. Just try to make it so everyone comes on the same day so I'm not running around every morning thinking, I've got to get my drawers on pronto cos the bleeding plumber's on his way.'

'OK,' she said quietly.

'And *smile*, for fuck's sake. Crack a bleeding smile. It's like looking at a shagging slapped arse, looking at you—'

He broke off and jerked to his feet, staring at the CCTV monitor on the wall. 'Holy Jesus,' he muttered under his breath. 'The scabby little bumsucker.'

On the lane outside was parked a small Japanese jeep in a metallic purple, with shiny chrome bull-bars. Sally stared at it. The dealer from Kingsmead? It couldn't be. Here at David Goldrab's? As if he'd *followed* them? The window opened and an arm came out, jabbing at the keypad on the gate. It was him. She recognized the hair and the suntan. She spun round and stared out of the window. Millie had appeared on the lawn. Maybe she'd already seen the pheasants, maybe she wasn't interested anyway, but for some reason she had settled on the grass, lying on her stomach, her phone in both hands, busily texting or browsing, or updating her Facebook page. Sally got up, dithering, not sure what to do, whether to run through the kitchen and yell, or to get her phone and call her.

On screen the man was still jabbing in numbers, though evidently he didn't know the code, because the gates stayed resolutely closed. David didn't seem perturbed in the slightest. He was leaning back in his chair, his hands behind his head, a nasty smile on his face. 'Oh, Jake,' he said, to the monitor. 'Jake the Peg. You didn't ought to be coming back here, mate. No. You really didn't ought to be doing that.'

24

Taking casts of footprints and comparing them to shoes was generally one of the quicker jobs forensics teams did. No waiting around for lengthy lab tests. By eleven o'clock that morning the results from the canal path had come back. The prints Zoë had found last night had been made by Lorne Wood. And when the police looked at the path that led away from the gap in the trees they saw there was only one route she could have taken to get there. From the canal the track led through a small wooded area, then along a path that ran between two horse paddocks, under a railway bridge and out to a bus stop. Nowhere near the shops. Lorne had lied to her mother about where she had been that Saturday and, in Zoë's book, if a person could lie about something like that, there was no knowing what else they could lie about – the fibs could roll on and on, as far as the horizon.

She got one of the DCs to start warrants on the bus companies' CCTV, then spent some time in the office looking at all the routes that passed through the stop near the canal. They snaked out for miles in every direction – there was no knowing which she'd come from. She could have been travelling from almost any direction, she could have changed routes – she could even have gone as far afield as Bristol in the time she'd been away from home. Zoë fished out the camera chip she'd found in Lorne's bedroom and balanced it thoughtfully on her finger, considering it. Twice already she'd almost taken it into Ben's office. But each time she'd stopped herself. She wasn't sure who she was protecting by not speaking up – Lorne or herself. In the end she got up and pulled on her jacket. She needed to know more before she did anything.

The agency was in the centre of Bath. 'No. 1, Milsom Street', said the sign, and under it, written in tall, thin letters, 'The Zebedee Juice Agency'. It was above a boutique, and when Zoë came up the stairs she found a wide room, daylight pouring into it through a vast glass dome in the ceiling. There was no reception desk, just an array of red sofas dotted with *faux*-fur cushions and piles of magazines on black lacquer tables. On the wall in an unframed LCD screen a video played silently – faces, boys and girls, morphing one into another.

The manager, a girl dressed in a polo-neck, denim shorts and spiked heels with metallic shadow on her eyelids, jumped up to greet Zoë with a neurotic-sounding 'Hi, hi hi!' She was twitchy, kept rubbing her nose and swallowing, and it didn't take a genius to see she was itching to get to her next line of coke. Still, Zoë supposed, you didn't get that super-thin look without a bit of help.

She poured two long glasses of Bottlegreen lemon grass pressé and took Zoë to sit near the window. In the street below shoppers and tourists bustled in and out of the shops. The manager admitted she'd half been expecting a visit from the police – she added that maybe she should have called them herself, because she remembered Lorne well. She'd come in with her mother a month ago. She'd been a very nice-looking girl, if a bit short and a little on the heavy side for the catwalk. And her eyebrows had been plucked to within an inch of their lives. 'Most of our models aren't what you or I would call convention-ally pretty. Some of them, if you saw them in the street, you'd almost call ugly. What's hot at the moment is a very animal look. You want to be able to see the ethnicity of a model. If someone walks in the room and I think, Yeah, he's got all the anger of his race behind him, that's when I know I'm on to a winner.'

'Lorne wasn't like that?'

'No. Glamour, maybe, but not right for the ramp. Never.'

'Did you tell her that?'

'Yes.'

'And how did she react?'

'She was upset. But it's what happens all the time, girls coming in here all hopeful, going away com-pletely miserable, rejected.'

'What about Mrs Wood? What was her reaction?'

'Oh, relief. You'd be surprised – I get that reaction more than anything else. Mothers just humouring their daughters, but they're over the moon when someone else points out what they've secretly thought all along and just can't bring themselves to say. The girls, though . . .' She gave a small shake of her head. 'Even when you've said it over and over some of the girls still won't listen to you. For some of them it's like a hunger – eats away at them. They won't take no for an answer. All they care about is seeing themselves staring up out of some glossy page somewhere. Those are the ones I worry about. Those are the ones that'll end up places they really don't want to be.'

'Places they don't want to be?'

The manager wrinkled her brow. 'Yes – you know what I mean.'

Zoë held her eyes. For a moment she'd thought the emphasis in that sentence had been on 'you'. As in *You, DI Benedict, know exactly what I'm talking about. So don't pretend you don't.* She found herself wanting an explanation – wanting to say, 'What the hell do you mean?', but then she caught herself. This girl was twenty if she was a day. There was no way she knew anything about what had happened all those years ago.

'So,' she said levelly, 'what do you do if you get a girl like that who won't be put off?'

The agency manager picked up a little pile of business cards in a plastic holder on one of the tables. She pulled one out and passed it to Zoë. 'We tell them they're better off doing glamour and give them one of these. Want one?'

Zoë took the card. Studied it. It was shaped like a pair of lips. It read: 'Holden's Agency. Where dreams come true'. 'Did you give one to Lorne?'

The manager ran a finger inside her polo-neck, thinking about this. 'I don't know,' she said, after a while. 'Probably not, because her mum was here. I can't recall exactly.'

'She didn't take one anyway?'

'Maybe. I honestly couldn't say.'

Zoë tucked the card into her wallet. She sipped her drink thoughtfully, her eyes on the windows in the department store opposite. Something was niggling at her, something she'd seen, or something the manager had said in the last ten minutes. It wouldn't come to her. She put her glass on the table. 'Lorne didn't mention a boyfriend, did she? At any point when she was here did she mention any names?'

'No. Not that I can recall.'

'Do you have a catalogue? Of your models?'

'Sure.' She opened a drawer to show Zoë a stack of pink-bound notebooks and a box of pink memory sticks. All with the name 'Zebedee Juice' emblazoned in lime green. 'Hard copy or a stick?'

'One of these'll do.' She took a book. 'I want to check if you've got any models with the initials "RH".'

'RH?' While Zoë flicked through the catalogue the manager sat with her thumb in her mouth, her eyes to the ceiling, mentally running a tally of her clients. By the time Zoë got to the end she was shaking her head. 'No. And not even with their real names.'

'Staff?'

'No. There's only me, and Moonshine who comes in in the afternoon. Her real name is Sarah Brown.'

'Nothing else you can remember that sticks in your mind about Lorne? Anything that you think could be important? Anyone she spoke about?'

'No. I've been thinking about it. Ever since I saw the news and put two and two together about it being the same girl who was here, I've been going through it. And I honestly can't remember anything about the meeting that was odd.'

'OK. Can I keep this book?'

'Of course – please. Be my guest.'

'One last thing, and then I'll go. What do you think about Lorne? Do you think she was one of the ones who'd end up in *those* places you were talking about? Did she have the *hunger*?'

The manager gave a short laugh. 'Did she have the hunger? My God. I don't think there's a girl who walked through that door in the last two years who had it any worse.'

25

David Goldrab spoke into the intercom, released the gates and told Jake to park at the front, come in through the front door, which was open, and wait in the hall. Then he disappeared upstairs to the bedroom to get dressed. The moment he left the office Sally dialled Millie's number, her fingers shaking on the keypad. She stood at the window as the call went through and watched Millie on the lawn, frowning down at the phone. She seemed to be considering ignoring it. After a moment, though, she changed her mind and held it to her ear.

'Yeah, what?'

'He's followed us. He's here.'

'Who?'

'The guy in the jeep. Jake. That's his name. Jake.'

Millie jolted at that. She got to her feet and stood for a moment, half frozen, not knowing which way to go.

'It's OK.' Sally crept to the doorway and put her head into the gap, peering down the corridor. She could just see the hallway – a huge, galleried atrium

177

with a central staircase done in granite and marble with black and white tiles on the floor. Jake was near the front door. His ebony hair was gelled into spikes, his distressed jeans and T-shirt showing off his muscles and the trim line of his belly.

'He's in the house,' she whispered into the phone. 'Don't worry – he's in the hall at the front. He can't see you.'

She held the phone to her chest and cautiously leaned out of the doorway again to watch him. He seemed smaller and much less confident now he wasn't in his car. He kept bending a little to crane his neck up the stairs to see where David had disappeared to.

Sally ducked back into the office. 'I'm not sure what he's up to,' she hissed. 'It's weird – maybe he's here just to see David. Go and hide somewhere – somewhere in the trees where he won't see you from the back of the house. I'll call you as soon as I know something.'

The noise of a door closing upstairs echoed down the stairs. Sally ended the call and jerked her head back through the door. Jake was still in the hall, tightening his belt, pulling his shoulders back, watching David come along the landing.

'Jake! Jake the Peg!' David smiled expansively from the top of the stairs. He was wearing a well-cut white shirt over jeans. His feet were bare as he padded down, his arms open as if greeting a long-lost friend. He stopped a few stairs from the bottom and sat so he was a little above Jake's eye level, forcing

178

him to look up. 'It's been too long. How's things? How's the extra leg, mate?' He held his hands at his crotch to mime an enormous phallus. 'Still getting out and about, is it? Making lots of new friends?'

'Yeah, yeah.' Jake nodded nervously. He folded his arms tight across his chest, his hands tucked under them. 'Everything's wicked. Ticking over. Had a bit of a business proposal and thought I'd – y'know – *drop* in. Talk to you about it.'

'Yeah – I saw you "dropping in". I'll be honest – I was a bit taken aback you'd think I had the same gate code six months on. Thought that was a bit dis-respectful, but . . . you know how I am. Never dwell on things. If you feel at home enough to plug my code into my gate, after not seeing me in all this time, I reckoned that means you just feel comfortable around me.' He took a toothpick from his pocket and began studiously picking his teeth, his hand over his mouth, his eyes on Jake. 'So, Jakey, Jakey, Jakey, my extra-legged boy, Jake. What you bin up to, boyo? Just, from time to time you do hear some stupid rumours. Last I heard you were up to a bit of jiggery-pokery with the old no-no stuff. Selling it on to the rich kids – hanging around outside the posh schools, like a lonely turd in a lake, or so I've heard. Course I never listen to that nonsense, cos I'm sure it ain't true.'

'Nah . . .' Jake shifted anxiously. 'Course it ain't.'

'So how you bringing home the corn, these days, then, matey boy? Now that you're not cracking off the money shots for me?'

'Oh, you know. Been – doing my thing. Hoeing my row.'

David made a small sound in his throat as if he found this incredibly funny. He had to put a finger to his head and bend slightly at the waist to stop himself laughing like a horse.

'What?'

'Nothing. It's just . . .' He wiped his eyes with the back of his hand, then gave in to another spasm of giggles. He checked it and sat straight, his face still twitching. 'It's just "hoeing my row". The images it conjures up, mate. Hoeing my—' He couldn't get the words out. Again he doubled up with silent contortions.

Jake watched stonily, the huge muscles in his arms twitching slightly. 'Sounds like they're funny. The images.'

'They are,' David said, his voice tight, as if he was on the verge of hysteria. 'Very funny. They're poof images. One poof hoeing the other poof's row. You know, one poof ploughing into another's glory hole. That's what it made me think of.' David wiped his eyes again. Got himself under control. 'My mother is a relatively intelligent woman. I mean, apart from the three times she opened her legs to my father, she isn't altogether thick. Do you know what she used to say to me when I was a nipper? She used to say, "There are several people you should never trust, son. You should never trust a cop, you should never trust a skinny chef, you should never trust a fat beggar. Never trust an Arab or a bloke whose eyebrows meet

180

in the middle. Never trust a man in black shoes and white socks and never trust a black man in a fez. But do you know who was at the top of her never-trust list? The *crème de la crème* of untrustworthiness?'

'No.' Jake said it almost soundlessly.

'The poofs. The fucking poofters.'

'What're you talking about?'

David gave a slow smile. 'You're a fucking queer, Jake. A bum-boy, a shirt-lifting faggoty shit-stirrer. Now, I ain't saying that's your fault. What the scientists are saying, these days, and I don't know if you've heard this, but what they're saying is that *you can't help it*. Apparently it's in your biology. You can't be blamed for it – it's in your genes.' He held his hands out in amazement, as if to say, 'How weird is that?' 'Yeah, according to the mad professors it's nothing to do with you all being a bunch of perverts, it's all down to some fuck-up in the chromosome department. So I can't blame you, Jake, for the simple fact of you being a turd-tickler – what you do with your arse is your lookout – but I *can* blame you, and this is where I start to feel twitchy, like, what I can blame you for . . .' he leaned forward '. . . is not having the fucking good manners to *mention* it to me. Jake the Peg with his extra leg – and turns out the leg's not got its lead up for the bit of gash lying on the bed. It's got it up maybe for one of the *crew* members. Or, God forgive me for saying it, maybe even for *me*. And he never mentions it. *That*, you see,' he jabbed his fingers in the air, '*that* is what I call ignorance.'

David lowered his hand and put it on the banister.

For a moment it looked as if he might swing his legs up and kick Jake in the chin. But he didn't. He simply pulled himself to his feet.

Jake swallowed. He didn't step back. He put his hands into his jeans pockets defiantly. 'I'm not a poof.'

'Liar.' David's face didn't change. 'You are.'

'OK – so what if I *was*? Don't mean anything, does it? This isn't the Stone Age – there's human rights now. You can't get away with calling me a poof.'

David made a tutting noise. He shook his head disapprovingly. 'Playing the poofter discrimination card? It's against the rules, boyo. As bad as playing the race card.' He dropped his head to one side and put on a fake bright voice: 'We are sorry, your poof card has been denied. Please be advised that your poof card account has been closed. This decision was based on your account history of excessive over-limit spending. Please destroy your card immediately as it will no longer be honoured. Now, see that crossbow on the wall? Up there.'

Jake raised his eyes. Sally couldn't see up to the galleried landing, but she knew what was up there. A crossbow mounted in a cabinet with a picture light trained above it. In the back of the cabinet there was a framed photograph of the sun setting over the African bush.

'I shot a fucking hippo with that. Back in the days when white law-abiding people who worked hard had rights, before someone took them away from us and started handing them out to animals and blacks

and poofters – and I don't care *how* politically in-
correct you think I am, *you*, my son, are not welcome
here. Now –' he gave a peremptory jerk of the head,
indicating the door '– now, get that tart of a car off
my gravel before I get my friend up there off its stand
and shoot you in your fancy little pink-boy *derrière*.'

Jake kept his chin up, staring at the crossbow.
There was a long silence. Sally could see his Adam's
apple going up and down, as if he wanted to speak.
Then he seemed to change his mind. He dropped his
chin and without another word, without meeting
David's eyes one more time, he turned and left the
house. There was the sound of his feet crunching on
the gravel, the high-pitched squeak of a remote locking device, and the slam of a car door. Then the
sound of the car leaving, going slowly.

Shakily, Sally separated herself from the wall and
dialled Millie's number.

26

The incident stayed with Sally all day. Even when Jake had gone, and she'd spoken to Millie and knew she was safe out in the garden, even when she'd spent three hours struggling with the database and things at Lightpil House had quietened down, with David wandering around, champagne in hand, muttering incessantly about class and the immorality of homosexuality, she was still uneasy. There wasn't really any doubt in her mind now that Steve had been right, that what lay under the surface of David Goldrab's life was wide and deep. She had the feeling it could all just crack open at a moment's notice.

She gave Millie a long lecture about it in the car on the way back. 'This is serious stuff. Jake is *not* good news. These are really unpleasant people you're getting involved with.'

'Well, you're the one working for one of them,' Millie replied sullenly, and, of course, Sally couldn't argue with that. Now Julian wasn't around to shelter them, she and Millie had crossed that line and she was beginning to see how different everything on this side was.

'I'm thinking of a solution. I will come up with something.'

'Will you?' Millie stared out of the window, a bored, disbelieving expression on her face. 'Will you really?'

Sally was exhausted by the time they turned into the driveway at Peppercorn, and the last thing she felt like was seeing people. But there were two camper-vans parked in the garden – Isabelle and the teenagers were standing there, waiting for her. She pulled on the handbrake. She'd completely forgotten that today was the day Peter and Nial would pick up the camper-vans they'd been saving for. Two rusting old heaps with mud and manure all the way up to the wheel arches. She had to force a smile on to her face as she got out. But as it turned out no one else was in the party mood either. They might have pretended they were celebrating the vans' arrival, but there was an underlying tension. An unspoken ghost flitting between them. Lorne Wood. Dead at sixteen.

'Their first lesson in mortality,' Isabelle said, when she and Sally were on their own at last. They'd each poured a glass of the nice wine Steve was always bringing to Peppercorn, and had gone into the living room. 'It's a difficult one. They're taking this badly.'

'Millie didn't want to go to school today. She said it was because the police might be there. Were they?'

'No. But they were at Faulkener's the second day in a row. Sophie got a text from one of the girls.

185

Apparently the place came to a standstill – the police think one of the boys did it.'

'*One of the boys?*' Sally looked at Isabelle's face, the salt-and-pepper strands of hair and the clear blue eyes. 'Seriously?'

'The police stopped the kids using their phones. They kept them shut in the school all day. It sounded like a frenzy – some of the parents have been complaining to the head.'

The two women stood at the french windows, gazing out reflectively at the kids and the vans. Sally had painted each of the kids several times. She'd loved doing it – it was like capturing their emerging personalities, tethering a tiny piece of their fleeting souls to something, even if it was just oil paint and canvas. Because, she thought now, if there was one thing she knew for sure, things were changing for them fast. Faster than anyone could have predicted.

'Nial says the girls are scared.' Isabelle gave a sad smile. Outside, Nial was bent over, using a Magic Marker to sketch on his van the patterns he was going to paint. 'He half thinks he's going to be the white knight – just the way you painted him in those cards. Protect them all. Like that's going to happen with Pete around.'

It sounded about right, Sally thought. Sweet little Nial, secretly her favourite of the boys. Too small, too timid, he was totally overshadowed by Peter. He was good-looking, but in the way that wouldn't show itself properly until he was in his thirties. When handsome boys like Peter would be getting heavy and

186

losing their hair, the boys like Nial would be growing into their looks. Just now he was still too small and feminine for the girls to notice him. Her favourite tarot card depicted him as the Prince of Swords, on the one hand angry and sometimes vengeful, on the other reserved and hugely intelligent. The sort who could lead rebellions with his insightful ideas. She'd chosen to clothe him in a robe of velvet and brocade, blue, to bring out his eyes.

'Do you think they're right?' she said. 'To be scared, I mean. Do you think it was one of the other schoolkids?'

'God, I don't know. But there is one thing I can tell you.' She nodded at the teenagers. 'There's something they're not saying.'

'What do you mean?'

'I don't know, but I do know my son. And there's something he's not saying. Something he really wants to say but can't. He and Peter are really secretive at the moment.' She used her toe to push the glass door open a little more. The sound of birds singing came through it, with the bleat of lambs and the distant noise of traffic on the motorway. She was silent for a while. Then she said, 'Peter was in love with Lorne – did you know that?'

'Yes. I mean, I suppose everyone was in a way.'

'I think she wasn't interested in him, but he loved her. So did Nial, I imagine. But . . .' she said, lowering her voice a little '. . . I think the thing with Peter was what really finished Millie's friendship with her.'

187

Sally shot her a look. '*Millie*'s friendship?'

'You mean you don't know?'

'Know *what*?'

'Look at them out there, Sally. Really look at them.'

Sally did. Millie had separated from the group and was under a tree about ten yards away, sitting on the swing, one toe on the grass, twisting round and round, making her shadow twirl on the ground. Now, as she watched, Millie raised sullen eyes to the others. Sally followed the direction of her gaze and saw Peter, crouched next to the van, examining something in the tyre. She looked back at Millie and saw the expression on her face. It hit her like a train. That was what Isabelle meant. Millie was in love. In love with Peter. Good-looking, brazen, self-assured Peter, who was completely wrapped up in himself, and completely oblivious to Millie.

'Is that . . .' She paused, feeling stupid again. 'Is that why Millie stopped seeing Lorne? Because he was in love with her?'

'Did you really not know?'

'Uh,' she said dumbly. She rubbed her arms. 'Yes. I mean, I suppose.'

The two women were silent for a while, watching the kids. Something sad and lonely and familiar was thumping in Sally's stomach. The sick knockings of being the loser – the way Millie must feel about Peter. It had been the same for her at boarding-school, where she'd learned early to exist at the bottom of the winning pile. While Zoë, of course, at

188

the other school, knew what it was like at the top.

   'Oh, Isabelle,' she murmured sadly. 'They're growing up. It's happened right under our noses.'

27

Sally had put the dinner in the oven and was making chocolate fudge for Isabelle to take home, cutting it into squares and putting it on greaseproof paper. Isabelle was outside but now she came in through the back door, huffing and puffing and kicking at the grass clippings that clung to her bare feet. Sally smiled at her, but Isabelle put a finger to her mouth and shook her head seriously.

'What?'

She turned to reveal Nial and Millie standing behind her in the doorway, sheepish expressions on their faces. Sally set down the knife, wiped her apron and made herself smile at them. She was thinking of the conversation earlier – Isabelle insisting the teenagers were keeping a secret. 'Millie?' she said warily. 'What is it?'

'Look, Sally.' Isabelle closed the door behind the teenagers and crossed to the table, holding Sally's eyes seriously. 'There's a problem.'

'Is it Lorne?'

'No. Thank God, no.' She raised her eyebrows at

her son in the doorway. 'Nial? Come on – explain.'

Nial came forward and sat down, casting a tentative glance at Sally. Millie followed hurriedly, pulling up a chair next to him – sitting with her shoulder touching his, her hands between her knees, her eyes lowered. She might be in love with Peter, but Isabelle was right: when it came to knights in shining armour Nial was always there, hoping all the girls would want to hide behind him. Of course, he'd puff himself up to make himself look as big as he could and they'd walk straight past him, their arms open to drape around Peter's neck.

'What happened,' Isabelle said, 'is they got their Glastonbury tickets a couple of months ago. You knew that, didn't you? With Peter's big brother?'

'Of course. That's what you're painting the vans up for, isn't it? Why? What's the problem?'

Isabelle dug her finger into the wood grain of the table. Gave Millie an embarrassed sideways glance. 'Millie hasn't paid for her ticket.'

'Her *ticket*?' Sally turned her eyes to Millie. 'What *ticket*? Millie, we talked about this. You were never going to have a ticket – you weren't going with them.'

'Mum, please. Don't go off on one.' She looked as if she might cry. 'Peter paid for them online. Now I've got to give him my share of the money.'

'But . . .' Sally sat down, shaking her head. 'Sweetheart, I've told you over and over again, I just can't afford for you to go to Glastonbury. We talked about this.'

'Everyone else's parents are paying.'

191

'Yes, but everyone else's parents . . .' She stopped herself. She'd almost said: 'Everyone else's parents know what they're doing.'

Isabelle put her hand on Sally's arm. 'Nial and I want to pay for it. That's why we're here. Seriously – I'm happy. If you're happy for her to go, then I'm happy to pay.'

'I can't do that.'

'Why not?'

'I just can't. You've already helped me out more than I deserve.'

'But think of everything you've done for me over the years. You've helped me – given me so much. I've lost count of the number of presents you've given me, all the paintings you've done for us. You must let me help you out.'

Sally gave a long sigh. She bit her lip and looked out of the window. The second time in less than twenty-four hours that she'd sat here and insisted she could do this alone. She turned back to where Isabelle and Nial were watching her with expectant faces. 'I can't take your money,' she said. 'Thank you for offering, but I really can't. Millie will have to find a way of earning it. Or she'll have to send the ticket back.'

'*Mum!* I can't *believe* you sometimes.'

Millie pushed her chair back and ran out of the cottage, slamming the door. Isabelle and Nial sat in silence, eyes lowered.

'Sally,' Isabelle said eventually. 'Are you sure we can't help?'

192

'Absolutely. I've got to find my own way through it.'

She got up and carried the glasses to the sink, turning her back to them. Her shoulders were sagging with tiredness. God, she thought bitterly, I'm even starting to bore myself saying it.

28

One of the cats that crowded around Zoë's back door had injured its foot. She noticed it as she stood there late that night after work, sipping a long-overdue Jerry's rum mixed with ginger, watching them all swarming around her, eager for the food she put out every night. The little one hung back from the group, peering nervously at her. It looked skinny, as if it hadn't been eating.

She drained the Jerry's, went back inside for more cat biscuits and coaxed it out of the shadows. She managed to catch it and take it inside to examine under the light. It had a rubber band looped around its back legs. No wonder it couldn't walk. The band had rubbed, but it hadn't yet broken the skin. She cut it carefully, and peeled it away. Then she put her hands under the cat's front legs and held it up in front of her to check it everywhere else. It gazed back at her, its legs dangling idiotically.

'Don't look at me like that,' she said, and put it on the floor. She found a litter tray and some cat litter in the back of the shed and put it with a bowl of food and some water on the floor in the downstairs loo. Then she carried the cat over and placed it next to the food. 'One night only, just until you're better. Don't even think about getting used to it – this is not a hotel.'

The cat ate hungrily. Zoë straightened to leave and, as she did, caught sight of her reflection in the mirror above the washbasin. She stopped and stared at herself. Red shaggy hair. High cheekbones and sun-damaged skin. She looked half wild. Eighteen years ago in the clubs she had worn her hair cut short and white-blonde. Only one person had known her real name – the manager of the club, who was long gone, overseas somewhere. No one would recognize DI Benedict as the girl on that stage all those years ago. She was the master of disguise. She could hide anything she chose to.

She pushed up her sleeve, and stared at all the welts and scars. Unevenly shaped wounds made by her own nails. Something else she'd been clever at hiding. Ben had never noticed these all the time they'd been together. She'd covered them with makeup, made sure he never got a good look at the worst ones. The marks were the evidence of a trick she'd learned at boarding-school in her first term: whenever she thought of Mum and Dad and Sally, the way they could sit contentedly next to a fire, arms around each other, the feelings that came up in her used to make her cry softly into the pillow. Slowly she found that the only way to make the awful raw spot in her chest go away was to hurt another part of her body. She'd do it anywhere Matron wouldn't notice – the tops of her thighs, her stomach. Sometimes there would be blood on her pyjamas in the morning, and then she'd make an excuse to creep off to the showers, where she'd stand, shivering, soaping away the evidence. The habit had never left her.

Stop it, she thought, yanking the sleeve down. *Stupid stupid stupid.* Stop it. This wasn't her. She was the person who'd survived boarding-school, who'd fought her way across continents, who'd worked her way up the ranks in a male-dominated world. It didn't matter that tonight was the second in a row Ben had suddenly become 'too busy' to come back to hers. She didn't own him. It really didn't matter. And none of her past was going to come back to get her just because of those photos of Lorne.

She switched off the light, closed the door on the cat, washed her dinner plate and the pots, then went to bed. She lay for a long time in the darkness, resisting the urge to touch her arms. When she did at last sleep, it was uneasy, ruptured, infected with dreams and discomfort.

She dreamed of clouds and mountains and rushing rivers. She dreamed of falling buildings and of a barge, tilting on its side, taking on water. And then, as the sun rose and her bedroom began to fill with light, she dreamed of a room like a Victorian nursery, with children's number and letter charts on the wall and a rocking horse in the corner. Outside, an old-fashioned streetlight cast its yellow glow on the snow that was being driven by a wind, the flakes racing in horizontal streaks past the panes. Although there was nothing familiar about the setting, somehow she knew this was the childhood bedroom she had shared with Sally. And she also knew, with absolute clarity, that it was the day of the 'accident'. The day she'd come upstairs and found, to her fury, her bed, her toys and all her belongings painted by Sally with idiotic yellow flowers. A 'surprise'. To please her.

But in the dream Zoë didn't feel rage. Instead she felt fear. Real terror. Something about the snow and the nursery and the numbers on the wall was crowding at her, trying to close in on her. And behind her a child was screaming. She turned and saw it was Sally, her face a mask of terror, something red leaking from her hand. With the other hand she was pointing anxiously at the numbers on the wall, as if it was of vital importance that Zoë saw them. 'Look,' she was screaming. 'Look at the numbers. Number one, number two, number three.'

Zoë looked again at the number chart and saw it had changed. Now it wasn't numbers written out for children to learn: it was the sign at the Zebedee Juice Agency, No. 1 Milsom Street.

No. 1 . . . No. 1.

She sat up quickly, gulping air, her heart racing. It took her a moment to realize where she was – in her bed at home.

It was light outside and sunlight dappled the ceiling. *No. 1. Number one.* Now she got it. It had niggled at her when she was at Zebedee Juice and now she understood why. It was what the killer had written on Lorne's stomach. She snatched up her phone. The display read ten to eight. She'd been asleep for seven hours. There was a team meeting in forty minutes. But this time it wasn't going to be Debbie Harry speaking at the front of the room. It was going to be Zoë.

She raced through the shower, guzzled two cups of coffee, let the cat out, shooing it when it tried to nuzzle her ankle, and got to work at exactly half past to find the meeting had already started. Someone had blown up a series of photos – all registered sex offenders under the age of twenty-five who lived in the area – and had pinned them to the wall. One of the DSs was talking the team through the history of each one. When Zoë came in, flushed, hair still wet from the shower, clutching her bike helmet, the DS stopped talking and stared at her dumbly.

'Sorry, mate,' She dumped the helmet and her keys on a chair and came to the front of the room. 'I've got to say something. Just before you go any further.' She uncapped a marker pen and drew a circle on the whiteboard. 'We're looking at it all wrong.'

In the circle she carefully wrote: *No. One.*

Then she moved one of Lorne's post-mortem pictures – the one with the message on her stomach – and stuck it on the board next to the words. 'Look at the picture,' she said. 'Look at her belly button. Right here, after the "No".'

The team gawped at the whiteboard, not a flicker of recognition in their faces.

'It doesn't mean no one understands him. It doesn't mean that Lorne is no one to him. He's telling us she is *number one*. Just one of many. He means there are going to be more. A number two. A number three.'

There was a long, stunned silence. Then, at the edge of the room, the superintendent cleared his throat. 'Great – thanks, Zoë. Everyone – take that on board, OK? You hear me? Now.' He nodded at the DS. 'Have you finished, mate? Because I want to get on to this thing with British Waterways. I want a complete list of anyone who was mooring in the canal on Saturday so we can—'

'Hang on, hang on.' Zoë held up her hand. 'I'm still here, you know. I haven't left the room.'

'I'm sorry?'

'I'm still here. Or are you going to ignore what I just said?'

'I haven't ignored it. I've told everyone to keep it in mind.'

'Would you like me to *finish* what I was going to say? Or shall I not bother?'

The superintendent looked at her, a baleful light in his eyes. But he knew Zoë of old, knew sometimes it was easier to roll over, and eventually he took a step back, holding his hands up in surrender.

'OK.' She turned back to the team. She knew the blood had come to her face and that Ben was watching her steadily from the corner. 'We've got to take this seriously, because – who knows? – I might even be right. He could intend doing this again. It could

199

already have happened. Has anyone gone to Intelligence to find out if there're any other forces dealing with anything like this?'

'We'd know if there were,' said the superintendent.

'Would we? What if the body hasn't been found?'

'There'd be a missing-persons case.'

'No – that's rubbish. How many women in their late teens, early twenties, go missing every month?'

'Yes – but you're not talking about girls like Lorne.'

Zoë looked back at him with a level gaze. She knew what he meant – that the girls who went missing without making headlines were the prostitutes, the drug addicts, the runaways, the strippers and the dregs. She'd get it through to them if she showed them the photos of Lorne. But she couldn't. Just couldn't do it.

'You mean,' the superintendent said, lowering his chin and looking over his glasses at her, 'there's a pile of dead bodies somewhere? Just no one's noticed?'

'No. I'm saying that up to now we're pushing this investigation towards it being someone she knows, a teenager. I'm asking you to reconsider. I'm asking you to think outside those parameters. And to do it quickly – because, honestly, I think this could be a warning.'

Debbie Harry, who had been sitting at the back of the room in silence, gave a delicate little cough. She looked very young and fresh and pretty, dressed in a white lace blouse, her hair tied back. 'While speculation is a good thing, it is just that. Speculation.'

'More speculative than saying "all like her" means everyone likes her? What if it means he's going to go after anyone who's like Lorne?'

'Well,' Debbie said, suddenly soothing, 'I've always been very clear in stating my case in this forum: that my opinions are only guidance. That you really, really – *all of you* – must form your own conclusions. And always keep an open mind.'

'Yes. And I heard you say that. But I might be the only one who did, because I look around and I see a whole room full of investigators all too happy to accept a bit of guidance from you because it means they don't need to use their brains. Sorry, guys, it's true. You've accepted her parameters, so if we're really going to work this case like a psychology seminar, then let's go for it. Let's all of us write up a thousand interpretations of these sentences. Then have a seance to decide which is right.'

'Hang on, hang on.' The superintendent held up his hand. 'There's vindictiveness creeping in here. It's the last thing we need.'

'Vindictiveness?'

Debbie nodded regretfully. As if it hurt her to be attacked, but that she, the adult, was prepared to be grown-up about it. She gave Zoë a sympathetic smile. 'Well, I didn't want to be the one to say it, but I have wondered if I'm stirring things up for you, Detective Benedict. Just a feeling that something about me is tapping into something very painful for you.'

Zoë opened her mouth to answer, then saw that

everyone was staring at her. She got it. They all thought she was jealous. Jealous of this idiotic jumped-up psychology student with her one-size-too-tight blouses and her soft hair. She shot Ben a look, half expecting, or hoping, he'd say something in her defence, but he wouldn't meet her gaze. He had focused his eyes on the photos of the sex offenders on the board as if he was far more interested in them.

'Jesus.' Bad-temperedly she snatched up her keys and her helmet. 'Welcome to the new age of policing. Anyone in here who gives a shit about justice, you'd better start saying your prayers.' She saluted the superintendent, clicked her heels together and, the team staring at her as if she was completely mad, left the room, slamming the door behind her.

29

Sally had decided that Millie had to go to school, whatever happened. She had some free slots at work that morning, so she drove her to Kingsmead, and promised to pick her up next to the sports hall at home time. Jake the Peg's purple jeep was nowhere to be seen. Even so, she watched Millie all the way until she'd gone into the building.

Her job that morning was just around the corner from the school – in one of the most expensive streets in the city. Most of the houses were elegant detached villas, built in Victorian times. The Farrow and Ball paint fad had arrived here, and all the doors and windows seemed to be painted in muted greys and greens; bay trees in *faux*-lead pots lined either side of neat gravel paths while pots of woody lavender and rosemary were dotted everywhere. Steve had a house at the other end of the road from Sally's cleaning job, so on Wednesdays she'd got into the habit of going on to his afterwards. Sometimes they'd eat lunch. More often they'd end up in bed.

His house was a little smaller than the others in the

street, but otherwise very similar – a stone-flagged doorstep, an old-fashioned bell with a wire pulley that rang a proper chime inside. At one o'clock she stood outside, listening to the bell in the hallway and thinking about David and what had happened with Jake. She was ready to tell Steve all about it. But the moment he opened the front door, she saw the mood was all wrong.

'Hi, gorgeous.' He kissed her briefly, but it was a distracted kiss. Just a peck on the side of the face before he turned and went back down the corridor towards the kitchen.

She followed him thoughtfully, watching his retreating back. He was dressed in shorts and a paint-spattered T-shirt with 'Queensland: beautiful one day, perfect the next' printed across the back. There was something heavy about his shoulders, which wasn't right. 'Are you OK?' she said, when they got into the kitchen.

'Hmm?'

'I said, is everything all right?'

'Yes, yes. I was going to make you lunch – there's tuna in the fridge – but I got busy sorting out all the tools you need for the house. And while I was going through them I got hit.' He slapped the back of his neck, as if a mosquito had landed there. 'Right here, by the bloody carpentry muse.' He gestured to the adjoining living room, where dustsheets lay on the floor covered with curls of planed wood. A nail gun had been balanced on a Black & Decker Workmate and a toolkit sat under it. 'Trying to fix that doorframe, but I'm just making a cock-up of it.'

'I'll cook.' Sally unfastened her HomeMaids tabard. 'You get on with it.'

'Sally, I—'

'What?'

He shook his head. Turned away. 'Nothing. There's, uh . . .' he waved a hand vaguely at the cupboards '. . . sesame oil in the one at the end, if you want it.'

He went back to the living room. Sally folded the tabard and put it on the worktop, watching him carefully. He stopped in the doorway, looped up a professional-style tool-belt, bristling with chisels and hammer handles, and strapped it to his waist. Then he picked up the nail gun, switched it on, and began firing nails into the doorframe. He didn't once turn to look at her. Over the months she'd learned that, from time to time, Steve had moods like this, when something would preoccupy him. One or two clients would leave him quiet and introspective for days, as if he'd peeped into a world he wished he hadn't known about. Maybe now he was thinking about an upcoming trip he was supposed to be making on Saturday – a client in Seattle he needed to visit. That, or maybe the meeting he'd had yesterday in London: he'd been anxious about that before he'd left, before Millie had got up. He'd been vague about who he was meeting – perhaps it had been Mooney. The one whose name she was supposed to forget.

She went back to the fridge. Tuna steaks in grease-proof paper oozed red on the middle shelf. There was a pot of basil that looked to have been bought from the farmers' market, some gherkins and, when she delved deep, an old jar of capers. She'd make *salsa verde*. She took the ingredients out and began to chop, her eyes sliding across the room to Steve as she worked. Every time he drove a nail into the door-frame she jumped.

She'd finished the sauce and was heating the oil in the pan with her back to the room when the sound of a nail being fired was followed by a loud clatter. She put down the pan and turned. He was standing with his side to her, his left hand placed high on the door-frame, the other pressed against the wall. The nail gun was on the floor where it had fallen, turning slowly on its axis. He had his head down and was perfectly still, except for his left leg, which was moving spasmodically up and down as if he was kicking himself. He looked sideways at her, his face grey, pinched.

'Think I've fucked my hand, Sally, if you'll forgive the expression.' His teeth were clenched. He jerked his head in the direction of his left hand, not raising his eyes to it. 'Gun hit a knot, slipped. I've got to assume I've really fucked it. Would you have a look?'

She turned off the gas and hurried across to him. The hand looked normal at first glance, just as if it was resting there, the fingers pointing up to the ceiling, but, closer to it, she saw what had happened. He'd skewered himself to the wall. She stood on tiptoe and examined it.

'What?' he said tightly. 'What can you see?'

She could see the steely gleam of a nail head poking out from the fleshy pad below his thumb. She could see a single, oily line of blood running from the site of the wound to the wrist, where it split into a delta that continued down through the hair on his arm. And she could picture more – she could imagine the musculature and bone structure inside, because it was what she'd seen almost thirty years ago on the X-ray of her own hand after the accident with Zoë. She closed her eyes for a moment and tried to get past that image. It always made her feel inescapably sad. 'I'm not sure,' she said. 'I don't know about these things.'

'OK.' He wiped his face with his free hand. 'See that hacksaw?'

She crouched and rummaged through the toolkit. 'This?'

'No. That one.'

'What?' She picked it up shakily. 'What've I got to do?'

'Cut the nail. Between my hand and the wall.'

'Cut it?'

'*Yes*. Please, Sally, just do it. I'm not asking you to cut my hand off.'

'OK, OK.' She went quickly to the cupboard under the sink and pulled out two rolls of kitchen towel. She got a chair, scraped it up to where he stood and climbed on it to inspect the wound. Tongue between her teeth, she pressed the area around it. Steve winced and sucked in a breath, rolled his head around once

207

or twice as if he was trying to release a crick in his neck. The skin on his thumb was stretched sideways: the nail had only pierced the side of the muscle. It wasn't as bad as she'd thought.

'OK.' Her heart was thumping. 'I don't think it's too serious.'

'Just do it.'

Her hands were slippery with sweat but she pushed her fingers between the wall and his flesh and gently pulled at it, pushing it along the nail away from the wall, until about a centimetre of the shaft was visible between skin and wall.

'*Jesus*.' He dropped his head, teeth clenched, and his foot kicked harder. 'Jesus fucking Christ.'

Tentatively she raised the hacksaw, edging the blade into the space between the wall and the hand, lowering it until it bit into the shaft of the nail. Steve stopped talking and went still. His eyes rested on her face. She moved the saw back and forth experimentally once or twice. He'd gone curiously quiet. She adjusted the blade and felt it lock into the metal, knew it was right, and began to saw.

'Sally,' he whispered suddenly, while she worked, 'I really need you.'

Her eyes shot to him and she saw something she'd never seen in them before – something naked and scared. When he had said 'need' he had meant more than just needing her to cut him away from the wall. It was a bigger 'need' than that. She opened her mouth to reply, but before she could the blade slipped through the metal and the nail came apart. Steve's

208

hand dropped and the head of the nail fell out of it. He took a couple of steps back and she jumped off the chair and caught him, lifted the hand and held wads of kitchen towels round it to stem the blood. She made him sit down, his hand positioned on his shoulder.

'Take deep breaths.'

He shook his head. His T-shirt had dark circles of sweat at the neck and under the arms. There was a fine spatter of blood on the floor and the tools were scattered all over the place. After a minute or two, he spoke. 'Yesterday was the most fucking awful day, Sally.'

'Yes.' She crouched, peering up into his grey face. 'Something's happened, hasn't it?'

He looked up at the ceiling as if he was trying to find a steady place to rest his eyes and keep everything together. 'It's work. Fucking *crap crap crap*.'

'Is it America?'

'No. God, no – that's a breeze. It was the meeting. In London. With . . . You know who I was meeting.'

Mooney, she thought. I was right. 'What happened?'

There was a long silence. Then he turned his grey eyes back to her and looked at her seriously. 'I got offered a novel way to earn thirty K. No tax. Would solve all your problems in the blink of an eye.'

'What?'

'Killing David Goldrab.'

She put her head to one side and gave a small smile. 'Yeah,' she said. 'Right. I'll kill him and you

209

steal all his champagne.' Steve didn't laugh, just went on staring at her.

'What? You look weird, Steve. Don't scare me.'

'But I'm serious. That's what they offered me at the meeting yesterday. I sat in the Wolseley in Piccadilly drinking two-hundred-quid-a-bottle champagne and got offered thirty K to off David Goldrab. I told you it was going to be dark.'

They stared at each other, stony-faced with shock.

After a moment he shook his head. 'No – forget it. I didn't say that.'

'Yes, you did.' She straightened, groped blindly for the sofa behind her. Sat down with a bump on the arm. 'It's not true – is it?'

His eyes flickered across her face. 'Good God, Sally, what the hell have I wandered into?' His shoulders slumped wearily. 'It's like being in a bloody Tarantino movie.'

'You're serious? You're really serious?'

'Fuck, yes. *Yes*.'

'Do people really do things like that? In real life?'

He shrugged, as mystified as she was. 'Apparently. I mean, Christ, I always kind of knew it happened from time to time to people in my job. You'd hear about it – this and that bent PI giving some ex-IRA guy ten K to drive a Range Rover over someone's wife in their driveway. Just like I always knew the really shit stuff in life existed. The reality of all the bastards who walk the streets unchallenged. They're not stopped because they're dressed in Armani suits, drive high-end Audis and get called "sir", but they're psychos just the same, for their ruthlessness and for the scalps they take. I knew all that – that lives were being destroyed under the veneer. I knew complete and utter bare-faced greed really existed. And on some level I knew things like this must happen. People must get killed – for a price.' He leaned back in the chair, clutching his hand. 'I just never, *ever*, thought it would come near me.'

Sally let all her breath out. She gazed up at the ceiling, spent time fitting this into her head. After a while, when neither of them had moved, she said, 'Steve?'

'What?'

'Those people. Weren't they nervous when you said no?'

He was silent for a moment. Then he unwrapped his hand and inspected the wound. Licked his finger and rubbed at the blood.

She lowered her chin and squinted at him. 'Steve?'

'What?'

'You did say no. Didn't you?'

'Of course I did.' He didn't meet her eyes. 'What else do you think I'd have said?'

30

Zoë strode down the corridor from the incident room to find five teenagers standing moodily outside her office. The three boys had spiked hair and wore their school trousers belted under their skinny buttocks. The girls were straight out of St Trinian's, with school skirts rolled up at the waist to show their legs and shirts tied at the waist like Daisy Duke.

'Auntie Zoë?' said the smaller of the two girls. 'I'm sorry to bother you.'

That stopped Zoë in her tracks. She leaned a little closer, peering at the girl. '*Millie?* Jesus. I didn't recognize you.'

'What's wrong with me?' Millie put both hands on her hair, as if to check it was still there. 'What?'

'Nothing. I just . . .' She'd only ever seen Millie in photos Mum and Dad had sent, and twice in the flesh, in the street, just in passing. But she was pretty – really pretty. It took a moment for Zoë to gather her wits. 'What do you want? Aren't you supposed to be in school?'

'The headmaster let us come here. We've been

waiting to speak to you. Can we do it in private?'

'Yes. Of course. Come in, come in.' She unlocked her office and kicked the door open, scanned the room quickly for anything the kids shouldn't see – post-mortem photos or notes on Lorne's case. 'There aren't any chairs. Sorry about that.'

''S OK,' said the tallest boy. 'We won't be staying.'

Zoë closed the door. Then she sat on the desk and regarded them all carefully. She had to stop herself staring directly at Millie, though she monitored her out of the corner of her eye. Was it her imagination or did Millie look more like her, Zoë, and less like Sally? 'What can I do for you all?'

'We need some help,' said the tall boy. He was blond and good-looking. You could tell from the body language of the rest of the group that he was the alpha male. That he threw his weight around and generally got what he wanted. 'It's about Lorne Wood.'

'Right.' Zoë glanced cautiously from face to face. 'OK. And I take it from the way we're all standing here, the way that you approached me, that you want, for the time being, to have a private chat?'

'For the time being.'

'That's fair enough. But before we start I'd like to get your names. I give you my word it won't go any further. Here.' She pulled out a spiral-bound jotter and handed the bigger boy a pen. He studied it for a moment, unsure. Zoë nodded. 'You have my word,' she repeated. 'You really do.'

Reluctantly he took it, bent over the desk and

wrote *Peter Cyrus*. He handed the pen to Millie, who glanced at Zoë, looked about to say something, but instead bent over and wrote *Millie Benedict*. Benedict, Zoë noticed, not Cassidy. So it was true what she'd heard: Sally really had divorced Julian. And here was Millie – using Sally's name instead of her father's. What did that say about the separation?

The other teenagers lined up and took turns to write on the pad.

Nial Sweetman, Sophie Sweetman, Ralph Hernandez.

Ralph Hernandez.

Zoë stared at the name, moving her jaw from side to side. She put on a calm smile and raised her head to him. She hadn't taken much notice of him until now. He was slight, medium height, with wiry dark hair and olive skin. Apart from his tie, which was knotted the way they all seemed to these days, puffed up and wide, like some seventies TV cop's, he was dressed more conventionally than the others, in that at least his trousers appeared to almost fit him and the spikes in his hair weren't totally outlandish. His fierce brown eyes were bloodshot.

'So.' She forced her voice to sound casual. 'What can I do for you all?'

There was a moment's silence. Then the one called Nial nudged the one called Peter. Sophie and Millie kept still, their eyes on the floor. Ralph rubbed the back of his sleeve nervously across his forehead.

'It's like this,' said Peter. 'Ralph's scared.'

'Concerned,' Ralph corrected. 'A little concerned. That's all.'

'I see. And why are you concerned?'

'I was . . .' He scratched his arms. 'I was . . .'

'He was with Lorne,' Peter said, 'the night she was killed.'

Zoë cupped her chin with her fingers. Gave the teenagers a ruminative look. In her chest her heart was knocking like a tom-tom. Here was Debbie and Ben's 'killer'. All five foot ten of him. And meanwhile, if she was right about that message on Lorne, the real killer was out there somewhere. Maybe thinking about number two. 'OK,' she said calmly. 'And obviously there was a reason you didn't mention this before.'

'I've never told my parents I'd got a girlfriend. And Lorne never told anyone about me either. It was supposed to be a secret.'

'His parents are Catholic. They find that sort of thing a bit – you know.'

'Can you help him?' Nial asked. 'He doesn't know what to do.'

'Help? I'm not sure about help. This is serious. I know you know that – you're not stupid. But we'll take this slowly. Ralph, Lorne was your girlfriend. How long had you been seeing her?'

'Only a couple of weeks. But I loved her. I mean that. She was the one for me.' There was something tight in his voice that said he wasn't lying. 'Please,' he said, and for a moment he sounded like a little kid. A kid left out in the rain and begging to come inside.

215

'Please, I just don't know what to do.' He straightened against the wall and put his head back against the plaster, shaking it. 'Honestly, I think I'd be better off dead.'

'Come on,' she said, leaning forward, 'let's take a deep breath, shall we?' Technically she should be thinking about calling in the child-protection units, with a minor saying things about wanting to die, but she'd never get the story out of him if she did that. 'OK? You OK?'

After a moment or two he licked his lips and muttered, 'Yeah.'

'And calmly now, Ralph, just calmly, knowing how awful you feel about all of this, and knowing how much you want to help us catch whoever did this to Lorne, take me through what happened that night.'

The room fell quiet. All the other teenagers had their attention on him. He lowered his eyes to his hands, which he held in tight fists. 'She told her mum she was shopping, but actually she was meeting me. Up near Beckford's Tower. Where we always met.'

Beckford's. The great Victorian monument that drunken farmers were supposed to have used to find their way home at night, with its neoclassical belvedere, its gilded lantern. It stood in a cemetery at the top of Lansdown and could be seen from all across the city. It was also on one of the bus routes that came through the stop near the canal. Zoë sighed. Lorne must have been on the bus because

216

she'd been up at Beckford's with Ralph. 'So, what time was that?'

'About five thirty, I think.'

'How long were you there?'

'I'm really not sure. It could have been an hour. It could have been an hour and a half.'

'You don't know?'

'I didn't check my watch. I just didn't. Otherwise I'd tell you.'

So, up to ninety minutes maximum. Add to that the ten minutes or so bus ride to the centre of town and there was still the outside chance Lorne had gone somewhere after leaving Ralph – before going to the canal.

'And then?'

'And then she left. And I walked into town. I met up with, uh—' he rubbed his arms again '—with Peter and Nial.'

'We went out for a beer,' Nial said hurriedly. 'The school had won a cricket match the day before so we felt like having a little celebration.'

'The three of you?'

'That's right.'

'Are you old enough to be cruising round the local pubs?'

'Well – no. Not really. We kind of used fake IDs.'

'Kind of?'

'Yes. Why? Are you going to give us a lecture on it?'

Zoë raised her eyebrows at him. Impressed by his guts. 'No,' she said. 'Of course I'm not. In the scheme of things it's not exactly the crime of the century. So what time did your little fake-ID celebration finish?'

Nial shot Peter a look. Peter scratched his head. 'What time was it? About midnight?'

'About that, yeah.'

'Where did you go, Ralph?'

'Home. Weston.'

'How did you get there?'

'I walked.'

'Did anything unusual happen on the way? Did you see anyone you knew?'

'No.'

'So let's backtrack a bit. You met Lorne. What happened while you were together?'

There was a silence. Ralph's head was quite still but his hands weren't. They made little trembling movements. His shoulders were shaking. He shook his head imploringly – as if he couldn't trust himself to speak without crying.

Zoë met Peter's eyes. She jerked a thumb at the door. 'Give us a few moments here?' she mouthed. 'Some privacy.'

The other two boys and the two girls exchanged glances. Then, as if they were a single organism, capable of reaching decisions without words, they filed out. In the corridor they stood with their hands in their pockets, each with one foot up against the wall. Like the cover of a Ramones album. It never went out of style to be skinny and sullen.

Zoë kicked the door closed, grabbed a handful of tissues from the box on the window-sill and turned

218

back to Ralph. He had slid down the wall and was in a little huddled squat, his hands over his face. 'OK, OK.' She crouched next to him, put a hand on his shoulder and felt the warmth of his skin through the thin shirt. The tremor of his breath coming in and out. 'Look, you've done the right thing by coming to me.' She handed him a tissue. He took it and crammed it against his face. 'You can be proud of that.'

He nodded and wiped his nose. His breathing was thick and nasal.

'But I need to get it all clear in my thoughts, Ralph. I asked you if something particular happened at Beckford's Tower and that seemed to upset you.'

He nodded miserably. 'We had an argument. She wanted to tell everyone about us and I . . .' He had to take deep breaths to calm himself. 'We split up. We split up and she said she never wanted to see me again and . . . And . . . And that's what happened. And it's all my fucking fault. All because I'm scared of my fucking parents.'

'It's not your fault, Ralph. It's really not your fault.'

'What's going to happen? Do I have to go to court? Are my parents going to know about it? My father'll be furious. He thinks lying should be counted as a mortal sin.'

She rested her arm on his shoulders. He really was just a little boy. She could see the faint white of his scalp at the neat parting of his black hair. 'I think, Ralph, that most parents would be more concerned about your welfare. And that you've had the courage to tell the truth.'

'Christ.' He'd used up the tissues so he wiped his nose on the shoulder of his shirt. 'I wish you were my mother.'

'Oh, no, no. I'd be a terrible mother. You can trust me on that one. Now, coming here was a huge decision for you, but it was the right one. This information is really, really important. With it we can build a picture of what happened to Lorne. But there's not a lot I can do with the information if I can't share it with my colleagues. If I gave you a guarantee that nothing will be said to your parents until you're happy for them to hear, would you come and tell the rest of the team? The ones who can make a difference? You could stop this happening again. To someone else.'

There was a silence. It took her a moment to realize he was nodding.

31

The Police and Criminal Evidence Act of 1984 had dictated that all interviews of suspects had to take place in a specially designated room – well lit, well ventilated, soundproofed, with embedded recording facilities and access to a neutral 'break-out' space should the interviewee decide he or she didn't like the way the interview was going. Councils around the country had had to dig deep to install PACE rooms – and at Bath police station there were two.

Zoë sat at her desk with the door open so she could monitor the passageway. Her office was at the place where the corridor branched off to lead to the interview rooms. If Ralph was moved from the side office near the incident room where Ben was speaking to him, it meant they had gone against every one of her instincts, every one of her requests, and were interviewing him as a possible suspect in the murder. But the station was silent for a long time. Hours. God only knew what they were doing with him.

She tried to concentrate on other tasks. She set up

an intelligence request for missing women aged between sixteen and twenty-one. When she'd told Debbie that 'all like her' meant the killer was going to target girls like Lorne, she'd plucked it out of the air. But what if she hadn't been so far off the mark? It was worth thinking about. Except that, looking at the screen, it wasn't going to be easy – the result of the search was terrifying. Name after name after name. Of course she knew most of the girls on the list were probably alive and well and had simply lost contact with their families, or were avoiding them. A good proportion would have returned and the police not been notified. Even so there were hundreds and hundreds and hundreds. One person couldn't work through all of those on their own. She sat back in her chair and folded her arms. Shit. If one of those names had belonged to a victim of Lorne's killer and their body hadn't been found, there was no earthly chance the police would pick up on it.

At a quarter to ten Ben walked past, going fast, carrying a stack of files. He didn't pay her any attention, but went into his office. She heard the door slam. She waited for a moment or two, then got up, went along the corridor and knocked on the door.

'Who is it?'

'Me. Zoë.'

A pause. A hesitation? Then, 'Come in.'

She pushed the door open. He was sitting at his desk, his elbows planted on either side of the stack of paperwork. He faced her but, she noticed, his eyes didn't meet hers. There was a blank, polite smile pasted on his face. 'What's happening?' she said.

'With?'

'You know what with. With Ralph. Are you still interviewing him? Did you get him an appropriate adult from Social Services?'

'He's seventeen. Doesn't need one.'

'I promised him his parents wouldn't be involved. Not unless he agreed to it.'

'Yes. And that's what we're working on. Him agreeing to it. They're going to find out eventually.'

Zoë let all the air out of her lungs. She came forward and sat on the chair opposite him. Ben eyed her, one of his eyebrows slightly raised, as if he really didn't appreciate the way she was making herself at home. 'It's not him,' she said. 'It's just not. He's too *young*. Don't you remember, all those courses – how these sorts of crimes take time to build? He's just a kid. He nicely and neatly fits a profile you've been sold, but it's a *flawed* profile. Please see that. It's flawed.'

Ben gave her a calm smile. 'I like to think I'm too much of a professional to be trammelled by psychological profiling, flawed or not. That would be a huge mistake – remember what our trainers used to say? "To assume makes an ass out of you and me."'

Zoë sighed. 'Come on, Ben – I know you too well.'

He tapped his pen on the desk. 'Ralph Hernandez is a person of interest. That's all I can say at this point.'

'A "person of interest"? Oh, for God's sake – you are such a bloody moron it's just not true.'

223

'Am I, Zoë? Have you got any better leads than this?'

'I gave you this "lead". I handed it to you on a plate and I really, really thought you'd do the honourable thing. Just goes to show how much I know about the world, doesn't it?'

At that moment the door opened. Zoë swivelled round. Debbie was standing there, serene in her white lacy clothes. She had started to speak, but when she saw Zoë her face changed. 'Aaah,' she said apologetically. 'Sorry.' She held up a hand and backed out of the room. 'Crap timing – not my strong point.'

She closed the door. There was a moment's silence. Then Zoë turned back to face Ben. She shook her head and gave a small, mirthless laugh. 'Funny,' she said. 'You never usually let anyone in without knocking. Unless they're . . . you know . . .' She made her hands into a cup on the desk. 'Unless they're inner circle. Is she inner circle now?'

Ben stared back at her stonily. 'Have you got any better leads than Ralph Hernandez?'

'So whatever she says you'll believe it? You'll convict that kid in there because of it?'

'My alternative is what? Choosing anyone, any route, any lead, just anyone because they *don't* fit the profile she drew up? I've been watching your inquiries, Zoë, and what it boils down to is that you'd rather let the killer go free than have Debbie be right. So who is worse? You or me?'

Zoë's face burned. 'This is all because of whatever it was I said the other night, isn't it?'

'I don't know what you mean.'

'Well, Ben, let's be honest. One minute we were fine – doing fine. The next, everything's gone. Just . . .' she flattened her hand and mimed an aeroplane flying '. . . like that. Gone. And you're hostile and distant, and, frankly, acting like a dickhead.'

Ben gave her a cold look. 'We've got no future, Zoë.'

'What? Because I don't *pretend* to give a shit about people I really *don't* give a shit about? Because I don't make a pantomime about how caring and *simpatico* I bloody am? Is that my sin?'

'Why do you have to insist you're bad?'

'Because I am.'

'Why do you insist you don't care for anything?'

'Because I don't. Because I don't *care* for anything and I don't *need* anything.'

'Well,' he said quietly, 'don't jump all over me and make me feel small when I say this, but, Zoë, some people like to be needed.'

'Like to be needed? Well, that's not me.'

'Bullshit.'

'It's *not* fucking *bullshit*.' She pushed her chair back and leaned across the desk, putting her face close to his. 'I drove around the world on my own. I don't need you or anyone else. That's why *I*'m solid and *I*'m efficient. And anyway . . .' She took a breath. Tried to put a bit more width and height into her shoulders. 'It doesn't matter because next thing we know you'll be having it off with Miss Cracker out there.'

He held her gaze. He had still, clear green eyes. 'Actually,' he said, 'I already am.'

Zoë stared at him. Something inside her was falling away. Dropping and dropping down into the floor. 'What?' she murmured. 'What did you say?'

'I'm sorry,' he said. 'But it's true.'

She was motionless, absolutely speechless. The scars on her arms ached, made her want to rip her sleeves up, but she held herself steady. She wouldn't let him know he'd poleaxed her.

'OK,' she managed to say. 'Then I suppose it's time I went.'

He nodded. The politeness, the openness of the nod, was the worst of it. This wasn't hurting him at all.

'But I'm right about Ralph,' she said. 'One hundred per cent right. He didn't kill Lorne.'

'Of course, Zoë.' He turned his computer screen around and put on his glasses. 'You're always right.'

32

Sally called the NHS helpline. The woman she spoke to said Steve should go to his GP, but Steve had looked carefully at the wound and said that would be over-reacting, that really it was just a hole in the skin, nothing more. Together they disinfected and bandaged it, cleared up the blood and put the nail gun, chisels and hacksaw into the boot of her car ready for the DIY on her house. After that they got on with lunch – eating the tuna, picking through a bowlful of mango and raspberry sorbet, drinking coffee, and loading the dishwasher shoulder to shoulder, all without alluding to the conversation about David Goldrab. As if they'd decided, in a curious telepathic manner, to pretend it hadn't happened. It wasn't that they were solemn either – in fact, they were light-hearted, making jokes about Steve's wound going gangrenous. How would it be if he lost his arm and had to walk around like Nelson for the rest of his life? Sally wondered if she'd dreamed the whole thing. If shady, raw acts like contract killings really happened, or if she'd somehow misunderstood what Steve was saying.

She got a text from Millie, who said she was getting a lift home in Nial's camper-van, and not to worry about coming to school, she'd see her at Peppercorn. She sounded happy, not nervous. Even so, Sally still made sure she was home by four thirty, waiting by the window in plenty of time to see Nial's half-painted van trundling along the driveway. Peter was sitting on the back seat, shades on, one arm draped casually around Sophie's shoulders. All of them were in summer school uniform, their hair gelled, spiked and decorated as much as they could get away with at Kingsmead. The van stopped and Millie got out without a word to the others. She slammed the door and strode up the path, her face like thunder.

'What's going on?'

She walked straight past Sally, down the corridor, into the bedroom and slammed the door. When Sally padded softly after her and listened, she could hear muffled sobbing coming from inside. As if Millie was crying into the pillow. She opened the door, tiptoed in and sat on the end of the bed, resting her hand on Millie's ankle. 'Millie?'

At first Sally thought she hadn't heard. Then Millie sat up and threw herself at her mother, arms round her neck, head pressed against her chest, like a drowning victim. Sobbing as if her heart would break.

'What on earth's happened?' Sally pushed her back so she could see her face. 'Is it him? Jake? Did you see him?'

'No,' she sobbed. 'No, Mum. I can't handle it any more. Now he's with *Sophie* of all people. She's not even that pretty.'

'Who's not even that . . . ?' She thought about Sophie, with a dreamy look on her face in the back of the van, Peter's arm around her. She remembered what Isabelle had said about Peter being in love with Lorne and how it had upset Millie. This was all about him. Half of her was bewildered that her daughter couldn't see past Peter's blond hair and height, couldn't look into the future and see his beery red face at forty, his thick torso and rugby-club nights. The other half was relieved that this wasn't anything to do with Jake. Or Lorne.

'Hey.' She kissed Millie's head, smoothed her hair. 'You know what I've always told you. It's not what's on the outside, it's what's on the inside.'

'Don't be stupid. That's just crap. No one looks on the inside. You're just saying that because you're *old*.'

'OK, OK.' She rested her chin on Millie's head. Looked out at the fields and the trees and the clouds piled up like castles in the sky and tried to span her memory across the distance between fifteen and thirty-five. It didn't seem an eternity. But when she put herself in Millie's shoes and thought about her own mother fifteen years ago she saw how honest and clear that comment was. She let Millie cry, let her soak the front of her blouse.

Eventually the sobs died down to the occasional hiccup and Millie straightened up, her bottom lip sticking out. She wiped her nose with her sleeve.

'I don't really like him. Honestly. I really don't.'

'Is that it? Is that all that's upsetting you?'

'All?' Millie echoed. '*All?* Isn't that enough?'

'I didn't mean it was nothing. I was just thinking – you're so unhappy. Unsettled.'

Millie shivered. 'Yeah – it's been such a bloody horrible day. Everything's wrong. It's been just pants.'

'Everything?'

She nodded miserably.

'Like what?'

'I don't think you want to know that.'

'I do.'

Millie gave a long-suffering sigh and stretched her blouse so the cuff came down over her knuckles and drew her knees up to her chest, hugging them. 'OK – but I warned you.'

'What?'

'I saw Auntie Zoë.'

Sally had opened her mouth to reply before what Millie had said sunk in. When it did she closed it. It was the last thing she'd expected. Zoë hadn't been mentioned in their house for years. Years and years. In all of Millie's lifetime they'd run into her twice – once in the high street, when Millie had been about five. That time Zoë had stopped and smiled at Millie, said, 'You must be Millie,' then looked at her watch, and added, 'Well, got to go.' The second time, two years later, the two women had simply nodded in acknowledgement and carried on their way. Afterwards Sally had been quiet for hours. These days, sometimes, she dreamed about Zoë – wondered

230

what it would be like to see her again. Now she pushed the hair gently out of Millie's face. She hadn't even realized she knew Zoë's name. 'You mean you – uh – saw her walking down the street? Or you spoke to her?'

'We went to see her at the police station. The head said we could take the morning off to do it. Nial and Peter and Ralph had something to tell her.'

'Ralph? The Spanish one?'

'He's *half* Spanish. And he was seeing Lorne.'

'*Seeing* her?'

'Yes, and he tried to keep it secret. But it's out now and it's no big deal. I mean, he was seeing her, but he didn't *kill* her, Mum. He didn't have anything to do with it.'

So Isabelle had been right, Sally thought. About the secrets. The whispering. She wondered how it could be that the children they'd given birth to could have gone from curly-haired toddlers sitting on their laps to complete human beings with secrets and codes and plans.

'He stayed at the station. With Auntie Zoë. She was, like, *so* nice to him. So nice.'

Sally heard the admiration in her voice. Unmistakable. She knew what it felt like to admire Zoë. 'How is she? Zoë, I mean.'

'She's fine.' Millie sniffed. 'Fine.'

'Fine?'

'That's what I said.'

'How did she look?'

'What do you mean?'

231

'I don't know.' Sally hesitated. 'Is she tall? Years ago she always seemed quite tall to me.'

'Yeah,' Millie said. 'She is. Really tall. Really, *really* tall. The way I'd like to be.'

'What's her hair like? She had amazing hair.'

'Still has. It's like mine – sort of reddy colour. A bit mad, actually – and it looked wet. Why?'

'I don't know. Just wondering.' She gave a small, rueful smile, then said, 'She's doing well in her job, I suppose. She's really clever, you know. You'd never think we were related.'

'She's got her own office and stuff. She doesn't seem the type to be in an office, though.'

'Why?'

'Oh, I don't know. She's . . .' Millie searched for the right word and failed to find it. 'She's just too cool to be in the police. That's all. She's just too cool.'

33

The most private ladies' toilet at Bath police station was on the ground floor, just past the front office. Zoë walked through the foyer with her head lowered, in case anyone saw her, and pushed the door open. The toilets were empty. Just the smell of bleach and the vague plink-plink of a leaky cistern in one of the cubicles. She ignored her reflection and went straight along the line of doors, choosing the last one, furthest from the entrance. She went inside, closed the toilet lid, locked the door, pulled off her jacket and dropped it on the floor. She sat down, her elbows on her knees, her head in her hands.

Actually, I already am . . .

It was none of her business who Ben slept with. There had never been any promises like that. It had never been part of the deal. But it had never been part of the deal either that he'd freeze over the way he had. She'd known him for years. Years and years they'd worked together before they'd started sleeping together – he should know every inch of her personality by now. So what had changed? It couldn't be

233

that he'd got a glimpse inside her, seen the nasty dark thing she worked so hard to keep down. No, it couldn't. She was sure he couldn't see that. Then what?

She dragged her sleeve up, rolled it tightly at the biceps, the way an addict would. She found a spare centimetre of skin and used the nails on her thumb and forefinger to find a demi-lune of flesh. She closed her eyes and dug them in. Harder and harder. The pain was like a sweet black thread moving through her body. Like a drug. She put her head back and breathed slowly while it moved up to her chest, wrapped itself round her lungs and heart and made everything go dark and still. The blood rose up in the pinched flesh and slid coldly down her arm to splash on to the white tiles. She didn't let go. Just held it there. Held it and held it.

And then, when she was sure the scream had been stopped, she dropped her hand. She opened her eyes and blinked at the white light, the blood all over her nails, the cold Formica of the toilet door.

Ben was nothing. He didn't matter. It would be a battle, but slowly it would pass. She was exhausted, wrung out with the case, and she needed space to breathe. She would take some time off work – God knew, she had enough time owing. She'd take the Shovelhead and disappear for a while. Sleep rough and drink Guinness out of the can. Forget the case, lose interest in who had killed Lorne, let the memory of that nightclub in Bristol be whipped out of her head by the slipstream on the motorway.

She unravelled some toilet tissue and began to clean herself up. She bent over to wipe the blood off the floor and saw her wallet had spilled out of her jacket. She paused, the tissue wodged on the floor. Peeping out from one of the compartments was a curved pink sliver of card: the top of the business card she'd been given at Zebedee Juice.

'*Shit.*' She sat up again, leaning back against the cistern, the bloody tissue hanging limp in her hand, her head lolling. The fluorescent tubes pulsed on the ceiling above her. 'OK, Lorne,' she muttered. 'OK. I'll give you one more day. Twelve more hours. And then, I'm sorry, but I'm out of it.'

34

When Sally came out of Millie's room she was surprised to find Nial in the kitchen, standing awkwardly near the table, arms folded, head lowered. 'I thought you'd gone.'

'Yeah I . . . I sort of needed to make myself scarce.' He gestured out of the window to where the van was parked. 'They needed a bit of time. You know, before I drop Peter home.'

She looked up and saw Peter and Sophie on the back seat of the van, locked together in a kiss. Peter must have been standing up because he looked much bigger and taller than Sophie, bearing down on her, pushing her into the seat with his mouth. Sophie wasn't resisting. In fact, quite the opposite. She was clinging to his neck as if she was afraid he'd disappear. There were a few moments of uneasy silence. Then Nial cleared his throat, said in a small voice, 'She's in love with him, isn't she?'

'It certainly looks like it.'

'I don't mean Sophie, I mean Millie. Millie's in love with Peter.'

She turned woodenly to him, hardly believing what she thought he was saying. 'Nial?' she said curiously. 'You don't mean you . . .'

He gave a weak, embarrassed smile. 'Yeah, well – nothing I can do about it, is there?'

She stared back at him. Good God, what a mess. No reciprocity – no returns. Sophie in love with Peter, Millie in love with Peter, and Nial in love with Millie. Poor little Nial. It was like watching elephants in a circus ring, each with its trunk linked round the tail of the animal in front, plodding on, blind to the futility of it all. Really and truly, life just wasn't fair.

She sighed. 'Oh, God, you're probably right. At the moment. But you wait. You wait.'

'What?'

'One day, Nial, Millie will see you in a different light. I promise you that.'

He blinked. 'Do you?'

'Oh, yes – oh, yes.' And in saying it she prayed, with all the hope in the world, that she was right.

35

Zoë had taken a sleeping pill last night – she'd needed something, anything, to help escape the persistent voice in her head. At first it had been bliss, sending her sliding over the edge into oblivion. But she woke with a jolt five hours later, the first light of dawn at the window and the same clawing pain in her centre that she'd gone to sleep with. She didn't look at her reflection when she got dressed. She sat on the edge of the bed and carefully wound a bandage around the wound on her arm, holding its end in her teeth. She selected a heavy black-cotton shirt with sleeves that buttoned securely at the wrists. She pushed her arm into it gingerly, not wanting to make it bleed again. She was an old hand at this.

She drove across town with the radio on, trying to keep her mood up, but the sight of the battered sign in the doorway of Holden's Agency, the steps up to it, covered with chewing gum and stained with God only knew what, sent her resilience for the day down another notch. She hesitated – suddenly reluctant. But it was too late. Through the wire-meshed glass the man inside had noticed her. He came to the door and swung it open. He was suntanned, in his sixties, wearing a cheap pinstriped suit and a neat white shirt that were both a size too small. He was obviously trying to beat the smoking habit, because he had a Nicorette inhalator tucked in his breast pocket and the faint tang of tobacco smoke lingering around him.

'Hi.' He gave her his hand to shake. It was huge and meaty and he had the big grin of a Texan car salesman. She expected him to say, 'How can I be of assistance to you, ma'am?'

'Zoë,' she said.

'Mike. Mike Holden. What can I do you for? You're not looking for the health-food shop, are you? It's round the corner.'

'No – I—' She fumbled for her warrant card. Gave it a quick flash. 'I'm from CID. In Bath.'

Holden paused at the sight of it. 'Wendy? Is it Wendy? Has something happened to her? Just say it if it has. I've been preparing myself.'

'Wendy? No. It's an investigation. Something that happened in Bath. No bad news.'

He took a step back, breathing slowly, calming himself. 'That's good. Good.' He looked her up and down – seemed to notice her for the first time. 'I'm sorry – no manners. You'd better come in.'

The office was clean and less depressing than it was on the outside. It had the smell of a kitchen show-room, with industrial-grade brown carpet and a few pieces of furniture that looked a little lost in the large area. On one wall there was a line of framed black-and-white prints. Girls in bikinis, girls in swimsuits. Nothing topless.

'You're a model agency.'

Holden nodded. He sat at his desk, gestured for her to take a chair and turned a book towards her. 'Our portfolio.'

She leafed through it and saw what the manager at Zebedee Juice had meant. These were nothing like the feral, challenging creatures on the morphing screen. These were pretty, sexy and well fed. Lorne would fit well in this portfolio. 'Some of them are topless.'

He nodded. 'That's what we do. Everything from swimsuits to lingerie to page three. This year we've had two girls in the Pirelli calendar and we've had page three eighteen times. The West Country produces some of the best-looking girls in the land. It's the warmth and the rain.' He winked. 'And the clotted cream. You know – all that fat.'

'These girls, these models, do they go further than topless?'

'Of course. The human body is a great instrument for artistic expression. If a girl is liberated, comfortable being naked, then she can get a lot of satisfaction from this sort of work. Most of them love it – really love it.'

'Do you believe that? Or, rather, do you expect me to believe that? I mean, really they're in it for the money.'

He was silent. Only his jaw showed agitation: it

240

moved, very slightly, from side to side, as if he was working a piece of food out from his teeth. At last he raised his hands. 'You're not stupid and neither am I. Of course not. They do it for the money. And most of the time it's not cos they have to – it's not cos they were trafficked, or cos they're having to put food in the mouths of their disabled babies or their dying mothers or whatever. Not even to feed their drug addiction, because most of them are clean. No – in my experience most of the time they're doing it cos it's easier than standing behind a till at Top Shop for eight hours a day. Quicker and easier – and, honestly, you get more respect from the photographer than you do from your average shopper. And I say hats off to them. Not that I've ever, in my ten years in the business, *ever* seen a girl do something sensible with the money. No investing it or anything like that. They spend it on clothes and, frankly, tit jobs. So they can – what? Go on doing modelling. A bit of a mindless cycle, if you think about it – men getting what they think they want from women, women getting what they think they want from men.'

Actually, Mr Holden, Zoë thought, not all of them spend their money on clothes and tit jobs. Some of them spend it on escaping something. Buying their freedom. 'Have you been watching the news? The local news? There was a murder in Bath the other day.'

'I know. Young girl. Pretty. Lorraine, was it? Lorraine someone.'

'Lorne. Lorne Wood. The name doesn't ring a bell?'

He frowned. 'I don't think so.'

'You don't remember her coming to you?'

'She was a schoolgirl, I thought.'

'Yes, but she wanted to model. And she might not have used her real name.'

She pulled from her satchel a laminated set of pictures that the reprographics unit had produced. A set of photos of Lorne. The billions poured into developing facial-recognition technology had done little more than raise an important issue: the human face is so multi-faceted that it can vary wildly just from the smallest change in angle and lighting. The chief constable had picked up on this and now the force was inclined to use a selection of photographs for identification purposes. On this sheet many of the photos collected from Lorne's wall had been collaged. Zoë leaned half out of her chair and placed the sheet under Holden's nose.

He looked at them. Frowned. Shook his head slowly. 'Don't think so. I get scores of photos from girls who think they're going to be on page three, or the cover of *FHM*. The faces, I'll be honest, merge into one eventually, but I don't think I remember her.'

She took the sheet back and sat for a moment, eyes on Lorne's Hollywood smile. None of these looked anything like the photos on the camera chip. They were in a totally different mood. She reached into her pocket for her iPhone, to which she'd transferred all the photos from Lorne's chip, and brought up one of Lorne in underwear on the bed. Not the topless one. She'd protect Lorne from that at least. 'How about that?'

This time Holden's face changed. 'OK,' he said quietly. 'That alters things. I do recognize her.' He went to a filing cabinet and pulled out a folder, riffled through the photos and printed pages in it. 'I would never have recognized her from the other photos – but seeing that, I remember.' He pulled out a photo and held it up. It was one of the topless ones from the camera chip, printed out. 'She emailed it to me – didn't use that name, though. Called herself –' he checked on the back '– Cherie. Cherie Garnett.'

Zoë's whole body felt tired. She wasn't glad she'd been right, just enormously depressed. 'And? What did you say?'

'Nah. I thought there was something a bit suspicious about it, to be honest. I thought right away she was younger than she said she was.'

'That stopped you, did it?'

He raised his eyebrows. 'It's a serious offence. You really can't be too careful. I told her I'd keep her on file.'

'So you told her no. Are you sure?'

'I'm sure.'

She looked at him, trying to get the measure of him. She thought he was telling the truth. 'Do you think she'd have gone somewhere else when you turned her down?'

He was silent for a moment. Then he got to his feet and opened a filing cabinet. He took out a written list and handed it to her. 'Listen,' he said seriously, 'I don't know you and you don't owe me a thing. But if you tell any of them who put you in touch

243

and it comes out it's me – well, I'm just saying.'

Zoë scanned the sheet. It had about fifty names printed on it with contact details. A lot of them seemed to be agents around the West Country, but several were lap-dance clubs. 'Did you give her this list?'

'I didn't. I give you my word on that. But I'm not the only show in town. Someone else may have.'

She folded the page of addresses, put it into her pocket and got to her feet. 'Just one last thing,' she said.

'Yes?'

'If you have any more thoughts on this don't call the police station. None of the others are working on this lead so you need to speak to me direct.' She pulled a business card out of her pocket and laid it on his desk. 'And don't leave any messages except on my personal voicemail. If you do that for me . . .'

'Yes?'

'Your name won't be mentioned to anyone on this list.'

36

Sally found herself staring at David Goldrab as she cleaned his house that day. She kept trying to catch glimpses of him as he wandered around after his visit to the stables, opening a bottle of champagne, tapping his whip on his calf as if keeping rhythm with some song he was humming. She stood at the sink opposite him, in her rubber gloves, wiping the surface over and over, not looking at it but at him – his skin, his hands, his arms. The moving parts of him that made him living. Someone wanted him dead. Actually dead. Not pretend dead. Really.

She finished her cleaning chores and went to the office to start entering the household expenses into the database. She'd been there for about ten minutes when she heard him go upstairs to the gym, which faced out over the front of the property. Soon she heard the familiar whirr of the treadmill, then the thud-thud-thud of him running. Her eyes drifted to the bank of computers on the other desk. His 'business' section. She thought about what Steve had said. Porn. But nasty porn. Something dark and enveloping. She bit her lip and tried to concentrate on the column of figures. Earlier she'd noticed a light on the other computer. It meant it was on standby – not actually switched off.

After a while she couldn't stop her attention wandering to it. She stood up and, tongue between her teeth, leaned over and touched the mouse. The computer whirred and began to come to life. Suddenly scared, she got up and went to the open door, looking up at the ceiling. Bang-bang-bang, came the noise from the treadmill.

Quickly she went back into the office and to the computer. David hadn't logged out of the session – everything on the screen was plain to see. The wallpaper for the desktop was a scanned newspaper page. It showed a man in his forties, heavy chin, thinning hair, dressed in a suit. The photo seemed to have been taken in the street somewhere: he was holding his hand up to the camera as if he'd been caught by photographers. The headline read: 'Top MoD man Mooney heads Kosovan sex unit'. It looked as if the article had come from the *Sun* or the *Mirror* or another tabloid. She scanned the article – something about a unit that had been set up within the United Nations to stop women being brought in as prostitutes for the peace-keeping forces. Then she examined the man's face. Mooney. Steve's client. Did the fact it was on his computer mean David knew Mooney was watching him?

She bit her lip and glanced up at the doorway. Overlying the photo on the screen there were ten icons on the desktop, each with the file extension *'mov'*. Videos. Still David was pounding on the tread-mill. She let the mouse trail over the icons. It was ridiculous, when she thought about it, but she was thirty-five and she didn't remember ever having seen a porn movie from beginning to end. She must have seen snippets, though, somewhere along the line, because if she really concentrated she had an idea of what to expect – very tanned women with blonde hair and bouncy breasts and lips painted pillar-box red. She thought of faces contorted in ecstasy. What she didn't expect was what she saw when she got up the courage to click on the first icon.

It was set in what looked like a large livestock pen, with whitewashed concrete walls and grid-shaped floodlights suspended overhead. At first all Sally could see were the backs of people gathered around, as if they were watching something on the floor in the centre of the pen. They were all men, dressed averagely enough from the neck down – jeans, shirts, sweaters. Their faces were covered – some wore scarves tied so that only their eyes showed, others had ski masks or balaclavas. A few wore rubber party masks: Osama bin Laden, Michael Jackson, Elvis Presley, Barack Obama. It would seem bizarre and even comical if it hadn't been for the fact that all the men had their flies undone and were openly masturbating.

The camera panned up, the picture became clearer, and Sally felt herself go numb. In the centre of the ring someone lay naked on a tattered mattress – a girl, though at first it was difficult to see her sex, she was so emaciated. Her tiny ankles were manacled to the floor, her legs forced apart. Her face wasn't visible, but Sally could tell she was young. Very young. Not much older than Millie, maybe.

A man wearing sunglasses and a baseball cap pulled low over his face pushed his way through the crowd. He wore jeans and a tight T-shirt and, although his face was half covered, she immediately recognized him as Jake. It was the tan and the muscular arms that did it. He approached the girl and straddled her, one foot on either side of each shoulder, so he was looking down at her head. He began to unzip his flies – and as he did Sally realized the noise of the treadmill had stopped.

She clicked off the video and hurriedly went to the shut-down button. And as she did she remembered it had been on standby, not shut down. Quickly she changed her mind. Chose *Sleep*. She jumped up from the seat and went to sit at the other desk, her back to the computer, willing it to close down faster – wishing she'd just unplugged it. But then David appeared in the office doorway, dressed in his jogging pants and trainers. The postman must have been because he had a glass of pink champagne in one hand and a stack of letters in the other. More letters still were wedged under his chin. He was shuffling through the envelopes, murmuring under his breath, 'Bill, begging letter, sell sell sell, fucking credit-card company shite.'

Then he saw that the computer was alive and that

Sally was sitting, stony and still, eyes locked on the database, her face flushed.

Slowly, he lowered the handful of letters. 'Uh, 'scuse me for pointing this out, but someone's been titting with my computer.' He stood in front of it, frowning, watching the screen whirr itself into darkness. There was a long silence, in which all Sally could think about was her heart thudding. Then David turned.

'Sally?'

She was silent.

'Sally? I'm speaking to you. Look me in the eye.' He reached over and pulled her shoulder. Reluctantly she turned. He made a bull's horn with his pinkie and his thumb, jabbed his hand at his eyes. 'Look me in the eye, and tell me why you did that.' A vein was pulsing in his forehead. 'Eh? When I told you to keep away from that side of the room.'

She didn't answer. She couldn't. She thought she might be sick, any moment.

'Don't give me that patronizing look. I'm not the lowlife shit on your shoes, Sally, it's the other way round. Has it escaped your attention that *I*'m the one employing *you*? Just cos you speak like you got coughed out of some hoity-toity fucking finishing school that teaches you how not to flash your snatch when you're getting out of a Ferrari doesn't make you better than I am – you still gotta pretend to like me. Because you're desperate and you—'

He broke off. Something else had caught his attention. The TV monitor on the wall. He raised his chin, gazed at it, his mouth open. Shakily, Sally looked up and saw on screen, behind the electronic gate, the familiar metallic purple jeep. Jake was leaning out of the window, pushing the buzzer.

'Well, that's fucking mint.' He slammed the post down. 'That has really made my day.' He snatched up a riding whip that was propped against the wall and strode into the hallway, bending every three steps to slap it furiously on the floor. The gate buzzer echoed through the hallway. David didn't go upstairs to get the crossbow. Instead he went straight to the door and pressed the button to open the gates. Seeing her chance, Sally silently grabbed her bag and jacket and crept down the corridor. She came into the kitchen as she heard the jeep pulling into the driveway. She grabbed her cleaning kit from the work-surface, went quickly to the door that led out across the terrace, and put her hand on it, expecting it to open.

It didn't. It was locked.

She jiggled it and tugged, but there was no mistake: it was locked. She hunted around for a key, picking up pots and vases to check under them. The utility room. She knew for sure that that door was open – it always was. But before she could get across the kitchen the front door slammed and the two men came into the hallway. She stood, frozen, her heart thumping. There wasn't any escape from this – she couldn't go back to the office without passing the hallway. She couldn't get to the utility room either. She was trapped.

Quickly she slipped into the huge glass atrium that

was tacked on to the back of the house. The doors that opened from it five yards away were closed, but she couldn't risk crossing it to check if they were locked because the men were nearly in the kitchen and they'd spot her. A chaise-longue was set against the wall, just out of sight of the kitchen – she could hide there for the time being. She sat down silently. The men came into the kitchen and at the same time a long bar of light moved across the atrium windows. A reflection. She realized she could see all the familiar things across the kitchen and into the hall: mirrored in the panes. If the men stood at the right place and glanced across they'd see her reflected back at them, but it was too late to move. She pulled her feet up tighter, her case and jacket crunched against her stomach, and kept as still and quiet as she could.

'Jake.' David stood a few steps back from the doorway, silhouetted in the sunlight, his feet planted wide, his arms folded. Sally couldn't see Jake's face clearly in the reflection, but she could feel the seriousness of his mood. He was wearing a leather jacket and gloves, and was carrying a large holdall. He kept his chin down slightly. She thought of him straddling the girl in the video. She couldn't get it out of her head how thin the girl had been.

'David.'

'What do you want?'

'I want to talk to you.'

There was a long pause. Sally's attention stayed on that holdall. It had caught David's eye too. He

251

nodded at it. 'What's in there, Jake? Brought me a present, have you?'

'In a manner of speaking. Can I sit down?'

'If you tell me what you want to talk about.'

'This.' He raised the bag. 'I want to show you.'

For a few seconds David didn't move. Then he stood back and held out his hand towards the table. 'I've just opened a bottle of champagne. You've always had a taste for champagne, Jakey boyo.'

The two men moved to the table, their reflections a shoulder's width apart. David pulled back a chair and Jake sat down, the holdall in his lap. David got the champagne bottle out of the cooler and unstoppered it, then poured some into a long flute. 'Just the one, mind. Don't want my Jakey boy driving under the influence. Would never do. Terrible waste of talent, you with your brains smeared all over the M4.'

David got himself comfortable, raised the glass. Jake raised his in reply, drank. Even in the conservatory Sally heard the hard, metallic clink of it knocking against his teeth. He was nervous. He didn't know she was here – her car was parked at the bottom of the grounds, out of sight. As far as he was concerned he was on his own with David.

'Nice camera system you've got out front. Records everything, does it?'

'Oh, yes. Records everything.'

'I've got a system like that. After a week the image gets recorded over. Unless you wipe it.'

'Yes,' David said reasonably. 'But to do that you'd have to have a code.'

'Yeah. A code.'

'Which the owner of the system would change on a regular basis. The same way he'd change the code on the security gates. I mean, say, there was someone that person had had confidence in at one point. Such confidence that they gave him – or her – their security code. Say, then, those two people developed differences, little niggles they couldn't iron out – well, the system owner would be a mug, wouldn't he, not to change the codes? Otherwise what's to stop the guy with the codes coming in and misbehaving in the house? Even, God forbid, doing something silly to the owner.'

'Something silly.'

'Something silly.' There was another silence, then he said, 'What's in the bag, Jake?'

Sally closed her eyes for a moment, put her head back and drew a slow, silent breath – tried to get her heart to stop throwing itself against her ribcage. When she opened her eyes Jake was opening the bag and everything in the house had a vague silvery glaze, as if it was holding its breath too. Even the big clock on the conservatory wall seemed to hesitate, hold its hand still, reluctant to click forward.

Then Jake pulled a DVD out of the bag. He placed it on the table. David looked at it in silence. After a moment or two, he held out his hand.

'And the rest,' he said. 'Show me whatever else is in there. I ain't scared of you.'

'There's nothing. Just more of the same.'

David nodded. 'Yeah. Of course. Let me see.'

Jake held the bag out. David took it, gave it a

shake, peered inside. Put his hands in and sifted around. He raised puzzled eyes to Jake, as if he still suspected him of something underhand. Jake shrugged. 'What? What now?'

David gave him a suspicious glare, but he handed the bag back. Sally slowly let out her breath. In her chest her heart was still bouncing around like a rubber ball.

'DVDs? What are they?'

'My latest venture.' Jake inched forward on his chair, suddenly enthusiastic. 'Jake the Peg's done every city in the UK – I couldn't afford to take it out of the country so I had to look for something cheap and I thought, Hey, old man, how about Jake the Peg does the alphabet?'

'The alphabet?'

'A girl whose name starts with every letter of the alphabet. She wears the letter on her outfit here.' He put a hand to his stomach. 'I got one of those basque things and had a letter A stitched on. A for Amber. B for Brittany. C for Cindi. We've got to F for Faith so far. Her real name was Veronica. But serious mahongas. The type they like in the States.'

'Shows a touching faith in your audience, boyo, thinking they know the alphabet.'

'If I put the letter on the spine they become a set – a collection. The real fans'll want to have the whole lot – A to Z – on their shelves.'

David turned one of the DVDs over, studied the back. 'Very creative. But they do say that about you lot, don't they? Good with colours, wallpaper, soft furnishings, that sort of thing.'

'I need some start-up capital.'

'From me? Well, I would, my old friend, but they say bukkake doesn't sell any more. Did you know that? Apparently more women are watching porn. Apparently they don't get off on seeing some slag getting wanked over by twenty men. God knows why, it's a mystery to me, but you do hear the word "degrading" bandied around, these days.'

Sally massaged her temples. So what she'd seen on the video had a name. Bukkake. Somehow it made it worse, to put a word to it, made it more real. No pretending she'd dreamed it.

'Course, maybe you could flog it to the gay market – could be a new opening. I mean, it was always beyond me why any red-blooded male would want to watch a bunch of other men jacking off. Where's the hetero in that formula, eh?'

Jake ignored the dig. 'I was thinking we'd go forty:sixty. You put in the copying facility, the packaging and the marketing. I put in the product.'

David was still for a moment. 'Forty:sixty? Who's the forty?'

'You. Let them go out at six ninety-nine. The same strategy we had with the last series.'

David got to his feet. He went to the fridge and poured himself another glass of champagne. He closed the door and stood for a moment or two, his back to Jake, as if he was composing himself. Then he came back and sat down. 'Look, boyo, we had a

255

falling-out the other day when you were here. I was rude, I grant you.'

'Yeah – you were pissed off.'

'Pissed off. That's right. And I told you not to come back. You chose to ignore that. So you must, I think, be asking yourself why the hell I let you back in today. Aren't you?'

'I dunno. Maybe.'

'Let me explain. I opened the door to you for one reason. Curiosity. I'm a curious man, see, always have been. Used to love, as a child, going to the zoo. Nice family outing to see the monkeys playing with their peckers, know what I mean? Used to be curious about that and I'm like that even now. For example, I'm intrigued by the amazing variety of things some of the Kosovan slags'll shove up their snatches for a few euro. That, believe me, never fails to make me curious. And Jake, my old friend, that's why I'm welcoming you in here.'

'Because you're curious?'

David laughed expansively. He leaned over and slapped Jake on the knee. 'Oh, I love it – I love your expression. You think I'm going to ask you to pull out your pecker like those monkeys, doncha? Or ram an onion up your jacksy? Don't worry – I'm not going to ask you that, though I'm sure you would, you being a bum-boy and all. No – I've seen your legendary whanger enough times to satisfy that curiosity, eh? Like half of Britain. Sad your one-handed audience can't applaud, isn't it? Might make you feel better about yourself. No, Jake, I'm not

256

curious about any of that. And yet I am still curious. Still curious . . .'

'About what?' Jake blurted.

'About what the *fuck* you were *thinking*!' He rammed a finger hard into his temple. Spittle flew out of his mouth. 'Have you fucking *lost* it up here in old Mission Command, boyo, mincing back, trying to sell me my own fucking speciality? *I'm* the bukkake king, you queer piece of shit. *I'm* the one got you started. I *made* you, Jake. *I. Made. You.*' He shook his head sorrowfully. Let out all his breath wearily and opened his hands as if he despaired. 'Honestly, Jake, if you had an extra brain it'd be lonely. Now, get the fuck out of my house. And this time don't come back.'

Jake stared at him.

'What're you fucking looking at? You deaf or something?' David slammed a fist on the table, making the DVDs rattle. Jake jumped to his feet and hastily swept the DVDs into the bag. Throwing it over his shoulder, he backed out towards the door, his hands up. David followed him as far as the hallway, then swung loosely around the banister and disappeared from Sally's view up the stairs.

Going for the crossbow. He had to be.

She got up and went quietly to the door. Jake was outside on the gravel, patting his coat, trying to find his keys, glancing anxiously at David, who had come downstairs and was standing a few feet away in the sunshine, his back to her, the crossbow raised. She looked across the kitchen to the utility room – just ten feet to cover, then she'd be out. She was about to scamper across when there was a loud thwack and a bolt was fired. A fountain of gravel spurted into the air about ten feet away on the driveway near the jeep. Jake put his hands in the air defensively.

'What's wrong, boyo?' David called pleasantly. 'Still struggling with the meaning of "fuck off"?'

In an act of defiance, Jake stooped, snatched up a handful of gravel, and threw it at him. Then, before David could react, he was in the jeep, powering up the driveway, the automatic gates swinging open to let him go. And Jake was gone, the butterfly flash of his jeep bumping along the tiny lane that wound down to the road.

David trudged back into the house. Immediately he caught sight of Sally shrinking back into the atrium.

'What're you staring at?' He glanced over his shoulder as if there might be someone else in the hallway who was making her gawp like that. 'What? So I lost my temper. Don't get all weepy on me, Princess – if you hadn't been cunting around with my private affairs I wouldn't've been so pissed off in the first place.'

Sally gaped at him, lost for words. Her face was on fire. She was thinking about the girl in the video, strapped to the floor.

'*What?*' His chin jutted forward aggressively. 'Don't give me that fucking superior-bitch look – I'm fed up with seeing it. You stand here in *my* house judging me? Well, there's a simple solution to that. You fuck off. If you don't like it, then just fuck right off.'

258

She was still for a moment longer. Then she turned on her heel and began to walk towards the utility room. 'You bastard,' she muttered, under her breath.

'I beg your pardon?'

She shook her head. Kept walking.

'You'll apologize for that,' he yelled behind her. 'You'll fucking apologize.'

She got to the door of the utility room. Mercifully it opened smoothly and she was out in the sun, her bag over her shoulder, her jacket bundled up in the cleaning kit. She was trembling but she didn't run, just went fast and steady, her head up and straight, ferreting around with one hand in her bag for her keys. She could hear him behind her. Also not running. But keeping pace.

'I said *apologize*. Say it. Tell you what, I'll make it easy for you – give you the script. "I'm truly sorry, David, for calling you a bastard. I'm sorry." Just say it and it's over.'

As she got to the bottom of the path and swung the little gate open, the keys in her bag suddenly seemed to leap into her hand. Thank you, thank you, thank you, she thought, hoisting them out and aiming them at the car. The locking system beeped and clunked reassuringly; the indicators flashed. The gap from the parking area to the gate was only a few yards. As soon as she was in the car she'd be fine.

But David caught up with her on the gravel. 'You really take the fucking biscuit, Sally.' He ran forward a little so he was in front of her. He wanted her to look at him. 'Never known anyone like you for bare-faced stupid cuntness.'

She dodged past him, opening the car and throwing her jacket and bag on to the passenger seat. Then she went round to the back, weaving past him, still not meeting his eye. She opened the boot and threw her kit inside. As she was straightening, he came up behind her and struck her on the back of the head with such force that her face went forward, her cheek hitting the underside of the opened boot lid. As she bounced back, her left elbow slammed the inside of the boot at speed, breaking the motion. She jerked sideways in an undignified scramble to right herself. Before she could catch her breath and twist to face him he was on her back, gripping her by the throat from behind, pinning her face down into the boot.

'You fucking *apologize*. What do you take me for? Eh?' He shook her forcefully. '*Apologize now*.'

She scrabbled at his fingers. Felt the hot, fat pressure of blood squeezed into her brain. Her arms tingled – static crackled in her ears. This was insane. It couldn't be happening.

'I ought to fucking take you out here and now, you bitch. Taking my fucking money and judging me at the same time?' He shook her, his body weighing flat against her back. 'I ought to rip your head off and shit down your neck. I thought Jake was bad.'

She couldn't swallow. There was blood in her mouth from where she'd bitten her tongue – it dribbled out of her lips and down her chin. All the objects in the boot seemed to bulge out at her, as though behind a fish-eye lens. Then she realized what she was looking at. Something smooth and black. She recalled Steve, standing at the wall, bouncing nails into the door frame. The nail gun, a dim red light on the base. Steve had shown her how to use it before he'd put it in here, and he'd said the light only came if it was switched on. Maybe it had been switched on all this time.

'Apologize.'

'No.' Her speech was slurred with the blood that webbed her mouth. She tightened her fingers around the gun. It felt smooth. Curiously warm. 'I won't.'

He kicked the car, making it rock. '*Don't* take the fucking piss. You're worse than Jake for not knowing when you've got shit all over your face. Now apologize.'

Her finger found the trigger. Found the parts that Steve had used to start it. You had to pull back the guard on it, make sure the nail strip was in place, hold the muzzle flush against the surface and depress the trigger. If she could find a place on David's arms, or his legs. Somewhere that would hurt, but not injure him seriously. Just stop him long enough for her to get into the car.

'You know what happens to tarts like you who take the piss?' He gave her another shake. 'Say it,' he hissed in her ear. His breath was sour and hot. 'Say it now. Cunt.'

Sally took a breath and wrenched her body sideways out of his grip. The car suspension creaked, she staggered against the bumper, waving the nail gun at

261

David. He came at her again and she lashed out blindly – at the first and easiest place she could reach. His leg. Before he could react there was a loud *whoomp* and she had landed a nail in his thigh. He crumpled with the pain, wheeling away. Took a few staggering steps away from the car, clutching his leg. She tottered sideways, staring at him, hardly believing she'd done it.

'Fuck. What the fuck did you do that for?' He sank to the ground, scrabbling at his jogging trousers, pulling frantically at the nail. She dropped the nail gun and stood there, like a dummy, mouth open, knowing she'd hit something big because blood was already soaking his jeans. Thick pulses of it ran over his hands. 'You made your point, Sally. You made your point.'

'No,' she said, horrified. 'What have I done?'

'I don't fucking know, do I? Get the fucking thing out.'

She crouched, fumbling for his leg, trying to find where the wound was, but the blood seemed to be everywhere, mushrooming up like a spring. On Wednesday when Steve had nailed himself to the wall she'd been completely calm. Now her body was seized up in panic. She seemed to move in creaky slow motion, pushing herself upright and stumbling to the front of the car to get her jacket. She came back, threw it on to the wound and groped around helplessly, trying to tighten it.

'Call an ambulance.'

To Sally's horror she saw his lips had gone blue.

262

His hands were flailing, trying to grab her wrist. They kept slipping in the blood and losing their grip.

'Get me back to the house.'

'*Keep still*,' she panted. '*Keep still*.'

He lay there for a moment, breathing hard, while she wrapped the jacket around his thigh. But even before she could tie it at the back she saw it was useless – the blood had soaked through the fabric, pushing through the herringbone stitch as if it was squeezing through a grid. And then that awful pulsing fountain of red again.

'*God God God*.' She glanced frantically up at the house. Jake? No – he was long gone. '*What do I do? Tell me what to do now!*'

'*I don't know.*'

She leaped up and grabbed her bag, tipped out the contents and snatched up her mobile. With shaking fingers she began to dial, but before she'd got to the second nine, David let out an odd whine. He half sat up – his mouth open in a grimace as if he wanted to bite her. He froze like that for a moment then fell back, jerking and spasming, as if an electric current was going through him. His legs kicked involuntarily, making him circle like a broken Catherine wheel. Then his back arched, his head twisted painfully, as if he was trying to look over his shoulder at the wheel of the car, and he went limp, lying on his back, one arm trapped under him, the other stretched out to the side.

There was silence. She stood, the phone forgotten in her hand, staring at him. He wasn't breathing. Or moving. A smell of urine and blood rose up off him.

'David?' she whispered. 'David?'

Silence.

Shaking, she fell to her knees in the spreading pool of blood, her heart beating like thunder. His eyes were open, his mouth too, as if he was shouting. It was like seeing a machine stopped in mid-action. She sat back on her heels. Numb. No, she thought. Christ, no. Not this on top of everything else.

The evening sun shone warm on the back of her head, and a sudden gust sent a swirl of blossom dancing past her gently, as though this was just another late-spring evening. Nothing unusual about it – nothing unusual about a small woman in her thirties killing a man, quite unabashedly, out in the open air.

37

It took all of Zoë's reserves, that day of work. It took going into the sort of places she'd hoped for years she'd never have to see again. The club she'd worked at in the nineties was closed now – it had turned into a betting shop – but driving round the streets of Bristol that day, the list Holden had given her taped to the dashboard, the sheer misery of it came back to her like a slap. Nightclub after nightclub after night-club, all across the city. Most of them were just opening in the afternoon, and from some the cleaners were coming out, dragging their heels, knowing their lot in life was to wash floors that had had every kind of bodily fluid spilled on them. The places smelt of bleach, stale perfume and stomach acid. The majority of the girls were East European. They were generally open and pleasant, unobstructive, but none of them had ever seen Lorne Wood, except on the front page of the newspapers. When Zoë mentioned there was a chance Lorne had wandered into topless modelling, maybe into the clubs, one or two of the girls had given her a look as if to say, was she nuts?

Someone like Lorne ending up in a place like this?

By nine that evening, when she'd got to the end of the list, she was starting to think the girls were right, that Holden's agency really was where Lorne's trail had run cold. She was coming to the end of the day – the end of her promise to Lorne. Just one more knock and she'd admit defeat. Go home and watch TV. Go to a movie. Call one of the biker friends she sometimes met up with for a beer and sit in a bar planning her week's bike ride.

Jacqui Sereno's was the last name. She lived in Frome and had cropped up in a conversation with a bouncer at one of the clubs. Zoë drove the old Mondeo out there, both hands on the steering-wheel, her eyes fixed doggedly on the road. The address was a private house – and for a moment she thought she'd got the wrong place. But she checked the list and it was right. Apparently Jacqui operated a webcam service, letting out rooms, computer equipment and bandwidth, from this small, ordinary house, only distinguishable from all the others on the estate by its tattiness. The door of the gas meter hung open at an angle, broken on the hinges, and a dustbin overflowed on the front path. The windows hadn't been cleaned in years. With a deep sigh, Zoë swung her legs out of the car and walked up the path.

The woman who opened the door was in her fifties, small, thin and bitter, with a dark suntan and an old-fashioned beehive she had decorated with plastic flowers. She wore tight black leggings, a T-shirt and red high-heeled mules. She was sucking at a cigarette, as if she needed the nicotine so much she'd like to swallow the thing whole.

'Jacqui?'

'Yeah? What?'

'Police.'

'Oh, yeah?'

'Have you got a few moments?'

'S'pose.'

Jacqui kicked aside a fluffy pink draught-excluder and opened the door. Zoë stepped inside. It was hot – the central heating was on high although it was spring. She followed the woman into the kitchen at the back of the house. It was neater inside than out – there were lace curtains in the windows, with a mug tree, matching tea-towels, and biscuit tins piled in a pyramid on top of the fridge. The only thing out of place was a yellow and black sharps bin on the work-surface.

'Insulin,' Jacqui said. 'I'm a diabetic.'

'Really?'

'Really. Now, make yourself comfortable, pet, and I'll put on the kettle because you'll be here a while.'

'What does that mean?'

'You're going to sit here and threaten me, pet, and I'm going to come back at you over and again, explaining how I'm not running a brothel. How what I'm doing here is not illegal. How you have to define what the girls are doing as lewd or likely to cause offence. You're police but you're out of your depth.' She smiled and plugged the kettle in. Threw a couple of teabags into mugs. 'I mean no personal offence,

267

pet, but since they've got rid of the specialized cops – the street-offences crew – I've been able to run rings around you CID muppets. Shame, I had a lot of friends in that team.'

Zoë didn't want to get into the small print of the Sexual Offences Act. From her own experiences, she knew the earlier legislation – a lot of it was written in stone on her heart – but over the years her knowledge had slipped. A lot of the stuff relating to lap-dancing clubs was governed by local bylaws, and a huge Act had been passed in 2003 that overturned a lot of what she'd learned. The only part of the new Act she could quote for sure was the bit about assault by penetration with an object – and she only knew that from the discussions in the incident room over what Act they might charge Lorne's killer under. She'd be no match for the hard-bitten Jacqui.

'I've been over and over this. The point is that no sexual gratification actually takes place on the premises.' She dug a wrinkled finger at the table. 'I can promise you that. If there is any sexual gratification occurring it ain't here. It's happening in New York or Peru or bleeding Dunstable, for all I know.'

Zoë raised her chin and looked at the ceiling, imagining a warren of rooms up there. 'How does it work?'

'They're "chat hostesses". That's all. Sitting in front of a web cam and "chatting" – or whatever they have a mind to do, if you get my drift. Catering to the more discerning gentleman who's had his fill of the Asian girls. A little pricey, but you get what you pay for. Two dollars a minute. Not that I see a penny of it. Because this ain't a brothel. My only comeback is the rental of the equipment and bandwidth with it. What they do ain't my affair.' She put a mug on the table. 'There you are, pet. Drink up. You look like you need it.'

'Are they up there now?'

'Just one. Our big clients are South America and Japan.' She looked at her watch. 'South America's in the office now, and doesn't like to get caught with his trousers round his ankles by the boss, and Japan? Well, he's only just waking up. We won't catch him at his randiest for another twelve hours. So?' She gave Zoë a friendly smile. There was a smudge of red lipstick on her front teeth. 'What section of the law do you want to argue about? You see, me,' she held the hand with the smouldering cigarette against her chest, 'I love a good debate. I should have been on *Question Time*, me. One day they'll ask me.'

'They will. They surely will.' Zoë cleared her throat and reached, for the hundredth time, into her satchel. Pulled out the photos of Lorne. 'Jacqui. Look, I'd love to have a debate. But I'm not here about the setup you're operating.'

'Operating? Be careful the vocabulary you use.'

'The equipment you're renting.' She rubbed her forehead. She was hot and sticky in this shirt, and Jacqui's tea tasted awful. She so, so wanted to go home – forget all this. 'What I really want to know is if this girl ever passed across your radar screen.'

She spread the photos out. Jacqui took a long puff

of the cigarette, pushed the smoke out of her mouth in a thin, straight stream, and squinted down at the photos, taking in every detail. She'd done this before, Zoë thought. Probably, if she'd been in the business a while, she'd done it a lot of times – speaking to the police about the victims of rape, abuse, domestic violence. Prostitution, lap-dancing, pole-dancing. Lying naked on a bed in front of a tiny video camera and a mic. All these things lived in a hinterland just on the other side of the law – sharing boundaries with the dangerous and the violent.

'No.' She sat back, closed her eyes and took another puff. 'Never seen her.'

'OK.' Zoë put the wallet into the satchel and began to get up. She'd done what she could.

'But . . .' Jacqui said. 'But wait . . .'

'But?'

'But I know who would like her. For his videos. He's cornered the young totty market, hasn't he? He likes them to look like teenagers.'

'Who's that?'

'I don't know his name. Not his real name. London Tarn they always called him. London Tarn.'

Zoë sank slowly back into her seat. 'London Tarn?'

'It's London Town,' Jacqui explained. 'Just "Tarn" because of the accent. You know – like in *EastEnders*, but he—' She broke off, squinting at Zoë suspiciously. 'What? You look like someone just sucked the blood out of you. You've heard of him, have you?'

'No.' She clutched the satchel to her chest. Drew her knees together. 'No. I've never heard of him.'

'You sure?'

'I'm sure.'

'It's just that for a minute there, when I said his name, you looked like—'

'I'm *sure*.' She started tapping her foot, suddenly irritable. She was awake now. Wide awake. 'Tell me about him. London Tarn. He makes videos?'

Jacqui took another slug of smoke and eyed her. 'Yeah – he's been around years now, must be pushing sixty. When he started, he used to be just soft porn. Hi Eight. He used to run a club too – out in Bristol, one of your old-fashioned strip clubs – and when that closed down he put everything into the videos. He didn't have any proper production equipment – the only time I went to his place it was just him in a flat in Fishponds, with one VHS here,' she put a hand out, 'and another here, and a bit of wire between them, and that's how he'd copy them. Then he'd sell them in the markets. You know, the stalls at St Nicholas.'

'And after that?'

'After that he was a gonzo.'

'A *gonzo*?'

'Yeah. He'd make vids of himself. This was in the nineties, mind.' She tapped her ash into the ashtray and crossed her legs – getting comfortable for this reminiscence. 'I never knew him then, that was after my time, but I seen the movies. He'd be there in his glory with some poor girl he'd talked into doing

271

whatever. Never bothered with lighting or anything, which I always thought wasn't professional. A bit slack, if you want my way of looking at it. But they do say, don't they, some people like it – the, you know, warts-'n'-all look. Either way up, it was a seller. And on the back of that he picked up pretty swift on the Internet deal. Give him his due, he was in there. And after that came the bukkake stuff.'

'Bukkake?'

Jacqui laughed. 'Doncha know what that is?'

'No.'

'It's all about humiliating the woman. They say it was an old Japanese custom – what they'd to do to the womenfolk if they got caught putting it around. The men of the village would take them out and bury them up to their necks. Except instead of stoning . . .' She broke off. Gave a nasty smile. 'Nah, you're the detective. You go and find out. But, anyway, it's what he built his empire on. Bukkake, the nastier the better. I've seen some of it – looked like some sort of snuff movie, really dirty. Gritty. You'd think looking at it the girl was going to be butchered. Still, it sold by the shedload – just stacks of the stuff. Makes you wonder about human nature, don't it?'

'OK,' Zoë said, very slowly, 'what's he doing now? Where is he?'

'Oh, he's mega. Mega-mega.' She waved a hand in the air as if they were talking about a different universe. 'Private jet, probably, servants. The works. He's up there, now, sweetie, and there's no taking him down.'

272

'Which country?'

'Here. In the UK.'

In the UK. Zoë cleared her throat. She'd just changed her mind about having a week off. 'You mean, in this area?'

'I think so, yes. And, believe me, if he set his eyes on a girl like that one on your photos he'd get dollar signs lighting up in his eyes. Why? What's happened to her? Is she hurt?'

'You don't know his real name? Do you? London Tarn?'

Jacqui gave a low, guttural laugh. 'No. If I knew his real name I'd be after him. For that tenner he borrowed off me in the nineties.' She tapped another column of ash off her cigarette. 'I mean, fifteen years. The interest he owes me, I could fly round the world. Go and say hi to my customers in South America, eh?'

273

38

The sun had already left the north-facing slopes outside Bath. The garden at Peppercorn Cottage would
be in darkness. But the fields up at Lightpil House
were slightly angled towards the sun and got more
daytime. Another two or three minutes. The sun
melted down over the hill, spread itself out, and then
it was gone, leaving just a few flecks of grey cloud in
the amber sky.

Sally couldn't move David Goldrab's body so she'd
reversed her car to block the entrance to the parking
area so it couldn't be seen. Not that anyone ever came
up here. Then she found a cardigan in the Ka, pulled it
on and sat on the bonnet with her knees drawn up. She
wondered what on earth to do. The muscles in David's
face had tightened, drawing his eyes wider and wider
open, as if he was amazed by a rock that lay a few feet
from his face. It was cold. She could hear everything
around her, as if her ears were on stalks –
the hedgerows, the fields, the faint shift of breeze in the
grass, the dry rustle of a bird moving in the branches.

After a while she saw that the blood on her hands

had dried. She did her best to flake some of it off with her nails. She cleaned off the phone, too, on the sleeves of her cardigan and dialled Isabelle's number. 'It's me.'

'Hey.' A pause. 'Sally? You OK?'

'Yes. I mean – I'm . . .' She used her fingers to press her lips together for a moment. 'I'm fine.'

'You don't sound it.'

'I'm a bit . . . Issie, did you pick up Millie from school like you said?'

'Yes – she's fine.'

'They haven't gone out?'

'No – they're all watching TV. Why?'

'Can she stay with you tonight?'

'Of course. Sally? Is there anything I can do? You sound terrible.'

'No. I'm fine. I'll come and get her in the morning. And . . . Issie?'

'Yes?'

'Thank you, Issie. For everything you are. And everything you do.'

'Sally? Are you sure everything's all right?'

'I'm fine. I promise. Absolutely fine.'

She hung up. Her hands were trembling so much she had to put the phone down on the car bonnet to jab the next number into it. Steve answered after three rings and she snatched it up.

'It's me.'

'Yes. I know.'

'Something's happened. We need to speak. You need to come to me.'

'OK . . .' he said cautiously. 'Where are you?'

'No. I can't – I mean, I suppose I shouldn't say on the phone.'

There was a pause while Steve seemed to think about this. Then he said, 'OK. Don't. Think carefully about every word. Are you near your place?'

'Further.'

'Further south? Further north?'

'North. But not far.'

'Then you're . . .' He trailed off. 'Oh,' he said dully. 'Do you mean you're at the house of someone we've spoken about recently?'

'Yes. There's a car-parking place. Take a right fork as you come to the house. Don't go past the front, there are cameras. Steve, can you – can you hurry?'

She hung up. A sound – very distant in the evening air – of a car revving on the road to the racecourse. Then headlights coming through the tree-line. She lowered her head, cowering, even though it would come nowhere near Lightpil. It changed gear and continued up the hill. But she pressed her forehead against the cold windscreen, trying to disappear, trying to bring something peaceful into her head. Millie's face, maybe.

It wouldn't come. All that came was a bright zigzagging light, like the after-image of a firework.

About ten minutes later another car on the main road indicated left and came off on the small turning. Slowly it climbed the road that snaked around the bottom of Hanging Hill. She saw the sweep of head-lights and slithered off the bonnet, going to crouch behind the shrubbery at the edge of the parking area as the lights came nearer. The lights turned into the track, rattled over the cattle grid, then came to a halt. It was Steve.

He got out, and, silhouetted, tall against the darkening sky, pulled on a fleece, glancing around himself. She pushed herself out of the hedge and stood there, the cardigan wrapped tight around her to cover the blood on her clothes.

'What?' he whispered. 'What's happening?'

She didn't answer. Head down, hands tucked into her armpits, she walked around her car and led the way into the parking area. He followed without a word, his feet crunching in the gravel. At the back of the Ford Sally stopped. Steve stood next to her and they were silent for a long time, looking at David Goldrab's body. His running T-shirt was rucked up, showing his thick, tanned torso, his hair matted with blood. His face seemed calcified, his mouth widening around his gums. She realized she could still smell him. Just a little of his essence, streaking the grey air.

Steve crouched next to the body. Putting his bandaged hand tentatively in the gravel he leaned closer, peering at David's face. Then he rocked back on his heels and wiped his hands. 'Jesus. Jesus.'

'There was an argument. He followed me out to the car and hit me on the back of the head. He was forcing me into the boot. Your nail gun was in there and I had to—' She drew her hands down her face, felt the soreness where he'd pushed her into the boot

277

lid. 'My God, my God, Steve. It was over so quickly. It wasn't what I meant to happen.'

Steve let all his breath out at once. He came and hugged her. She could feel his pulse jack-hammering against her own. The awful crackle of David's dried blood on her clothing.

'It just happened,' she said. 'Just like that.'

'It's OK.'

'No one's going to believe it was an accident.'

She cried then – long, drawn-out sobs. Steve said nothing, just kept his hands on her back, rubbing her soothingly. When at last she'd stopped, he let her go and walked back to the parking area's entrance. He stood with his hands in his pockets, looking out at the landscape. She knew what he was seeing – the whole of the valley spread out. The beginnings of the city on the horizon. Her childhood land. The places she'd dreamed in, the places she'd cried and had hopes and fears in. All the valleys and the brooks and the glades – all the places she'd been and never spied this future crouching in wait for her behind the trees.

After a long time he turned round and came back down the slope. 'What have you got in the car? Have you got your cleaning kit?'

'Yes.'

'Rubber gloves?'

'Yes.' She opened the boot, rummaged in her cleaning kit and held out a pair still in their pack. Steve took them. His face was white and controlled. He ripped the pack with his teeth and began pulling on the gloves.

'*Steve?* What're you doing?'

'I've got a meeting at nine in the morning. That means we've got thirteen hours.'

39

Steve's plan, he said, was the best possible solution. But if they were going to do it, it would have to be done quickly, and to start with they needed to find some plastic. Sally knew David kept a lot of his equipment in the garage, but it was at the side of the house where the camera was, and she worried they'd be caught on video. She wanted to check on the monitor inside what could be seen so she and Steve went back up to the house. Even in the daytime David was in the habit of leaving lights and TVs on, and now that it was getting dark the place seemed to be lit up like a bonfire. The halogens in the glass atrium blazed, casting the shadows of huge potted plants out into the garden. The utility-room door stood open, the TV blasting out from inside.

Steve waited on the deck, keeping an eye on the road, while she crept in alone. It seemed so hot inside, stifling, as if the heating had been turned up high. The air was as still as the grave, and even in the familiar rooms and corridors, she found herself jumping at every shadow, as if David's's ghost was waiting to leap out at her. She wondered if it would be like this for ever, if she'd be driven mad by the guilt. You heard about that happening, people haunted all their lives by the spirit of the person who'd died.

When she checked the monitor in the office she saw that a huge part of the driveway wasn't covered by the camera – plenty of room to get into the garage without being seen – so she collected a bunch of keys from the hooks in the kitchen where David kept them and went with Steve around the side of the house.

'Holy shit,' he muttered, when she pressed the fob and the door opened to reveal a huge, shiny car. 'It's only a Bentley.'

'Is that good?'

He gave a small wry smile. 'Come on.'

Behind a row of motor-oil cans they found a roll of plastic and some old ballast bags, some tape and a Stanley knife. They carried it all back to the parking area and unrolled the plastic on the ground next to the body.

'Take his feet.'

'Oh, God.' She stood a yard away, staring at the body. Her teeth were chattering. 'I don't know if I can.'

'Sally,' Steve said steadily. 'You can do it. I know you can – I saw you the other day with that hacksaw. You can do this.'

'We're really going to do it, then? Really not report it – and just get the money?'

He raised an eyebrow. 'You tell me. You could have called the police but you didn't.'

281

She closed her eyes and put her fingers on her temples. He was right, of course. She could have called the police at any time. Had she decided already – subconsciously – that this was what they'd do?

'But . . .' She opened her eyes. 'Is it the right thing? Steve? Is it?'

'How do you quantify right? Is it the legal thing? No. But is it the best thing? You'll get thirty K for offing this old pervert. Is that the best thing? You tell me.'

Sally didn't answer. She kept her attention on David's face. Pale and rigid now. His eyes had changed. They no longer had a shine to them, the way normal eyes did. They were cloudier and flatter, she thought, as if they were sinking backwards into his skull. Earlier she'd seen a fly try to land on the right one. An image popped into her mind. A bruise. It was on the thigh of the girl that had been on the floor of the livestock pen. Just a single bruise, but it came at her like a punch.

'OK.' She came forward, rolling up her sleeves. 'What do I do?'

David was heavy, but he wasn't going stiff the way she'd imagined he would. Steve said not enough time had passed for that to happen. The body flopped around as they tried to move it, his arms lolling all over the place, but eventually they got him on to the plastic sheet. They folded it around him like a cocoon and lifted him into the boot of Steve's Audi. Then Steve searched in the pool-maintenance shed until he found two buckets and, for the next twenty minutes, the two of them toiled up and down the path from the outdoor tap to where the body had lain, sluicing the ground with bucket after bucket of water until the blood, hair and urine had been rinsed into the ground.

Steve got into the Audi and put the key in the ignition. 'Is there a back way to yours? A way we don't have to use main roads?'

'Yes. Follow me.'

She got into the Ka and reversed back along the track to the lane. The Audi headlights followed her. The countryside was pitch black now, a low cloud covering the moon. She took the switchbacks and narrow lanes that crisscrossed the land. They got back to Peppercorn Cottage without seeing another car. The porch light was on – it looked so welcoming that she had to remind herself there was nothing warm on the stove, no candles in the window or fires in the grates. That she and Steve weren't going to spend the evening eating a meal or watching TV or chatting over a glass of wine. She stopped the car in the driveway, got out and pushed wide the doors of the huge garage for Steve to drive the Audi through. He cut the engine and got out, pulling off his gloves.

'I never noticed this before.'

'Because I never use it.' She switched on the light – just a bare bulb in the rafters that did nothing except illuminate the spiders' webs and fossilized swifts' nests. There were a few rusty tools that the previous owner had left. Steve walked along the racks, checking them all. He stopped at a chainsaw, took it off its hook and examined it.

'Steve?'

He looked round at her. 'Get us a drink.'

'What would you like?'

'Something clean. Whisky. Not brandy.'

Inside the cottage smelt of candlewax and the blue hyacinths Millie had potted. They sat on one of the window-sills, drooping. Sally stood for a moment, her head resting against the cool plaster wall, looking at the flowers. After a while she took off her shoes and rested them on a carrier bag in the corridor, then rolled up her coat and pushed it into a bin liner. She walked in her socks to her bedroom with the bag and stripped to her underwear, adding all her blood-soaked clothes to the bin liner. Then she found a T-shirt and a pair of ski pants she'd bought for one of Julian's business trips to Austria, pulled them on, shoved her feet into trainers, and went back down the corridor, looping her hair into a ponytail. She got towels from the airing cupboard and a pile of tea-towels from the cupboard under the sink. The whisky was at the back of the cupboard, behind all of Millie's school books. Sally hadn't touched it since they'd arrived, she only really kept it for visitors. She rested the bottle on the towels, added two glasses to the pile, a plastic bottle of sparkling water, and carried it outside.

The moon had broken through the clouds and as she crossed the lawn the awful beauty of the garden hit her. It had always reflected warmth and health back to her, even in the depth of winter, but now it seemed to be the silvery reflection of something old and sickly. She stopped for a moment and turned her face to the west, thinking she might catch something watching her. The fields on the other side of the hedge, which always seemed friendly, tonight were full of shadows she didn't recognize.

Steve was standing in the garage with the boot open. In the electric light his face was yellow – hollow under the eyes. She put down the towels and poured two glasses of whisky – not too much – and handed one to him. They stood facing each other, held up their drinks – as if they were toasting something good – and drained the tumblers. She grimaced at the taste of it and took a hurried swig of the water.

'We've got to put him outside. On the grass.'

Sally lowered the water bottle. 'Why?'

'Just help me. Get the plastic.'

They put the bottle and the empty tumblers on the window-sill and pulled on their rubber gloves. Together they went to the boot, got hold of each end of the plastic cocoon and pulled. David's body came rolling forward with one hand up, almost as if he knew he was toppling on to the ground. Steve caught his weight, wincing at the pressure on his wounded hand, then together they lowered the body. Through the plastic David's face was visible, as though he was pressing it against a window.

'Jesus.' Steve wiped his forehead with the back of his hand. He looked sick. 'Jesus.'

Sally stared at him. He couldn't give in. Not now,

after what they'd already done. There was no going back.

'*Steve?*'

'Yeah.' He wiped his forehead again. Gave himself a shake. 'OK,' he said, suddenly sharp. 'Roll up your end.'

'Right. Yes. Of course.'

They knotted the ends of the plastic and between them shuffled the body out of the garage on to the driveway. They walked sideways, down the two stone steps that led to the lawn, struggling with the weight.

'Here,' Steve said, and they dropped the bundle in the middle of the grass.

He straightened and looked around him. There were no lights as far as the eye could see, only the first stars pricking at the sky. He felt in his pocket and brought out his phone, flicked it on with his thumb. Holding it in one hand, he walked around the body, firing off photos, making sure he got the face from every angle.

'What're you doing?'

He gave a grim smile. 'I haven't a clue. I'm just pretending I'm in the movies. Pretending I'm de Niro. Or Scorsese. Doing what one of their hitmen would do.'

'Oh,' She rubbed her arms. '*God.*'

He crouched again, and gingerly inspected David's right hand.

'What is it?'

'His signet ring. With four diamonds and an emerald. It identifies him.' He took several photos of the ring then pulled it off and slipped it into his pocket. Then he pocketed the camera and shuffled sideways. He hooked his index finger behind David's front teeth and, with his other hand, cautiously prised the lower jaw open. He pulled the face to one side. The corpse gave a long, soft sigh.

Sally shrank back against the car. David's head fell sideways, slack on the ground, his eyes staring.

'It's OK,' Steve murmured. 'Really – it's OK. It's just air coming out of his lungs.'

Sally sank to a crouch, trembling. Steve licked his lips and went back to exploring inside David's mouth. He tilted his chin down and squinted inside, grunted approvingly.

'That'll do.'

He put his elbow on the grass and lay almost full length next to David's body, facing him as if they were going to have a long and involved conversation. With his free hand he fumbled out the phone again and spent almost five minutes photographing the face and teeth. When he had finished he got to his feet and looked at Sally.

'What?' she hissed. 'What now? What happens now?'

'I told you – I haven't done this before.'

He went back into the garage and pulled more things from the shelves. She saw him in the weak light pouring petrol from a plastic container into a power tool. The chainsaw. He brought it out and stood in front of the corpse.

'No,' she whispered. 'No. We can't.'

'We haven't got a choice. Not any more.'

She closed her eyes and took a long deep breath. Something was trying to thump its way out through her chest. She breathed hard, counting to twenty, until the static in her head eased and the thing in her chest stopped moving.

She opened her eyes and found Steve watching her expectantly.

'OK,' she murmured. 'OK. Where do we start?'

'His face,' he said tightly. 'Because that's the worst part. We start with his face.'

40

The whisky wore off quickly. They kept themselves together by setting a timer to fifteen minutes. They'd force themselves to work for those minutes, but the moment the timer went off they'd rip off their gloves, drop them on the plastic next to the remains of David Goldrab, and go back into the garage, where they'd stand with their backs to the mess in the garden, drinking another whisky, washing it down with water. They didn't speak, just drank in silence, holding each other's eyes as if they needed to look at a living human being. To see flesh that had blood and heat and life moving through it.

'We can't go on drinking,' Steve said. 'We've got to drive.'

Sally let her eyes stray outside to the plastic mat – slick purple lumps shining in the moonlight. Steve kept saying he had good reason to know what the police were like – that without a body and a motive they'd have nowhere to start. He said that human remains were easier to hide than anyone believed – that most criminals just lacked the time, resources and basic balls to hide their victims properly. That it was easy as long as you had the stomach to make the remains unrecognizable as human. Then you could hide them under the noses of the law and they'd walk straight past them. Sally thought he was only talking as if he knew what he was doing to reassure her, but she said nothing. 'It's easier from now,' he said. 'The worst bit's over. We can stop the whisky. And we should try to eat something.'

She shook her head. 'I'm never going to eat again.'

'Me neither. I'm just saying we should.'

They went back outside and began dividing the pieces into eight piles. Steve had a pair of pliers, which he used to remove some teeth from David's broken bottom jaw. There was no vice in the garage so he had to hold the jaw between his knees to get a purchase on it. Sally took photos using his camera. She heard the noise of gristle tearing as the teeth came from their sockets, and knew she'd never forget it. To the electric drill he fitted an attachment with a helical blade, meant for mixing paint, then together they loaded joints of bone and flesh into a bucket. They used more plastic sheet taped down around the drill to stop the contents spraying out and Steve switched it on, ramming it into the bucket over and over again, pulverizing the pieces.

By one in the morning he was covered with sweat and ten Lidl carrier bags sat on the lawn, each bulging with an unrecognizable red paste. Sally said they should say a prayer or something. Or make some sort of gesture to mark the death.

'You think anyone's up there to hear a prayer like that?'

'I don't know.' She stood on the driveway, transfixed by the bags. 'Maybe it doesn't matter if we believe – maybe it only matters if *he* did. David.'

Steve shook his head. 'Forgive me, Sally, but we just don't have time for a morality lesson. If there is a God up there, then don't waste His time praying for David Goldrab's soul. Just pray – as hard as you can.'

'For what?'

'For us.'

41

The clouds cleared and the moon sat, low and dazzling, over the Somerset countryside. Sally arranged her jam-making pans outside on the lawn, filled them with limescale remover and cleaned everything they'd used – the drill, the chainsaw, the plastic sheet, the plastic bags. Then she cut all the plastic into small squares the size of postage stamps and placed them in a bin liner. Meanwhile Steve piled up the clothing they'd worn – with the shoes, the towels – heaped it in a flowerbed on the west side of the house, poured paraffin on it and set it alight. When the fire had died and they'd dug the ashes into the soil, they spread more plastic in the boot of the Audi and loaded in the carrier bags. An eleventh, containing hair and larger pieces of bone that hadn't been pulverized by the mixer, went into the well below the back passenger seats. The remains filled the car with a foul mixture of offal and faeces. Sally and Steve kept their coats on, the heater up high, the windows wide open.

Steve was from the countryside outside Taunton.

He was a rambler – someone who had every Ordnance Survey map of the British Isles ordered neatly according to their code number on his book-shelves. He knew the border lands of Somerset, Gloucestershire and Wiltshire better than Sally did and he had a route already planned. It took in rivers and canals, forests where badgers foraged at night. It took in the Severn estuary – Steve waded out into the mud in the giant grey shadow of the decommissioned nuclear power plant at Berkeley. They stopped on the outskirts of villages and squeezed dollops through sewage grates in the road; they tramped across fields in the Mendips to press the contents of the last bag through the meshes that protected disused Roman mineshafts. Steve stood in the silent darkness, his ear close to the mesh, straining to hear the soft wet patter of the tissue hitting the sides of the shaft.

From time to time Sally turned and looked at his face as he drove, the glow of the dashboard lighting it. She watched his eyes on the road and a strange thought came to her – that for the first time in her life she'd done something as a partnership. An ugly, perverse, unthinkable thing, but it had been done by equals. Crazy though it all was, she decided it was the closest she'd ever been to anyone in her life.

He turned and caught her looking at him. He held her eyes, just for a second, and in that moment some-thing passed between them. Something that made her stomach stir, as if an odd strength was gathering. Like the beginnings of excitement on a holiday, the desire to yell and dance. She opened the window and threw a handful of the shredded plastic into the slipstream, watched it in the wing-mirror, like confetti, lit red by the rear lights. It was so beautiful it could have belonged to a celebration. Funny, she thought, how everything in life was so deceptive.

Part Two

Part Two

1

'I've got something for you.'

'About time too.'

'These things don't just happen overnight. It's not the way it works.'

The guy at the other end of the phone – a clerk at SOCA, the Serious Organized Crime Agency – was getting a little weary of Zoë and the way she kept pressing him for an answer. It was Monday and in the last four days she'd called at least twice a day to find out if he had any results for the search she'd requested on a pornographer from London, nicknamed London Tarn.

'Maybe not overnight, but within the next year isn't too much to expect, is it?'

'There's no need to be sarcastic.'

'Well, if you weren't so fucking slow I wouldn't have to be,' she wanted to say, but she pressed her lips together, tapped her finger on the desk and kept her control. London Tarn had been the manager of the Bristol club she'd worked in – the only person from that time who'd known her real name. She'd never thought she'd hear of him again – she thought

297

he had disappeared abroad, but no. Apparently all these years she'd been living on borrowed time, because he'd been in the UK all the while, somewhere in this area, and if he ever had any cause to be called into the nick and heard the name Zoë Benedict attached to the title 'Detective Inspector' – she'd be screwed, so screwed. That was the thing about the past. You never really appreciated its power until it was too late.

She swung the chair back and forth impatiently. At least her energy was back. Finding him was helping her not to think about Ben. 'Fair enough,' she said. 'Fair dos. Thank you for what you've done. How's it going to come to me?'

'Email. It should be on your system now. Unless your webmaster is being a jobsworth.'

She tapped in her password and scanned her inbox. It was there – an email loaded with attachments. 'Yup – I've got it.'

'There are some pieces missing. If they've got form you'll get a mug shot – but some haven't been convicted and we're building intelligence packages on them, so on those the photos might be missing. Do you want me to take you through what's there?'

'Sure – I mean . . .' She put her tongue between her teeth and began scrolling down the list of attachments. SOCA gathered information from an array of agencies: the old Vice and Street Offences squads, Serious Crime groups across the country, Customs and Excise, Trading Standards, even the Department of Work and Pensions. Sometimes the files they sent looked like ancient computer MS DOS printouts. She found one that looked promising and clicked on it. A list of names reeled down the screen. 'It looks like a hell of a lot. Are there really that many pornographers in this country?'

'I've narrowed it down for you best I could. I couldn't find the name London Town anywhere.'

'No – that was probably just a nickname he picked up out here.'

'But you wanted me to look at Londoners, right?'

'Londoners who came out to the west in the nineties.'

'Well, as you can see there were lots. And a few I thought you might want to look at closely. There's a Franc Kaminski. Made a fortune from an online porn site called Myrichdaddy. Serious Crime have been after him for years – the website's got a portal to a newsgroup that's basically a kiddie-porn site.'

'Franc Kaminski? Polish?'

'Maybe his parents. But he's a Londoner.'

'Kaminski?' She tapped her teeth thoughtfully with her pen. 'I don't know. When did he come out west?'

'1998.'

'Nope. It's not him. This guy arrived in 1993. And child porn sounds wrong.'

'OK. Scratch him, and the next two – they're definitely child porn. Look at Mike Beckton. He was there some time in the early eighties, hard to be specific. He's in the slammer at the moment. There's a photo.'

'Yup – I can see that. It's not him. And this guy under him?' She was looking at a picture of a Middle

Eastern guy. 'Halim something or other, can't pronounce it, that's not him. The one I'm looking for is pretty much completely white bread. If he's anything at all he might be Jewish.'

'Right – that rules out some of these. Tell you what, keep scrolling down. There are four at the bottom who both came to Bristol from London. No photos but they're all listed as IC ones – white.'

'Yup. I see them. Jo Gordon-Catling? Doesn't sound right – but I'd like to see him.'

'I've just had his photo come through this morning. I'll scan it when we get off the line and send it over to you. The last three photos are coming directly from your force targeting team. The case officer's got your email address. He'll send you photos later.'

She put her finger on the screen, looking at the last names. 'Mark Rainer?'

'Yup. They still haven't nicked him but he's wanted for importing porn that breached the Sexual Offences Act – S and M stuff and, of course, the law's all changed on that. Richard Rose – he's small-time, hasn't been active for years; we think he's gone straight, but might be worth a look. The last one's the biggest hitter of the lot – got overseas connections. Military. In the late nineties he was using Special Boat Squadron guys to smuggle nasty stuff into the country – paying them a grand a pop to bring a launch in through Poole, used a mooring in one of those millionaire pads on Sandbanks. The Met's Organized Crime Group has got him firmly on their radar, not to mention their e-crime unit – even the

Specialist Investigations Directorate at the Inland Revenue have given him a good hiding. But this boy's as slippery as a butcher's you-know-what. They just can't make it stick.'

'OK. What's his name?'

'Goldrab.'

'Goldrab?'

'That's right. David Adam Goldrab.'

2

It was hot in the office. The printer was still whirring, churning out hot sheets of paper. Zoë stared at the names, willing them to mean something – to convey something to her. Marc Rainer, Jo Gordon-Catling, Richard Rose, David Goldrab. 'Come on, London Tarn,' she murmured. 'Which one is you?'

None of the documentation helped. She needed a face to put to the details. But the emails from SOCA and the targeting team could take ages. She pushed back her chair, wandered out into the kitchen at the end of the corridor and put on the kettle. Waiting for it to boil, she stood at the window, idly looking down into the car park. There were marked vehicles moving around down there, in and out, pedestrians coming and going. Finding London Tarn, after all these years? She wasn't sure how she felt about that at all.

She was about to turn away when she noticed an officer and a teenage boy in school uniform coming across the forecourt. She put her forehead against the window. She recognized the thatch of blond hair. It was Peter Cyrus – Millie's friend. Frowning, she switched off the kettle and went out into the corridor. DC Goods was coming out of the incident room, scanning a memo.

'Goodsy?'

He looked up. 'Hmm?'

'One of Ralph Hernandez's friends is in the building. Peter Cyrus. Any idea what that's about?'

He cocked his head on one side. 'Don't you know?'

'Don't I know what?'

'About the CCTV.'

'What CCTV?'

'I thought everyone knew.'

'Well, probably *everyone* does. Just not *me*. You know.' She tapped her forehead. 'I've got that sign here that says, "Important information to share? Please ensure I'm the last person you tell."'

He shrugged apologetically. 'Ben's had a team trawling the pubs. The ones Hernandez was supposed to be drinking in with his mates?'

'Ye-es,' she said cautiously.

'Well, he wasn't there. None of them were. We've interviewed regulars and the bar staff, who've checked till receipts and CCTV. They've all been lying.'

303

3

Zoë couldn't see Peter Cyrus anywhere, but she found Nial Sweetman sitting in a surly huddle in the reception area. She saw him through the glass door as she came down the corridor and knew from his face he'd rather be anywhere than there. He glanced up at the sound of the door opening, and when he saw it was her, a faint ray of hope crossed his face. She shook her head. 'No. It's not me who's interviewing you. I'm sorry.'

He drooped back, elbows on knees, staring at the floor. Zoë glanced at the desk sergeant, who was speaking on the phone, standing staring out of the window, not paying attention. She stood near Nial, her arms crossed, monitoring the sergeant out of the corner of her eye, speaking in a low whisper out of the side of her mouth.

'I shouldn't talk to you. I could get into serious trouble. They could even charge you with obstruction.'

'I know,' he muttered. 'That's what my dad said might happen.'

'Why the hell did you do it?'

Nial shrugged. 'Because he's a mate? Because I thought it was a good idea. That's what I'm going to tell them. That it was my idea.'

'Well, *was* it?'

'Of course,' he said evasively. 'And that's what Ralph's going to say. And Peter.'

'You know the shit load of trouble you're going to be in.'

'He's a mate,' he said fiercely, 'and mates look out for each other.'

Zoë shook her head. When would people learn? The desk sergeant was yawning now, scratching his chest as he talked. 'So, Nial,' she murmured, 'when they ask you where you really were that night, what're you going to say?'

'That I was at home.'

'With Ralph?'

'Well . . .' Nial shifted uneasily.

'Well?'

He rubbed his nose and glanced at the open door, the sunlight coming down in the street outside. He gave it a hungry look, as if he was going to sign a pact with the devil and knew that might be the last daylight he ever saw.

'Nial?'

'No,' he admitted. 'Not with him. I don't know where he was. But I can promise you this.' He stared up at her. There were red patches on his face. 'I can promise you he wasn't out hurting Lorne Wood.'

4

Zoë went back to her office, clenching her teeth so hard they hurt. She couldn't get Ralph's face out of her head, how he'd been so scared of his parents. She couldn't get Nial out of her head either – *He wasn't out hurting Lorne Wood*. Nial *knew* what she only had a hunch about: that Ralph wasn't a killer.

The door to the incident room stood open, the whiteboard covered with scribbles, Ralph's photo pinned up. She passed it, went into her office and stared at the reams of paperwork among which there *might* be a person who *might* know something that *might* prove them all wrong. Something that would let Ralph off the hook. She sank into her chair, a sense of defeat creeping over her. A lot of 'mights' and no 'concretes'. Ralph didn't stand a chance. Didn't stand a sodding chance.

Somewhere outside the office a door slammed. She didn't get up but used her toe to pull her door open a fraction. Ben was coming along the corridor. He was holding a folder under his arm, his glasses in the other hand, a strained look on his face, as if this case was really doing his head in. Behind him came Nial, slouching along uneasily, trying to act nonchalant and doing such a bad job of it that he only managed to look furtive. The two weren't exchanging a word.

Zoë was about to retreat when Ben's office door opened and Debbie came out. She was wearing a creamy lace dress – feminine and innocent – high green sandals on her tanned feet. There was a bit of a sway in her step, as if she was enjoying life. Her face changed when she saw Nial. She stopped in front of the door, crossed her arms and frowned at him as he passed. Like a headmistress who'd just come face to face with the biggest troublemaker in the whole school. He raised his eyes sullenly to her and, very, very slowly, Debbie shook her head. If the gesture had had words they'd have been: *you silly, silly little boy*. Then, as if there was nothing more disappointing to her in the whole world, she turned on a heel and walked away in the opposite direction.

Before anyone could see her, Zoë kicked the door closed and turned her chair back to the computer. Her face was hot. She rolled up her right sleeve and studied the skin. Covered with marks and scabs. She found a piece of flesh that wasn't marked. It would be easy to dig her nails into it – so easy. She closed her eyes. You don't have to, Zoë. Don't.

The computer beeped to let her know an email had arrived. She opened her eyes, blinked at the screen. It was from a DS in the targeting team. There was a paperclip next to the subject line. She rolled down her sleeve and clicked on the attachment. It was a PDF file with three main spreads: on Marc Rainer, Richard Rose and David Goldrab.

She clicked on Marc Rainer first. He was pictured leaving a café on a nondescript street with two black guys who wore tight trousers and Afro hair, as if they wanted to be in a blaxploitation movie. Rainer was thick-set and wearing a mustard turtle-neck under a brown leather jacket. He wasn't London Tarn. The second was a custody photograph. Richard Rose. An English name, but his heritage was from somewhere in the Levant: Turkey maybe, or Cyprus. She clicked on the third. And sat, hardly breathing, looking into his eyes.

London Tarn. Unmistakably, London Tarn. Years and years had passed but she'd have known him anywhere.

His name was David Goldrab.

5

'Have you ever heard of David Goldrab?' The uniformed inspector looked up from the overtime sheets he was signing off. Zoë stood in the doorway, her arms folded. 'David Goldrab. Apparently he's got connections on our patch.'

The inspector put down his pen and looked at her levelly. 'Ye-es,' he said cautiously. 'Why?'

'Oh, nothing. Just his name came up. I'm having a little look at him.' She broke off. The inspector's face was twisting unhappily. 'What is it?' she asked. 'What've I said?'

'Nothing. It's just that . . .' He glanced at the telephone. 'David Goldrab?'

'That's the one.'

'I put down the phone to his brother about an hour ago. Nice piece of work – calling from London. Called me a "fucking woolly" and a few other things. Made a few allegations about my feelings towards sheep.'

'His brother?'

'Yup. Goldrab's not been heard from for nearly

four days. He lives up near Hanging Hill, and usually he speaks to his mother in London every day, morning and night. But he hasn't answered his calls and now she's having epis right, left and centre, the brother's going ballistic and apparently we're supposed to get every officer in Avon and Somerset Constabulary out hunting for this jerk. So he's got form, has he? I didn't know.'

'He hasn't,' Zoë said distantly. She was thinking about Hanging Hill. North of the city. It faced north, looking out towards the Caterpillar. It was a weird place, damp and a little lonely. There was a bus stop there, on the same route that took in Beckford's Tower – where Ralph claimed to have met Lorne on the night of her death – and continued to the bus stop at the canal. 'Or, rather, he should have form but he flew under the radar. Clever man. Have you actioned anything yet?'

'Someone in Intelligence is going to look at his phone later, and his bank account – but he's not exactly vulnerable. One of the cars'll swing by and do a welfare check.'

'Have they left?'

He stood up and craned his neck to look out of the window at the car park. 'Nope. They're taking the GP car. It's still there.'

'OK. Call down. Tell them not to bother. I've got to drive through Hanging Hill in about twenty minutes. I'll save them the hassle.'

'You're not getting all helpful on us, are you?'

'Helpful? Christ, no.' She patted her pockets, looking for her keys. 'Like I said, I just happen to be going that way.'

6

The West Country got the first of the weather from the Atlantic. It got the first of the winds and the first of the Gulf Stream. Its job was to tame the systems for the rest of the country, to filter them out before they passed over to the powerful cities in the east. But the west had got used to waiting until last for the sun. Dawn took its time over Russia, over the Continent, creeping across France and over the ferries and small boats of the Channel, moving inland over London with its glass towers and steel buildings grazing the underside of the sky. By the time daylight found Bath it was weary of the land and anxious for the blue of the Atlantic. Evenings in Peppercorn Cottage were like fiestas, flame-coloured and long, but mornings seemed tired, half-hearted and flat, as if the light was only there because it had nowhere better to be.

That Monday morning it was misty. Millie had gone to school and Sally and Steve had breakfast at the kitchen table, beside the window. Afterwards they sat there, not talking, just staring out at the garden and fields. On the table between them was an empty cafetière and an untouched plate of croissants. Neither of them had much appetite – since Thursday they'd both felt tired, constantly tired. Sally had taken Friday off work and Steve had postponed his trip to Seattle. It seemed neither of them had the energy for anything.

A deer appeared outside, nosing the hedge at the bottom of the garden, its outline faint and blurred in the morning mist. Neither Sally nor Steve moved, but maybe it sensed them there – or maybe it could smell the traces of David Goldrab, reduced to ten knotted, bulging carrier bags – because, without warning, it startled, turned to look directly at the window, then bounded away.

Sally got to her feet and went to the Welsh dresser. She took a small key from her pocket, unlocked a drawer and took out a tin, which she opened and carried to the table. It contained an assortment of objects: some photos; David Goldrab's signet ring with the four diamonds and the emerald – one diamond for every million he'd made in profit, the emerald for when he'd hit five million; the keys to his house, bristling with electronic fobs, two solid gold dice hanging from the ring; and five teeth. Steve had chosen the ones that were the most distinctive and had been the most visible in the photos: two incisors, which were filled with white composite, and another three, all molars, with gold fillings across the crowns. Their fine sharp roots were dull and brown with blood. 'I can't keep these things here any longer. You never know, with Millie in the house.'

313

'I'll find somewhere to hide them. Somewhere safe.'

'Are we . . . going ahead? You know, with—' She bit her tongue. She'd nearly said Mooney. 'With the people in London.'

'I'm seeing them tomorrow. Then it will all be sorted.' He looked at the date on his watch. 'I was supposed to be coming home from America today.'

'I know.'

'I'm still going to have to make that trip. And soon. I've postponed it once, but I can't again. I've got to keep going on with my life. We both do. We have to behave as if it never happened.'

'Yes.' Sally nodded. 'I know that too. It's OK.' She pushed her chair back, got to her feet and began pulling on the HomeMaids tabard. When David had hired her, he'd asked the agency to adjust the days she and the Polish girls went in. Today was the day the management had chosen. There had been nothing in the news about David Goldrab, so she knew she had to go along to Lightpil House as if nothing had happened. If she cancelled, or did anything out of the ordinary, the police would be bound to turn their attention to her. The slight bruise on her cheek left from David pushing her into the boot lid had already disappeared. Really, there was no excuse now. 'You go to America. I'll be OK.'

'Sally?'

She looked up. 'What?'

'You know it's all going to work itself out?' In the morning light Steve's face was older. His beard coming through made him look as if he'd lived a hard life for many years. 'Don't you?'

'Is it?'

'You made the best of a bad situation. And there isn't going to be some sort of divine retribution for it. You won't get punished. Do you believe me?'

She closed her eyes. Then opened them slowly. 'Maybe,' she said. 'Maybe.'

7

The moment Zoë crested the horizon on the lane at Lightpil House she knew Jacqui had been right and that something along the line had changed seriously for the London boy who'd come out west in the 1990s. The house on the other side of the wall looked more like a Mediterranean palace than anything else, with its white walls and balustraded terrace basking in the sun. David Goldrab must have discovered someone in Bath's Planning Department on his porn mailing list to have got Lightpil House through the application. It was horrific. Truly horrific.

She slowed about twenty yards from the front gates, pulled the Mondeo into a small layby and studied her reflection in the mirror on the sun visor. If he was at home he would never recognize her after all these years. But he might recall the name Zoë Benedict. In her pocket she had her own police warrant card, but there was a second one too, with the name Evie Nichols on it. She'd found it years ago, kicked under a table at a riotous police party. She should have done the right thing and given it back,

316

but she hadn't: she'd kept it all these years, sure one day it would come in handy. Anyway, she told herself, she was fairly sure she wasn't going to need it. If phone calls were going unanswered Goldrab probably wasn't there. Even so, she was shaking as she nosed the Mondeo forward to the gate, leaned out and pressed the buzzer.

No one answered. She waited two minutes, then rang again. When still no one answered, she parked the car on the side of the lane and wandered along the perimeter fence until she found a gap in the hedge. She squeezed through, emerging in the garden, and stood on the lawn, brushing off her clothes, looking up at the house with its enormous windows and glass atrium. Lorne, she thought, did you ever stand in this garden? Or on that patio? Or behind one of those windows? Wouldn't it be something if your life turned out to have this in common with mine, as well as all the rest?

She went silently up the steps on to the huge sandstone terrace, and wandered along the back of the house, peering into the two-storey conservatory at the tall palms and the wicker furniture. The place was flooded with sunlight. She put a hand against the window to shade her eyes, and saw the filaments of the halogen lamps all lit, a newspaper discarded on one of the cushions. A little bud of curiosity opened in her. She went to the glass door and tried it. It was unlocked. She put her head inside, looking up at the glass ceiling, waiting for the familiar beep-beep-beep of an alarm system. But there was nothing.

'Hello?' she called. 'Anyone home?'

Silence. She sniffed. The air was stale and the house was hot, as if the heating had been left on. There was condensation on the ceiling panes of the atrium. Missing, huh? Missing? She ferreted around in her pockets and found a pair of latex gloves. Pulled them on and stepped inside, looking around at the huge space. Amazing, she thought. All this because people liked to watch other people having sex. She went into the huge kitchen and looked at all the gilt and marble and downlighting. Two glasses sat on the kitchen table, one half full of champagne. There was a half-eaten sandwich on a plate next to the fridge, going hard and grey. In the microwave oven she found a plate of pasta, also dried up and congealed. She opened the fridge and saw a bottle of champagne with no cork in it. She sifted through the other things in there – bottles of vitamins, cartons of orange juice, packets of bacon and sausages. There was a marble cheeseboard with four wedges of cheese on it, covered with clingfilm. She picked up a bag of salad and checked the date: 15 May. Yesterday.

'Hello?' She stood in the hallway and called up the stairs. 'Mr Goldrab?'

No answer. She went up the marble staircase, her footsteps echoing round the hall, and checked all along the first floor, both wings of the house, opening doors and peering into rooms that looked as if they'd never been set foot in since the day the house was finished. There was a gym, a home cinema, a clawed bath with a tap in the shape of a swan, and

318

a four-poster bed in one room that could have slept ten people. No David Goldrab. Back on the landing she noticed a glass case standing open, a picture of a night safari in the back of it. Two aluminium arms were mounted in the picture. It was a display cabinet. Empty. Zoë experimentally opened and closed the glass door, looking at the lock, then at the stand. Whatever was missing from it was important.

She searched downstairs and still found no sign of him. Overlooking the back garden, an office was filled with banks of computers and DVD players – all black, red lights blinking from their shiny surfaces. A bespoke bookcase made of a reddish wood, maybe walnut, lined one wall, full of photos. There were two computers, each with a light on. When she touched the mouse of the first, the screen came to life. A spreadsheet with figures entered in three columns. The second PC also sprang to life with a quick nudge. This one showed an array of video icons. She peered at the titles: *Bukkake in Gateshead*; *Bukkake in Mayfair*. Bukkake – like Jacqui had said. Christ, she thought. Lorne, if I see your face in any of these, I promise I'll find a way to keep it secret.

She closed the blinds, sat down in the swivel chair, and began opening files, watching them with her elbows planted on the desk, her mouth tight. Jacqui had been right about how nasty bukkake was. None of it actually broke any laws that she could think of, but it was pretty disgusting nonetheless, and Zoë had a high threshold for things like this. She truly, truly hoped she wasn't going to see Lorne staring back at her from the floor of one of these bear-pits.

She was concentrating so hard on the faces of the girls that it wasn't until the third video that she recognized the male star of the show. Jake the Peg. Jake the Peg! God, she thought, she could be as dumb as a bag of hammers sometimes. The whole station had been wondering how Jake had sharpened up his act lately – knowing he had to be up to something more than just dealing to the schoolkids. But a porn star? Old Peggie? No one had guessed that one. And no one would have guessed how he'd got his nickname. She gave a small, dry laugh. 'So, Peggie,' she murmured, looking at the screen, '*that's* your secret.' Christ, the world was a screwy place.

Zoë spent two hours going through the hard drives with a fine-tooth comb and by the end of it she was about 99.9 per cent sure Lorne wasn't in the videos. The faces of one or two actresses who'd made brief appearances weren't completely distinct. She made notes of the frames they appeared in. The girls weren't blonde, like Lorne, but she could have been wearing a wig. When someone from HQ came over to pick up the computers Zoë'd ask for those faces to be enhanced. She pushed the keyboard away and gave the swivel chair a push with her foot, making it twirl. The bookcases sped by, then the window, with a view over the lawns, the swimming-pool and the trees outside. All the DVDs and the computers.

She brought the chair to a stop. Folded her arms and sat there, considering this situation. Half-eaten food? A computer like this left on standby with all the sensitive shit on it? Doors unlocked? Lights on and phone calls not answered? She didn't know, just didn't know, but if it wasn't too good to be true, just too damned convenient for words, then the cop in Zoë would have guessed that Mr Goldrab, the only man who could link her back to that Bristol club, was no longer alive.

8

Even though their hours at David's had been cut, the
Polish girls were in a good mood that morning.
Marysieńka was going on holiday with her bus driver
boyfriend next week, and Danuta had met a nice
Englishman in Back to Mine, a nightclub in the centre
of Bath. He was tall and he had plenty of . . . She
rubbed her fingers together. 'If you got that,' she told
Sally, on the back seat, 'then you don't gotta have
that.' She held her hands apart about nine inches,
then shortened the distance to two inches. 'It don't
matter.' Next to her Marysieńka let out a howl of
laughter and banged the steering-wheel with the palm
of her hand. 'It really don't matter!' She laughed.
'Don't matter if you got a cocktail sausage down
there.'

The sun was high in the sky when they arrived at
Lightpil House. They stopped the little pink Smart
car in the gravel car park at the foot of the estate.
Sally couldn't take her eyes off the ground. But there
was no blood left, no stain. Nothing. She got out and
gazed up at the house. The place seemed much

quieter than usual but, of course, that was because she knew. She followed the other women up the path. Danuta had taken off her high heels and put them in her cleaning kit so she could walk barefoot. Everywhere flowers were coming out – the fluffy purple balls of allium, and already some bleeding hearts, their white drooping flowers like little bells. You'd never guess what had happened here. It would be the last thing you'd picture.

The utility-room door stood open, as it often did. They walked in, putting down their cleaning kits. The place was exactly as Sally had left it. Maybe cobwebs were already forming, growing on the ornate wall lamps, maybe dust was settling on the surfaces, the computers and huge TVs, but it all looked exactly the way it had been. The champagne glasses were still on the table where David and Jake had sat drinking.

'No list,' Danuta said, lifting a couple of newspapers and checking under them. 'Bloody fat man, you didn't leave a list.'

'Dum-de-dum-de-dah,' Marysieńka hummed. She went to the doorway and shouted into the hall, 'Mr Goldrab?'

Silence.

'Mr Goldrab?' She wandered to the bottom of the stairs, pulling on her rubber gloves, looking up to the landing. 'You there?' She waited a moment. When there was no answer she wandered back into the kitchen, shrugging. 'Not here.'

She flicked on the coffee-maker, opened the fridge, got out some milk and filled the frother while Danuta rummaged for mugs. Sally put her kit down and made a play of pulling things out, getting ready for a job that wasn't going to happen. She was concentrating so hard on making it look natural that it took her a moment to realize the girls had gone quiet. They had stopped what they were doing and were standing, hands frozen on milk bottles and coffee cups, their faces turned to the door.

When she turned she saw why. A woman was standing in the doorway. Very tall, dressed in jeans, her red hair loose across her shoulders, a police card thrust out at arm's length. Sally stared at her, her heart doing a low, disorienting swoop in her chest.

There was a moment's silence. Then the woman lowered the card with a frown. 'Sally?' she said. '*Sally?*'

9

'Sally Cassidy.' Zoë wrote the name. She'd inter-viewed both the Polish girls already and let them go. Now she and Sally were in her office, the door closed. 'I'm using your married name.'

'I'm not married any more.'

'No.' Zoë raised her head and studied her. Sally sat on the other side of the desk, her hands in her lap. She had her hair tied back, no makeup on, and she was wearing a little pink tabard with 'HomeMaids' emblazoned on it. In front of her was a Lucozade bottle one of the Polish girls had given her for the shock because she was taking it badly, Goldrab going missing. Her face was pale under the freckles, and her lips had a bluish tinge. 'But I'll still use it. Because I shouldn't be interviewing you, you being my sister.'

'OK. I understand.'

Zoë put a line under the name. Then another. This was weird. So weird. 'Sally,' she said, 'how long has it been now?'

'I don't know.'

'Years. Must be.'

'Must be.'

'Yes. Well.' She tapped her pen on the desk. 'We don't have to take all day about this. I'll ask you the same questions I asked Danuta and Marysieńka. Then you can go.'

'My answers won't be the same.'

'Why not?'

'Because I've been working for David privately. We had an arrangement.'

'An arrangement?'

'I didn't tell the girls and I didn't tell the agency, but yes. I worked for him and he was paying me direct.'

'The girls said he cut their hours recently – changed their day?'

'Yes, because I'd started working for him.' Sally linked her hands on the table. 'He didn't need them.'

Zoë's eyes went to the hands, to the little finger on the right, which was crooked. You had to know it was there – it was just the faintest deviation in the joint, making the finger turn in on itself. She dragged her eyes away, concentrated on her notes. It would be so easy to go back to that hand, back to the accident and the moment her life had changed. She tapped her biro harder on the desk. One, two, three. Snapped herself back to the interview. 'When you say working, what were you doing exactly?'

'He called me the housekeeper. I was cleaning, like before, but I was doing admin for him too. I've only done a few days so far.'

'A few.'

'Yes.'

'Over how many days?'

Sally hesitated. 'One. Just the one.'

'One. You don't seem sure about that.'

'No, I am sure. Quite sure.'

'What day was it?'

'Last Tuesday. A week ago.'

'Tuesday. You're certain it was Tuesday?'

'Yes.'

'And you haven't been back since?'

'No.'

'And you worked for his business?'

'For the house. I was paying bills, hiring people to do jobs around the place.'

'Lightpil House is huge. The gardens – he must have needed someone to maintain them?'

'The gardeners come once a week. The Pultman brothers. They're from Swindon.'

'Pultman.' Zoë noted it carefully. 'And the pool man. He was from a company in Keynsham. Anyone else?'

'Not that I can think of.'

'Does David talk to you a lot?'

'Not really.'

'Not really? What does that mean?'

Sally picked at the label on the bottle. 'Just means not a lot.'

Zoë's attention wandered distractedly back to Sally's hands. The faintly deformed finger. God, but the past was coming back in droves these days. Just like the snow outside the window in her dream. 'So?

Apart from today, the last time you were there was when?'

'Last Tuesday. Like I said.'

'You didn't notice anything suspicious?'

Sally fiddled more with the label. 'No. Not really.'

'And he didn't say anything about planning to go away?'

She shook her head.

'You see,' Zoë said, 'everything in that house is telling me something's happened to Mr Goldrab. Now, I'll be honest, I'm floundering a bit. If he's come to harm I'm stuck – because I don't know where to start. So if you remember anything, *anything* at all – doesn't matter how small or insignificant it is, just something that you can add to this – please say it because I—'

'Jake,' Sally said abruptly. 'Jake.'

Zoë stopped writing. 'I beg your pardon?'

'He turned up when I was there. David called him Jake the Peg.'

'What did he look like?'

'Not very tall. His hair cut quite short. Maybe mixed race, I wasn't quite sure.'

'Drives a purple Shogun jeep?'

'Yes. Do you know him?'

'You could say that.' She tipped her head on one side. 'So, Sally. When Jake turned up, what exactly happened?'

'It got nasty. There was an argument. Then he went.'

'An argument? About what?'

328

'Jake hadn't been over for months – then he turned up and tried to use David's gate code. I think that's what it was about. I was in the office and they were in the hallway so I couldn't hear it all. They were shouting for a while – then Jake left.'

'He didn't say he'd be back later in the week? No chance he could have come over again on Thursday to finish the argument?'

'I don't know. I didn't hear him say he would.'

'We found a crossbow in the utility room. You saw that this morning, didn't you – saw where we found it?'

Sally nodded.

'You don't know how it came to be in there, do you?' She was monitoring Sally's fingers. They were tearing at the label now. 'Seems a strange place to put a crossbow. And then leave all your doors open and go out for a drive.'

'It was always on the stand on the landing. I used to clean the case.'

'You never saw him use it?'

'No.'

'And you haven't been back to Lightpil since last Tuesday? And you weren't there Thursday, for example? That was the last time anyone spoke to him.'

She shook her head. Wrapped her arms around herself as if someone had suddenly opened the window.

'What's making you nervous, Sally? Why the nerves?'

'What?'

'You're shaking.'

'No, I'm not.'

'Yes, you are. You're shaking like a leaf. And fidgeting.'

'It's been a shock.'

'Goldrab going missing? The Lucozade's supposed to help you with that. Isn't it working?'

'I didn't expect to see you.' She shivered, looked away again and hugged herself harder, rubbing her hands up and down her arms. 'That's all. Can I go now?'

Zoë didn't speak for a moment or two. She twirled the pen thoughtfully. 'I heard about the divorce,' she said eventually. 'Mum and Dad didn't say, but you do hear things around this town, don't you? I was sorry about it all.'

'Yes. Well. That was a long time ago now.'

'If you don't mind me asking, why did you leave?'

'I didn't leave. He left me.'

Zoë stopped twirling the pen. '*He* left *you*?'

'Yes. More than a year and a half ago.'

She didn't know what to say. She studied her sister – really studied her. An attractive woman coming up for middle age, but no stunning beauty. Her hair had lost the pure, lemony blonde streaks of childhood and was coarser now. The clothing under the tabard, though nice, was well-worn and threadbare. She was working as a cleaner – a cleaner and housekeeper for a pornographer. Julian had left her and she was bringing up Millie alone. Out of nowhere, an enormous, awful wave came up inside Zoë. An overwhelming urge to stand and hug her sister.

She coughed. Pushed her hair out of her eyes.

'Right.' She handed Sally the statement. 'If you'd just put a signature there, you can go. Told you it wouldn't take long, didn't I?'

10

When Sally had gone, Zoë sat staring into space. It was ten minutes before she shook herself, and began to think about Lorne and Goldrab again.

She started by doling out some tasks for her DCs. Then she leafed through her messages, checked her emails and put in a request to reclassify David Goldrab's status as a misper. If he really was dead, the question remained: why? If he'd had a hand in Lorne's death, could he have been killed *because* of it? In revenge? Lorne's dad, maybe? Or had Goldrab known who Lorne's killer was and died because he'd threatened to reveal what he knew? Or – and this was the eventuality she was struggling with – maybe Lorne's connection to the porn industry really had stopped with the approach to Holden's Agency and Goldrab's disappearance was entirely unconnected. Either way she wouldn't be completely at rest until she knew for sure he was dead – until she had seen his body on a slab in the mortuary, seen it cut down the middle the way Lorne's had been. Perhaps then that jumpy thing in her would roll back a bit. Keep its peace.

But what about Sally? And all that had happened in their pasts? What would make *that* poisonous thorn go away? An apology? she thought, rubbing her knuckles. How the hell did you go about apologizing for something like that?

Another message popped up – this time from the high-tech unit who, in less than two hours, had cracked through the administrator password page on the CCTV and analysed the footage from the front of Lightpil House. She read the email quickly: the team had found no record of Goldrab leaving the house on the Thursday. He'd been out to the stables in the morning, had come back at ten and hadn't been picked up by the CCTV camera since. Which must mean he'd exited through the side entrance not covered by the camera. What the team had found, however, was five-minute footage of a serious altercation that had taken place outside the house at about three p.m. that same day. She closed the office blinds again, and watched the segments of video they'd attached to the email. A suntanned young man next to a jeep, dodging crossbow bolts. Jake the Peg jumping like a monkey on hot coals.

Jake, she thought, tapping the screen. Jake the Peg. Sally was right, you naughty boy.

11

Jake the Peg's home was on the road from Bath to Bristol and didn't look as if it belonged to a porn star. Apart from the small security camera trained on the jeep that stood outside, it was an ordinary thirties house with metal lattice windows and deco-inspired stained-glass porches – the type of building that had survived the bombing during the war because it was part of the suburban sprawl and too remote from the vital organs of the city to have interested the Germans. Zoë pulled up at just after four o'clock to find the curtains still closed. She sat for a while, considering the house. It was a bit like her parents' place had been. People who lived in a place like that shouldn't have been able to afford to send two children to boarding-school. Not unless they had very good reason to separate them. Very good reason. Earlier today in the office Sally had looked broken. Really broken. *Julian* had left *her*. Not the other way round. That didn't fit at all.

Zoë locked the car, went up the path, rang the bell and stood on the doorstep, listening for movement inside. After three or four minutes had elapsed she rang the bell again. This time there was a muffled thump, then someone called out, 'Coming, coming.'

The boy who answered the door couldn't have been much more than seventeen. But what he lacked in maturity he made up for in sass. Dusky brown – maybe from Vietnam or the Philippines – his hair was shaved at the sides and neck, with an area on top that had been teased into a small pompadour. He wore a gold chain and an iPhone holder velcroed to his upper arm. Aside from that, he was naked except for a pair of tight pink boxers, with 'Wow' printed across the crotch. When he saw Zoë's warrant card he laid a hand on his chest as if to say this just wasn't the sort of thing that happened to him every day – did anyone mind if he fainted?

'Is Mr Drago here?'

'No! Him asleep.' He eyed the card warily. 'You police?'

'That's right. What's your name?'

'Angel. Why?'

'OK, Angel. I think I'll come in, if you don't mind.'

He tutted, but swivelled haughtily on his heels and disappeared into the house. She followed. The underpants, she saw, had 'Kitty' emblazoned on the buttocks.

If the place was a typical thirties house on the outside, inside it was anything but. The front room – where most families would have had a gas fire, a TV, a sofa – had been turned into a gym with lots of black and chrome equipment. One wall was painted lime green, with a blown-up black-and-white image of a young man looking coquettishly over his shoulder. The back room, which led out to the kitchen, was the living area, with sixties geometric wallpaper, suede furniture and different-coloured neon tubes suspended from the ceiling. It was very cold, but Angel didn't seem to notice. He yelled up at the ceiling, 'JAAAAKE. JAAAKE. Important you come now.' Then he went into the little kitchenette and began making tea, breaking off every now and again to execute a demi-plié, holding the fridge handle to balance himself.

There was the sound of someone falling out of bed overhead. Zoë found a seat and sat with her back to the wall, in the corner, where there was a precious pocket of warmth. No wonder it was cold – the windows were open. Original thirties leaded panes, propped open on metal latches. When they were kids, at Christmas Sally would paint each pane of glass in their bedroom windows. Every one a different colour. Silver, green, red.

''S bloody freezing in here.' Jake came in, swaddled in a duvet, his teeth chattering. He scowled at Zoë, but he wasn't awake enough for a fight. He seemed more worried about the heating. 'What've you got against a bit of warmth?' he yelled at Angel. 'You fucking freak of nature.'

'Listen her,' Angel said sarcastically. 'She Wicked White Witch on the sleigh. Ice Queen.'

'Shut up,' Jake said. 'Shut up.'

'Ooh – *crooooooel*. Yours is a problem in the

336

blood.' He pronounced it *blod*. 'Not enough to go round your whole body. Problem starts in the little fingers and we all know where it ends.'

'Shut *up*.'

Angel made a small disgusted click in the back of his throat, put his chin up and flicked back a hand, as if it was no surprise to him, none at all, that a person as ignorant and crude as Jake would have brought the police to his house – as if that was to be expected of people like him. He turned on a heel, his nose in the air, and disappeared upstairs, slamming the door.

'Ignore him.' Jake closed the window bad-temperedly and put his hand on the radiator to check it for warmth. He found none. He bent and turned the valve on full. 'Tried to teach him some manners, didn't I? But with his lot, what do you expect?'

Zoë examined the mug she'd been given. It had pictures of Billie Holiday hand-painted in pinks and greens. 'How did you keep this secret from us all these years?' She nodded to the door through which Angel had huffed off. 'Jake the Peg and his boyfriend. I admit it wasn't what I'd expected. And even more spectacular, in the revelations stakes, Jake the Peg *the porn star*? You slipped that one by us, no pun intended. But you're a celebrity! I've been watching some of your appearances recently. At the office. They all have. Funny, thinking about it now, but you always seemed so much smaller in the flesh.'

Jake looked steadily at her. He sat down. 'I know why you're here.'

'Do you? Go on, then. Tell me.'

'Jake does barely legals, innit? Because there was them schoolgirls in it? But see that vid with the yellow spine over there? On the shelf? Get it out. Go on. It's a vid of each of them girls, with their passports held up to the camera. Proof they was all eighteen.'

'Barely legals? Funny – that's not why I'm here.'

Jake frowned. 'I'm telling you – I do my homework, man, learn the law. This is proper business now and I'm clean. Easy.'

'I'm sure you are, Jake, I'm sure you are. I've always had absolute faith in you. But that's not why I'm here. I want to talk to you about Lorne Wood.'

He sucked his teeth, rolled his eyes. 'Yeah. You asked me about her already. What do you want to know now?'

'I want you to revisit your memory. Have a double-check in the grey matter. Sometimes things slip our minds.'

'We talked about this.'

'Yes, but I asked you whether you saw her outside the school. What I didn't ask you was whether she ever turned up on one of your sets.'

'Her?' Jake gave a short sarcastic laugh. 'No fucking way. Too classy.'

'You sure? You sure David Goldrab never introduced you two?'

Jake's face changed. It went flat. 'Goldrab? What's he got to do with anything?'

'You do know him? Don't you?'

'See, you ask that question like I'm some kind of

eejit, man. Like I'm some eight-year-old. But I ain't. Because what I worked out is I don't got to answer that. And I don't got to because you already know the answer. Or else you wouldn't've asked it.'

'I'm impressed. Is there no end to your talents?'

'And whatever he's said about me, whatever he's told you, it's because he hates me.'

'He hasn't said anything about you.'

'It should be him you're nosing around, not me. He's a homophobe. You can get him for discrimination and that.'

'You obviously didn't hear me. I said, he hasn't said anything about you. Because, at the moment, he's not saying very much at all.'

Jake creased his forehead. He pulled the duvet tightly around him. His feet poking out of the bottom were bottle-tanned, the nails neatly cut and shining subtly with clear varnish. 'What's that supposed to mean?'

'It means that the last trace we have of him is Thursday, the twelfth of May. His mother spoke to him in the morning, didn't hear from him again. Nobody has.'

That stopped Jake in his tracks. 'Right,' he said slowly. 'Right.'

'When was the last time you saw him?'

'Thursday, the twelfth of May. Four days ago. I've tried to wipe it from my mind. He stopped giving me my proper respect, know what I mean?'

'That'll be the day he went missing.' She sipped her tea. 'Did you have an amicable meeting that day?'

'No. But you know that because you got it all on camera – on his spy cameras. Like when he assaulted me? Saw that, did you?'

'We did. Care to tell me what the disagreement was about?'

'About him being fucked up. Bein' a homophobe. Can't stand the sight of me since he heard about—' He jerked his head to the ceiling to indicate Angel.

'And he tried to shoot you because of it?'

'Yeah.'

'Did you come back later that day? Or had your meeting come to a – how can we put it? – a natural conclusion at that point?'

Jake rolled his eyes again. 'You having a joke? No – I never went back. Never will.'

'I don't know about this, Jake. Something's not right. You were the last person to see this guy alive.'

'Yes, except there are whole streetfuls of people who'd like to see that dick go missing. Why are you chewing *me* out about it?'

'Streetfuls of people want him to go missing?' Zoë scooped out her iPhone. 'That sounds interesting. I'm sure you won't take offence if I record this.'

'I would.'

She lowered the phone. 'That's fair, Jake, not to want to have your voice on record. But let me put it on my notepad. You have my guarantee it won't have your voice on it.'

He raised his nose disdainfully. He unfurled a hand in her direction, held it open. She looked at it for a moment. Then she clicked the phone into *Notes* and passed it to him. He gave the phone a brief derisory scan, as if it was a bit of roadkill she'd brought in for him to inspect, then thrust it back at her. She took it and began tapping in words as he spoke.

'He's got enemies.' He gave the phone a suspicious look, but began to reel off names anyway, counting them on his fingers. 'There's this girl from Essex called Candi. I'm telling you, she would *shoot* him. In the street, tomorrow, if she saw him.'

'A girl? A woman? Making a grown man disappear? I don't know – we don't usually put women in the frame for something like this.'

'Candi? I mean, fuck, man, she'd eat your eyes out, that one. She's got a habit and she lives with some guy called Fraser, I don't know where exactly – somewhere over that side of the world. Then there's this ex-SAS guy. Built like that.' He held out his arms to indicate the man's height and size. 'Always used to hang around the shoots – he's got an itch about David, know what I mean? Spanner, they called him. Don't know why. Think his real name was Anthony or something. But . . . nah – he'd never have the balls for it. But there's another one. One I really think is whacked enough to do it.'

Zoë stopped tapping and looked up at him.

'I never knew his name.' Jake's voice was sober and low when he said 'his', as if speaking the word alone could bring hellfire down into his little thirties semi. 'But he was the type, you know. He'd get in and out and no one would've seen a thing.'

'Who was he?'

'Dunno. Only met him once when he was down for a shoot. That's how David done his business, innit? He's got some gamekeeper raises pheasants for him and these dudes visit when there's a shoot organized. This guy came down and was mouthing off. He was something in the military. The – what d'ya call it? – Ministry of you know . . .'

'Defence? The Ministry of Defence?'

'Yeah.'

'Christian name?'

'Dunno. David just called him "mate". They knew each other in Kosovo. And that's all I know about him. Otherwise, swear' – he held his hands up – 'I'd give it to you.'

'Any others?'

'No.'

Zoë tapped the last few words in, saved it, then clicked the phone off and put it into her pocket. She took a moment or two to regroup, then leaned forward to him, her elbows on her knees.

'What?'

'I've still got a problem, Jake. I mean, meet my eyes and tell me I look convinced you had nothing to do with Goldrab going missing.'

'What the fuck're you talking about?'

'None of those names gets you off the hook. Do they?'

'But I've got an alibi for that afternoon. Which is good news.'

'Depending on your perspective. Who is it? Angel? Because *he*'d convince a jury.'

342

Jake gave her a sly smile, the diamond in his front tooth glinting at her, as if this was the most satisfying thing he'd done in years. 'That's the easiest question you've asked, sista. I tore my jeans when David was shooting at me. When I seen what I done I go straight into town and buy a new pair. River Island. Their workers'll remember me and for sure they've got a CCTV there.'

'But as an alibi it doesn't work because, of course, we don't know exactly when Goldrab went missing. It was probably that afternoon some time, because his mother couldn't reach him on the phone in the evening, but we can't say for sure. You could have come back later and dealt with him then. Say, six or seven o'clock.'

'That's OK too. Straight after I got the new jeans I went to the cinema. With my mates. I used my credit card and there were six of us. And then we spent the rest of the night in the Slug on George Street. So wherever David Goldrab was going that night, who-ever he met, it weren't me. But none of that matters, does it?'

Zoë raised an eyebrow. 'Doesn't it?'

'Nah,' he said, with a smug smile. 'Because David hasn't been *killed*. David – Mr clever fucking Goldrab – oh, no, not him. *He* has *disappeared* himself.'

343

12

The air above the field was full of drifting white butterflies. Like fairies floating on the wind, they trailed past Sally's face, blocking the sunlight, alighting on her shoulders and hands. To her right she could see shapes, indistinct in the blizzard. They were important, instinctively she knew they were, and she began to walk towards them, her hands shielding her face from the insects. The first shape was big, standing high, a giant, moving white mass. A car, she saw, as she got nearer – she could make out wing mirrors and headlights through the throng. She clapped her hands and the butterflies lifted in a cloud, spun and flapped. Underneath them the car bonnet was black and shiny, and Sally saw it was Steve's Audi. Which meant, she was sure, that the shape on the ground, ten feet away, cocooned in white, was David Goldrab.

Her heart began to pound, a giant drum, filling her chest. She took a few steps, crunching on butterflies, breaking their bodies under her shoes. David lay on his back, motionless, his arms folded across his chest, as if he was in a sarcophagus, butterflies covering his face. She didn't want to approach, but she knew she had to. She got to within a foot, and although every sense was telling her not to, she crouched near his head, stretched her hand out towards him.

The body moved. It rolled towards her and began to sit up. A hand shot out and gripped her. The butterflies swarmed away from the face but it wasn't David under there. It was Zoë, sitting up and looking beseechingly at Sally, as if she was at the bottom of a very deep hole, and Sally was the only light she could see.

'Sally?' A hand was shaking her. 'Sally? Wake up.'

She covered her face with her hands. 'What?' she mumbled.

'You were crying.'

She opened her eyes. The room was dark, the bed-side clock casting just a faint glow. Three o'clock. Steve was lying behind her, his hand on her shoulder. She touched her fingers lightly to her face and found her cheeks were wet.

13

He has disappeared himself . . .

Jake's words kept knocking at Zoë. She'd been almost certain for a while that Goldrab was dead, but now she wasn't so sure. It hadn't occurred to her before that he could disappear himself. But now she saw it was feasible, and the thought made her more than uneasy. If he wasn't dead it meant he could come back at any time, walk into her life and cut her down in one swipe. Because that was the sort of bastard he was.

The next day she got straight to work, ploughing through the list Jake had given her, putting out feelers – calls to Essex Police to track down Candi and Fraser, and to SOCA to see if there were any clues as to who 'Spanner' might be. She used the parliamentary website, Dodspeople, to search hundreds of CVs for MoD people who'd done time in Kosovo, and the more digging she did the more convinced she became that the person to start with was a guy named Dominic Mooney. Mooney was now head of intelligence at one of the Foreign Office departments, but what interested her was that he had spent time with the Civil Secretariat in Kosovo at the beginning of the decade and had done three years as the director of a unit set up in Priština to monitor and investigate prostitution and trafficking. If any of his staff in Kosovo had had contact with Goldrab, or had been up to anything suspicious, Mooney would be the one to know.

She put in a call to him in Whitehall, but he was out at a meeting, so she left a message with his secretary, then began systematically working her way through her list of other tasks. She spoke to the gardening company in Swindon, but they didn't have much to tell her – Goldrab was reclusive, paid them by direct debit, and often the workers would be at Lightpil for eight hours solid without seeing or speaking to him. It was much the same story at the pool company, and at the stables where Goldrab kept his horse, Bruiser. He rode most days, though usually on his own, and paid the livery fees also by direct debit. In fact, no one Zoë spoke to had had any inkling of what Goldrab was like as a person, let alone any idea if he was unhappy or making plans to leave.

DC Goods called from town. Zoë had told him that Jake the Peg was in trouble again and given him the task of finding support for Jake's alibi. Already he was unearthing evidence: the staff at River Island remembered him, and they had the CCTV footage to prove it. From a glance at the photo, the manager of the cinema too was almost certain she remembered Jake. She was having a look at the time-coded CCTV footage even as they spoke. His alibi for that night seemed watertight. Zoë found she wasn't much surprised at that: it had felt too easy a solution for Jake to have been the one who had made Goldrab disappear.

She opened an email from the technical team at HQ. The freeze frames of the porn footage lifted from Goldrab's computers had come back and none of the women was Lorne. She stared at the images, trying to force Lorne's features into the girls' faces, but she couldn't. Again, she wondered if Goldrab's disappearance was totally coincidental. Did that mean she was leaving Lorne behind by chasing what had happened to Goldrab? She looked at the photo of Lorne pinned to the wall. Come on, she thought, you brought me here, so you tell me – what do I do now? You know I really want David Goldrab. Do I go after it? Or is he nothing to do with you?

There was a knock at the door. She made sure her shirt was straight and tucked in and that her cuffs were buttoned, then swivelled the chair to the door. 'Yup?'

Ben put his head round the door.

'Oh.' Her head felt suddenly heavy, her feet like lead. 'Ben.'

'Hi.'

They regarded each other without speaking. Somewhere down the corridor a phone rang. A door at the other end of the building banged. What, she wondered, was the grown-up way to deal with Ben? How would a normal person address what had

348

happened between them? She didn't know. Hadn't a clue.

Eventually Ben saved her by speaking. 'Have you heard?'

'Heard what?'

'About Ralph?'

'What about him?'

'I thought you should be the first to know.' He glanced up at her whiteboard, where Ralph's name was written with a big red line through it. For the first time she noticed dark rings under Ben's eyes. He'd been working hard. 'He tried to commit suicide. Two hours ago. His mother found him.'

'Christ.' She remembered Ralph crouching here on the floor, his back to the wall, his tears wetting the carpet. 'Is he going to be OK?'

'They don't know yet. He left a note, though. It said, "Lorne, I'm sorry."'

Zoë leaned back in the chair, her hands resting on her thighs, her eyes closed. She felt the long, hard drag of the past few days hanging on her.

'Zoë?'

She dropped her chin. Opened one eye and locked it on him. 'What?'

He scratched his head, glanced at the whiteboard, then back at her. 'Nothing,' he said. 'Nothing. Just thought you should know.'

14

Sally took a long time to go back to sleep after the dream. It seemed she'd slept only minutes before Steve's alarm was going off. He had a meeting to attend, he'd told her, in London. He hadn't said what, but they both knew it was with Mooney. To get the money. He showered and dressed while Sally lay in bed, trying to get rid of the dregs of the dream. He didn't eat breakfast, but walked around anxiously, drinking a mug of coffee, hunting for his keys and his sat nav. He told Sally not to call him, he'd call her.

She sat at the window in her dressing-gown and watched the car pull left out of the driveway, which led away from the lane along a narrow track into the woods. It was down there, in true Famous Five style, that they'd dug a hole under the trunk of a tree and buried David's teeth and ring in a tin. She waited at the window until, twenty minutes later, Steve's car reappeared from the woods and sailed past the drive. Yes. He was going to see Mooney. He was going to get the money. And tomorrow he was going to America to get his other business finished. He was good at keeping things contained, she thought. He had to be, with his job. She envied that. He had no idea what it was like in her head at the moment. The mess and the confusion. The awfulness of being interviewed yesterday by Zoë.

There was a pile of dead brushwood that she'd collected back in December and hadn't got round to burning. During the winter it had become wet and rotten, but over the last few days the high, bright sunshine had dried it out. She didn't have to be at work until lunchtime, and she didn't want to stay in the cottage thinking about Steve going away tomorrow, or about the curious light in Zoë's eyes when she had said, 'Why are you nervous, Sally?', so she pulled on jeans and wellingtons and assembled the things she needed to make a bonfire. In the garage she found the can of paraffin they'd used to burn David's belongings and all their bloodied clothes. Her old gardening gloves were in the greenhouse. They had been sitting on the window-sill for months and had dried into stiff leather claws. She had to crack and soften them before they'd slip on to her hands.

The place they'd had the fire five nights ago was still black and grey with ash. There was a screw or a nail from something, she wasn't sure what, embedded in the soil. She pushed it further into the earth with her toe, then piled the brushwood on top of it, going back and forth across the garden, until there was lichen on her clothes and a long trail of debris across the lawn where she'd walked. The paraffin was easier to manage than she'd expected. As she worked some

351

of the resolve she'd felt the other night in the car came back to her. She could do things. She could do this on her own. She could keep going as if nothing had happened. She could maybe even do some research and make a start on the thatch – wouldn't that be something! She could be as strong as Zoë. She watched the embers lift off, borne on the oily flame tips, watched them take to the air and whisk away to the fields, leaving grey speckles on the new skin of green. When the fire had reached its peak and was starting to die a little, she turned away to get a rake to keep it all together and saw a car sitting in the driveway behind her.

She hadn't heard it over the roar and crackle of the flames. It was blue and beaten up and she recognized it from yesterday. In the driver's seat – as if Sally had magicked her there – was Zoë, in a white T-shirt and a leather jacket, a beanie pulled down over her mad splay of red hair. Sally stared at her as she swung out of the car. The confidence of a cowboy. It must be so nice to be in that body, with those well-spaced legs, those capable arms. No clothes that felt too tight around the waist or old, frayed bras stretching and sagging.

Zoë looked serious as she came towards her. 'Where's Millie?'

'At Julian's. Why?'

'Have you got time to talk?'

'I've . . .' She glanced at the can of paraffin. 'I've got this to burn.' She pushed her hair off her face with the back of her wrist. 'Then I've got work.'

'That's OK. I won't be long.'

'I've got to wash all Millie's school clothes too.'

'Like I said, I won't be long.'

Sally was silent for a moment. She looked out at the fields. She saw the lane that wound its way up to the motorway. Steve would be at Victoria by now. 'What do you want to talk about?'

'Oh, this and that. Actually . . .' she glanced at the cottage '. . . I'd like a cup of tea. If that's not too much trouble.'

Sally kept her gaze on the fields, trying to guess what was coming. She'd never been any good at reading her sister. That was just the way it was. She put down her rake and went towards the cottage, pulling off her gloves. Zoë followed, stooping to get through the low doorway. While Sally boiled the kettle, scooped tea into the pot, Zoë wandered around the kitchen, picking up things from the shelves and examining them, stopping to peer at a painting Sally had done of a tulip tree. 'So,' she said, 'this is where you live now.' She studied a photo of Millie and the other kids – Sophie, Nial and Peter – pictured walking in a line across a ploughed field. 'You going to tell me about it? What happened to Julian?'

'There's nothing to tell. He found a girlfriend. They've got a baby.'

'Is Millie OK with it?'

'I don't know.'

'I saw her the other day, Millie.'

'I know.'

'She looked well. She's growing up fast. She's very pretty. Is she well behaved?

'Not really. No.'

Zoë gave a small smile and Sally stopped spooning tea.

'What?'

'Nothing.'

'Is that what you came to talk about? Millie?'

'In a way. There's some news. Ralph Hernandez – her friend? He's going to be OK but he tried to kill himself this morning.'

'*Ralph?*' She put the tin down with a clunk. 'Oh, good Lord,' she muttered. 'It just doesn't seem to stop.'

'We've got someone talking to the headmaster at Kingsmead. I guess he'll decide how to break the news to the kids.'

'But is it Ralph's way of . . .' she tried to find the right word '. . . his way of *admitting* that he had something to do with Lorne?'

'Some people think so.'

Sally lowered her eyes and put the lid back on the tea tin. She'd never met Ralph, but she knew all about him. She pictured him tall and dark. So, then, a suicide attempt. Another thing for Millie to carry. As if this household didn't have enough weighing on it. She cut slices of an orange-iced almond cake she'd made at the weekend in an optimistic attempt to cheer herself up. She got out plates, napkins, forks, and had turned to the fridge for the milk when behind her Zoë said, 'But that's not really why I'm here.'

354

She stopped then, her hand on the fridge door, her back to the room. Not moving. David, she thought. Now you're going to ask me about David. You're so clever, Zoë. I'm no match for you. Her head drooped so her forehead was almost touching the fridge. Waiting for the axe to fall. 'Oh,' she said quietly. 'Then why are you *really* here?'

There was a moment's silence. Then behind her Zoë said quietly, 'To apologize, I suppose.'

Sally stiffened slightly. 'To . . . I beg your pardon?'

'You know – about your hand.'

She had to swallow hard. It was the last thing. The very last thing . . . The accident with her hand hadn't been referred to by anyone in the Benedict family since the day it had happened, nearly thirty years ago. To mention it was like saying the name of the devil aloud. 'Don't be silly,' she managed to say. 'There's nothing to apologize about. It was an accident.'

'It wasn't an accident.'

'But it was. An accident. And all a long time ago. Really, so long ago we hardly need to go back and—'

'It wasn't an accident, Sally. You know it, I know it. We've spent nearly thirty years pretending it didn't happen, but it did. I pushed you off that bed because I hated you. Mum and Dad knew it wasn't an accident too. That's why we got sent to separate schools.'

'No.' Sally closed her eyes, rested her fingers on the lids and tried hard to keep the facts straight. 'We got

355

sent to separate schools because I wasn't clever enough for yours. I failed the test.'

'You could hardly hold the damn pen, probably, because your finger was broken.'

'I *could* hold the pen. I didn't get into the school because I was stupid.'

'Don't talk bullshit.'

'It's not bullshit.'

'Yes, it is. And you know it.'

There was a long, hard choke wanting to come up from Sally's stomach. She struggled to keep it under control. Finally, and with an immense effort of will, she opened her eyes and turned. Zoë was standing awkwardly on the other side of the table. There were red patches on her cheeks as if she was ill.

'I need to make amends, Sally. Everyone does. If we want to live well in the present we need to face the failings of our past.'

'Do we?'

'Yes. We have to. We have to make sure we . . . make sure we *connect* to other people. Be sure we never forget that we're part of a bigger pattern.'

Sally was silent. It sounded so weird, words like that coming out of Zoë's mouth. She'd never thought of her sister as connected to other people. She was something quite out on her own. A lone planet. She needed nothing. No people. It was what Sally envied most, maybe.

'Yeah, well.' Zoë cleared her throat. Raised a dismissive hand. 'I've said my piece, but now I'd better go. Villains to catch. Kittens to rescue from trees. You know how it is.'

And she was gone, out of the kitchen, out of the cottage, striding across the gravel, spinning her keys on her hands. She didn't look back as she drove out on to the lane so she didn't see Sally watching her from inside the kitchen. Didn't see that she didn't move for several minutes afterwards. A passer-by, if there had been any passers-by in that remote place, would have thought she was frozen there. A fuzzy white face on the other side of the leaded panes.

15

Just as Sally's job was finishing that afternoon, Steve called and asked her to meet him in town. There wasn't enough time to get to his house before she picked up Millie so he suggested they met at the Moon and Sixpence, the place they'd first had dinner together. She used the bathroom she'd just cleaned to have a hurried wash, and straightened her clothes. She put on a little makeup, but in the mirror her reflection was still tired and drawn. She couldn't stop turning over what Zoë had said that morning. About amends and patterns and the past.

She got to the café by four and found him sitting on the terrace, dressed in a suit and camel overcoat, drinking coffee. She sat down opposite him. He turned his grey eyes to her and studied her. 'Are you OK?'

'I think so. How was the meeting?'

He nodded in the direction of the third seat at the table. 'In there.' He had the weary, resigned look of a man who'd just woken up to the fact that the world was going to disappoint him for ever. 'In there.'

She saw a rucksack on the seat. 'Is that . . . ?'

He nodded. 'I got paid in Krugerrands.'

'Krugerrands?'

He nodded. 'Had to go and change it in Hatton Garden. I got a good deal – there's more than thirty-two K in there.'

Sally shivered. Thirty-two thousand pounds for killing a man. Blood money, they'd call this. She should be revolted by it, but she wasn't. She just felt numb. 'What are you going to do with it?'

'I'm not going to do anything with it. It's yours.'

'But—'

'Really. You did the job.'

'But you helped. We did it together. Like partners.'

'Don't argue. Just take it.'

She bit her lip. Looked at the rucksack. It was bulging. Ever since Thursday night she hadn't been able to look at a bag stuffed full of anything without picturing those carrier bags lined up on the lawn at Peppercorn. The red paste pressing against the plastic. She pulled her eyes away. Fiddled with the lid of Steve's cafetière.

'Millie got another call today from Jake.'

'That's fine. We'll sort it tonight.'

'I don't know if I want to.'

'Well, we're going to have to. We'll do it tonight and tomorrow I'm going to America. You know that, don't you, that I'm still going to America?'

She nodded.

'Are you going to be OK?'

'Yes,' she said distantly. 'I'll be fine.'

But she wasn't fine, of course. Her head was full of static and images. David Goldrab. The smells. The way the colour had crept into Zoë's cheeks when she was standing in the kitchen this morning. The 'pattern'. And now she thought that, whatever part of the pattern between humans she and Steve had made in the last few days, it was ugly and wrong. And that whatever happened now, it couldn't be changed. The ugly, knobbly part would become an uneven, deviating vein in the fabric that would, with time, be woven over and built on, as the generations kept moving. On down the line.

16

Zoë spent the rest of the day in the office, following up leads and answering emails. She still hadn't heard from Dominic Mooney so she put in one last call but was told he was still 'in a meeting'. By the time she left the office the sun was low, the roofs and high windows of Bath gilded with the last of the light, as if they'd been dipped in gold. It would be dark by the time she got home. She could have a Jerry's and ginger and watch the stars come out – on her own, while Ben and Debbie were doing whatever it was they did, wherever it was they did it. The welts and sores on her arms ached dully as she went into the car park.

She came to a halt. A guy dressed in red chinos and a blazer was standing in her way. He was very tall and thin and looked like an Asian version of David Bowie, with his jet-black hair gelled up in spikes. Even in her heeled boots she stood an inch or so shorter than him – not usual for her. She took a side-step to go round him and he mirrored her movement, blocking her. She did it again, going left this time, and again he barred her way.

She laughed. 'Very good. I like the way you do that.'

'I wouldn't laugh if I were you.' He was from Scotland. Somewhere posh, Edinburgh perhaps. 'If this was the movies it'd be the bit where I hit you on the head and throw you in the back of the Chrysler.'

She put her head on one side and scrutinized him. 'Do I know you?'

'Captain Zhang.' He produced a card and held it up to her. 'In the movie you'd wake up tied to a chair, a spotlight on your face. Never trust the Chinaman – don't they teach you anything in your job?'

'Give me that.' She made a grab for his card, but he returned it neatly to his pocket. 'Special Investigative Branch. SIB. But you can call us the Feds.'

'The *Feds*? Oh, please. I thought you said this wasn't the movies. Special Investigative B—' She broke off. Of course – she should have known he was military from the way he was dressed: typical Sandhurst graduate get-up. 'SIB – I know who you are. Military Police. They call you the Stab in the Backs – the squaddie rubber-heelers. Standing here making out you're in the fucking Special Forces, but you're just a squaddie spy. Stopping me getting to my bike? I don't think so.'

'Well, I do.'

She shrugged, tried to walk round him. He barred her way again.

362

'Do you want a fight?' she asked. 'See who wins?'

'I'd win.'

'No, you wouldn't.'

Zhang sighed, as if he was trying to keep his patience. 'We need to speak to you, Inspector Benedict. We need a frank and meaningful talk about Dominic Mooney. I think if you're patient you'll find we're all singing off the same hymn sheet – no need for any arm-wrestling.'

She looked at Zhang very carefully. Dominic Mooney. The MoD guy she'd called. 'OK. You've got my attention now. You really have.'

'Good.' He fastened his blazer and smoothed the front, as if something in the encounter had made it go awry. 'That's what I was hoping for.'

'So?' She turned, opening her hand to indicate all the vehicles lined up in the car park. 'Which boot are you going to lock me in?'

17

Twerton was Bath's crippled cousin. Its hump-backed secret brother. No one in the nice northern squares and crescents of the city could say the name without putting on a cod country-bumpkin accent and tucking their tongue in the corner of their mouth like a congenital idiot. Anything that went wrong in the city seemed to emanate from there, or have a connection. It was where Jake the Peg could be found when he wasn't loitering outside one of the classier public schools.

'Whatever happens, you stay in your seat.'

In the passenger seat Sally shot a sideways look at Steve. 'Why? What're you going to do?'

'Don't worry. I've done this before, trust me.'

She clenched the envelope between her knees, her palms sweating and slick. She'd got Millie to call Jake to tell him the money was ready, then driven her over to Isabelle's for the evening. She and Steve had directions to where Jake was waiting, but in truth, she thought, as they pulled up, you could have found him by instinct alone. He was parked at a bus stop in front of a row of shops. One or two were open, lit with pools of light – a fish-and-chip shop, an off-licence, an all-night convenience store. Otherwise the street was dark.

Steve pulled the car up alongside so it was partly blocking the road. He didn't seem to mind other traffic getting stuck. He didn't seem to mind witnesses.

'Hello.' Engine still running, he wound down the window and held up his mobile phone to Jake. Clicked the *Record* icon.

Jake jerked a hand in front of his face. He opened the window and leaned over, yelling, 'What the fuck you think you're doing? Turn the fucking thing off.'

'Not if you want your money back.'

'*Jesuuuuus.*' He got out of the jeep, slamming the door, and strode over to them, his hand up in front of his face. He was wearing a gym vest and jeans that hung so low they gathered in folds around his trainers. He seemed like a different person now he was on his own territory and not on David's. More confident, swaggering. 'You are doing my head, man. Doing my head. Keep that thing outta my face.'

He leaned through the window to grab the phone, but Steve held it out of his reach. 'You take the phone, you don't get the money.'

'Give me the fucking phone.' He made a swipe for it. 'Or you can double what you owe me.'

'Do you want the money or not?'

'Giss the fucking phone.'

He leaned in again and this time Steve pressed the

365

electric-window button. Jake realized what was happening just in time and pulled back to avoid being squashed. 'Shit. *You wankers.*' He bounced his hands off the window in fury. Thumped the roof. 'You wankers.'

He went around all the doors, pulling at the handles. When he couldn't get in he went back to his jeep and opened the rear door. Rummaged inside.

'What's he doing?'

'I don't know.' Steve didn't turn. He handed Sally the phone, then tipped the rear-view mirror down and watched Jake. 'When he comes back don't stop filming, but keep the camera on his face. Don't have it on me – OK?'

She knelt up on the seat and swivelled round, aiming the camera out of the back window. As she did, Jake emerged from the jeep. He was holding something long and metal, lit red by the car lights. It took her a couple of moments to realize it was a tyre iron.

'Steve,' she began, but Jake had already lifted the tyre iron and swung it down on the roof of the Audi.

'Fuck.' Steve slammed his hand on the horn. 'You shithead.'

The noise was deafening. A group of kids in the stairwell of the block of flats opposite stopped what they were doing and turned to watch. Steve took his hand off the horn, opened the window and leaned out. 'Hey! What the fuck do you think you're doing?'

Jake reappeared next to him, bending down and grinning at them nastily. With one hand he dangled the tyre iron. The other he extended for the phone. Steve gave the hand a contemptuous look. 'I really don't think so.'

'Well,' Jake said, 'I do.'

He raised the tyre iron again, ready to bring it down on the car, but this time something stopped him. It had been a quick movement, like lightning. Steve had leaned back in the car and straightened himself enough for his jacket to fall briefly back from his stomach. It happened so fast that Sally thought she'd imagined it, but she hadn't. Jake had seen what was there too, and his face changed instantly. It was the butt of a gun, tucked in Steve's waistband.

Jake lowered the tyre iron and stood awkwardly, uncertain what to do. For a moment he was the same fidgety person she'd seen at David's. 'Yeah, well.' He glanced around, checking up and down the street who was watching, giving the kids in the stairwell a look that made them all turn away. He licked his lips and made a circling motion with his hand. 'OK, man. Let's just do it – just do it and put it to bed, eh?'

'Thank you,' Steve said. 'Thank you very much.' He closed the window again. 'You can turn the camera off, Sally, and count out the money.'

'W-what?'

'You heard.'

Shakily she switched off the phone, reached down to the bag at her feet and began counting the stacks of twenties. She kept trying to see into Steve's waistband, covered now by his jacket. 'Was that what I thought it was?' she murmured.

'It's decommissioned. Don't worry, I'm not going to shoot my nuts off.'

'I can't believe this.' She glanced up at Jake, who was standing a few feet away, arms folded, bouncing his head back and forth as if he was moving to music no one else could hear. 'I can't believe any of it.'

'Neither can I. Just count the money.'

She did, and passed it hurriedly to him.

'OK. Start filming again. When we leave, get a good shot of the jeep. The licence plate especially.'

She turned on the phone and scrunched back in the seat, holding it in front of her like a shield. Steve wound down the window. Jake came forward, glowering at him. He snatched the money and sauntered back to the jeep. He slammed his door and sat for a moment, lit by the interior light, bent over as he counted the blocks of cash. When he had finished, he didn't look at them, just reached up to switch off the light, started the jeep and roared away, narrowly missing taking their front bumper with him.

'Did you get his number?'

Sally nodded. She stopped the video and sank back in the seat, breathing hard. 'God,' she muttered. 'Is this the end of it now? Is this really the end?'

'Shit. I hope so.' Steve readjusted the mirror and started the engine. 'I really, really hope so.'

18

Captain Charlie Zhang was based temporarily in an old Victorian red-brick villa, set, incongruously, in a garrison to the east of Salisbury Plain. It might have been a military base, but when Zhang led her along the cool, carpeted corridors, Zoë decided the Military Police definitely had it better than the common-or-garden cops. There were fitted carpets and panelled walls, and the doors all closed with a reassuring *shush* as if they were on the *Starship Enterprise*.

Zhang's commanding officer was a cool-looking woman in late middle age, Lieutenant Colonel Teresa Watling – the army equivalent of a chief super-intendent and fairly heavy hitting in the grand scheme of things. With her blow-dried grey hair, the gold pendant over her black turtle-neck and her black reptile-skin heels, she looked like a Manhattan businesswoman. In fact, she explained to Zoë, as they went along the passageways, it was far more pedestrian than that. She had been born and brought up in the home counties.

'Cool.' Zoë swung the ID they'd issued her at the control gate. 'Can I ask you something?'

'Anything.'

'When I get tied to the chair, are you going to be the bad cop or the good cop?'

Lieutenant Colonel Watling ignored that. She stopped at a door and pushed it open. The room inside resembled a boardroom at an oil company, with a polished walnut table and twelve hand-carved teak chairs. There were water glasses and leather notepads at each place setting, so clearly the cutbacks that were axing thousands of backroom staff in the civilian police hadn't reached here yet. The three of them filed in. Zoë chose the seat at the head of the table, furthest from the door, and Captain Zhang sat next to her, his long, delicate hands folded one on top of the other. Six large files were placed down the centre of the table. It would have taken a long time to amass that lot, Zoë thought. A long time.

Lieutenant Colonel Watling opened a sleek black box and offered it to Zoë. At first she thought it was a humidor – it seemed somehow appropriate to light up a stogie in a place like this, kick back a little and watch the sky out of the window go indigo. She wasn't going to say no if that was the way the evening was going to work. Maybe a little snifter of Talisker on the side. But it wasn't cigars in the box: it was coffee capsules, in rainbow colours. She looked at the key and chose the strongest.

'Black, please. Two sugars.'

Watling began to make the coffee. Zoë watched

370

her, wondering how she'd got this job. It would be cool to wear Jimmy Choos to work, she thought. Maybe swap them now and again for combats and a quick, safe investigation at one of the bases in Iraq or Afghanistan. She'd heard they had a Piacetto café in Camp Bastion that did the best cakes. 'I know your boss,' Watling said. 'I worked with him on a couple of operations in Wiltshire.'

'Was he into psychological profiling in those days?'

'I'm sorry?'

'Nothing. He's a nice guy. What do you want to talk about?'

'Oh, just this and that.'

'This and that?'

Watling gave Zoë her coffee and lined up her own cup next to the leather writing pad. She sat down and clasped her elegant hands on the pad. 'Zoë,' she said. 'Do you remember those good old days when the Crime Squad and the Intelligence Service combined forces and SOCA came on line? How we were told it was going to revolutionize our lives? The right hand was at last going to know what the left hand was doing?'

'Did you believe it?'

She gave a cold laugh. 'I'm a post-menopausal woman who's lived in a man's world for twenty years. A more cynical, cruel creature it's hard to find. But it's true, I thought SOCA might help. I believed that at least other agencies would check it – make sure a target they were looking at didn't have a great big flag marked "SIB" waving over it. Why didn't

371

you *check* before you started leaving messages at Mr Mooney's office?'

'You're telling me Mooney's in trouble?'

'Yes.' Watling splayed her hand out to indicate the long line of folders. 'These represent almost two years of work – they're ready to go to the Service Prosecuting Authority, which is our version of the Crown Prosecution Service, and, believe me, just as anal about procedure and—'

'Hold on, hold on. Correct me if I'm wrong here, but Mooney – he's a big cheese, isn't he?'

'Extremely. Doesn't mean he can't be a naughty boy.'

Zoë stirred her coffee thoughtfully. She watched the sugar dissolve and waited for this new information to move itself into line. 'OK,' she said eventually. 'I get it now. I've stumbled into something and I apologize for that. I didn't check SOCA because it never occurred to me – I just pulled Mooney's name out of a hat, from Dodspeople, because he'd done some time in Kosovo. I thought he might give me some information, point me in the right direction. I'm working on a misper on my patch, a pornographer who had something a bit moody going on with someone connected to the UN in Priština. I followed my nose, came up with Mooney as a starting point.'

'Look,' Watling folded her arms, 'you know, of course, because it's unspoken conventional wisdom by now, that where the United Nations goes, human trafficking goes too. That it makes a kind of hole in the ground, and all the women in the region who aren't weighted down just roll into it.'

'Yup.'

'Well, that's what happened in Priština. The floodgates opened, the prostitutes poured in. Except this time the UN got smart and set up a unit to monitor it. The Trafficking and Prostitution Investigation Unit.'

'Yeah – I saw that. Mooney headed it up.'

'And, as it turned out, made a few inroads into the local population himself.'

'Inroads?'

'That's a euphemism. To make what he did sound less horrible, the way he abused his position.'

'Like?'

'Oh – no limits. Selling girls to the highest bidder, offering protection from criminal prosecution for sex, arranging abortions – some of the babies were his. The list is mind-boggling.'

'It's funny.' Zhang rubbed his head, perplexed. 'To meet the guy you'd think he was the kindest person on the planet.'

'OK,' Zoë said slowly. 'I'm getting the drift now. I'm going to take a stab in the dark and say I bet he persuaded them to do porn movies too.'

'Very good. *Very* good. You should charge for that.'

'Thank you. And for my second trick, he wasn't actually making the movies, was he? Doing the nuts-and-bolts lighting and camera work? He was just providing the flesh.'

373

'We don't know. We think so. It's one of the areas we haven't put a line under yet.'

'Well, let me help you put a line there. Let me make a guess and say that's how he links to my man Goldrab. Who probably, at a guess, *did* provide all the technical stuff. David Goldrab? Ring any bells? Gold-rab. British citizen, had a lucrative market in the nineties bringing porn in from Kosovo. It was cheaper to make it out there, of course.'

'Goldrab?' Zhang glanced up at Watling questioningly. 'Ma'am? Didn't that name come up somewhere?' He pulled a file towards him and shuffled through the papers. 'I'm sure I've seen it.'

Watling pulled one of the other files across. 'Was it in the . . . ? No. It was one of those payments, wasn't it? One of the companies.'

'Ding-dong.' Zhang shot a finger at her. 'That's it.' He put down the file and snatched up another, moving through the pages at lightning speed, muttering names under his breath. At last he came to a Companies House certificate. He pulled it out. 'There you go. DGE Enterprises. The director and company secretary? Mr David Goldrab. Registered address in London – but that's probably an accountant, or a solicitor maybe.'

'What sort of company is it? Purveyors of the finest-quality filth? By Appointment to Her Majesty Queen Elizabeth II?'

'Nope. Containers. Food containers to the catering industry. And in 2008 Dominic Mooney bought twenty thousand units of Kilner jam jars from DGE.'

374

Zoë raised an eyebrow. 'Now, that's a lot of jam. He must run a fruit farm.'

'From his city house in Finchley?'

The three of them looked at each other.

'So,' Zhang smiled, 'who's going to be the first to say it?'

'Bagsy me.' Zoë put her hand up. 'Blackmail. Years ago Goldrab was making porn in Kosovo and Mooney was supplying the girls – using the ones his unit was *supposed* to be protecting. The relationship breaks down and years later, long after they've been in Kosovo, it occurs to Goldrab that blackmailing an old friend is a legit way to turn a dime.'

'That's what Mooney's payments are – to his dodgy "catering" company.'

Zoë nodded. If Goldrab had been blackmailing Mooney he'd be a very happy person indeed for Goldrab to be dead. He could only win from a situation like that. She looked from Watling to Zhang and back again. 'What's Mooney like? I mean apart from what he did in Kosovo. Is he meaty in other arenas? What's he capable of? Is he capable of murder?'

Watling gave a dry laugh. '*Very* capable. It wouldn't be the first time. Not from what our investigations are showing – we're seeing links to at least two missing persons, here and in Kosovo.'

'And the name Lorne Wood hasn't cropped up, has it?'

Watling raised her eyebrows. 'No – I mean, I know the name. It's the murder you're dealing with in Bath,

375

isn't it? Surprisingly, at SIB we do take an interest in what the provincial police are doing, even if that interest isn't reciprocated. But Lorne hasn't featured with Mooney. Not at all. Why do you ask?'

'Where was he a week last Saturday? The seventh of May? The day Lorne died?'

'London.'

'You sure?'

'One hundred per cent. I can assure you he's got nothing to do with Lorne Wood's death.'

'But he is a killer.'

Watling sucked a breath in through her teeth. 'Let's get this straight – yes, he's a killer, but not that sort. If Mooney wants to off someone it'll be a cold, calculating business contract, not a sex killing. Lorne Wood? Never. Goldrab? Maybe. But he certainly wouldn't be getting his own hands dirty. He'd contract it out.'

'Contract it? Then there'd be a record of payment.' Zoë stood and leaned over Zhang to look at the file. 'Don't suppose you've got Mooney's bank statements there?'

He closed the folder, turned away slightly in his chair, crossing his leg and raising his shoulder protectively so she couldn't see it.

'There's nothing in there,' said Watling. Trust me. We'd know. If there had been a payment recently it wouldn't be paper-based – he'd use hard currency so there's no trace. My guess? He'd use Krugerrands – he had links to that RAF currency scam years ago, remember? The humble Kruger was a very hot ticket in those days.'

'What sort of person would he hire?'

'Usually ex-military. At the moment the market's flooded with ex-IRA boys – they'll drop someone for ten K. But it's not Mooney's style. They're loose cannons, too unreliable, too flappy with the old gums in the pub afterwards. He'd pay more and get someone he could trust.'

Zoë put her elbows on the table, her chin in her hands, and stared at the files, thinking about this. A hired gun. If Goldrab really had been offed by Mooney, and she could find out whom he had paid to do it, the whole thing might start to unravel. If there was a connection between Goldrab, Mooney and Lorne that SIB hadn't uncovered it would pop out in no time. If not, at the very worst she'd be sure Goldrab was really gone.

'And where is Mooney at the moment?'

'He's on holiday with his wife – soon to be his ex-wife when this thing breaks.'

'Anywhere I could go and visit him?'

Zhang snorted. 'Yeah – hang on a minute. I'll just write the address down.'

'What I mean,' Zoë said slowly, 'is how do we work it from here? Who backs off? Who scratches whose back? I mean, I've got primacy on Goldrab, which means I've got a right to investigate his connection to Mooney.'

'And we've got primacy on what Mooney did in Kosovo. And the bulk of the evidence.' Watling shook her head. 'Please – we've spent years on this, Zoë. Years. You can't calculate the man hours.

Everything's in place – just teetering like that.' She held up a hand and seesawed it, like a car on a clifftop. 'Mooney's arrest's scheduled for next week. But he's a flight risk – if he gets even a *whiff* of this there's any number of ways he can disappear out of the country. His secretary's already getting windy from your phone calls because you said the CID word, didn't you? Forgive me but you've already jeopardized the case. One more cock-up now and we're going to lose the whole thing. No.' She placed two hands on the desk. As if she'd made up her mind and it was all over. 'We'll take on Goldrab's disappearance, share our SPA disclosure files when it's all tied up. You get the results without the work. Goldrab can't be that important to you, can he?'

'Yes. He can.'

'Why?'

'For all the usual reasons,' she said sweetly. 'Like when I close the case and my superintendent hangs out the bunting for me. When every plain-clothed officer in Bath lines up and sings, "We love you, Zoë," as I walk through the briefing room. When bluebirds come in and tidy my desk every morning.'

'Any of the glory we can spare we'll pass on to you. You have my word. You'll get your bunting, Zoë. You will. Bluebirds and whatever.'

She nodded and smiled. If they were in the movies, the way Zhang said, this would be the point at which she'd argue, refuse to have the case wrested from her. Why did they always do it like that? she thought. What did people have against just nodding, making a promise, then getting the hell on with whatever they'd intended doing in the first place? In her experience it saved a lot of trouble.

She gave a long sigh and sat back in her chair, arms flopping open. 'OK. OK. But if there's going to be bunting, I get to choose the colour.'

19

It was late and Millie wanted to stay with the Sweetmans, have a sleepover with Sophie. Apparently they were friends again. Sally wouldn't have agreed after what had happened tonight, but maybe, she thought a little hopefully, Millie would spend time not just with Sophie but with Nial too. Get Peter Cyrus out of her head. And anyway, Steve insisted, Jake wasn't a problem now: Sally could relax, she could come to his place and they could get drunk, celebrate the end of the whole bloody awful affair. Secretly she was glad. It gave her a chance to escape the silences that seemed to be building in the fields surrounding Peppercorn Cottage.

They stayed up late drinking a sweet dessert wine Steve had found for ten euros a bottle in a supermarket in Bergerac. They had sex twice – once on the kitchen counter with their clothes still on, and once much later in bed, under the covers, when they were very drunk and Sally couldn't stop hiccuping or giggling. Things seemed almost normal on the surface. Even so, the last thing she did before she

went to sleep was open the windows so the un-
familiar city noises would come into the room and
get into her dreams – maybe stop Zoë, or David
Goldrab sitting up in the field and grabbing her arm.

She woke late, her head thick and heavy, to a
morning as hot as midsummer. She and Steve ate
breakfast on the terrace. They drank cranberry juice
and ate fresh raspberries. Today he was going to
America and she had thought she was ready for that,
but when, after breakfast, she came into the hallway
to find him dressed in a suit, luggage on the floor
next to him, she felt suddenly cold.

'What if something happens? What if I get
questioned again? I won't know what to say.'

'You won't get questioned again. It won't happen.'

'What happens if someone traces that money you
changed?'

'The Krugerrands? They won't. Trust me.' He
picked up his suitcase. 'It's going to be OK.'

Sally was subdued on the drive to the airport. The
Audi would need to be repaired so they took her car,
Steve driving, the window open, the radio on full
blast, as if he didn't have a worry in the world. She
sat hunched on the passenger seat, her handbag
clenched on her lap, staring out of the window at the
Bristol suburbs, at the sunshine in sharp, blocky
shapes on the dingy houses. She wondered whether
Zoë sometimes came to Bristol. Of course she must –
all the time. She'd been all around the world. Zoë's
face as she had stood at the table came back to Sally
then, saying, 'I apologize.' She tried to imagine the

image being taken away from her, pulled like a grey thread out of her head, out of the car window, whipped away by the slipstream, like a twisting ghost.

She and Steve didn't speak much as they parked, made their way out of the sunshine into the terminal, through Check-in and up the escalator. They were already calling his flight, so he went straight to Security. It was after she'd kissed him goodbye and was walking away, her head down, that he stopped her.

'Sally?'

She came to a halt, ten feet away, and turned. He was standing in the security line, facing her, the other passengers streaming past him. He wore an odd expression. He was rubbing his fingers together, studying them curiously. 'What? What is it?'

He was frowning. He opened his hand to show her. 'Lipstick?'

She walked back to him and together they looked at the lipstick on his fingers. A sort of orangey-red. 'Where did that come from?'

'I don't know. Just from when I kissed you . . .' He put his hand on her shoulder and rotated her away from him, looking at her back. 'It's on your dress. Look.'

Sally craned around, pulling the seat of the dress out to inspect. He was right – the back of her dress was covered with lipstick. A very distinct orange-red colour.

'Did you brush up against something?'

'I don't think so.' She strained to see it. 'There's lots of it.'

'You have – you've leaned up against something. Here.' Steve pulled out a folded handkerchief, made to rub at the cloth.

'It's OK. Don't.' She took it from him, let go of her dress and put the handkerchief back in his top pocket. 'Don't worry, I'll sort it out. You'll be late.' She kissed his cheek and gave him a gentle push towards the security checkpoint. 'Go on.'

He took one last look at her dress. 'You sure?'

'Of course. Safe journey. Call me when you get there.'

20

Dominic Mooney's *Who's Who* entry hadn't been updated since his return from Kosovo. It read:

*Born: Hong Kong, 20 Sept. 1955; s of Paul and
Jean Mooney; m 1990, Paulette Frampton; one s
Education: Kings, Canterbury; Edinburgh Univ,
BA Hons; RMA Sandhurst
Career: Military service 1976–1988, UK, Belize and
Northern Ireland (1979–80). Civil service
1986–present: 1986–99 Defence Procurement
Agency; 1999–2001 Civil Secretariat, Kosovo;
2001–2004 TPIU Priština
Address: 3 Rightstock Gardens, Finchley, London
N3*

Zoë knew that on the second line 'one s' meant that
Mooney had one son – who was probably a teenager
and too old to go on holiday with his parents. It took
her no time to find him online. She started after the
morning meeting, searched Mooney/Kosovo and
found him within ten minutes: Jason Mooney. He

had posted just about his entire life story online, including the time his dad had spent in Kosovo. (No mention of the women and the aborted half-brothers and sisters.) He was a nice-looking boy, suntanned in the way happy students always seemed to be in their Facebook pictures. He liked swimming, and Punk, a club in Soho Street, and thought Pixie Lott was about the hottest woman on the planet. He had tattoos in Hindi on his left ankle, still wore a friendship bracelet his best mate had given him when he was twelve and was a fresher at City University, studying aeronautical engineering. His shoot-for-the-stars ambition was to work on a privately financed team sending a probe into outer space. But his number one love, his truly, truly highest devotion, the thing that would take his soul with it if he ever lost it, was his hog: a 71 FX Harley Super Glide. He was pictured with it, standing on a sunlit country lane, looking so happy his heart could burst. The photo had a soft focus to it, as if it was a picture of newly weds. The moment Zoë saw it a bright clean path opened up in front of her. So clear it almost seemed to have beacons at either side of it.

Watling had said there was no one in the wide world as cynical as she was. But she'd been wrong. Zoë beat the shit out of her for cynicism. She knew that the polite goodbye handshake of Watling and Zhang would be the last she'd ever hear from 'the Feds'. There wasn't going to be any bunting coming from the commanding officer's desk on Salisbury Plain. She didn't want to rattle the case for them, but she was still going to get what she needed from it.

Bring me the head of David Goldrab, she thought, snatching up her helmet, balaclava, credit cards and keys. She trotted down the stairs. No Zhang standing like a giant irritable spider in the car park today. She climbed on to the Shovelhead, opened up the choke and pressed the starter. She'd be in London by midday.

It was a sunny day – great riding weather. The M4 was clear, only one hold-up outside Swindon that she shimmied her way through. She got plenty of glances from men in their cars, the sun glinting off her Oakley dirt goggles like she was in some seventies road movie, the opening guitar riff from a Steppenwolf track looping through her head as she drove. The Mooneys lived in Finchley, north London, near the North Circular, where the packed terraces of the inner city began to give way to lawns and drive-ways and garages, lots of yew hedges and leylandii. She found the road easily – the sort of place you had to take only one step into to know you'd walked into Moneyville. High walls, electronic gates and security systems dozed in the sun. It wasn't that far from Bishop's Avenue, after all, where the zillionaires lived.

The numbers at this end were high, so the Mooneys' would be at the other. She swung the Shovelhead into a U-turn and nosed it out of the street back on to the North Circular. Took a right then another right until she came to the other end of the street, found a place to pull over. She put down the kickstand, pulled out the key, and walked back a few yards, taking off her helmet. From the cover of a curved brick wall she could peer down the road to the houses. The Mooneys' was the big fifties detached thing, with spike-topped walls and a brick driveway, the borders planted with kerria, its egg-yolk-yellow blossom balls motionless in the sun. No civil servant should live in a place like that – even the ones who made more than the Prime Minister.

She weighed up her options. There were no cars on the driveway, the doors were closed on the double garage and the gates were closed too. One of the windows on the first floor stood open. Just a crack. She inched forward a little, out of the din of the traffic on the main road, and concentrated on that open window. The Steppenwolf guitar was still grinding in her head, but there was something else. She was sure of it. Something frenetic pounding out of the house. A woman's voice, rapping out South-London-gone-Hollywood R&B. The sort of thing those who really lived on those streets shrank from, and only rich suburban white kids thought was radical. Zoë gave the open window a small ironic smile. Jason. It had to be. Sometimes things were just too damned easy.

She sauntered back to the bike, pulling on her helmet, bounced it off its kickstand and pulled the Leatherman knife she carried everywhere out of her jacket pocket. She bent over, reached into the space above the cylinder head and gave one of the ceramic spark-plug insulators a sharp tap. It cracked instantly. She got back on the Shovelhead, started the engine and headed into the avenue, the bike's full-throated roar bouncing off the houses beyond their big front gardens. About fifty yards up, the roar became a cough, then a stuttering choke. It died to nothing and the bike freewheeled to a stop about ten yards past the Mooneys' driveway. She climbed off it, removed her helmet, shook out her hair, opened the saddlebag and began pulling out tools. A set of pipe grips – completely the wrong thing for the job. She got down on the pavement, lay on her side and began struggling to get the grips around the insulator.

She didn't hear Jason approaching. The first she knew of it was when his feet appeared about a yard away: tanned, in a pair of battered Ripcurl sandals, their braiding bleached to shreds by sun and sand. She looked at them for a few seconds. Then she pushed herself away from the bike and rolled herself up to a sitting position, her feet in the gutter.

'I'm sorry. Hope I'm not inconveniencing anyone. I should be out of your way in less than ten.'

'It's misfiring. I can tell just by the sound.' Jason looked thinner than he did on his Facebook pictures. And the photos he'd chosen had made his lower jaw look squarer than it was in real life. But his face was open, his eyes wide-spaced and pale blue. No trace of malice or slyness in them. He was wearing a T-shirt with the logo 'Oh Christ. You're going to try and cheer me up. Aren't you?' 'I heard you coming down the street. I closed my eyes and I thought, It's an FXE Superglide Shovelhead, isn't it? An '80. I was wrong about the year, but I got the make and model.' Jason

388

shook his head. He looked awestruck. 'And of all the houses you could have broken down in front of – I mean, I'm a *total* hog *insect*. You couldn't have planned it any better. Have you looked at the plugs?'

'It's what I'm doing now. I could have had it sorted in a couple of seconds if I had a plug socket. Have to make do with these.' She held up the grips.

'Jesus. You've got to see my workshop. It's got everything. Come on, come on.'

She hesitated. Looked around the avenue. 'You sure?'

'Of course. Come on. I swear this is pure karma at work.'

Together, they wheeled the Shovelhead into the driveway, the cast-iron gates sliding closed behind them. There was the sound of a water feature coming from somewhere at the side of the house. 'Great place,' Zoë said, as Jason opened the garage door. 'Someone's doing very nicely.'

'My parents. They're away. It's just me and the tortoises. Have you ever tried to have a conversation with a tortoise? Trust me, they don't know their hogs.'

'I don't know many people who know their hogs. Not the way you do.'

That pleased him. He gave a broad smile and held out his hand. 'I'm Jason.'

'Evie.' She shook it. 'It's nice to meet another hog freak. You total nerd.'

He grinned and pointed a finger at himself. 'Remember this face. Technical genius. One day I'm going to land a probe on Mars. You see if I don't.'

Inside the garage there was a red four-by-four and the Harley. He spent some time showing it to her, letting her run her fingers over a welding job he'd done himself to see just how 'awesomely smooth' it was. Then he went to his workbench at the back of the garage and scanned the tools mounted on the wall, murmuring under his breath until he came to the item he wanted. 'A magnetic one for this, I think,' he said, selecting a plug socket. He knelt down on the cool garage floor next to the bike. While he tinkered Zoë unzipped her jacket and made a show of wandering along the workbench, pretending to study the labels and the mountings. With her back turned to him she slipped the pipe grips from out of her T-shirt, crouched and left them on the floor. She might need to come back. Then she leaned against the bench, arms folded, head tilted back. From here she could see through the door that led into the house. It was slightly ajar. Beyond it there were glimpses of Dominic Mooney's life – a pale-blue carpet, a polished mahogany hall table, artificial arum lilies in a vase. Jason must have turned the hip-hop off, because the place was quiet, just the sound of a grandfather clock ticking somewhere.

'It won't take long. The insulation's cracked.'

'Is it? Good job you were here, eh?' She nodded into the house. 'I don't suppose I could . . . uh?' She held out her hands to show how grimy they were. 'I've been in the saddle all day and I'd love to just wash my hands.'

'First on the left.' He didn't look up. 'Use the towel on the metal ring and not the folded ones, the ones with the lace and shit. Those are for guests. Mum'll castrate me if they get used.'

Zoë sauntered into the house, the zips on her jacket jingling. She went into the cloakroom and splashed her face. There were nice toiletries – good stuff, like Champney's handwash and an Italian moisturizer in a stone bottle with gold script on it. She took the towel off the ring and wandered into the hallway, drying her hands. The noises of Jason tinkering came from the garage. He was totally absorbed, so she quickly put her head round all of the doors leading from the hall. The living room was huge, carpeted with something patterned and furnished like a hotel, with ornately upholstered sofas. The fitted mahogany shelves were crammed with books and photo albums. French windows led on to a large, walled garden, filled with sunshine. Leaning against the windows was a tennis racket and a tube of balls. Funny, she thought, eyeing them. She'd never really given much thought to how many people had tennis balls knocking around their house.

She went to the kitchen doorway and gave that a quick scan: country-style with wooden units, dried hops draped across the pelmets, utensils in a rustic terracotta jug. A gingham tea-towel. It didn't seem like the house of a person who'd kill someone or pay someone else to do it. Even so, there was something, just something, about this place that said Mooney could easily be responsible for David

Goldrab's microwave dinner going hard back in Bath.

In the garage the engine came to life. Jason gave a little yelp of victory. Zoë came back into the doorway, still drying her hands. He was standing next to the bike, grinning all over his face, turning the throttle, making the engine roar. 'Told you, didn't I?' he shouted, over the noise. 'Remember this face. Remember me!'

She put the towel down on the workbench and came over to the bike, shaking her head admiringly. 'Great,' she yelled. 'Do I owe you anything?'

'A ride? That is—' Remembering his manners, he stopped revving and let his face go sober. 'A ride? If you don't mind.'

'You want to drive my Shovelhead?'

'No – I mean, not if it's a problem. Really. Forget I asked.'

'No, no – I mean, it's . . .' She nibbled her lip. Pretended to be struggling with this. Then, at length she said, 'It's fine. Are you insured?'

'I'll only take it up the road and back. I won't take it out of the street.'

'OK. I s'pose it's the least I can do. But take care of her, eh?'

'I will.'

Jason ran inside and came hurrying back out with a black Shoei open-face helmet. He kicked off his sandals and zipped boots on to his bare feet. He looked faintly insane in his T-shirt and the beetle headgear as he clambered on to the bike. He wobbled a bit coming out of the gates, then got into his stride. He turned out on to the street in second and was gone. She could hear the blast of the engine coming over the hedges and gardens as he sped up the road. She turned and went quickly back into the house.

The bookshelves in the living room didn't contain anything special. A few photos of the family, the Mooneys on their wedding day, Jason as a baby, a tall thin girl in a bridesmaid's dress. The books were mostly non-fiction, on domestic policy and languages – Spanish, Russian, Arabic. Nothing that looked like business files. She went into the hallway and opened all the other doors. A utility room, a studio with half-finished pottery dotted around, a dining room with the curtains closed to stop the sun fading the furniture. And a room that was locked.

She rattled the door. She ran her fingers over the frame, feeling for a key. Checked in the bowl on the hallstand, picking up car keys on a springy spiral rubber ring, a gas-meter key, some petrol receipts. No key.

She went back through the garage, across the driveway and through the wooden side gate. Here, the houses stood quite close to each other, and the side access was in shadow. On this wall there were only two windows in the Mooneys' house, one frosted, with the overflow from the toilet below it, the second the window into the locked room. She put her hand against it and peered inside. She could make out a big mahogany leather-topped desk with a green banker's lamp on it, a leather armchair and a footstool. On the shelves beyond the desk she could plainly see the box files lined up. 'Kosovo', one said, 'Priština' another. Maybe some record of whom he'd paid. And how. She drummed her fingers on the glass. She could smash the window now, be in and out in no time.

The noise of the bike coming back echoed down into the gap between the buildings, and she stepped back from the window, her hands itching to just do it. But the bike was getting louder and louder and at the last second she changed her mind. She went back to the gate leading to the driveway and found it had become stuck. She yanked at it, rattled the handle, but it wouldn't budge. The bike was nearer now. She glanced over her shoulder at the back garden. It'd take too long to go that way. She gave the gate one last tug. This time it opened, and she stepped outside, just in time for Jason to sweep into the driveway.

He stopped the bike, took off his helmet and looked at her curiously.

'Hi.' She patted the bike's handlebars. 'You enjoy her? You not enjoy?'

His eyes went from her to the side door. 'You OK?'

'Eh?' She glanced over her shoulder. 'Yeah. I was looking for a hosepipe. Wanted to give her a wash-down.'

'A wash-down? She doesn't look like she needs one.'

'I think she does.'

'There's a hosepipe there.' He gestured at the tap mounted on the front of the house, the hose carefully wound away on a green and yellow reel. 'Didn't you notice that before you went round the back?'

'No.'

Jason scratched his head thoughtfully, wrinkled his mouth. Then he swung his leg off the bike and looped his helmet around his wrist – the way she'd seen bikers loop helmets when they were getting ready to swing them as a weapon.

'Jason?'

'Who are you?'

'Who *am* I? I told you. I'm Evie.'

'Well, Evie, you'll regret it if you've taken anything out of the house. I've got your number-plate. And you have no idea how tenacious my father is when it comes to things like that.'

'I'm sure he is.'

'You really don't want to mess with my father.'

'I'm not messing with anyone.' She held up her hands. 'I'm going.'

She walked past him, half expecting to hear the whistle of his helmet cracking down on her head, he'd changed so quickly. Respect to you, Jason. You're not the pushover I thought. She scooped up her own helmet from the driveway, Jason shadowing her, arms folded, watching her zip her jacket, swing her leg over the Shovelhead.

'I left the towel on the workbench.' She revved the engine, held up a hand and flashed him a smile. 'You might want to hang it up, keep Mum happy, eh? See you around, Jason. Nice knowing you.'

21

In the Ladies at Bristol airport Sally stood with her back to the mirror, holding her dress out to study the lipstick. In the reflection she could make out what she thought were letters, as if she had leaned on something. A display or some graffiti. But where? Most were smudged and indecipherable, but she was sure she could make out 'AW'. And maybe 'G'.

She went into one of the cubicles, took off her dress and tried to clean it with a packet of wet wipes she had in her bag. But the lipstick wouldn't come off. It just smudged further into the fabric, and in the end she had to put it back on, take off her sweater and wrap it round her waist so that it hung down and covered the lipstick. She went back to the car park, goosebumps coming up on her arms in spite of the sun. She threw her handbag on the back seat of the Ka and was about to get into the driver's seat, when something occurred to her. Steve had driven here – she'd been in the passenger seat. She slammed the door and went round to the other side of the car, opened the door and dropped to a crouch, carefully touching the upholstery. Her finger came away red. She looked at it for a long time. Then, hurriedly, she pulled some more wipes out of the handbag and placed them so they were spread across the seat. She leaned a small amount of weight on to them with her hands, and counted in her head up to a hundred. She could hear other people, trundling their suitcases across the car park behind her. Could hear the pause in their steps as they stopped to look at her crouched in the opened door.

She turned over the wipes and studied them. For this to have been imprinted on her dress it must have been there since she'd got into the car. It had been parked overnight at Steve's, on his driveway. She tried to recall if she'd locked it. She never did at Peppercorn, so maybe she hadn't last night. Maybe kids had got into it.

She spread out the wipes and moved them around until they fitted together. The letters were blurred, some of them missing, and the ones she could work out were in reverse. She found a 'Y', then a 'G' and then a 'W'. She saw 'ITCH', the letters in sequence, and, quite clearly, 'EVIL'. Another 'Y' and 'ITH', then the whole thing tumbled suddenly into place.

You won't get away with it. You evil bitch.

Trembling she shot to her feet, almost banging her head against the car roof. She spun round, as if someone might be standing behind her, watching. All she could see for hundreds of yards in every direction were cars, the heads of one or two travellers moving among them. She slammed the door and started off towards the terminal at a trot. Then, realizing Steve had already gone through into Departures, she raced back to the car and fumbled her phone out of the bag, dropping things in her haste. She dialled his number, her fingers like jelly. There was a pause, then an electronic hum, and the phone connected to his voicemail.

'This is Steve. If you'd like to leave a message I'll . . .'

She cancelled the call and stood in the glaring sunshine, her hands on the roof of the car, breathing hard, the truth coming down on her like a cloud.

Someone, somehow, knew exactly what she and Steve had done to David Goldrab.

22

The motel was one of those places with sealed windows to stop the traffic noise, squeezy soap mounted on the walls and vending machines in the foyer. Signs everywhere guaranteed your money back if you didn't get a good night's sleep. It was ten miles outside London on the M4, and the moment Zoë saw it she pulled off the motorway and booked a room. She didn't intend to sleep there – all she needed was a place to lie down for a couple of hours and think – but she dutifully carried her helmet and few belongings in, and asked the receptionist for a toothbrush in a plastic wrap.

In the room she opened the window a crack, took off her boots and lay on her back, legs crossed. She draped her bike balaclava over her eyes, crossed her hands over her chest and began shuffling her thoughts around, trying to make them sit down in a proper straight line so she could decide what to do next. Whether to keep champing at the Mooney bit or call it a day and head back to Bath. What would it mean to her if she saw Goldrab dead, and all the things he knew

399

about her past locked away? Did she think that now she'd apologized to Sally it was going to make her *clean* suddenly? Clean like Debbie Harry? The sort of clean Ben would like? She had the idea that uncleanness was a state of mind, which, once installed, never went away. Like Lady Macbeth's spot of blood.

She took long, calming breaths. Began working it all out. But the travel and the last few sleepless nights got the better of her. Within five minutes she was asleep.

She dreamed of the room again, the nursery with the snow falling outside. Except this time she was on the floor, feeling very small and very scared and, terrifyingly, Sally was standing above her. She was holding the broken hand over Zoë. It was wrecked, with bones sticking out at all angles, and the blood dripped out of it, rolling in fat plops on to Zoë's face.

She pushed her legs out, scrambling away from Sally, flipping herself over and stumbling for the door. Sally followed close behind, her hand raised. 'No!' she was crying. 'Don't go – don't go!'

But Zoë was out of the door, tumbling down the stairs, breaking into a run, pelting through the streets. It was Bristol, she realized. St Paul's. Ahead she saw a doorway, a red light coming from it, a hand beckoning her. *Hurry up*, someone yelled. *Hurry up! This is the way through. In here!* And then, suddenly, she was standing on a stage, an audience looking expectantly up at her. In the front row were her parents, her first-form teacher and the super-intendent. *Do something*, shouted the superintendant. *Do something good*. The lighting man frowned from the box at her, and at the back the maintenance man leaned on his broom, grinning up at her. *Get on with it*, someone yelled. *Do something good*. Someone was pushing her from behind. When she turned she saw David Goldrab, as a young man, London Tarn.

Zoë, he said. *Lovely to see you again, Zoë!*

She woke in the hotel room, her hands clutching the sides of the bed, her eyes wide. Her head was aching. She breathed in and out, in and out, staring at the headlights racing to and fro across the wall. After a while she rolled over. The display on the bed-side table said 11:09. She groped for her phone – the signal was strong, but no one in that time had tried to call her or text. She wondered who she'd been hoping for. Ben? It was eleven o'clock. He and Debbie would be in bed, maybe sharing a nightcap or cocoa. Or something else.

Debbie. Clean, clean, clean.

She put the phone into her pocket, swung her legs off the bed, went into the bathroom and splashed cold water on her face. Then she straightened and considered her reflection. 'Damn it,' she hissed. 'Damn it and fuck it to all hell.'

She knew what she was going to do. She was going to go back to Mooney's.

401

23

'Millie, go to bed.' A hundred miles to the west, Sally sat at the kitchen table in Peppercorn Cottage, watching her daughter rummage in the fridge for a late-night snack. 'You've got school in the morning. Go on. It's late.'

'Jesus.' She gave her mother a disdainful look. 'What's the matter with you? You're *so* messing with my head.'

'I'm only asking you to go to bed.'

'But you're acting totally weird.' She turned from the fridge with a carton of milk and gave the wine glass next to Sally's elbow an accusatory nod. 'And you've drunk tons. I mean *tons*.'

Sally put a hand protectively over the glass. It was true: she'd drunk the whole bottle and it hadn't changed a thing. Not a thing. Her head was still hard and taut, her heart racing. 'Just pour a glass of milk,' she said, in a controlled voice, 'and take it to bed.'

'And how come all the doors are locked? It's like being in a prison. I mean, it's not like he's going to find us all the way out here, for Christ's sake.'

'What did you say?'

'He doesn't know where I live.'

'*Who* doesn't know where you live?'

Millie blinked, as if she wasn't quite sure whether she'd heard Sally right. 'Jake, of course. You've paid him now. He'll leave me alone.'

Sally didn't answer. The muscles under her ribs were aching, she'd been so scared all day. It was an effort to hold the panic locked inside. After a while she pushed the chair back and went to the pantry for another bottle of Steve's wine. 'Just pour the milk. Take it to your room. And leave the windows closed. It's going to rain tonight.'

Millie banged around the kitchen, getting a glass, pouring the milk. She slammed the carton down on the worktop and disappeared. Sally stood motionless in the pantry, listening to her clump off down the corridor, and slam her bedroom door. She took a breath, rested her head against the wall, and counted to ten.

It was nearly nine hours since Steve's plane had taken off in Bristol. Nine hours and it seemed like nine years. Nine centuries. Wearily, she pushed herself away from the door, uncorked the wine, carried it to the table and filled her glass. She sat down and checked the display on her mobile. Nothing. He'd be landing in fifty minutes. She'd left several messages on his voicemail. If he switched on his phone before he got into Immigration he'd get them all within the hour. He'd know something was wrong. She raised her eyes to the window, the lighted kitchen reflected in the dark panes. All the surfaces and cupboards and her own face, white as a moon, in the middle of it. Earlier, after picking up Millie from school, she'd gone round the house and locked all the doors and windows, closed all the curtains. But then the idea that someone could be standing unseen outside one of the windows had crept into her head and eventually she'd thrown the curtains open again. When it came to the choice of being watched or not being able to see what was happening outside, she'd chosen being watched.

Watched . . .

She'd been sure, so sure, that night that no one could be watching her and Steve in the garden. So how could it be? How *could* it be? What had she overlooked?

She pulled the laptop towards her and opened Google. When Google Earth had first come out she and Millie used to spend hours looking at it – zooming in on friends' houses, going into street view and taking virtual walks down streets they knew. Streets they didn't know. Streets they might never visit. Now she zoomed it in on Peppercorn. The familiar double-pitched roof of the garage, the grey gables – three at back and front – the stone chimney and the thatch. The photo had been taken in midsummer and the trees were as fluffy and fat as dandelion clocks, casting short, puffy shadows on the lawn. She traced her finger across the screen in a huge circle around the cottage. There was nothing, no overlooking buildings. She zoomed the image out and still there was nothing. Just the familiar planting lines through the crops in the neighbouring fields.

She pushed the computer away and sat for a while, a finger on her lips, thinking. She got up, switched off the light and went to stand at the window. There was nothing out there. No movement or change. Only the distant twinkle of cars on the motorway and the faint grey of the moon behind the clouds. She took off her shoes and padded silently down the corridor, into Millie's room. She was asleep in bed, her breath coming evenly in and out, so she went back to the hallway, put on her wellingtons and a duffel coat and found the big, high-powered torch that Steve had insisted on buying her from Maplins, because he said it was craziness her being out in the middle of nowhere when there were power cuts all the time. Steve. God, she wished he was here now.

Silently she let herself out of the back door. It was cool – very cool, almost cold after the unseasonable heat of the day. She stood for a moment looking around at the familiar surroundings, the great line of silver birch on the north perimeter, the patch of wood to the east, the top garden where a kiwi tree grew, its fruit hard and bitter. Her car was parked at the place she and Steve had stood six nights ago, shaking and sick with what they had done.

She locked the door behind her and went to the car. She stood with her back to it and slowly, slowly, scanned the horizon. Nothing. She moved around the car and did the same on the other side. There was nothing there. No building or place someone could have stood and watched. She crossed the lawn to the flowerbed where she'd made the bonfire yesterday. The earth was still grey and luminous with the ash and she could smell the faintest trace of carbonized wood in the air. She hefted up the huge torch, switched it on and aimed the beam into the trees. She'd never used the light before and it was so powerful she could make out details hundreds of yards away. If it found glass, a window-pane she'd overlooked, it would flash back at her. She swept the torch across the fields, going in a wide circle up the side of the cottage, the garage, bumping over the hedgerows. She could see individual leaves and branches in the forest, the trees bending and whispering. In the copse at the top of the property the beam glanced across twin green spots. Eyes looking at her steadily. She came to a halt, her heart thudding. The eyes moved slightly, ducked a little, turned. It was just a deer, startled in the middle of grazing.

Sally let out all her breath and lowered the torch. There was nothing – no building, no concealed layby or bird hide or tree-house or farm building. Nowhere someone could have hidden to watch what they'd done. And then something occurred to her. Something that should have been clear all along if she'd only been thinking straight. The car. Whoever had sent the message had chosen to put it in the car when it was parked at Steve's. What did that mean? Why hadn't they come to Peppercorn? Why go to the trouble of following her to Steve's if . . .

Of course. She switched off the torch, went fast

across the lawn to the cottage. Unlocked the front door and, without taking off her wellingtons or switching on the lights, went into the kitchen and opened the laptop. The screen came to life – all the thick midsummer fields green and vibrant with light. She zoomed out, clawed the image to the left, moving north, pausing when she came to the faint, blurred line of the Caterpillar opposite Hanging Hill.

'There,' she breathed, sinking into her chair. 'There.'

The photograph had been taken in, she guessed, late June. A pinkish floating haze of poppies hung over the fields. Among them, Lightpil House – a huge yellow slash on the green, its fountains and terraces reflecting the sun. To its north the almost triangular wedge of the parking space where David Goldrab had died. To its south, near the perimeter, half hidden by towering poplars, the roof of a cottage.

Whoever had left the note knew nothing about Peppercorn Cottage: they'd seen her at David's. She'd thought they couldn't be overlooked where the killing happened, but she hadn't thought about the gardens of the houses at the top of Lightpil Lane. The bottom of the land attached to the cottage on the screen stretched along the northern wall of Lightpil House and came out at the bottom in a spoon shape, bordered by a low hedge. If someone had been standing there at the right time, if they had looked across the dip in the land . . .

The phone rang in her pocket, making her jump. She snatched it out with trembling hands.

'Steve. *Steve?*'

'Christ, Sally, what the hell's going on?'

'It's all gone wrong. I told you it would go wrong and it has.'

'OK, OK, calm down. Now, first of all, we're speaking on an international line. You know what I mean by that – can you hear it humming?'

She took deep breaths, still staring at the cottage roof. 'Yes,' she said shakily, thinking of those vast domed listening stations. And Cheltenham GCHQ not far from here. Did phone calls really get monitored? Maybe in Steve's job they did. 'I think I know what you mean.'

'Explain, carefully, what's happened.'

She licked her lips. 'I got a message when I got back into the car. The lipstick I leaned on – it was a message. It said—' She swallowed. 'It said I wouldn't get away with it.'

There was a long silence at the end of the line as Steve digested this. 'Right,' he said, sounding as if he wasn't just thousands of miles away but millions. In a different galaxy. 'Right.'

'But if anyone has . . . you know, witnessed anything, it wasn't here at Pepp— at my place, so I don't think they know where I am. It must have been at the . . .' She hesitated. 'The first place. I think they must have seen my car – and then they saw it outside your place and planted the message. I've looked at Google Earth and I think I know where they were standing . . .'

'OK. I'm coming straight back. I'm not even going

408

to leave the airport – I'll just turn right around and get the first flight back. OK?'

'No,' she said. 'No. You can't.'

'I can.'

'Yes. But I don't want you to.'

'Don't be ridiculous.'

'I mean it. I'm going to be OK.'

'Well, I don't care what you say, I'm coming back.'

'No.' This time her voice was so firm Steve went silent. 'I really, really have to do this on my own. And, Steve, please don't ask again.'

24

The air was colder now that it was past midnight, and the roads were almost empty. Gliding into London on the overpasses to the west was like a magic-carpet ride over an enchanted city. All the buildings were lit up like palaces. The Ark on Zoë's right, bulging out over the road, the blue-tiled onion dome of a mosque on her left. She had to get into a single-lane queue for a while to go past a traffic stop in Paddington, with two police cars pulled over, their lights flashing, but apart from that nothing delayed her and she sailed on to Finchley.

She stopped the bike, cut the engine and stood on tiptoe next to the brick wall at the end of the road. The Mooneys' house blazed with light. Every window seemed to be open, voices and music floating out through the night. The music was so loud she imagined she could feel it in her feet. On the drive-way someone was revving a motorbike engine. She was surprised the cops weren't there because the neighbours couldn't be putting up with this, but when she looked around at the silent houses, one or two with coach lamps on, the gates all locked, it occurred to her that people didn't *live* there. It was one of those streets where the owners lived in Dubai or Hong Kong and only kept a London residence to impress business colleagues. It could be that the Mooneys' was the only occupied house in the street. No wonder Jason was having a party.

Cautiously she got on the bike again and started it. She drove slowly down the road, keeping her face forward, her eyes left. The gates to the Mooneys' house stood open and seven large West Coast choppers were parked on the brick driveway. Behind them in the garage, lit like a tableau in a nativity scene, two men in sleeveless T-shirts stood drinking beer from cans and examining Jason's Harley. They didn't stop talking as she went by but one of the men lifted his head and followed her progress until she was out of sight.

She got a hundred yards down the road and swung the Shovelhead into a U-turn, came back to the house and let it cruise into the driveway alongside all the choppers. She parked near the hosepipe, hooked up to the front wall as obvious as could be, then swung her leg off and wandered into the garage, tugging at her helmet.

'All right?' said the bigger of the T-shirts. 'OK there?'

'Guess.' She ran her fingers wearily through her hair and walked past them. They didn't stop her, so she continued on through the door she'd gone through earlier and into the house. Everything inside

411

was different. Dominic Mooney's lifestyle was being systematically trashed. Every piece of furniture was draped with bike leathers and helmets. The kitchen was full of people drinking beer; girls, with barbed-wire tats on their arms and stilettos under their skinny jeans, were perched on the counters. Someone else was using one of Mrs Mooney's wooden spoons to beat out an imaginary drum track. Zoë wandered around, peering into rooms, counting the nose rings and the forehead studs and the number of feet in oily boots resting on the Mooneys' nice sofas. Her parents hadn't thrown a single party for her – not after what she'd done to Sally. Certainly they'd never have trusted her alone in the house while they were away.

Jason she found in a bathroom on the first floor, lying fully dressed in the bath with a tin of Gaymer's in one hand and an iPhone in the other, his head lolling on his shoulder, his mouth open. He was completely wasted.

'Hello, Jason.'

His eyes flew open. He shot forward in the bath, splashing cider everywhere. When he saw who it was he gathered himself, made a vague attempt to wipe the cider away. Pushed his hair off his face. 'Hello,' he said, in a wavering voice. 'Why did you come back?'

'I had to. I dropped the pipe grips in the garage.'

'I know. I found them.'

'Didn't know if I'd be welcome.'

He looked at her as if she perplexed him. 'What did you want? What were you doing, sneaking around our back garden?'

412

'I needed a pee, Jason. That was why I was round the back. And I'm sorry.'

'OK, OK,' he muttered, his mouth moving as if he was testing this excuse. Too pissed, though, to realize she could have just used the loo in the house, where she'd washed her hands. He shrugged. 'Yeah – well, that's cool, I s'pose.'

'But, Jason, peeing on your mum's roses kind of pales into insignificance when you look at the people down there drinking beer in your kitchen.'

Jason stared up at her. 'What are they doing? I told them a couple of beers and then it was goodbye.'

'A couple of beers . . . Jason? Do you know how many people are down there?'

'Five?'

'Five? Try fifty.'

'Are you serious?'

'Serious? Uh, ye-*es*. I mean serious to the point of you'd better think hard about halls of residence and getting a job to make it through your smarty-pants science degree. Because I don't know any mummy and daddy sainted enough to ignore this mess. Have you looked downstairs? Seen the cigarette burns on the carpet?'

'Burns? *Shit*.' He scrambled out of the bath. 'Did they get the guest towels?'

'The guest towels are the least of your worries. It's like happy hour at Wetherspoon's.'

Jason stood for a moment, his legs in their skinny jeans doing a little panicked dance. He was drenched with cider. 'Is it that bad?' He put his hands up to his face, gave her a look like that Munch painting you saw everywhere. *The Scream.* Horrified. Truly horrified. 'What am I going to do? I didn't ask them. I didn't.'

'Do you want me to scatter them? Make them run away in twenty different directions?'

'Can you?'

She shrugged. 'Only if you want me to.'

'Can I stay here? Can I put the lock on the door and stay here?'

'If you want.'

'Then yes. Do it.'

Zoë hoisted up her trousers, tightened the belt a notch and felt in her pocket for her warrant card. 'Are you ready to close the door?'

'I'm ready.'

'Then here goes.'

God knew, Zoë had cleared enough rooms in her life, and on a scale of one to ten the bikers rated pretty low. They didn't exactly scatter to the four winds, hands over their faces in shame, but at least they didn't jump up and get in her face, poke fingers at her, like some people did. The bikers were old hands at this: they knew how far the *craic* could go and when to back off. So when she walked round the house unplugging lights and CD players, dropping the place into silence, yelling, 'Police,' at the top of her voice, the bikers did the right thing. They picked up their lids, gloves and tobacco tins and slouched, grumbling, to the door. She stood on the driveway and watched them, talking politely to them – even helped one to get his sluggish chopper going.

When she went back inside Jason was sitting on the stairs. He'd stripped off his wet jeans and was wrapped in a fluffy white bath sheet. With the goose-bumps on his bare legs and the way the towel peaked in a cowl above his head, he looked as wretched as a refugee. His eyes were like holes in his face. She had to stop herself sitting down and putting an arm round his shoulders.

'You OK?'

'You never said you were police.'

'Because I'm not. I'm a veterinary nurse.'

'A veterinary . . .' He shut his mouth hard with a clunk of his teeth. Frowned. 'But how did you make them think you . . .'

'Showed them my driver's licence. Said it was police ID.'

'What? And they believed it?'

'Yup.' She pulled her licence out of her wallet and waved it in front of his face so fast he couldn't read the name. 'You'd be amazed what people will fall for. Just got to style it right.'

Jason gulped and put his hands to his temples. 'Christ. This is all going so fast.'

'I know. Have you seen the mess?'

'I am so not going to survive this. What'm I going to do?'

'You're going to have a cup of coffee. It won't make you less drunk, but it might wake you up a bit. We're going to clean the place up.' She helped him down the stairs, one hand under his elbow. Once or twice he lost his balance and nearly dropped the towel. She got glimpses of his pale body, the sparse hair, underneath, his old-fashioned lilac underpants, with a damp patch on the crotch. She got him downstairs, wedged him upright on a chair just inside the kitchen doorway and switched the kettle on.

She went back past him to the hall and tried the door of the study. 'No one been in here?'

'Eh? I dunno. I hope not.'

'I can't tell. It's locked.'

'No. It's just stiff. Give it a boot.'

She blinked at him, then let out a laugh. A slow, huffing laugh of disbelief.

'What?' he said.

'Nothing.' She shook her head. The door had been open all the time – she could have walked straight in this afternoon and not gone to all this trouble. 'Believe me. It's nothing.'

She put a shoulder against the door, turned the handle three hundred and sixty degrees, and hefted all her weight into it. The door gave a clunk, then swung open. Everything was there – the banker's lamp on the desk, the leather armchair and footstool. The files. 'You just about got away with that one. No casualties in there – or nothing serious.' She came out and drew the door towards her, leaving it slightly ajar. 'Tell you what – are you sure you want that coffee? You look like you should just lie down. I'll do the rest. You helped me earlier.'

Jason nodded numbly. He let her lead him into the

living room and settle him on the sofa. She found some coats hanging in the cloakroom and piled them on top of him. 'And if you're going to be sick, don't make it any worse for yourself – at least get yourself to the toilet.'

'I'm not going to be *sick*. I'm just tired.'

'Then sleep.' She stood in the doorway, her hand resting on the wall and watched him for a while. The french windows faced east, and before long the room was filled with pink first light. Like someone igniting a bonfire out in the garden. It didn't disturb Jason. He closed his eyes and within seconds was breathing low and hard. 'Suppose you won't be needing the coffee, then.' She waited another five minutes to be sure, then, very quietly, moved down the corridor, picking up a couple of beer cans as she went.

The study was the only place people hadn't been smoking. She propped the door open, so the smell could permeate from the hallway, dropped a couple of the cans on the desk, pushed the armchair to one side and scuffed the rug so it would look as if the bikers had been in there. Then she began to sift through the files. There were whole boxes devoted to Jason's schooling – he'd gone to St Paul's and the invoices were eye-watering. She wondered if Julian was still paying Millie's fees at Kingsmead. Report cards, sports-day cards, uniform lists and details of overseas school trips were all tucked together. Whatever unpleasantness Mooney had inflicted on the women of Priština, he did at least love his son. Or, rather, he had ambitions for him. In other boxes she found details of pension plans, with the MoD and a private company, mortgage papers, rental papers on a property the Mooneys seemed to own in Salamanca. There were medical reports and details of a legal case relating to a car accident Mrs Mooney had had in 2005. His bank statements were there. Zoë took them to the armchair and sat down with them, began to sift through them.

Over the impossibly expensive tiles of the next-door roof the sky was brightening by the minute, one or two clouds, still with their grey night pelts on them, hanging above the chimney pots. As she worked it grew lighter and lighter, until the sun found its way into the gap between the houses, and crept through the leaded window into the study. She searched the accounts for almost an hour and found nothing. Her heart was sinking. After all this, the answer wasn't here. Zhang and Watling had been right: if Mooney had paid someone to drop Goldrab, he'd brushed the ground clean behind him with his tail. She rested her chin in her hands and stared blankly at the photos on the wall. Pictures of Mr and Mrs Mooney holding hands in front of the Taj Mahal. One of Mooney shaking hands with someone she thought was high up in the US government – Alan Greenspan or someone. Krugerrands, she wondered. Who the hell in the West Country would take Krugerrands and know what to do with them? You'd have to go to one of those bloody horrible streets in Bristol or Birmingham. Going round those with a warrant card in her hand would be a nightmare. Impossible—

Something in one of the photos struck her. She pushed the chair back and went to the picture. It showed Dominic Mooney, wearing a standard Barbour and green Hunters. A Holland and Holland shotgun, the breech cracked open, dangled from one hand. He was smiling into the camera. Behind him a snatch of horizon was visible, a distinctive shape black against the blue of the sky. The Caterpillar opposite Hanging Hill. And in his hand, which was lifted to the camera, a brace of pheasants.

The gamekeeper. She pushed aside the file. The fucking gamekeeper. Jake had said someone was raising pheasants for Goldrab. Mooney had been shooting at Lightpil House and had to have spoken to the gamekeeper. She put the file away, shoved the photo into her jacket and buttoned it up. *Jesus Jesus Jesus*. Everyone knew what gamekeepers were like – mad as fishes. And dangerous. With gun licences and plenty of ways for disappearing bodies. If she was Mooney and wanted something done to Goldrab, the gamekeeper would be the first place she'd start.

She went into the living room. Jason was still asleep. She leaned over, put her head close to his face and listened to his breathing. Low and steady. He wasn't that pissed. Not die-in-a-ditch pissed. He'd live. She crouched and hoisted him further on to the sofa so he wouldn't roll off in his sleep. 'Night, dude,' she murmured. 'And Godspeed to Mars. You're going to need that rocket when Mum and Dad get home.'

25

Sally didn't go to bed. She snoozed for an hour or so on the sofa in the living room, but woke, her heart thumping, thinking about that cottage. The snaking path that led down to the bottom garden. She showered and dressed. Steve must have listened to her and gone on to that dinner meeting, because he hadn't called. And she was determined not to call him. There was a sweater of his he'd left lying around and she pulled it on, stopping for a moment to sniff the sleeve. Then she went into the kitchen and began to get breakfast ready. Millie appeared in the doorway, yawning and rubbing her eyes.

'Hi.' Sally stood at the sink, feeling as stiff as a wooden doll. Sore-eyed. 'Did you sleep OK?'

'Yeah.' Millie went to the fridge and poured a glass of juice. She sipped it for a while, then paused and glanced at her mother. 'Oh, no – you're looking at me funny again. Like you were last night.'

'I'm not.'

'You are. What the hell's going on?'

Sally filled the cafetière and placed it on the table.

Then she was still for a moment or two, contemplating Millie. 'Sweetheart,' she said. 'Remember that day last week when you came to work with me?'

'Yeah.' Millie used the back of her hand to wipe her mouth. 'The medallion man? I remember. Why?'

'What did you do while I was in the house? Where did you go?'

She frowned. 'Nothing. I wandered around. Walked to the bottom of the garden. There's a stream there, but it was too cold to paddle. I sat in a tree for a bit. Read on the lawn. Then Jake turned up.'

'Did you speak to anyone?'

'Only the freak.'

'The freak?' she said steadily.

'You know – the gamekeeper. He lives in that cottage.'

Sally's head seemed to lock in place on her neck. 'Gamekeeper?'

'Yeah. The one with the baby pheasants. Why? What're you giving me that look for?'

'I'm not. I'm just interested. I've never met him.'

'Well, you see him in town sometimes.' She put a finger to her temple and circled it. 'You know, few sandwiches short of a picnic.'

'No. I don't think I've seen him.'

'The one they said went to Iraq? Now he's got metal in his head? Ask Nial – he knows the whole story. Me and the others used to go over there, you know, in the old days if we were bored, except the metal in his head means he's nuts so we stopped. Peter and the others call him Metalhead.'

421

Metalhead. Sally knew who that was. Kelvin Burford. He'd been at the same nursery school she and Zoë had gone to as tiny children. Kelvin had been a funny little lad – always teased. She hadn't seen him much after nursery – he'd gone to one of the schools on the other side of Bath – and if she had seen him, it was only in the street, never to speak to. She'd have forgotten all about him if she hadn't read about him in the *Bath Chronicle* – how he'd got into the army, had been blown up in Iraq and nearly died. He'd been given a metal plate to replace parts of his skull, and although the doctors had thought he'd made a full recovery, the army wouldn't have him back because they said he'd gone mad. His talk was all about nightmares and people having their heads blown off. When she'd read in the papers about him being blown up she'd felt sorry for him – she'd even worried about him from time to time. But Kelvin Burford – the man in the cottage? The one who'd put the lipstick in the car? She wasn't sure if that made her feel better or worse.

'And the day I was working, did you speak to him? To Metalhead?'

'I just said I did.'

'What did you say? You didn't talk about why you were there?'

'No. I mean, I said hi and that. I said my mum was working at Medallion Man's house.'

'Does he know your name? Where you live?'

'I'm not completely thick, Mum. I went into his back garden. He showed me the baby pheasants and that was it. I came back. He let me put some hoods on them, which was kind of cool. Except you don't want to get too friendly with him. He attacked a girl in Radstock – went to prison for it. That's why I didn't tell you I'd been there. Thought you'd freak.' She lowered her chin and gave her mother an appraising look. 'And I was right.'

'Get dressed, Millie.' Sally gave an involuntary shiver. 'I'm taking you to school.'

26

Sally couldn't face parking in David's parking area again. It was as if the blood that had seeped out of sight into the ground might mysteriously find her car and soak its sly way up into the tyres, into the sills and the upholstery. So at half past nine, when she arrived after dropping Millie at school, she stopped the Ka twenty yards short and inched it into a passing space, out of sight.

She got out slowly, straightened, her back to the car, and scanned her surroundings. It was a clear day, just a few clouds on the horizon. The distant line of yews that marked the northern perimeter of Lightpil House seemed etched hard against the sky. The roof of the gamekeeper's cottage, with its mossy tiles, was just visible to her right beyond the trees that ran down to the valley.

She moved along the perimeter of David's property to where the wall ended and a hedge began, and peered over it. In front of her, surrounded by copper beech and leaning poplars, was the cottage. Small, stone-built, a typical eighteenth-century worker's home, with a low, tiled roof and chimneys. The gardens were a mess – overgrown and filled with junk; a yellow Fiat with a fading canvas roof was parked with its nose in a collapsed hay barn, some rusting disused chicken coops were piled against the far hedge, and, in the centre of the overgrown lawn, an old mower lay on its side, a roll of chicken wire abandoned next to it. Beyond the house was a huge mill shed. Maybe that was where the pheasants were reared. David had talked about his gamekeeper, but she'd forgotten about it until Millie had mentioned him.

After five minutes or more, when nothing in the house or garden had moved, she pushed through the hedge into the garden. The place was eerily quiet, just the faint sound of water running – maybe the stream that came down from Hanging Hill. The driveway was empty. No cars. She turned and went to the bottom of the land – the spoon shape she'd seen on Google Earth. The view here was quite different from up at Lightpil House: this land faced in a more westerly direction, towards Bristol. Where the trees bordering David's estate stopped, the land fell off, the garden giving way to patchwork farmland. And between them, wide and open like a wound, the yellowish smudge of gravel where it had happened.

She turned and looked up at the cottage. The windows were blank, the sky reflected in them. No movement. Nothing. She glanced again at the parking space, trying to judge what could have been seen. What if there were photographs? What if Kelvin hadn't only seen her and Steve but had made a record of the whole thing? She thought about Steve, thousands of miles away, sitting in a restaurant in Seattle, drinking wine and those endless glasses of iced water they served out there. She wished she'd asked him to come back, wished she hadn't been so proud and determined.

A breeze came through the wood, making the branches lift and sigh. Slowly she began to head up the hill towards the cottage. Closer, she saw how old and threadbare it was. There were animal traps everywhere and more bales of chicken wire piled against the wall. *He attacked a girl in Radstock – went to prison for it.*

The front door was flaked and old, with years of scuffing from wellingtons and maybe dogs. A name, faded by sun and rain to a pink, illegible smudge, had been written on paper and fastened under the bell with a rusting drawing pin. She stood on the step, put her head near the letterbox and listened. Silence. She went around to the back, looking up at the windows, trying to see a way in. Dirty scraps of lace curtain hung behind most of the panes, blocking her view, but she could see through the windows in the back extension – to a galley-shaped kitchen with yellow Formica cabinets. There was a packet of Weetabix on the table, a dirty plate next to it and a couple of Heineken tins flattened ready for the rubbish. No one to be seen. To her surprise, when she stepped back she noticed the door was open a fraction.

She stared at it, her legs suddenly like wood.

No. You can't . . .

But she did. She opened the door. The kitchen was small, the floor muddy, and the cupboards streaked with dirt at calf height, as if someone had been walking around wearing wellingtons. At the end a doorway led to the hall. Cautiously, she tiptoed over to it and peered through. It was a small hallway panelled in dark wood. No sound or movement. Just a curtain lifting lazily at the landing window.

There were two rooms opening from the main passageway. With a quick glance upstairs she went to the first, at the front, and peeped round the door. It was a small parlour, still with its picture rails and ornately tiled fireplace intact. The curtains were drawn but enough light was coming through for her to see it was almost empty – just an expensive TV on a black stand positioned about four feet in front of a sofa. The walls were bare, scruffy with years of grime. It didn't look like the home of someone organized, a person with the sort of technological know-how to have photographed or videoed people in a distant parking space.

The second room, at the back, had been turned into a makeshift office, with an IKEA flatpack desk, covered with piles of paperwork, and a swivel chair, all muddied and scuffed. She went to the desk and began opening drawers. In the top two she found a few boxes of shotgun cartridges and an oil-stained bandoleer. In the bottom one there was a small handbook, divided into sections marked 'Beaters', 'Dogs', 'Clients'. She was about to close it when she saw something gold glinting up at her. She squatted and tentatively moved things around it until she could see what it was. A lipstick case. She took it out, removed the lid and twisted up the lipstick. The little that was left of it was a distinct orange-red. She put her head against the desk and took long breaths, thinking of the little boy she'd played Lego with all those years ago, wondering why he'd grown up so angry and dangerous. And what he wanted from her.

A noise from the front of the house. Nothing much, just a vague whisper. Moving silently she closed the drawer, straightened and went to peer down the hall to the front door. The breeze outside was stronger now. It was making the curtains on the landing flutter, sending shadows like flapping wings on to the hall floor. A figure moved on the other side of the frosted glass.

She shot a glance behind her at the kitchen. The door was still open. Another noise and then, shattering the silence, the person began to knock at the door, the noise echoing through the house. It pushed her into action. She slid silently back the way she'd come, out of the kitchen, into the garden, walking fast in a straight line away from the house where she wouldn't be seen from the front, her hands in her pockets, her head down. It was only when she got to within ten yards of the gap in the hedge that she broke into a run.

She ran as fast as she could, fumbling in her pockets for her keys. The thorns in the hedge tore at her, the gravel in the parking space made her stumble.

She was sweating and trembling as she got to the car. She wrenched the door open and threw herself inside.

As she got the key in the ignition Steve's voice came back to her. *You won't get punished.*

'Steve, you were wrong,' she muttered, starting the engine. 'You couldn't have been more wrong.'

27

Zoë stood on the doorstep, her arms folded, her back to the gamekeeper's cottage, waiting for someone to answer the door. She surveyed the garden. It was a mess, with overgrown grass and a derelict garage, the weatherboarding rotting and hanging off. Over at the entrance, where a vegetable plot had been dug out, there was a stack of metal cages – fox 'trods' for trapping the animals. A keeper would need these especially at this time of the year. The foxes were only just recovering from the winter. This was their rebound time, and because it coincided with the young pheasants being at their most vulnerable, still too weak to fly into the trees, you'd often see keepers 'lamping' in their Land Rovers – bumping across the fields aiming their huge torches out into the darkness, attracting the foxes out of the hedges to be picked off one by one by a twelve-bore shotgun.

No one came to the door so she bent and looked through the letterbox. She could see a small hallway with dark polished floors and a patterned runner on the narrow staircase. No one in there. Strange. She'd had the sense there was. She checked her watch. Most people would be at work now, but a gamekeeper could keep any hours. If Goldrab had run a lot of driven pheasant hunts during the season they'd be breeding them on an intensive scale. A lot of places around here still did that in spite of the animal rights movement – and at this time of year there were scores of chicks at different stages of hatching. The keeper could be anywhere.

She realized she could hear water. Just a faint noise coming from somewhere behind the cottage. She went round the side and saw a dilapidated stone mill building with slate tiles stretching out at right angles to the cottage, spanning the stream, which rushed and echoed in a tunnel under the foundations. The braced redwood doors had been slid open to reveal the mill's concrete floor, lightly strewn with straw.

'Hello?' she called. 'Hello?'

No reply or movement, just the distant sound of a woodpigeon cooing, the constant undernote of running water.

'Hello?'

She stepped inside the mill. The air was warm, full of noise. A giant waterwheel would have once been mounted at the far end of the building where the stream rushed under the boards, but it had been dismantled and a floor put over the open area. A concrete aisle ran down the centre, on either side of which were four wire-mesh holding pens with aluminium drop pans and red heat lamps hanging above them. A murmur was rising from the scores of pheasant chicks in the pens that squeaked and shuffled and ruffled their feathers.

'Hey.' Zoë leaned over the pen and held her hand out to them. 'Hey, little guys.' They scattered away from her, running off, banging into each other and gathering in a group at the rear of the pen, eyeing her nervously. She wandered around a bit longer – found a large, netted cage at the end of the building with older pheasants, all fitted with little face masks to stop them pecking each other. They straightened their necks and blinked at her, ratcheting their heads from side to side.

Behind the pen was a bench with a vice, several jam-jars full of nails and screws and, mounted on a magnetic strip above the bench, a set of hunting knives – the type that could be used to field-dress and skin animals. Zoë studied them for a while, wondering if they'd been used to skin David Goldrab. She eyed the pheasants with the masks – were they fussy about what they ate? A body could disappear like that and never be found.

She went back into the open air. Near the mill doors, set at an angle in the grass, there was a hole with a grate – an entrance to an oubliette or an old ice house for a forgotten manor, maybe – with a big, padlocked chain linked through it. She made a mental note of it, then wandered back to the cottage, her hands in the pockets of her jeans, pausing to put her nose to the windows and peer inside. Idly she tried the back door. It opened. She hesitated, looking down at the handle, half surprised. Then she stepped inside.

'Hello?'

No reply, so she went into the kitchen and along the hallway, opening doors as she went, checking inside. No one here. She went upstairs, the curtain on the landing flapping and twisting like a ghost in front of her. She found two bedrooms – one with a bed against french windows that opened, improbably, on to a wrought-iron balcony overlooking the stream, the second empty save for a pile of cardboard boxes and an old poster of a football team Blu-tacked to the wall. A tube of tennis balls lay on the floor. Christ, there were bloody tennis balls everywhere she went, these days. Lorne. Don't think I've forgotten you. I'm going to find out if you're somewhere in all of this.

There was a bathroom with greying towels left to dry on the radiator, a framed needlework sampler resting on the window-sill that read 'I'm not a pheasant plucker, I'm a pheasant plucker's son. I'm only plucking pheasants till the pheasant plucker comes'. In the cabinet there was a box of medicine, open, the blister packs spilling out. 'Catapres', the label read. She'd heard of it. It was something to do with post-traumatic stress. She put the box back, leaned across the bath, opened the window and peered out at the tops of the trees. From here you could see parts of David Goldrab's house, with its reconstituted stone tiles, its coynes and laughable attempts to blend into the area. The panes of its huge atrium reflected lozenges of sunlight back through the yew trees. Yep, if she was Mooney, the gamekeeper would have been the first person she'd approach.

433

She went back downstairs. There was nothing much in the front room, just a wide-screen TV and a load of DVDs, but in the back there was an office with paperwork stacked in rickety heaps. She sat down and began leafing through them, hoping to get an idea of this guy. There was a pile of invoices from Mole Valley Farm Supplies with black fingerprints on them. A series of letters from the Royal United Hospital about medical treatment he was receiving. Something to do with a head injury. Sheet after sheet of details of operations and medication and X-rays and . . .

She stopped, half the pile of paper in one hand, half in the other. She was looking at an image she couldn't quite fathom. At first she thought it was some kind of Photoshopped joke, the sort of thing people loved to post online – outsize animals, one celebrity's head spliced on to another's body, ridiculous fake X-rays of all the weird objects a person had swallowed – because it seemed so outlandish. But when she studied it some more she saw it was real.

Watling and Zhang's unit would love to see this, she thought, a little shakily. It was the sort of photo there'd been a big thing about recently – the sort taken by servicemen on their mobiles. It showed a pile of bodies – men, skinny and half dressed, darkened by the sun and death into leathery strips of flesh. It looked like Iraq or Afghanistan, because there were plenty of *keffiyeh* scarves among the clothing of the corpses. Nasty, nasty. Maybe the gamekeeper had been a serviceman. *That* could be

434

another reason Mooney approached him. Ex-military, Watling had said. They were supposed to make the best assassins.

There was a noise from the doorway, and when she looked up a man was standing there, staring at her with his mouth wide open, as if he was more shocked to see her than she was to see him.

She dropped the photos and fumbled shakily inside her pocket for her warrant card, getting to her feet. 'You scared me for a moment there.'

He was tall and bearded, hair flecked with grey. He had a protruding stomach inside his checked lumberjack shirt, and he'd covered his jeans with snap-on waterproof leggings, like a cowboy's chaps. In his hand was a roll of garden twine. 'Don't think you'll get away with this again,' he said. 'Don't.'

'Sorry, I . . . ?' She trailed off. Her hand was frozen on the card, half in, half out of the pocket, as she stared at the scar on his head. 'Kelvin?' she said lamely. 'Kelvin?' It had taken a moment but she had recognized him. After eighteen years his name had popped into her head as if it was on a spring. Someone she'd been a tiny kid with at nursery school, and who, years later, had been a maintenance man in the Bristol strip club.

And at the moment she recognized him, he recognized her. He stepped forward, bent at the waist, an intrigued smile on his face. 'Zoë?'

She let the warrant card drop into her pocket. Slowly she took her hand out, holding his eyes. He knew her name. She couldn't show him the card, couldn't let him know she was a cop now. He knew everything about her. Everything.

'Wait there.' He smiled. He had good teeth. She remembered that from before. Above everything, she remembered his teeth. 'I'll be straight back. I've got something to show you.'

He ducked out of the door and was gone, leaving her in the room, idiotically frozen like a statue. Kelvin Burford. *Kelvin fucking Burford*. It had been eighteen years since she'd last spoken to him and yet she'd dreamed about him last night, leaning on his broom at the back of the audience, a sly smile on his face. He was a bastard. A scary bastard. *And he knew her bloody name*. All that time she'd thought it was just Goldrab, Kelvin had known it too. She went to the doorway and stood, looking left then right. She was still trying to get her numbed brain to decide which way to go when he reappeared in the hallway.

This time he didn't speak, just stood, filling the doorway. She'd never registered before quite how big he was, in girth and height. His belly in the lumberjack shirt hung over the top of his trousers. He was silhouetted by the sun that came through the back door and shone on to the filthy floor, and in his hand was a knife. One of the hunting knives she'd seen on the metallic strip in the mill building. Now she could see the long scar that started at his ear, went up around the top of his head and looped back down to the nape of his neck. It was square, with neat corners. She knew what that was – it was where metal had been inserted to replace his skull.

436

She glanced over her shoulder, calculating how far it was to the front door and if she could push past him. Then back at the knife. 'Kelvin,' she said, 'there's no need to be holding that now, is there? That's the sort of thing'll get you into a whole lorry-load of shit.'

'Zoë,' he said, 'I asked you before. What are you doing in my house?'

She took a breath, turned and bolted into the hall-way. She skidded along, taking up the rug with her and hitting the door with all her force. She threw the Yale lock and pulled, expecting the door to fly open. It didn't. The deadbolts were on. She grappled for them, throwing back the barrels, her hands shaking now. Still the door wouldn't budge. It was Chubb-locked. You could see the bolt between the jamb and the strike plate.

She turned. Kelvin stood behind her, blocking the path to the kitchen, his head down, as if in puzzled thought. He was looking at the knife, holding it angled with the blade facing upwards, as if the way the light glanced off it fascinated him. He didn't seem to be in a hurry. She threw herself away from the door and on to the stairs, flew up them, grabbing at the banister to pull herself faster. The french windows in the bedroom – they opened on to a small balcony. She got into the room, launched herself at the bed and scrabbled at the latch, but it was painted up and stiff. On the stairs Kelvin took a few heavy steps. Then stopped. As if he was shy or tired or unsure whether or not to follow.

She thumped at the windows with the heel of her hand. They had a stainless-steel lever handle with a keyhole in the back plate, but no key. Fucking locked. What was it with her and locked doors, these days? She looked around frantically for the keys. There was a dilapidated armoire against the far wall, and a bed-side cabinet. She wrenched the drawer open. Saw some screws, a phone battery, sex lube. No keys. Kelvin began to walk up the stairs again. His weight made the floorboards on the treads creak. Zoë got off the bed, and positioned herself in the way she'd been taught at police school. Sideways on, knees braced. She took long, slow breaths, trying to picture her centre of gravity sinking lower and lower, getting more and more solid and ready. Then, at the last minute, she lost her nerve. Dropped to her front on the floor and commando-crawled under the bed.

News about Kelvin had filtered through to her over the years – how he'd been driving through Basra in a Snatch Land Rover and an IED planted in a dead dog had detonated, killing everyone in the vehicle except him. So, yes, Iraq – that must have been when the photo of the bodies in a pile had been taken. For a while his accident had been all over the local news. Then, six months after his surgery, he'd attacked a teenage girl in Radstock. The story went that the girl had been baiting him – calling him Metalhead. He'd lost it and attacked her. He'd pinned her to a wall, got a plastic bag and wrapped it around her face. Later she testified he'd had his hand up her skirt while he was doing it, that he'd ejaculated into his trousers while he was strangling her. He denied that part of the story. Still, he got banged up for it. The girl's family wanted to sue the army for putting the madness into his head, but it had been thrown out of court.

Zoë had avoided Kelvin as much as she could when he'd been doing maintenance at the club. But in those days relationships had been formed, odd, handicapped friendships that limped along sometimes for weeks, sometimes for years. It must be how Kelvin knew David Goldrab. Maybe it was the reason he was working for him now.

She rolled on to her side, breathing hard, frantically looking around for something she could use to defend herself. Under the bed were the things you'd expect from a single man living on his own – dust balls, a pair of underpants, a pile of men's magazines. And bundled up in a ball next to the magazines, a few inches from Zoë's head, a woman's pink fleece.

She froze, staring at it, her heart thudding. A pink fleece.

It was the one Lorne Wood had been wearing the night she'd been murdered.

28

It was a strange thing, to have lost all sense of who you were and of what was right or wrong. Crouched in the damp-smelling woods, surrounded by the silence of the trees, one thought kept coming back to Sally, and that was how very much she envied Millie. Millie of all people. Millie who could find herself needing money and, instead of agonizing, just borrow it from the first person who offered. Millie who could drop in and out of a person's life and not think twice about it. She envied the simplicity of a teenager's mind – when you knew why you were doing what you were doing and could still follow the strand of reasoning back to its start point. When your motivations, goals and morals rested neat, un-crumpled and well spaced in your head. Before they began to knot together, lose their individual colour and become just a fat woolly ball.

She scraped at the earth beneath the tree with her bare fingers, burrowing through last year's leaves, warm and flaky, getting dirt under her nails. The court she'd summoned in her head had weighed

Kelvin against Sally as David Goldrab's killer and had found there was no contest. Kelvin Burford had a record of violence; he'd worked for David, and had severe mental problems. Of course he had killed David. Of course it couldn't have been the politely spoken, downtrodden housekeeper, with the nice accent and the teenage daughter in private school. And any way. There was evidence to prove it.

She found what she was searching for and sat back on her heels, resting it on her lap. The tin. She lifted it and blew off the earth. The few oddments inside rattled. David's teeth. His ring. She opened the lid and stared at them. Steve had called from the departures lounge at Sea-Tac. He'd finished the meeting, caught four hours' sleep in the hotel, then gone back to the airport and brought his flight back to England forward. It was going to Heathrow and was leaving Seattle in four hours. It would be early to-morrow morning before he was home. She'd told him about the lipstick at Kelvin's house, how it must have been him who'd left the message on her seat.

'But I told you. I can deal with it on my own. You didn't need to cut it short.'

'I know you can, but you don't have to. There are things you're going to have to do that I don't want you to do alone.'

'Things?'

'Sally, you and I have already done things neither of us ever thought we could. And it's not stopping now. We have to go on to the end of the road.'

We have to go on to the end of the road . . .

She knew what he meant. There were places at the gamekeeper's cottage she could leave the teeth. She could bury them, or wait until Kelvin was out and get into the house. Hide them somewhere careful. A place he wouldn't think to look, but a place the police would. And while she was there she could search the parts of the house she hadn't been able to earlier – check there really were no photos of her and Steve in the parking space. It was what Zoë would do, something clever like this. Zoë would do it, she would survive.

She got to her feet, put the lid back on the tin, slid it inside her jacket, and felt for her car keys. If she didn't do it now, she never would. She walked up the lane to the car, fast, her head down. Opened the door, threw the tin on to the passenger seat and swung inside. She started the engine and reversed up the drive, the familiar petrolly fumes coming in through the rattly back windows.

29

The boards outside creaked. Kelvin was walking leisurely along the landing, sauntering as if he was out in a park on a sunny day. He went to the front bedroom first. Zoë heard him throwing the boxes around. He was humming to himself. He had all the time in the world.

She grabbed the fleece, dragged it across the floorboards towards her and patted the pockets. Pulled out a mobile phone. Looked at it, her pulse racing. A white iPhone. It was Lorne's. She put her head back, her heart thudding like a jack-hammer. She'd been right. Right. Those arguments she'd had with Ben and Deborah, that Lorne's killer wasn't a teenager, *she'd been right*. And she'd been *right* to circle Goldrab and the porn industry – Lorne had met Kelvin through either Goldrab or the nightclubs. There couldn't be any other way a girl like her would have a connection to a man like Kelvin. God, Lorne, I'm sorry, she thought. For a while I lost sight of you. But you were there all along. I just never expected it to happen like this.

His footsteps stopped in the doorway. She tried the phone but the battery was dead, so she pushed it into the fleece pocket. She could see his blue Hunters in the doorway. Usually she'd be wearing a police radio, but she'd left it in the car. Stealthily she reached into her pocket for her own phone. The wellingtons came across the floor. Before she could even check the phone for a signal, Kelvin Burford crouched and his hands appeared, grabbing her ankles. She scrambled for the slats under the bed, dropping the phone in her haste. It skimmed across the floor, spinning, hitting the skirting-board. Kelvin braced one foot on the bed base to get leverage and pulled at her feet. She held on tight to the slats. He tugged again, and this time her grip weakened. The nail on her index finger tore away. She let go and he dragged her out, across the floor on her stomach, her T-shirt riding up.

He dropped her legs with a clatter. Instantly she slammed both hands on the floor, bunny-hopped to her feet and rounded on him, both hands out, her mouth open in a snarl. He stood against the wall, blinking at her, his hands half raised, as if he wasn't sure whether to laugh or not.

'Fucker.' She threw her hands at him, flapping them like birds. He reached up to keep them from his eyes, and she took the chance to bring her foot into his groin. She made contact, felt him begin to double over. He fell heavily against her, almost knocking her off balance, but she danced out of his way. He staggered a few steps forward, his head down as if he was going to ram the fireplace. She turned and clasped her hands together in a fist above his head, brought them down hard. She was aiming for the back of his neck but she got a point between his shoulder blades. He roared with pain, twisting and flailing with one hand to grab her leg. She wasn't expecting that – *you broke the first rule: never wait to see the effect of the punch, just get in there with the second.* He got her behind the knee and pulled so fast that she lost her balance and went down on her back with a thud.

He dropped to his knees next to her, his expression almost bored, as if this was too tiring, too wearying to be bothered with, and punched her hard in the face. Her head was thrown sideways with the force. Something flew out of her nose. Then he got a handful of her hair and lifted her head off the floor – there was the tiny *pop-popping* noise of a hundred hair follicles being yanked out – raised his fist and hit her again.

He dropped her head to the floor again and she lay there, panting thickly, staring through bleary eyes at a place about ten inches from her face where a spatter of blood had appeared on the bottom of the door. There was a noise – a wah-wah sound, as if someone in the room was squeezing out the air. The light coming through the french windows seemed suddenly greasy and unsteady, as if it was being manipulated. She tried to lift a hand to her face, but it wouldn't obey. It rose a short way then fell, like a piece of dead meat, and lay near her face as if it didn't belong to her. Kelvin was moving around the room, breathing hard. His weight on the floorboards tested the joists under her – as if the floor was bending slightly wherever he went. She thought about Lorne's face. The blood and the bruising. There was a tube of tennis balls in the next bedroom. How many game-keepers played tennis, for Christ's sake? How could she have been so fucking *stupid*?

Kelvin grunted. He got his hands under her armpits and lifted her on to the bed. She lay on her side, breathing rapidly, still unable to move. There was a pool of blood on the floor where her head had just been, bright red, like the ink from the luminous pens they used in the office. A clump of hair too, with something white attached to it. Her skin, she realized.

'I'm going to tie you up now. OK?'

She tried to move her legs. They wouldn't budge. They just hung down over the edge of the bed, no life, no feeling. She understood what was going to happen now.

'Come over here.'

He pushed her a little further onto the bed. She was shivering, cold and hot at the same time. Where his hands touched her they felt like warm muscle meeting glass.

'That's it,' he said. 'Now here.'

He lifted her numb legs and placed them on the sheets. She could see the veins in the whites of his eyes. An unhealthy yellowish film over the sclera. He smelt of woodsmoke and engine oil and dirty clothes. Zoë recalled the lines of blood running down Lorne's cheeks.

Her skin had split. Really *split*. 'It'sh OK,' she slurred.

He looked her in the eye, puzzled. 'What?'

'It'sh OK. You can do it to me.'

Kelvin kept his eyes on her, not expecting this. There was a white line on his lips, either from dried skin or toothpaste or spittle, she couldn't be sure. If she died now Ben would see the marks – everyone would know she'd put up some resistance. You were supposed to fight, weren't you? Fight for your honour. Except there were times that to win the war you had to lose the battle.

'It'sh what I want.'

He lowered his chin and looked at her steadily.

'I mean it.'

He sat on the bed, making the springs creak. 'You what?'

'I want it.'

He gave the sly grin he used to give her from the back of the audience, the one that made her sure the dirtiness in her was on the inside, deep, deep down, not something superficial she'd picked up from working in the club.

'You want what?'

She gritted her teeth.

'Say it. Say what you want.'

'I want you to fuck me.'

'Say, "*Kelvin*, I want you to fuck me." '

'I want you to fuck me, Kelvin.'

'No. Get it right. Say, "Kelvin, I really want you to fuck me." Lick your lips when you say it. Like you used to.'

447

She held his eyes. The trembling was starting under her ribs. 'Kelvin.' She put her tongue between her lips. Shakily moved it across them. 'I really want you to fuck me.'

He unlaced his boots and set them to one side. He stood and unsnapped the waterproof leggings, throwing them on to the floor. He unzipped his jeans and stepped out of them. He wasn't wearing anything underneath. No underwear. She could see his red testicles and penis dangling under the plaid shirt. He went to the dressing-table and sorted idly through the items on there. *Please not a tennis ball. Please not that . . .*

He found instead a condom and split open the packet. She followed it with her eyes as he came back and sat on the bed. He wasn't stupid: he wouldn't leave a trace. It was what he'd done with Lorne.

He sat down on the bed and began fumbling with her trousers. She didn't move – she couldn't. He got the zip undone and slid the jeans off, dragging her knickers with them. She kept her teeth clenched tight. Tried to shrink all her thoughts into a tight, hard knot in the centre of her mind. He pulled her sweater off over her head and dragged her bottom to the edge of the bed. Her feet clunked dully back on the floor. He knelt in front of her and put on the condom. 'Open your legs.'

The trembling under her ribs grew into a body-length spasm.

'Open your legs.'

She managed to get them a small way apart and he

448

used his knees to move them further, then pulled her closer and pushed himself inside her. He watched her closely while he worked at her, eyes on her face. She clamped her teeth together, and kept her eyes locked hard on a button on his breast pocket, holding them there, concentrating all the time on the tight place in her head. The feeling was coming back into her body now. She wished it wouldn't, she wished she could feel nothing. The blood from her nose ran down the back of her throat. The blood in Lorne's nose had congealed, blocked her nose. It had been what had killed her. What had Amy said in the barge? It seemed like an eternity ago. That rape was all about men and the way they secretly hated women?

Then, suddenly, it was over. He was finished. He pulled away from her and removed the condom. Tied it in a knot and dropped it on the floor. Then he sat on the bed next to her, almost companionably, reaching over, pushing a hand up inside her T-shirt to massage her breast. 'You liked that. Didn't you?'

She licked her lips. She could taste the blood. Salty, like sweat.

'I said – did you enjoy that?'

She closed her eyes and nodded.

'Your nose is bleeding.'

She raised a shaky hand, still weak, and wiped it. Kelvin stood and went out. She opened her eyes and blinked at the empty room. *The tennis ball*, she thought. *Now he's going to get the tennis ball*. But when he reappeared next to the bed he was holding a towel. He handed it to her. She tried to sit up but

449

failed. He pulled her upright and she sat there with the towel pressed on her nose. The feeling was coming back to her legs now, pricking like pins and needles.

'I'd like to come back another time.'

'What? What did you say?'

Once, years ago, Zoë had interviewed a rape victim. The girl had said the same thing to her attacker – she'd said afterwards, *I really like you – can we do this again?* He'd believed her and instead of hurting her, had let her go. Zoë swallowed more blood. Repeated it, louder this time: 'I'd like to come back another time. For more.'

He frowned, genuinely perplexed. 'You don't think I'm going to let you go – not now – do you?'

30

It was Zoë's face that stopped Sally. She'd got halfway up Hanging Hill, gripping the steering-wheel so hard her hands were white, leaning forward and staring out of the windscreen. The turning to Lightpil House and Kelvin's cottage was up ahead but, as she indicated to turn, out of nowhere Zoë's expression popped into her head. It was when she'd been standing at the table in the kitchen the day before yesterday, talking about patterns and the way we all connected to each other.

Sally faltered. Her foot twitched on the accelerator. She tried to picture Zoë with a tin full of a dead man's teeth, driving into the countryside with them. To do what? Point the finger at someone innocent. She couldn't conjure up the image. Just couldn't. Clever as Zoë was, it wasn't how she'd deal with this. And then Sally had a memory of Kelvin Burford at nursery school all those years ago – a fierce and sturdy little boy with the snot dried in crusts where he'd wiped it across his face, the feral sense of determination that stuck right out of his eyes whenever he looked at you.

As the turning to the gamekeeper's cottage came up to meet her, she flicked the indicator off. She let the car sail past it, continuing on along the main road. Scared as she was of Kelvin, she couldn't do something else this contorted. Whatever Steve said, she couldn't go on spoiling the pattern.

No. There had to be another way.

31

'What's the matter?' Kelvin had brought a bottle of cider up from the kitchen. He was standing at the window that looked out to the side of the house, unscrewing the bottle and pouring the contents into a cloudy glass. He lowered his chin and gave Zoë a long, measured look. 'What's the matter with you? You look weird.'

She lay in a curl against the bed head. She could no longer breathe through her nose: it had filled with compacted blood. Just like Lorne's had. She kept thinking about that pile of bodies in Iraq. She kept thinking that if Kelvin had seen things like that on a day-to-day basis then Lorne's death would have seemed like nothing.

All like her . . .

He knew Lorne as a stripper or topless model. The same way he'd known Zoë. Neither of them would matter much to someone this insane. They'd be just links in the sequence. The superintendent had laughed, and said, 'You're telling us there's a pile of bodies somewhere?' but Kelvin wouldn't see any difference between a pile of dead women and a pile of dead Iraqi insurgents. And to fight it she had nothing. Clever, clever Zoë. Spiky and cold, yes, but you couldn't take the clever out of her. Except now. When she just couldn't find a clever solution to this.

'I'm . . .' she began.

'What?' He looked up sharply. 'You're what?'

She hesitated. If she told him now she was police it could go either way. It could scare him into releasing her, or it could make him finish the job off even quicker.

'You're what?'

'I'm cold. Can I have my sweater back?'

He grabbed it from the floor and threw it at her, then sat down and drank the glass of cider in one gulp. He lit a cigarette and smoked for a while, his eyes on the wall, as if he was lost in thought. She clutched the sweater round her shoulders. Gave a small shiver. 'I have to go now.' Her voice was coming out a bit thick when she spoke, making her sound as though she was deaf. 'My husband's going to call the police – he'll be worried about me. I want to see you again. I'll come back.'

'You've said that already.'

'I meant it.'

He poured more cider, screwed the lid on the bottle and raised the glass, as if he'd lost interest in her. She dropped her head back and breathed slowly through her mouth. She'd noticed in the last ten minutes that the window-frame was weak. Maybe – maybe . . .

'You made me angry.' Kelvin didn't turn to her. 'You made me angry and you made me do it. There's a line, you know.' He tapped the cider glass rhythmically. 'A clear line. And once you cross it, once you've stepped into that other world, you have to accept the consequences. You have to take special measures.'

'I'll come back.'

'Shut up. I'm thinking.'

She lay in silence, her eyes going from him back to the window-frame. Magpies sat in the branches of the tree outside, the way they had outside Lorne's house. She wanted to shout to them, tell them to fetch someone, as if they could help her. Kelvin drank some more. He pulled up a chair and put it next to the chest of drawers, sat with his elbows on it, as if it was a desk. Lit another cigarette.

'Can I have some water?'

He lowered his chin and turned his eyes to her, his face serious. 'What?'

'Water? I'm thirsty.'

'Are you?'

'Please?'

He shrugged, pushed the chair back. 'Did you like me fucking you?'

She clenched her teeth.

'I said – did you like me fucking you?'

'Yes.'

He cocked his head, cupped his hand to his ear.

'I liked it. Kelvin.'

'Good. Then I'll get you some water.' He got up.

Halfway to the door he took a sudden sharp step towards her, his hands coming up as if he was going to attack. She jolted back into the headboard, her arms flying up to protect her face. Then she saw he was smiling. Cautiously, she lowered her hands. 'Don't be so jumpy.' He smiled. 'We'll get through this, babe.' He came back to the bed and squeezed her leg reassuringly. 'We'll get through this together.'

32

When he'd gone she worked fast. She pulled on her trousers, her sweater. No time for knickers. It seemed to take for ever to get the boots on to her numb feet. Downstairs Kelvin turned on the tap in the kitchen. The water pipes in the walls knocked and groaned. The condom she shoved into her back pocket. She'd been thinking hard. The frames between the panes in the french windows were fragile – little more than beading holding the glass in: she'd be able to fit through the hole made by three frames in a vertical row. The moment the first pane went he'd hear, though, so she'd have to do it fast. Bam bam. Like the karate experts she'd once sat and watched in a Japanese park at dawn. Like Uma Thurman in the yellow jumpsuit in that film years ago.

From the balcony the drop was ten feet. If she didn't land well she could forget it – her legs and feet were weak enough already without an injury and her only hope was to recover from the drop instantly and run straight into the forest before he could follow. Even when he had realized what the noise was it would take him time to get from the kitchen to the front of the house. The front door was locked – he'd have to find the key or go out of the back and round the cottage before she had time to reach the far trees.

The sound of him opening and closing the fridge door came up clearly from the kitchen. She heard him filling a kettle – doing what? Making tea for himself? He was so fucking calm that he was happily making tea, as if this was a normal Thursday for him. She flexed each muscle, checked it was working, wouldn't let her down. Then she linked her hands into the iron bed head to brace herself, lifted her right knee up to her chin and kicked. The glass broke instantly, falling outwards, tinkling on to the balcony. The cross brace above it needed a second thump. It splintered, taking the pane above with it. Another kick and the final pane toppled outwards from the frame. The hole was almost three foot deep.

Kelvin's footsteps were in the hallway; she heard him on the stairs, bellowing, '*Bitch! Bitch!*'

Good. Coming upstairs would cost him more time. With the sleeve of her sweater pulled down over her hand, she punched out the remaining slivers of glass and pushed her feet through. Then her hips. She heard Kelvin in the room, shouting and swearing, but she was gone, over the railings of the balcony, slithering down until she was dangling underneath it.

'Do it,' she hissed, looking at the ground, which seemed a million miles from her feet. 'Do it.'

Through the broken window she saw him appear in the doorway, his face contorted with rage. She let go of the railings and dropped. She landed on the weed-cracked concrete, her ankle twisting painfully under her. She stumbled, her knees making awful cracking noises as they hit the ground. But she was OK. She pushed herself up and ran. Kelvin was yelling somewhere inside the house, throwing furniture around in his fury. She pictured a shotgun being chambered as she flung herself into the trees, heading aimlessly into the forest.

The trees didn't quite have their full summer growth on them, and she could see a long way ahead. She could see the zigzaggy green splash of lawns. Maybe the edge of the estate that neighboured Goldrab's. She pushed her wobbly legs on, breathing through her swollen mouth, crashing through dead wood and leaves, waxy green carpets of wild garlic in the corners of her eyes. Eventually the wood gave out to a sweep of grass so clipped and green it could have been a golf course. Beyond it she saw a pale Cotswold chippings driveway and a spectacular stone mansion basking in the sun, with turrets and stone urns on the parapets. A Land Rover stood in the driveway. She ran to it and tugged at the doors – locked – continued, breathing hard now, past another car, past cold frames and a walled garden where white peonies and early roses grew, each neatly labelled. The front door had a huge old knocker – a Jacob Marley – and she hammered on it, the noise echoing through the house and out across the grounds. She glanced anxiously over her shoulder up the lawn. There was no sign of Kelvin in the trees.

'Hello?' She opened the letterbox and yelled through it. 'Anyone home?'

No answer. She limped along the front of the house, catching sight of tasselled curtains inside the leaded windows, her reflection moving across them – hair all over the place, her nose swollen to twice its normal size. She rounded the corner and made her way past dustbins, a pile of sawn logs, two cans of oil. She hammered on the back door, put her hand up to shade her eyes and peered through the windows. She saw an elegant painted kitchen, a central island, an Aga. No lights or sound. She went back to the corner of the house, and as she did she saw him. Just a blur in the trees, his red and black shirt a patch of moving colour – running down to the lawn with his arms out at his sides. She turned and began to head towards the front of the house, to the driveway that led to the road. Immediately she saw her mistake – she'd be in the open on the driveway. She hesitated. There was a wheelie bin next to one of the dustbins. She opened it and looked inside. It was almost empty – just one tied carrier bag of rubbish at the bottom – and it was solidly placed against the wall. It didn't move as she swung in one leg, then the other, landing in the bottom, reaching above her head to pull the lid closed.

It was dark and warm in the bin. She couldn't hear anything outside, just the hot percussive in and out of her own panting bouncing off the plastic walls. She wiped the sweat off her forehead and carefully lifted the carrier bag to her knees, silently using her

460

fingernails to slit a hole in the plastic. Inside were the remains of a kid's packed lunch – a couple of squashed drinks packets, a screwed-up ball of silver foil with crumbs on it, a wad of napkins printed with blue dinosaurs – and three baked-beans cans. She pulled the lid out of one of the cans and put it between her knees, crushing with all her might until it folded into two. Then she reversed it and folded it again. She did it three times before it split along the folded edge. She held it against her fingertip – sharp. It would work if she got the right angle.

Footsteps sounded on the gravel. Kelvin. She held her breath, raised the tin lid in both hands above her head. He went past getting so close she could hear his breathing, a raspy, deep-barrelled noise. He wasn't fit in spite of his job and his army background: the drink and the cigarettes had taken their toll. She could have outrun him, could have got to the road if she'd just had the confidence. She heard him go round the house twice, circling like a buzzard, passing so close to the bin she felt his clothing brush it. Then his footsteps disappeared towards the road.

After a long time she dared to look out. The long, sun-baked drive led to two stone newels, the gates standing wide open. She was just in time to see him exit and stand in the lane, looking up, then back down the hill. He hesitated, then turned and began to walk in the direction of his cottage.

When she was sure he had gone, she clambered out of the bin. She stood for a moment, unpicking the wad of dinosaur napkins, then carefully cleaned out the inside of a second beans can. She rinsed it under the garden tap, dried it with the napkins, pulled the knotted condom out of her pocket and dropped it in. She secured it by wadding a couple of napkins on top. Then she rinsed her hands again, splashed some cold water on her face, and began to hobble down the driveway towards the road.

33

Sally sat at the open kitchen window, an untouched cup of coffee at her elbow, and stared out across the fields. The Caterpillar opposite Hanging Hill had its new leaves on, and the outline it cast against the midday sky was thick. One day it had been a line of skeletons, stretching their hands to the sky, and the next they'd fattened into trees. Just like that, summer was on its way.

She picked up the phone and looked at it. No messages, no texts. Steve had already gone to the gate for his flight home. She unfolded the wet wipes, now dry, and flattened them on the table, tracing her fingers across the words.

Evil bitch.

There was a way of dealing with this. There was. She just couldn't see it yet.

The doorbell rang and she sat bolt upright. She hadn't heard a car. There definitely hadn't been a car. Hurriedly she folded the tissues, went to the window and leaned out. Standing on the porch with her back to the window was a woman, filthy dirty and dressed in torn jeans, hair straggling down her back.

'Hello?'

The woman turned, looked back at her without a word. Her face was bruised, her nose swollen; there was dried blood in her hair and on her face. Her eyes were dead black holes.

'Zoë?'

She shovelled the wipes into a drawer, slammed it closed, went into the hallway and unlocked the door. Zoë stood with one arm against the wall, her shoulders sagging, her head drooping. She gazed at Sally as if she was looking at her across a great, shattered expanse of desert. As if she'd found herself in a world so terrible that no one, no one, could ever adequately describe it.

She tried to smile. A twitch at the corner of her mouth. 'People keep telling me I should ask when I need help.'

Sally was silent for a moment. Then she stepped on to the porch and put her arms around her sister. Zoë stood there stiffly. She was shivering.

'Give me a bath, Sally. And something to drink. Will you? That's all. I need a little money to get home, but I'll pay it back.'

Sally shook her head. She held Zoë out at arm's length, studying her in the sunlight. Her nose was a bloodied ball. There were rivulets of blood running down her chin and her lips were swollen. She couldn't meet Sally's eyes.

'Please don't ask. Please. Just the bath.'

'Come on.'

She guided her inside, kicking the door closed, and helped her down the corridor. Zoë limped painfully along, grunting slightly with each step. In the bathroom Sally turned on the taps, then collected the towels Millie had left lying around that morning, and dumped them in the laundry basket.

'Here.' She put a clean towel around Zoë. 'You're shivering.'

'I won't outstay my welcome. I promise.'

'Shut up.' She switched on the heated towel rail, and brought flannels and clean towels from the airing cupboard. While the bath ran she went to the kitchen and prepared a tray with a tall jug of mineral water and a pot of coffee. Even as a child Zoë had drunk loads of coffee. Black and strong.

Back in the bathroom Zoë had peeled off her clothes and was climbing into the bath. Sally put the tray on the window-sill and watched her. It was strange enough to see another woman's naked body in her bathroom, but to see her own sister's. To see all the skin and muscle and flesh that Zoë walked around in, the covering that she lived in day to day and was so used to she didn't even look at. Not so different from Sally's, with the dimples and the small pouches and sags and records of life, except that Zoë was so tall and slim. And something else – she was covered with injuries. Welts and cuts and bruises everywhere. Some looked old, some new. She winced as she settled in the bath, soaked a flannel and held it to her face. The nails on her right hand were broken and black with blood.

'You're so beautiful,' Sally said. 'More beautiful than I ever was. Mum and Dad always said you were the beautiful one.'

There was a silence. Then Zoë began to cry. She pressed the flannel into her face, leaned forward and took long, convulsive breaths, her shoulders shaking and shuddering. Sally sat on the edge of the bath and put a hand on her sister's naked back, looking at the vertebrae standing white and sharp under her skin. She waited for the spasms to slow. For the awful, racking sobs to fade.

'It's OK now. It's OK.'

'I was raped, Sally. I was.'

Sally took a deep breath, held it, then exhaled. 'OK,' she said. 'Tell me.'

'The man who killed Lorne Wood. He raped me – I got away. I'm supposed to be dead.'

'The man who killed *Lorne*? But I thought Ralph Hernan—'

Zoë shook her head. 'It wasn't him.'

Sally didn't move for a few moments. Then she reached for the towel. 'You shouldn't be in the bath. Get out. They have to test you.'

'No.' She pulled her knees up to her chin and hugged them. 'No, Sally. I'm not going to the police.'

'You've got to.'

'I can't. I can't.' She dropped her forehead on to her knees and cried some more, shaking her head. 'You think I've been strong and independent all my life, don't you? But that's wrong. I was stupid. When I left school I was stupid. All the money I got to travel the world? I told Mum and Dad I'd got a magazine to pay for it – that I was working for them.'

'The travel magazine.'

'Oh, God – it never existed. I got the money from doing stupid stuff.'

'Stupid stuff,' Sally said hollowly. She was thinking about the way Millie had got her money, from Jake. That had been stupid. 'What stupid stuff?'

'Nightclubs. You know the sort of thing. The sort of place David Goldrab would have hung around. It was the stupidest thing I've ever done and I regret it. Oh, Christ.' She wiped her tears with the back of her hand, avoiding touching her nose. 'I've spent the rest of my life regretting it. The *rest of my life*.'

'You took your clothes off? Stripping? Or pole-dancing or something?'

She nodded miserably.

Sally frowned. 'But that's – that's *nothing*. I thought you meant something really serious.'

Zoë raised her tear-stained face, puzzled. Sally opened her hands apologetically. 'Well, I can think of worse. It's just . . .' She faltered. '*You*? It seems so . . .'

'I had to make some money fast. I had to get out of the house – you know why.'

'But it's the sort of thing someone would do if they . . .' Sally groped for the word. 'Well, if they didn't much like themselves.'

There was a beat of silence. Zoë's face was rigid. Then Sally got it.

'But, Zoë – how could you? I mean . . . you're beautiful and brave and you're clever. So *clever*.'

'Please stop saying that.'

'It's true.'

'Well, I'm not very clever now, am I? I've been raped and I can't do a thing about it.'

'You can. We're going to report it.'

'No! I *can't*. I can't go and report this bastard to them because . . .' She shook her head. 'He knows me, this guy. From the clubs – he used to work in one of them as a handyman. He gave me the creeps, the way he was always watching me. He'd use it in his defence. I'd have to stand up in the witness box and his fucking brief would point out to everyone that I used to . . .' She wiped her eyes angrily. 'I can't tell them. I can't say a thing.'

Sally tapped her mouth thoughtfully with her fingernails. 'There has to be a way. Who is he?'

'You know him. You won't remember him but we were at nursery school together, can you believe? Kelvin Burford. He—'

She broke off. Sally had sat forward and was gaping at her, her mouth open. 'You're not joking? Are you?'

'Of course I'm not jok— What is it?'

'Good God.' Sally stood up. 'Good God. *Kelvin?*'

'Yes. Christ almighty, Sally.' Zoë rubbed the tears off her face and stared at her sister. 'What the hell have I said?'

34

Zoë had drunk all the water and the coffee and life was coming back into her now that Kelvin was washed off her. She dried herself and carefully cleaned her face with tissues and cotton buds. She dabbed some antiseptic cream on the cuts, then put on a towelling robe she found hanging on the back of the door. She did it all without looking in the mirror. From time to time she opened the door a crack and peered out into the cottage, wondering where on earth Sally had gone, what was keeping her. What the hell had she said to make her jump up like that?

After a long time there was a knock at the door. When Zoë opened it Sally was standing there in silence, holding an open bottle of wine and two glasses between her fingers. Her face was very white and serious.

'Wine?' said Zoë. 'At two in the afternoon?'

'I've decided to become an alcoholic. Just for the duration of my middle years.' She filled a glass and rested it on the edge of the washbasin. 'That's yours.'

Zoë took it and sat on the rim of the bath,

studying her sister. Something had changed in her face. She was a different person from the one who'd opened the front door to her and run the bath. As if something important had happened in the ten minutes she'd been gone. 'Come on, then, Sally. What is it?'

There was a small pause. Then, without looking her in the eye, Sally pulled a handful of tissues out of her cardigan pocket. They were creased and dirty and had lipstick on them. She got down on the floor, pushed the bath mat away, and spread them out, making sure they were all lined up. Letters appeared – a phrase scribbled back to front. Zoë squinted and slowly made out the sentence: *You won't get away with it. Evil bitch.* She shook her head, mystified. 'I don't get it. What's this?'

'Kelvin Burford. He wrote it on the seat of my car.'

She squatted down. Read it again slowly. Her head began to throb. The lipstick was the same shade as the one Kelvin had used on Lorne. But that detail hadn't been given out to the public. No one knew about the messages in lipstick. 'What,' she said slowly, 'makes you think it was Kelvin?'

'Because of what I found when I was at his house. This morning.'

'You were there this morning? No – I was there this mor . . .' Her voice faded. '*I* was there, not *you*.'

'I was too. When you arrived I was in the back room. Did you knock?'

'Yes.'

'That's when I left.'

470

'Hang on, hang on.' She held up a hand. 'Slowly now. Why were you there?'

'He's trying to blackmail me. I found the lipstick he used to write this in. He's either blackmailing me or trying to scare me into giving myself up to the police.'

'Giving yourself up to the *police*?'

Sally nodded at her sister. Her expression was sad – determined, and brave, but very sad too.

'Sally? What the hell's going on? What is it?'

'I did it.'

'Did what?'

'David Goldrab. You want to know what happened to him, and I'm telling you. It was me. I killed him.'

'Yeah, *right*.'

'I mean it. I killed him and I didn't report it. Even though I should have. But I didn't. And then . . .' She rubbed her hands together nervously. 'I had to get rid of the body.'

Zoë snorted. 'Wish I'd been there. I'd've helped. He's an arse.'

'No, Zoë. I really mean it.'

Zoë became very still. She studied her sister's face. Her eyes had lost their usual soft smudgy blueness. As if they'd cracked somehow, like marbles. There was something tough and proud in them. Zoë gave a hesitant, uncertain smile. 'Sally?'

'Everyone thought you were really independent and clever and smart. Well, everyone thought I was really mild and harmless. And stupid. But it turns out

471

I'm not. I killed David Goldrab and I covered the whole thing up. It was me.'

'No. No. This is—'

'It was an accident. Sort of an accident. He attacked me when I was there working one day. I was on my own . . . It wasn't what I meant to happen. But it was me all the same.'

Zoë stared at her and Sally stared back. From the open window came the vaguely electronic-sounding twitter of a lark singing as it rose up through the air. Zoë thought about Jake the Peg, about Dominic Mooney. She thought of Jason sleeping on a sofa covered with coats. Lieutenant Colonel Watling and Captain Charlie Zhang and all the wrong turnings she'd taken. She bent her head, pressed her fingers to her eyelids, trying to get some clarity in her head. When she spoke her voice was thick. Unnaturally high.

'What did you – you know, how did you . . .'

'I killed him with a nail gun. And then I cut him up. I know it sounds insane but I did.' She jerked her chin at the window. 'Out there.'

'He's in your *garden*?'

'No. He's everywhere. All over the countryside.'

'Jesus.' She felt so, so cold, worn down to a thing that was transparent and wafer thin. 'This is craziness. This is . . .' She was lost for words. 'You're not joking,' she said eventually. 'You're really, really not joking. You mean all this. Don't you?'

'Yes.'

'You've never done anything like it before?'

'No. But when I'd done it I felt good. And I feel better. About everything. Look at me. I'm different.'

It was true, Zoë thought, she *was* different. As if the bones that had all her life lain deep under her soft, perfect skin had suddenly hefted themselves up to the surface and were pressing impatiently against it. All this time she'd been scared of Goldrab coming back when, in fact, he was dead. Very dead. And her own sister to thank for it. She gestured at the lipstick on the tissues. 'This was on your car seat?'

'On the passenger side.'

Zoë moved the tissues around with her finger. 'That little boy we knew at nursery?' she said, after a while. 'Kelvin? He's gone. You do know that, don't you? You know that he's a grown man, and whatever has happened to him, he's dangerous and, worse than that, he's insane.'

'I know.'

'And you understand that, whatever happens, we're going to have to find a way of getting him locked up? Without me saying what's happened to me – without you saying what happened with . . . with Goldrab.'

'Yes.'

'There are some things in his house that link him to Lorne.'

'We could somehow tip the police off? Anonymously? Can you do that?'

'You can. But it won't be that easy. My guess is he'll have hidden them all – destroyed them now that I've escaped. He'll know the police aren't far away.'

'Oh,' she said, deflated. 'Then what?'

'I don't know.' Zoë rubbed her ankle. It was aching from when she'd dropped off the balcony. 'Not completely yet. But I've got some ideas.'

35

An odd, non-reflective sky hung over Kelvin's cottage. As if the world sensed what lived there and wanted to blanket it. To suffocate it slowly. A few rooks cawed in the lime trees on the lane, and the mill stream babbled softly. The two women sat in Sally's Ka, parked at the top of the lane next to Zoë's car, abandoned this morning in her escape. They could see down past the hedgerow, with its new soft leaves, to the front of Kelvin's cottage. It was deserted.

'It's what I expected.' Next to her, Zoë took off the sunglasses Sally had lent her, tipped down the sun visor and checked her reflection in the mirror. She seemed in control but Sally knew it was an act. She used the cuff of the blouse – also Sally's – to dab at a cut on her mouth. She was wearing a little of Sally's makeup too – some concealer over the red and grey bruises that were already starting across her right cheekbone. Eventually she shook her head, as if her appearance was a losing battle, and closed the mirror. 'It's all gone wrong for him now because I survived. It wasn't supposed to happen that way. I was supposed to die. Now he's scared. He's on the run. It's like I guessed – there won't be any of Lorne's things in there. Or mine.'

Sally bit her lip and leaned forward a little, anxiously scanning the scene. An apple tree on the other side of David Goldrab's garden had dropped its blossom. It had blown in dirty white drifts along the lane and lay in complex scrawls around Kelvin's derelict garage. She didn't like this. Didn't like it at all. When he'd been here, in the cottage, her fear at least had been contained in one place. Now it could be anywhere – anywhere out there. Like a virus released on the wind.

'What about the photos though? If he's got any evidence against me – photos or something – they might still be in there.'

'I promise you, there's nothing in that house. I went through it. There were pictures . . . but not of you. Anyway, he's not organized enough to have done that. He'd have needed a long-range lens.'

'Are you sure?'

'I'm sure. I swear.'

Sally rubbed the goosebumps on her arms. 'Plan B, then?'

'Plan B it is. Just a few more hoops to jump through. Come on, let's get a wriggle on.'

She climbed out, got into her Mondeo and started the engine. Sally followed in the Ka, driving slowly down to the cottage. They parked at the top of the driveway. They left the doors open, keys in the ignition – if Kelvin did reappear he couldn't take both cars at once. They'd have a precious few seconds to start the engine of the other to make their escape. Anyway, Zoë insisted, he wasn't going to show his face again. Not round here.

They wandered around the house, trying to find a way in. But he'd worked fast, and since Zoë had escaped he'd padlocked everything – Sally had never seen so many padlocks. Some of the windows had been nailed closed, there were planks hammered across the back and front doors, and the french windows in the first-floor room had been boarded up. They found a garage neither of them had noticed before. According to Zoë, Kelvin drove a Land Rover – she'd made a call in the police station and had its registration number on a scrap of paper in her pocket – but it wasn't here now. There was just an oil stain on the floor and wheel tracks outside on the ground.

Zoë stopped near the mill. She squatted down and tugged at the rusty chain that wound through a grate covering a hole. She tested the padlock. It came open with a creak.

'You do your thing,' she told Sally. She dragged the chain out of the grate and lifted it off. 'I'm going to check in there.'

She bent double and went in, disappearing from view. Sally watched her go. Then, with a glance around at the stillness, she pulled on the nitrile gloves Zoë had given her, and began to dig with the gardening fork they'd brought. The ground was soft, if stony, and soon she'd created a yellowish scar. She felt in the pocket of her duffel coat for the tin. Fingers trembling, she removed the lid and tipped out the contents. Planting the teeth had been Zoë's suggestion, which was ironic, considering how Sally hadn't done it earlier because she'd thought Zoë would have found a better way. Now Sally knew about the rapes, though, she'd changed her mind about doing the right thing by Kelvin. Zoë hadn't asked how Sally had had the nerve to remove David's teeth – how she'd managed to mastermind getting rid of his body all on her own, or whether someone else was involved. Sally had a feeling she knew, though.

Now she dropped the teeth into the hole and stirred them a little, letting them mingle with the soil. She filled in the hole, covered it crudely with the turf she'd dug out. Seeing those human teeth, with their fillings and vulnerable roots, she felt nothing. Absolutely nothing. You're a monster, a voice said in her head. You've become a monster.

'Empty.' Zoë came out of the hole, doubled up, brushing cobwebs from her head. 'Nothing. It's an ice house.' She rattled the padlock. Opened and closed it a couple of times. 'I don't know if this was locked before or not. I didn't try.'

Sally straightened, pushed her hands into the small of her back and bent backwards a little to get the cricks from her muscles. 'Why? Do you think there was something in there?'

'I don't know. Maybe something was. Gone now. Taken away in the Land Rover.'

'What sort of thing?'

Zoë dusted her hands off. She touched her nose tentatively, and looked up. The clouds that all day had been loitering near the horizon had, in the last few minutes, slipped almost unnoticed across the sky, thinning themselves out in a flat, opaque blanket of grey. The air seemed to have dropped several degrees in temperature – almost as if winter had changed its mind and was coming back to claim the world.

'Zoë?'

She turned her eyes to Sally's. They were very dark and serious. 'Nothing. Nothing for you to worry about.'

36

It had taken some nerve, looking at her face in the mirror, but at least her nose wasn't broken, Zoë was sure of that, and when she'd cleared the blood away she saw it just looked fat – as if she'd been born that way, with a big nose and small eyes. There was a split at the top of her mouth, but it could pass as an infected cold sore. Even so she looked crazy in Sally's clothes. They were too wide in the waist and too short. After they'd been to Kelvin's the two women separated for a while – Sally to speak to Millie, and Zoë to go to her house to tidy up before they met again for the next step in the plan. Visiting Philippa Wood.

Zoë parked outside her house, checked the sun-glasses were straight in case any of the neighbours were home, jumped out of the car and went to the front door. She had the key in the lock when she heard a voice behind her.

'Zoë?'

She turned and saw Ben coming up the path.

'Zoë?'

'Oh, no,' she muttered. 'Not now.'

She got inside and turned to slam the door, but he was already there – his hand on the panel, pushing at it.

'Zoë? Where the hell have you been?'

'None of your business.' She tried to close the door, but he put his shoulder against it.

'I've tried calling.'

'My phone's broken. I dropped it. Please go away.'

'No. I want to speak to you.'

'Well, I don't want to speak to you. Go away. Please, Ben, please.'

'Only when you've listened to me.'

'Another time.'

She wedged her foot against the skirting-board of the small entrance hall and put all her weight behind the door. Ben answered with his own weight on the other side. There was a moment or two of silence when they concentrated on the struggle. Then, after a slight wavering, the door flew open and Ben walked in, his back straight, looking around as if he was quite at home and had been invited in.

'I don't appreciate this.' She walked past him, her head down. 'I really don't.'

'I'm sorry. Just let me speak. That's all I want.'

She went to the table and sat there, sunglasses on, head twisted away as if she was intent on looking out of the window. She kept her elbow on the table, and her hand on the side of her head to block his view of her face.

'Ralph Hernandez didn't do it.'

'Oh,' she said dully. 'Well, whoopee to that. How do you know? Did your little fortune teller look in her crystal ball?'

'No. He had an alibi for that night. Complete stranger saw him about the time Lorne was killed. He was in Clifton, seriously considering jumping off Suicide Bridge. He didn't tell us because he didn't want his parents to know. Catholics. He'd rather lie and tell them he was out with friends than admit what was going through his head. His friends told him to lie – said they'd back him up.'

'Great. Thanks for telling me.' She wriggled her fingers in a little wave. ''Bye.'

He didn't answer. A long silence rolled out. She was tempted to turn to him but she knew he'd be staring right at her.

'It seems weird saying this to the back of your head,' he said eventually, 'but I'm going to say it anyway and hope it sinks in. I'm going to say I'm sorry. About everything.'

She gave a careless shrug. 'Don't be sorry. It's a free world. You fuck, Ben, who you want to fuck. It was nice when you wanted it to be me. That changed, end of story.'

'It didn't change. That's just it. I never wanted it to be anyone but you I was fucking. Except, unlike you, I wanted it to be something more than just dick meeting pussy. I wanted more than that. Of course, in your world that's some kind of failure.'

Zoë didn't answer. She stared out of the window at the cars all parked there.

'But I've thought about it and thought about it, and from where I'm sitting I haven't committed a crime. It's not wrong to want something more, is it? I thought that was how the world went round.'

'I don't know,' she said, in a dry voice. 'Whatever floats your boat. But all of this is academic because it's too late now.'

'Debbie, you mean?'

'Miss Personality.'

'I'm not stupid, Zoë. I can see through her.'

'Can you? Interesting. What do you see?'

He sighed. 'Probably the same as you see. You can't trust anything she says. She didn't know what she was talking about with Ralph Hernandez and now she's walking round the office like she owns it, turning up to every meeting. A sterling careerist.'

'Oh, you noticed.'

'And the truth is, I don't even fancy her.'

'You did well, then, you know, to sleep with someone you didn't fancy.'

'You've never had an anger shag?'

She nearly turned to him then. 'A *what*?'

'I was angry with you. I was doing anything I could to get you out of my head. You're in my head, Zoë. I can't get you out. I wish I could, but I can't.'

'Sorry I'm not more impressed.' She shook her head. Her neck was stiff and painful. As if she had a fever. 'It's just if I was fixated on someone the last thing I could do is sleep with someone else.'

'Well, I'm a man and you're a woman. So maybe you wouldn't understand. And how the hell would you know what you could and couldn't do? You've never been fixated on anyone in your life.'

She was silent, her teeth clenched so tight she thought they might crack. 'Have you finished now?' she murmured eventually.

'Look at me, Zoë.' He sat down opposite her.

She twisted her head further away, bent it slightly and pretended to be scratching her scalp.

'Just look at me. Is that so difficult? Come on.' He reached out and took her arm. She snatched it away, but he leaned forward and grabbed it again, this time brushing against the sunglasses, knocking them slightly. She fumbled up her free hand to push them back on, but he'd already seen. He sat back on the chair, the air knocked out of him. '*Jesus*. What the hell?'

'Shit, Ben.' She sat with her head lowered, pressing the glasses against her face. 'I mean, shit, I asked you not to come in.'

'What the fuck happened to you?'

'It doesn't matter. Really – it doesn't matter.'

He slammed his hands on the table and stood up so he was towering above her. 'Yes, it *does* matter, Zoë. It *does* matter. I *am* allowed to give a toss about you. Handcuff me, read me my rights, but I do.'

She could feel herself trembling – could feel a cold, hard ball of something ease its way into her throat. 'There's no need to be like that,' she said evenly.

'Just tell me. Who did it? Where did you report it?'

'I haven't,' she mumbled.

'What?'

484

'*I said I haven't reported it*. OK?' She sat back a bit, rubbing her arms, embarrassed. She was going to end up crying again if she wasn't careful. 'And I'm not going to. I keep saying it doesn't matter. Please leave it.'

Ben was silent for a long time. Then he pulled his phone out of his pocket. 'I'm going to report it.' He was jabbing in a number. 'Whoever did that needs to be spoken to.'

'No.' She made a lunge for the phone, throwing herself across the table.

He twisted away, holding it out of her reach. 'Then tell me who did it. Or I report it.'

'Please, Ben.' She was definitely going to cry now. 'Jesus. Just – please.' She pushed her chair back with a squeal and stood up. Everything was spiralling away, getting out of control. 'Just please, *please*—'

'Please what?'

'Just please don't,' she begged. 'Don't call anyone.'

37

Sally felt like a wire stretched to its limit. She was shaking with tension and her jaw kept clicking as she drove, as if she was cold. The dark clouds had got even lower and were leaching a fine, almost invisible drizzle, but the lights were on in the windows when she arrived at the school, fighting the oncoming gloom. It looked so homely, the school, so normal that her throat tightened. That normality – the simple, unremarkable fact of doors closed, lights on, coats hanging on hooks and hockey boots lying in muddy heaps – all of that might never come back to her. She might have stepped out of its reach for ever.

She phoned and managed to catch Millie on her afternoon break. She said she could sneak out for a few minutes – no one would notice. Sally waited at the gate, clutching her umbrella. She couldn't help checking around the street to make sure no one was watching her. She wasn't good at hiding things – she didn't know how people did it.

'Hi, Mum.' Millie's expression was bright. But

when she saw her mother's face the smile dropped. 'Oh. Are you OK?'

'I'm fine. Are you?'

'No, you're not. What's up?'

'Nothing.' She ran her eyes over her daughter's face and hair. She wanted to hold her so much. She wanted to just grab her and carry her somewhere far away from here. She swallowed hard, and said conversationally, 'How did the test go?'

'Oh, pants. I revised the wrong page. Doh . . .'

'You've got prep after school tonight, haven't you?'

'Yes. Till five. Why?'

'Because I don't want you going home on your own tonight. I'm going to call Dad, get him to pick you up.'

'He can't. He's in London.'

'Then Isabelle.'

'She's at that gymnastics meet with Sophie. In Liverpool. It's OK, Mum – I'll get the bus. Don't worry about me, I'll—'

'No! For heaven's sake, will you *listen to me*? I've just told you – you're not going home on your own.'

Millie blinked at her, shocked. Neither of them spoke for a moment, embarrassed by Sally's sudden outburst. From the other side of the wall came the shrieks and yells of the other kids. They all believed they were grown-up, Sally thought, that they knew what they were doing – but they weren't and they didn't. Really and truly they were still babies. A car went by suddenly, its brakes screeching, and she jumped as if she'd been shot.

'Mum?' Millie frowned, her face curious. Suspicious. 'What's the matter with you?'

'Nothing.'

'Then *you* pick me up after school, if you're so worried. Don't you finish work early today? You usually do.'

'I'm not going to work. I'm busy.'

'Busy? Busy doing what?'

'It doesn't matter what.' She put a hand to her head and pressed hard. She thought of Peter Cyrus's mother. Dismissed the idea. Tried to think who else she could ask. Who else she could trust.

'Mum? Is this about what we were saying this morning? About that Metalhead muppet again? Why are you so scared of him?'

'I'm not. It's nothing to do with him. Just stay in the school after prep. I'll make sure someone's there to pick you up.'

'Come on, something's wrong.'

'It is *not*,' she snapped. 'Nothing is bloody wrong. Now please don't ask me again.'

Millie shrank back a little, her mouth open. She looked for a moment as if she was going to say something, and Sally took a step forward, wanting to say sorry. But Millie turned on a heel and marched back inside the school gates, leaving Sally standing in the rain, trembling under her umbrella.

Shit, she thought, feeling in her pocket for her car keys. Life really was turning out to be the closest thing to hell.

38

'I don't want to do this.' Zoë drew the curtains and switched on the overhead light. 'You're making me do this. So I'm asking you – as a fellow human being – to recognize that.'

Sitting on the chair at the end of the room Ben nodded dully. 'I recognize you as a human being, Zoë. Maybe more than you do yourself.'

She stood in front of him, unbuckled her boots and kicked them aside. She unzipped the trousers and stepped out of them. Her own knickers were still on the floor at Kelvin's so she was wearing a pair of Sally's, which were too wide and flopped around her hips as she undressed. She hiked them up and un-buttoned the shirt, threw it on the floor, and stood a step away from him, arms hanging at her sides. She felt totally foolish.

Ben sat forward, his elbows on his knees, his head up. He was expressionless, his mouth slightly open, as he moved his attention all over her face, over the swollen nose, the bruises on her cheeks, and down, over her bare arms, covered with bramble scratches.

Then the bruises and the scars. She held out her arms and sighed. 'This one.' She put a finger on the scabbed mess she'd made last week, the day he'd admitted sleeping with Debbie. 'This is recent, but I did it to myself. And these ones here? They're old. I did them too.'

Ben looked at her in absolute disbelief.

'This one.' She gently palpated a new bruise on her arm. She thought about the hatred that had caused it – Kelvin's need to harm. She wondered how her life had got so twisted that she'd ever imagined doing the same thing to herself. 'This was done this morning.'

'How?'

'When I was raped.'

There was a long, long silence. Then Ben dropped his head forward, put his hands on his temples and screwed up his eyes as if he had the world's worst headache. She thought for a moment he was going to get up and leave. Then she realized he was crying soundlessly, his shoulders shaking. After a few moments he wiped his face angrily with a palm and raised his eyes to her. There was an expression of such grief, such loss, such fury in his eyes that she had to turn away.

She went and sat down at the table, put her hands between her knees and stared at her thighs, mottled with bruises. She felt every inch of her sore body – the tiny, intense jets of fury at all the places where Kelvin's fingers had come into contact with her skin. There was a creak and Ben got up from the chair. He came to the table and dropped to a crouch next to her. He laid his hands gently on her knees.

'No.' She shook her head. 'Don't be kind, please. I can't bear it.' She couldn't get her throat to open enough to explain. 'It's all right. I mean, it's not your fault. How could you have been expected to know that I was the most pathetic excuse for a human being that ever walked this planet?'

'It's not true. Something's happened to you – but you're not to blame.'

She shook her head, bit her lip. A single tear came out of her eye and ran down her cheek. 'Ben,' she said, with an effort, 'you're going to have to listen. And you're going to have to forgive.'

39

As Sally got into the car outside the school, still trembling, a figure in a waterproof, hood up against the rain, stepped out towards her from near the school wall. It was Nial. He looked odd. Determined, but nervous. He glanced over his shoulder as if to make sure no one was behind him, then hurried over to her.

'Mrs Cassidy?' He bent and peered at her through the driver's window, raised his fist and mimed knocking on the glass. 'Can we speak?'

Sally rolled down the window. 'Nial? What is it?'

'I'll give her a lift home. I've got the van – it's parked round the corner.'

She stared at him. The gel in his hair and the way he'd knotted his tie, instead of making him look grown-up and cool, just made him seem younger and smaller. Even more inadequate.

'What?' he said.

She shook her head. 'Nothing. That would be very kind. I'll pick her up from yours. About seven.'

She started to wind up the window, but he gave a small polite cough. 'Uh – Mrs Cassidy?'

'What?'

He bit his lip and glanced over his shoulder again, as if he was sure someone was listening. 'Millie's . . .'

'Millie's what?'

'Honestly? Don't tell her I told you, but she's scared.'

'*Scared?* She's got nothing to be scared of.'

'She says you're acting weird and she's got it into her head you're being threatened by someone. Is that why you don't want her going home on the bus?'

'Why on earth would she think that?'

'I don't know – but she hasn't stopped talking about it all morning. She thinks someone's messing you around.'

'Listen to me, Nial. Millie doesn't need to worry about me, about anything. All that's wrong is I can't get here by five to collect her. That's all. Everything's fine.'

'OK,' he said, unconvinced. Then, 'Mrs Cassidy, I don't know what's going on with you, but I can tell you this. If anyone *ever* tried to hurt Millie . . .' he shook his head, sadly, as if he regretted having to say this '. . . then they'd have to get past me first. Nothing and no one is going to get to her as long as I'm around.'

Sally forced a smile and reached for the ignition key. She was getting a bit impatient with his hero act. He was too young to have any concept – any proper way of grasping the truth – of the awful, overwhelming reality of Kelvin Burford.

'Thank you, Nial,' she said patiently. She was tired. Very tired. 'Thank you. I'll pick her up before seven.'

40

Nothing in Lorne's bedroom had been touched since Zoë's last visit. She could tell that from the still, shuttered weight of the air. It needed stirring, needed human breath in it. She pushed her sunglasses on to her head, knelt, opened the lower drawer and began peeling away the layers of clothes. It was gone six o'clock and the rain had passed over the town. The lovely trees outside Lorne's window dripped with water. Beyond them was the driveway and, at the end of it, Sally waiting in her little Ka. She'd driven Zoë here and now she was as anxious as Zoë was to get this stage of the process right. Sally, little Sally, who was turning out not to be weak-willed and spoiled, but tougher and smarter than Zoë would ever have guessed. And then, good God, *then* there was Ben . . .

In spite of everything that had happened at Kelvin's, the part of Zoë that had been aching for years and years softened a little at the thought of Ben. He was . . . What was he? Too good to be true? A reality she couldn't push away with a sarcastic 'Yeah, right'? Earlier, at her house, instead of speaking, asking questions, he'd simply sat with his arms round her, his chin on her head, listening to the whole story. Everything. And afterwards – when she'd expected him to cough awkwardly, mutter something stiff about how her secret wouldn't go any further, that maybe she should think about counselling – he'd shrugged, got up, clicked on the kettle and said, 'Right, got time for a cuppa before we nail the dickhead?' Now he was in the car somewhere, on the way to Gloucester with a list of Kelvin's known associates in his pockets. She sighed. With all the wrong she'd done in the world, how had this right come to her so easily?

She shut the drawer and opened the next. There were some books in the back, and behind them a few oddments Zoë was sure Pippa hadn't paid much attention to when she'd done her hurried inventory of the room after Lorne's disappearance. She pushed aside a bra and knickers – Lorne's underwear had been found so that was no use. She examined a grey peaked cap with diamanté studs in it – no, too distinctive, someone would have remembered her wearing a hat like that. Then she saw an orange silk scarf.

She sat back on her heels and rested the scarf across her knees. It could have been tucked under Lorne's pink fleece that afternoon when she left the house and no one would have necessarily noticed it. It was distinctive enough – didn't look like something you picked up in Next, more like something that had come from a holiday. She checked the label. 'Sabra

Dreams', it said. 'Made in Morocco'. The pin board above the desk had a photo of Lorne on a family holiday in Marrakesh. Pippa would remember her buying this.

Zoë put the scarf in her jacket pocket and zipped it up. She closed the drawers, put the sunglasses back on, and went downstairs. She found Pippa sitting, bizarrely, on the chair in the hallway next to the front door. The chair was meant for coats and handbags and oddments to be thrown on to it, not to be sat on: it was in the wrong place. Pippa looked as if she was neither in nor out of the house. As if she was permanently waiting for something.

'Did you find what you wanted?'

'I just needed to look around again. I thought there was something I missed. I was wrong.' She stopped at the bottom step and studied Pippa.

'What?' She blinked stupidly. 'What is it?'

'I dunno. I guess I just wondered . . .'

'What?'

'I shouldn't ask it, it's not ethical, but I'd like to anyway. I want to know how you feel about the person who did this.'

Pippa's face fell. 'Oh, please – I can't stand another lecture on forgiveness. I won't forgive him. I know it's wrong, I know it goes against all the ideals I thought I had, but then it happens to you and all you want is for them to die. And die without being able to leave a final message. Without being able to have a final meal or hold someone's hand. That's all I could think – that she couldn't hold someone's hand when she died. And now I want his mother to feel the way I do. If it means I'll rot in hell I don't care. It's the way I feel.'

Zoë nodded. Pippa hadn't said it but she clearly still believed Ralph had killed Lorne. Earlier, when Ben had gone to the station to get her one of the unit mobiles to replace the one that was now in Kelvin's possession, they'd crept through a back door into Ben's office and done a quick intelligence search on Kelvin. They'd been stunned by what was there. He had been hauled in over and over again for petty offences. Even before enlisting – at about the same time she'd been travelling the world – he'd been a nightmare to the constabulary. Over and over again he'd sent up huge warning flares that he was dangerous. Yet over and over again he'd been freed on some technicality. Amazingly, it was only after the conviction for the assault in Radstock that his five-yearly application to renew his gun licence had been turned down. Up until that point he'd been allowed complete access to a twelve-bore shotgun. If Pippa was having trouble forgiving Ralph, how was she going to feel when she heard about Kelvin and how the entire system had failed her?

'I wasn't going to ask that,' Zoë said eventually. 'I was going to say sorry. About the way it's all gone.'

'Me too, Zoë. Me too.'

Wearily she got to her feet, and held the door open. Zoë zipped up her jacket and pulled up her hood even though it wasn't raining, Pippa put a hand on her arm and peered at her face. At her swollen nose and the red welts on her cheekbones. 'Zoë? Do people ever really walk into doors?'

'All the time.'

'*I* never have. Never at all.'

'Then you've never been as drunk as I was.'

Pippa tried to smile, but it was a twisted, sad thing. Something pitiful. Zoë pulled the hood tighter and pretended to be struggling with the zip. Then she held up a hand, goodbye, and walked quickly away down the wet path, the scarf snug in her pocket.

41

The rain had gone and the clouds had cleared but the sun was almost down now, the liquid orange light dissolving around the houses and churches on the hills above Bath. It was cold. Sally pulled her duffel coat around herself and watched Zoë come down the path from the Woods' house. She had her hood up but she'd taken off the sunglasses and her face was naked in the twilight. The bruises and swelling had got worse in the last two hours, yet somehow she didn't look broken any more. It was as if something in her had mended.

She got inside the car and slammed the door. 'You OK?'

'Yes.'

'Good. You can drive now. Go up to the main road and turn left so we stay close to the canal. I'll tell you where to stop.'

While Sally started the engine and pulled out of the drive into the evening traffic, Zoë took off her jacket and rummaged in the pockets. She placed a plastic bag on her lap and unravelled an orange scarf on top of it. Then she fumbled inside the jacket again, pulled out a tiny Ziplock bag, and opened it. Inside there was a condom, filled with semen.

'Oh, God,' Sally muttered.

'Well, don't look if you can't handle it.'

'I can handle it. I can.'

'Put the heater on.'

Sally turned it on full and concentrated on the traffic, glancing from time to time at her sister, who, biting her lip with concentration, was undoing the condom and carefully distributing the contents across the scarf. She folded the scarf and rubbed it together. Then she placed it on the carrier bag on the floor near the heater.

'Disgusting.' She returned the condom to the Ziplock bag, and used wet wipes to clean her hands. 'Disgusting.'

She sat back in the seat, pushed her hair out of her eyes and ratcheted the seat back so she had room to stretch her legs out. She was so tall, Sally thought, and her legs were amazing – so long and capable. If Sally had been given legs like that to go through life with she'd have taken on the world in the same way Zoë had. She wouldn't have shrunk back from it. She would have done all the things she'd done, and not regretted any of it. She wished she could explain it somehow – that she'd have been proud of everything. Even the pole-dancing. It seemed to her you needed real guts to do something like that.

'It's going to be OK,' Zoë said suddenly. 'It's all going to be OK now.'

'How do you know?'

She gave a small, wondering smile and shook her head. The headlights from the oncoming cars flickered across her face. 'It just is.'

The traffic was heavy at this time of night. Even heading back into town along the canal the roads were congested – it took nearly half an hour to get to the bus stop Lorne had used the night she'd been attacked by Kelvin. The women used torches to navigate through the trees to the canal. The rush-hour affected not only the roads: the Kennet and Avon towpath, too, was a swift route out of the city and workers often used it as a cycle route, their suits in bags on their backs, but by the time the sisters arrived even that surge of traffic was over and the path was empty. There was no noise except the sounds of people cooking evening meals in the barges.

They walked quickly, heads down. The crime scene had been released two days ago and as they approached they could see a few soggy bunches of flowers lying in the wet grass, brown inside the cellophane. Zoë gave a quick glance around and stepped off the towpath, crunching into the undergrowth. Sally followed. They stopped a few yards from a natural clearing surrounded by dripping branches and nettles. A cross embroidered with flowers had been nailed to a tree up ahead. Sally stared at it. It would have been the Woods who had left it. The family with the hole in the heart.

'This is going to get some CSI into a world of

trouble.' Zoë pulled the scarf out of her pocket. 'Don't like doing it.'

'CSI?'

'The crime-scene guys who are supposed to've searched this site. If it works I'm going to have some serious karma to pay back.' She bit her lip and surveyed the clearing, then nodded back towards the path. 'You stay here. Watch the canal. If anyone comes, don't shout, just walk back in here to me. We'll go out that way – between the trees. OK?'

'OK.'

Sally stood, hands in her pockets, glancing up and down the path where the puddles reflected the light of the barges. Behind her, Zoë made her way through the undergrowth. She'd told a colleague in her team what they were doing. Ben, his name was. He didn't know anything about what had happened to David Goldrab – that was always going to be a secret between the sisters – but he did know what Kelvin had done to Zoë and to Lorne. Sally felt a little better knowing someone else was helping; not that Zoë wasn't capable all on her own. She looked back and saw her in the clearing, on tiptoe, draping the scarf over a tree branch. Totally capable. A few moments later she trudged back to Sally, wiping her hands as she came.

'Anyone?'

'No.'

'I don't think it's going to rain again.' Zoë looked up at the sky as they began to walk to the car. A little cloudy still. The moon was sending down a cool, diffuse light that gave everything monster outlines. 'I

502

really don't.' She fished in her pocket for her phone and pushed a key. 'But I'll need to tell Ben to make sure someone finds it ASAP.'

Sally kept walking, watching her sister out of the corner of her eye. She sensed Ben was more than just a trusted friend to her.

Then the call connected and she heard a man's voice – Ben, she supposed – speaking excitedly. She heard the words 'I was just about to call you,' then something inaudible that made Zoë stop dead in her tracks. Sally paused too, and turned to her sister.

'*Are you sure?*' Zoë muttered into the phone. Her expression had changed completely. 'A hundred per cent?'

'What?' Sally hissed. 'What is it?'

Zoë flapped a hand at her to be quiet. She turned away and walked a few steps in the opposite direction, her finger in her ear so she could hear better what Ben was saying. She listened for a while, then muttered a few short questions. When she hung up, she came back at a trot, beckoning to Sally to get back to the car.

'Zoë?' she said, breaking into a jog alongside her. 'What?'

'Ben's in Gloucester docks.'

'And?'

'Kelvin's got a mate – a friend from the army who owns a barge moored there.'

'A barge?'

'We were looking for a barge right from the beginning. Thought there had been a houseboat here

503

that night. This *has* to be the same one. It's locked. Ben's waiting for Gloucestershire Support Group boys to arrive and break in but . . .'

'But what?'

'He thinks there's someone inside it. I think we've found him. I think we've found Kelvin.'

42

Sally drove fast up Lansdown Hill, Zoë in the passenger seat, drumming her fingers on the steering-wheel, glancing at the dashboard clock, calculating how long it would take to get to Gloucester. The traffic was thin now. It would take less than ten minutes to pick up Millie from the Sweetmans, then for Sally to drop Zoë off at her car. From there, with luck and a tailwind, Zoë could be at the docks within the hour.

Her mind was racing. Had the barge simply motored away, on the night of Lorne's killing, along the canal system? She scrabbled in her memory – trying to decide if the Kennet and Avon canal connected into Gloucester. She couldn't recall – but she could remember that the Gloucester docks were less than a mile from the red-light areas of Barton Street and Midland Road. She wondered if Kelvin's 'army friend' had taken the photo of that pile of dead bodies in Iraq, and what – *what* – would be on that barge? Her hand kept drifting to the pocket where her phone was, wanting to call Ben, because it seemed to her that whichever way she pictured the barge she also saw blood drifting away from it in the water, swirling in oily curlicues. She wanted to tell him to be careful, to wait until she got there.

Sally indicated left and turned the car into Isabelle's long driveway. Zoë's phone rang, making her jump. She snatched it out of her pocket. It was Ben.

'Are you OK?'

'I'm fine.' He sounded rushed. Excited. She could hear he was walking. Could hear traffic going past him as if he was on a busy city road. 'But, Zoë, where are you? Have you left yet?'

'I'm just picking up my niece. I'll be back at my car in five and on my way.'

'No. Don't come to Gloucester.'

'What?'

'He's not here.'

'*Shit.*' She sat back in her seat, deflated. She shot Sally a sideways glance as they bounced along the track. 'Not there,' she muttered. 'Not there.'

'How come?'

'How come, Ben?'

'The support team kicked the door in. His mate was on board, pissed as a parrot, but he hasn't seen Kelvin in weeks. The barge hasn't been anywhere near Bath, hasn't left Gloucester in over a year – the harbour master confirmed that. So I went back to the phone thing. You know I couldn't get anything about his mobile, needed superintendent authority on that. Well, someone at BT owes me a favour and—'

'And?'

'Burford made several calls to a number in Solihull this lunchtime. Turns out his sister lives there.'

'Solihull? That's about – what? A forty-minute drive if you take the—'

She broke off. Sally was slowing the car down and the headlights had picked out a vehicle, parked at an untidy angle up ahead in the driveway. A Land Rover.

'That's funny,' Sally began, as Zoë leaned forward. 'I thought Isabelle wasn't—'

'*Stop!*'

Sally slammed on the brakes. She stared out of the windscreen at the mud-covered Land Rover. Zoë made frantic motioning signals. '*Go back.*' She swivelled her head to look out of the back window. '*Go on. Do it.*'

Sally slammed the gearstick into reverse and the car lurched back twenty yards, bumping over potholes and the grass verge. Ben's voice was coming from the tinny little phone speaker. 'Zoë? What's happening?'

'In there. *Put it in there.* Fast.'

Sally jumped the car back another ten yards, shoving it in behind a row of laurels. She switched the engine off, and killed the headlights. Zoë sat forward in her seat, peering down the driveway.

'Zoë?'

She lifted the phone numbly, a ball of adrenalin clenched in her chest. 'Yes.'

'Are you OK?'

'We're OK,' she said dully. 'But listen. I really don't think Kelvin's in Solihull.'

43

The Sweetmans' house was big – a Victorian monstrosity, with three floors and a turret on the roof. There were lights on in some of the downstairs rooms and a window on the ground floor stood open. Zoë leaned out of the open passenger window and took in every detail. 'Isabelle doesn't know Kelvin.' She wound up the window and turned to her sister. 'Does she?'

'No.'

'Well, that's his Land Rover. That's the registration the PNC gave me this afternoon.'

Sally fumbled for her phone. Her face had gone pale. 'He doesn't know Isabelle, but he does know Millie.'

'He knows *Millie*? How come?'

She hit a fast-dial key and held it to her ear. 'She was up at his house one afternoon.'

'What the hell was she doing there?'

'She was with me one day when I was working for David – but she knew Kelvin before. She and the others used to go up there. I think they used to torment him. Peter and Nial and Sophie and Millie. And Lorne too, probably, they all used to—'

She put her finger to her lip. The phone must have been answered. She opened her mouth to speak, then closed it. Shut her eyes and put her fingers against her forehead. 'Uh, Millie,' she said, after a moment or two. 'It's Mum. I'm at Nial's. I need you to call me the moment you get this message. The moment.' She hung up and dug her thumbnail into the space between her two front teeth. 'The phone battery keeps running out. I've been meaning to replace it.'

Zoë was staring at Sally's face. 'Sally? Did you just tell me they used to *torment* Kelvin? And that Lorne went up there too?'

'Yes. Why?'

She turned and gazed back at the Land Rover. What, she thought, if all along Lorne hadn't met Kelvin through the clubs but through Millie's gang and the days they used to go up to the cottage and torment him? She could imagine someone like Peter Cyrus doing it – she could imagine Kelvin's rage. *All like her.* What if those words meant all the girls who'd been in that gang? The message in Sally's car had been on the passenger side – where Millie would have been sitting, which meant it could have been directed at Millie, not Sally at all.

'Shit,' she hissed. 'Call Nial.'

'What?' she said numbly. 'Sorry?'

'Just *do it*. Do it now.'

Shakily Sally scrolled through her contacts. She found the number and dialled.

'Put it on speaker.'

She did, and the two women sat, heads together, looking at the display flashing. After four rings the call connected.

There was a muffled noise at the other end. Then, clearly, someone breathing. A word, so slurred it was impossible to hear it. A male voice.

'*Nial?*' Sally whispered, horrified. '*Nial?*'

More breathing. A noise. Like something soft being banged against glass. Then the phone went dead. Sally turned her eyes to her sister.

'*What was that noise?*' she murmured, her eyes watering with fear. 'What the hell was that noise?'

'Shit.' Zoë slammed her hands on the dashboard. Her head dropped back against the seat. 'Jesus, *shit*, I can't believe this is happening.' She turned in her seat and peered back up the track towards the main road. Gloucester was a good forty miles away. Ben wouldn't be here for at least an hour. 'OK. Let's think.' No way was she calling the police. She could just see Kelvin being hauled off by some Support Group officers and yelling out everything he knew about her and about Sally's connection to Goldrab. She felt in her pockets. She'd left her expandable ASP baton in her car. All she had, tucked into her leather jacket, was the little CS gas spray canister issued to all officers. 'Where do the family keep their tools?'

But the shock had hit Sally. Her face was white and she had started to shake. '*It means Kelvin's got them,*' she said, her voice almost lapsing into hysteria. '*Both of them.*'

'No.' Zoë shook her head. 'It doesn't mean that at all.'

'*Yes, it does. You know it does. Millie's not answering her phone. He's done something to her. Call the police.*'

'Sally.' She grabbed her sister's arm. 'Keep it together. You know why I'm not calling the police. Ben's on his way and we can do this. We can.'

'Oh, God.' She put her face in her hands. 'Oh, God, I can't.'

'We *can*. You've got to listen. OK? We need tools. Where do I look?'

'There's a garage, but . . . ' She waved vaguely behind her. 'In the boot. There'll be something in there. Oh God, he's going to kill her.'

Zoë got out of the car. What warmth had accumulated during the day now radiated up into the open sky, as if it wanted to reach the stars. It was freezing. Really and truly freezing. She left the car door wide open and went silently to the back, throwing cautious glances at the lights of the Sweetmans' house shining through the trees. There wasn't a sound. All she could hear in this lonely farm land was the vague hum of cars going by on the distant road. But what kept reverberating in her ears was the noise in the background of that phone call. *Thud thud thud.* What the hell had that been? She went through the contents of the boot quickly. A few DIY tools – a ball-pein hammer, a pair of long-handled shears and a chisel. A small axe.

'Here.' She grabbed the hammer for herself and

carried the axe back to Sally, who took it dumbly, staring down at it as if she had no idea where it had come from or how it had got there.

'Call me on your phone. On my work number.'

She did as she was told, trembling. Zoë scooped the work phone out of her pocket and when it began to ring hit the *Accept call* button. 'Don't end the call, just leave the line open. That's how we're going to communicate.' She pushed the phone back into the pocket of her gilet. 'Now listen to me. Concentrate. Absolutely no chance Isabelle's back? Or her husband?'

'No. He's in Dubai and she's – I don't know. I don't know, I can't remember, but miles away.'

'Where's the main living area?'

'In the back. The kitchen.'

'What's on the next floor?'

'I d-don't know. Four bedrooms, I think. The front one on the left is Nial's and that's Sophie's on the right. There's a bathroom in between them.' She looked woodenly at the axe and at the phone in her hand. Still linked to Zoë's. 'What's going to happen, Zoë? What're we going to do?'

'I'm going to go into the house. We keep the line open. Don't, whatever you do, speak to me. No matter what. But do listen. If it sounds like I'm in trouble, all bets are off. Kill this call and get straight on to the police. It's the only way – we'll deal with the fallout later.'

'Oh, Christ.' Sally shook her head. Her teeth were chattering loudly. 'Oh Christ oh Christ oh Christ.'

44

Over her two years in uniform, and then on occasion in CID, Zoë had done hundreds of searches, not knowing what to expect. She'd lost count of the stairwells she'd crept down, CS gas at the ready, the car boots she'd clicked open, not knowing what might explode out at her. She'd always been rock steady. Not even a waver. Even when a crack addict in St Jude's had jumped out at her in a multi-storey car park waving a syringe in her face and screaming about the devil and Jesus and police cunts and *what does your pussy smell like, beeatch?* it hadn't wobbled her. Tonight, though, she felt as if she was coming face to face with God. Or with the devil. As if the whole sky was pressing down on her, squeezing the air out of her lungs.

The first thing she noticed when she got close to the house was that the front door was open. Just a crack, a tiny slice of the hall carpet visible. She dropped to a crouch with her back to the front wall. Somehow she'd pictured the house locked and shuttered, not open, like an invitation. She kept thinking of that awful sound, like meat being slapped against a wall.

Tentatively she craned her neck and peered round the door. She could see an umbrella stand, a table. She reached out and pushed the door open. It swung back on its hinges. The hallway was empty. Nothing moved inside. The only noise was the electronic hum of a fridge from the last doorway on the right, where Sally had said the kitchen was.

She hooked out the phone and whispered into it, 'Don't answer this, Sally. I'm at the front door, can't hear anything inside. I'm going to go in now. I'll be on the ground floor. Start counting slowly. I'll speak to you again before you get to three hundred. If I don't, make that call.'

She returned the phone to her pocket, straightened and stood in the doorway. Trying to put height and weight into her shoulders. It wasn't how you should enter premises, but police school and uniform seemed a lifetime ago and she had to struggle to recall the routine. She held the CS gas at arm's length and took two steps into the hallway. Waited. Took two more. She stood at the door to the living room, put her head round it, gave it a quick glance, snapped her head back. Nothing. Just a lot of chairs and tables sitting in a silent circle, as if they were having a quiet conversation in the absence of their owners. Then the music room – empty too.

She closed the doors – that much she did recall from training: *close the rooms you've cleared* – and continued down the hallway, checking, throwing switches, closing doors. By the time she got to the back of the house the ground floor was blazing with light. She lifted the phone to her mouth. 'Nothing so far,' she murmured. 'I'm going upstairs. Start counting again.'

The stairs creaked as she climbed, even though she tried to place her feet on the edges, where the boards were supported. This was an old house – it wasn't neat and painted and scrubbed and nailed down. It had nicks and bumps and the bruises of a lifetime. On the landing, a paper Chinese lantern hanging from the ceiling moved slowly from side to side as she disturbed the air. There were six doors. She worked through them methodically, pushing the ones that were nearly closed with her toe, holding up the CS gas as they swung open. In each one she left the light burning, the door closed. It wasn't until she came to the last bedroom, Nial's, that she found any sign of Millie. There, heaped on the bed, were a pair of girl's trainers and a sweater with Millie's name stitched on the label inside. She picked it up and went back downstairs.

The kitchen was the sort of middle-class kitchen you saw a lot in Bath, with cabinets painted a dull leaden green and lots of garden flowers in plain, clouded-glass bottles on every window-sill. Double doors led outside to a garden that was invisible behind the reflection of the room. On the bleached oak island in the middle sat two school rucksacks, the name 'Kingsmead' on them. A tin marked 'Cakes' was open, a solitary cupcake inside, and there were

515

two coffee cups in the sink. The tap dripped on them. A plinking punctuation to the silence.

'You can come in now,' she said, into her phone. 'No one here.'

She went to the table, where two opened cans of Stella Artois sat. She lifted one and shook it. Beer sloshed around on the inside. The drinks had just been left. Like the meals on the *Mary Celeste*. She saw a small door by the fridge, and when she tapped it with her foot it opened to reveal a utility room, with a sink, a washing-machine and the usual clutter – mops and buckets in the corner, a pair of secateurs on a hook on the wall. The door that led out of the room to the back caught her attention. It was ajar.

She went to it and pushed it open. There was a step down on to a stone patio and beyond it a wide black expanse that must be the lawn. It was surrounded by trees, the sky blocked by their huge inky crowns, the branches moving almost imperceptibly against the blue clouds. She stood for a moment in the doorway, listening to the night. The gentle *shush-shush* of the leaves. The *plink-plink* of the tap dripping behind her.

This house wasn't far from Pollock's Farm – in fact, the garden must back right on to it. She'd been called out here enough times to know. The last time had been in a thick autumn mist, the day old man Pollock's body had been hauled out by men who'd been wearing protective suits, he was so decayed. She'd vowed never to come back to that godforsaken place. It wasn't somewhere you'd want

516

to be at any time, let alone on a night like tonight.

She turned back to the kitchen and her foot hit something. Looking down she saw a phone. She crouched and picked it up. It was a black Nokia. She hit the on switch. Nothing happened. The battery was dead. She turned it over and saw the casing was cracked.

'Zoë?'

She jumped. Sally was standing in the kitchen doorway, her face white. Her hands were trembling. She was holding the axe.

'It's OK,' Zoë said. 'There's no one here.'

Sally's eyes darted around the utility room. Her jaw was clenched tight. She looked like she might snap in half.

'Put the axe down,' Zoë said. 'Put it down.'

Slowly she lowered it. 'That's hers,' she said, staring at the sweater Zoë was holding. 'It's the only one she's got. She'll be freezing without it.'

Zoë held the phone out. 'And this?'

Sally leaned over to peer at it. She gave a small twitch when she saw what it was and closed her eyes. She put her hand out to the wall, as if she was going to faint.

'Sally? *Sally?* Come on – keep it together.'

45

Sally blinked. She saw her sister's face close to hers. Behind her the little utility room was swaying, the colours bleary. She kept remembering Millie on the tarot card, her face, smudged and smeared and ruined. 'I'm sorry,' she said, and her voice sounded miles away. 'I'm sorry. I got it all so wrong.'

'Call Nial.'

Isabelle had been right that the tarot was a warning, but it hadn't been about Jake. It had been a warning about this: all along she'd been warned about tonight.

'Hey,' Zoë hissed. 'Did you hear what I said? Call him.'

'Yes. Yes.' She pulled out her phone and tried to dial but her fingers didn't seem to work. They seemed to be miles away – miles and miles away, as if her arms were very long.

'Give it to me.'

Zoë grabbed the phone, put it on speaker and dialled Nial's number. The ringing was distant and lonely. Like part of the invisible dark world out there, funnelling through this tiny channel to reach them. This time there was no answer. It rang four times. Five. Then it went to answerphone.

Zoë shook her head. She took the phone off speaker and dialled again, this time putting it in her pocket and holding it tight against her hip. She took a step out on to the patio, her eyes fixed on the trees.

'What is it?' Sally murmured. 'What's going on?'

Zoë put a finger to her mouth. 'Listen.'

Sally came to stand next to her sister and listened to the breathless night. Now she could hear it – a phone ringing faintly in the darkness. It was coming from somewhere far beyond the trees at the bottom of the garden. But just as she thought she'd got an exact direction on it, the ringing stopped. The answerphone again. Quickly Zoë scrabbled the phone out of her pocket and dialled again. The ghostly ringing came again, floating up from the darkness.

'Pollock's Farm,' Zoë murmured.

Sally's heart sank even lower. She thought about the acres of abandoned land. The decaying farm machinery. The drop and the deserted house at the bottom of it where a man had lain rotting for week after week. 'God, no,' she murmured. 'That's where they are. Isn't it?'

'Come on. Let's go.'

They checked in the garage and found a huge dragon lamp with a rubberized handle, like the one Steve had bought Sally – it seemed a million years ago. Zoë switched it on to check the battery was

519

charged – it sent a blinding white circle on to the wall, making both women squint. She used a canvas strap to loop it around her neck, and then they went around collecting everything they could carry. Zoë had the hammer in her belt, CS gas in her back pocket, and a large mallet – the type for knocking in fence posts – in her right hand. Sally carried a chisel in the pocket of her coat and the axe in one hand. In the other she had a child's wind-up torch – the sort that worked on a dynamo. She couldn't stop her teeth chattering. Her bones felt like water – for anything she'd just stop here and curl up on the ground and pretend none of it was happening. But when you couldn't bear the thoughts, the only thing to do was to act. To keep moving.

They set off along the path towards the farm. Zoë went in front, her back straight, the big torch beam flittering through the trees that bent around the path, the branches overhead. To the left this forest stretched as far as Hanging Hill, and to the right it continued for almost a mile, then on the outskirts of Bath began to give way to houses, playing fields, a rugby club, its spectral white goal posts rising above the hedge line. As the trees thinned out, the women stopped. Zoë switched off the dragon light and they stood in silence surveying what lay in front of them. The fields were paler than the woods, the dried remains of the dead crops like a mist hovering above the land. Here and there were dotted the shadows of broken machinery and burned-out car carcasses. At the far end the dark shapes of the old decaying silage bales were outlined against the horizon, silent and still as sleeping beasts. Beyond them, invisible to the uninitiated, was the drop into the quarry.

Zoë fished out the phone and dialled the number again. This time the noise was much louder. There wasn't any question where it was coming from. The other side of the silage. The quarry where Pollock's house was.

46

The moon broke free from its cloud cover as they crossed the farm and for a moment it was so bright they seemed to be under a giant spotlight. Two lonely figures casting long blue shadows where they walked, feet shushing the dead corn. They came through the gate at the top of the quarry and slowly, using their hands to steady themselves against the trees, joined the zigzag path, which meandered through thick trees down the cliff edge. At the foot of the path they paused. The valley floor stretched away, serene and motionless. To their right was the house. It was in darkness, but the moonlight picked out its shape and reflected off the broken windows in the top floor.

Zoë dialled Nial again. There was a pause, then it clicked through. This time the noise was so close it made them both jump. It was coming from the house, floating out across the frigid air like a plea. It rang five, six times, and went into answerphone.

'Come on,' she mouthed. 'Come on.'

They went, single file, heads lowered. The house

stood with its back just a few yards from the quarry wall – as if it had fallen from the top and landed there, miraculously upright. It was rendered and roofed, but since Zoë was last here it had been used by the meths addicts and now it had the feel of something built by the army as a training range, with its doorways stripped to the brick, a great pool of weed-pocked rainwater on the cracked concrete it stood on. Everything had been covered with graffiti – even the quarry wall behind it. There were a few grilles on the windows, but most had been wrenched off and scattered on the ground to rot.

The women got to the side of the house, and squatted, their backs to the filthy wall, while Zoë dialled the number again. They held their breath, listening. The ringing was coming from inside the house, at ground level, somewhere near the back. Zoë cut the call and pushed the phone into her pocket. She held her breath and listened again. This time she heard something else, coming from the same place inside the house. The noise, the rhythmic noise they'd heard on the phone. Like something soft being banged against glass.

She wiped her forehead. 'Christ. Christ.'

'Hey,' Sally whispered suddenly. 'We've got to keep going.'

Zoë shot her a look. Sally's eyes were clear, and her face was remarkably composed. Zoë got some strength from her expression. She took a moment, then nodded. She picked up the hammer and torch. 'Come on.'

Together they moved along the edge of the house, stopping at the corner, just ten inches from the front door. Zoë leaned her head back against the wall, took a few deep breaths, then swivelled, put her head into the doorway. She jerked back.

'Anything?'

She shook her head. 'But I can't see properly,' she murmured. 'It's too dark. I've got to use this.' She licked her lips, looked down and flicked the ready switch on the dragon light. 'It'll blind anyone in there. But only for about twenty seconds. Then they're going to know we're here. Are you ready for that?'

Sally pressed her eyelids down with her fingers. She was paler than a ghost, but she nodded. 'Yes. If you are.'

They turned into the entrance, Zoë holding up the light, shining it into the house, and the two women stared in, taking a mental snapshot of what lay in front of them. The hallway ran from the front door to the back, with two doors opening from it on the left. The place was completely stripped; only some parts of the wall still had chunks of plaster. There were the remains of a carpet in the hallway, but it had become so rotten and wet it looked more like mud and was dotted with puddles. This must have been the site of many a party – empty bottles and beer cans littered the place and something big lay next to the back door. At first Zoë took it for a bundled-up carpet, or clothes, half covered with leaves, but then she saw it was a human being. His shirt was half

524

lifted from his back to reveal long grazes that had leaked blood into the seat of his jeans.

She switched off the light and quickly flattened herself against the wall. Sally did the same and they stood there, breathing hard, closing their eyes and going back over what they'd seen.

'It's him,' Sally whispered. 'Nial.'

'Yes.'

He'd been lying on his side, his back to them so they couldn't see his face, but it was definitely him. Those injuries on his back could only have come from falling down the slope. Maybe with the last of his strength he'd crawled into the house through the back door. She switched the light on again, twisted back into the doorway and shone the torch on the two doorways to check Kelvin wasn't standing there. Then she moved the beam to the body at the end of the hall and saw it move slightly.

'Nial?' She cupped her hand around her mouth and hissed down the hallway. 'Nial? You OK? Where's Millie?'

Nial's hand lifted. Seemed to be trying to wave at them. It could have been a wave of acknowledgement, it could have been a warning, or it could have been him trying to direct them to Millie. It stayed in the air for a second or two, then collapsed. His leg twitched, he tried to roll sideways to face them, but the effort was too much. He gave up and just lay there, breathing slowly, his thin ribs rising and falling.

Thud. Thud. Thud, came the noise, from the second doorway. *Thud. Thud. Thud.*

Two lines of sweat broke from under Zoë's hair. It was the room where old man Pollock had been found.

Thud. Thud. Thud.

She nearly lost it then. She shrank out of sight and stood with her back to the wall, panting, wanting to run away. She put her hands up to her face and tried to calm her breathing. Slowly. In and out. In and out. She'd held it together this long. She could do this. She could.

'Zoë?'

A cool hand on her shoulder. She looked sideways. Sally was standing close to her. Her face calm, smooth. She reached down and gently prised the big torch from her sister's stiff fingers.

'It's OK.' She held Zoë's eyes. 'Really it's OK. I'm OK. Not scared. Not at all.'

47

As she'd walked across the fields, come down the quarry edge and approached the house, something had happened to Sally. The thing that had been coming up inside her for weeks at last reached the surface. It was the thing that had been able to say no to Steve when he'd offered her money, to say no when he'd said he was coming home from Seattle. The thing that had been able to keep filming Jake that night in Twerton, and had been able to cut David Goldrab into a million pieces. The thing was skinless and sharp-toothed, with the long face of a dragon, and had just shaken itself free of the old Sally, leaving her perfectly calm, perfectly focused. She was going to go in and get Millie out. Simple as that.

She examined the torch, flicked the switch back and forward, checking it carefully. Then she lifted the axe in the other hand, holding it over her shoulder like a woodcutter. Her face fixed, her heart beating slowly, she stepped into the hallway and crunched along the glass in the hall to the doorway where the noise was coming from.

She poked her head round the door, quite cool and unhurried now. There was no need for a torch – the moon from the window opposite lit up the room, wet and filthy. It was full of old furniture: a sideboard and a sofa that someone had tried to set fire to, a broken standard lamp leaning crookedly up against the wall. Scrappy blackened curtains hung at the window, which looked out at the cliff behind and, on the other side of the cracked glass, lit eerily by the moon, a man's dark, oval face. Kelvin. Banging his head monotonously into the glass, raw intent in his face. She didn't bolt back, just stood rooted in the doorway, staring at him. He wasn't looking at her. He hadn't even registered her presence, his eyes were so shuttered and blank in his brute need to get into the house.

He was smaller than she'd expected. He must be kneeling there, so close to the window, his hands out of sight below the sill. Whatever she'd imagined in his face – cunning or malice – it wasn't there. It was dull. Flaccid. She made up her mind right there and then. She was going to kill him. She'd done it to David Goldrab, but this was going to be easier. Much easier.

'What's wrong with him?' Zoë had crept up behind her and was looking over her shoulder. 'He looks weird. Is he drunk?'

'Yes,' she murmured. 'It's good. He's useless.' She put the dragon lamp on the floor and raised the axe. There was bile in her mouth. This was it, then. This was the moment. 'Don't look.'

'Wait.' Zoë grabbed her arm. 'Hang on. Something's wrong.'

Sally lowered the axe and Zoë hefted up the dragon lamp from the floor. It powered blindingly across the tiny room, illuminating the sofa and the sideboard and the tatty curtains, putting Kelvin's face into sharp relief against the rock. He didn't react to the light. Not at all. He remained in the same position, his lolling head banging rhythmically into the frame. There was a mark on his forehead where it was making contact, but no blood. And the banging was lackadaisical. More of a spasm than an intention.

'Why's he so low down?'

Sally shook her head, transfixed by his face. 'Isn't he kneeling?'

'No. It's something else.'

Together the two women took a step into the room. Zoë shook the torch, moved it randomly to create a strobe effect. Then she took another step forward and shone it straight into his eyes. Still he didn't react. His eyes stared forward, black and blank, as if focused on something in the window-frame.

Sally let out all her breath, walked to the window and put the axe straight through the glass. Kelvin's body swayed a little, but he didn't look up at her. His head jerked forward and made contact with the frame again, just inches from her face, then snapped back. She saw his eyes under the lowered lids. Saw the blackness. Saw the scar in his skull that snaked down from his ear into the collar of his checked shirt. His face was pulled back in a grimace. There was some blood on the front of his shirt, as if maybe it had come from his mouth.

'He's dead,' she said. 'Dead.'

She leaned out of the broken window, angled the torch down, and saw he wasn't kneeling at all. It was just that he had no legs. What had once been his lower body had concertinaed here. Into a bag of broken limbs half held together by his jeans. A tree branch growing out of the rock had caught him – suspended him there like a puppet, moving him back and forward into the window. Slowly, she raised the torch to the rockface. Saw a tree hanging half out of the rock, pale yellow earth spilling down. A long scar as if someone had tumbled down. She saw it all now – Kelvin and Nial struggling. A long, scrambling fall.

She pulled back from the window, and picked her way back across the litter of beer cans into the hallway. She dropped to a crouch next to Nial, where the ground was tacky with blood. She put her hand on his side, feeling it rapidly rise and fall under her fingers. His body was hot. As if the effort of the struggle with Kelvin was still being released.

He had a tiny ribcage, not much bigger than Millie's. She pulled his shirt down to cover him. 'Can you hear me? Where's Millie?'

He lifted his hands to his face and groaned. He half turned on to his back.

'Nial? It's OK. You can tell me – I'm prepared.'

'She's OK.' His voice was thick. 'She's safe. I did it.'

'Did it? Did what?'

'I saved her. I saved Millie.'

Sally rocked back and sat down, among the beer

cans, litter and broken glass. She sat there, holding her ankles, the floor and walls all moving around her. 'Where, Nial?' she heard Zoë say behind her. 'Where is she?'

'I locked her in the Glasto van. Up near the house. She hasn't got her phone – it all happened too fast. You must have driven right past her.'

Part Three

Part Three

1

Ben couldn't understand why Zoë wanted to go to Kelvin Burford's funeral. What did she think she was going to gain from it? Did she feel sorry for his family? Or did she simply want to be sure he was really dead and gone? Zoë couldn't answer the question, she just didn't know, but she went all the same: her, Sally and Steve. Millie, Nial and Peter had come too, still adamant they wanted to be there. So it was six of them that shuffled into a pew that day in the tiny chapel, each a little uncomfortable and awkward, fidgeting in their formal clothing, hoping the service wouldn't be too long and drawn out.

It was midsummer. The coroner had taken five weeks to call the final inquest on Kelvin Burford's death and reach the verdict of death by misadventure. The investigation into Lorne Wood's death, meanwhile, hadn't officially been closed, but Kelvin might as well have been tried and convicted of it because the whole world knew what he'd done. The scarf at the canal was positive for his DNA, and when his house was searched not only had Lorne's pink fleece and mobile phone been discovered under the bed, but also, in the desk drawer downstairs, the lipstick used to write on her body and the distinctive filigree earring that had been ripped from her ear. Ironic, really, when Zoë thought of all the planning she, Sally and Ben had put into getting Kelvin nailed – assuming he'd have disposed of the evidence at his cottage and would have to be nailed some other way.

There'd been story after story about the 'monster' Burford in the paper, detailing Kelvin's past, his injury in Basra, his assault on the girl in Radstock. There weren't many of his friends and family brave enough to turn up to the funeral so the congregation was small. Zoë glanced around – a few police, one or two colleagues who'd served with him in Basra wedged into the uncomfortable pews, not meeting anyone's eyes, as if they were ashamed. Then she realized with a jolt that the pew they'd chosen was directly behind Kelvin's sister. She stopped moving around then and, as silence fell in the chapel, studied the back of the woman's head. Fair hair curling out from under a black straw pillbox hat. It occurred then to Zoë that maybe guilt had sent her here. Shame at the number of ways she'd stepped outside the subtle moral framework of truth and lies that the police were supposed to know and respect. As well as Kelvin, David Goldrab's disappearance was on her conscience – repeatedly she'd reassured the family that everything possible was being done, while in truth she was silently helping the case to slide further and further down the force's must-do list.

Air wheezed into the organ pipes, a chord sounded. She picked up the order of service and fanned herself lightly, raising her eyes to the rafters overhead. The cobwebs and the dust. Maybe the eyes of God were beyond all that, peering down at her, seeing all these secrets. She'd been wrong that Lorne was just the tip of the iceberg, that Kelvin had already killed. There had been no traces of human remains anywhere in the house or in the Land Rover – and the photo from Iraq had been downloaded from a website that had got thousands of hits before it had been wiped from the server. Yes, she thought, she'd been wrong about a lot of things in the last few weeks. But some right had come out of it too. Her connection to Sally, to Millie. And maybe, through that, a new way of connecting to the rest of the world. A new dimension in the pattern she was leaving.

The doors at the back of the church opened and the funeral director's pall-bearers began the long walk up the aisle. Zoë looked down and saw Sally's hand resting on her lap. She looked to her left and saw Millie's hand on hers. On an impulse she reached out and took both, and as she did, the answer to Ben's question about the funeral popped into her head.

Solidarity. That was what it was. She was here to show the world, and Kelvin's memory, that this family, her family, wouldn't be pushed apart again. Ever.

2

When the service was over, the teenagers ran on ahead, though the adults lingered a while, waiting for Kelvin's sister to go before they got up and left by the east entrance, which led into the graveyard. They didn't want to bump into the press who were ranked outside the west gate, gathering around Kelvin's sister.

The three of them went to the bench under the buddleia tree to wait it out. Sally sat on Steve's knee, Zoë stood in front of them, smiling, a hand up to shade her eyes from the sun. She looked gorgeous, Sally thought, like an Amazon. Dressed in white from head to foot, with an incredible tan she'd picked up just from being on her bike. Her face had healed completely and she wore a solid cherry-red lipstick that hadn't smudged or faded.

'I like your dress,' Sally said. 'And the hat.'

'Thanks.' Zoë pulled off the hat and sat next to them. Tried to shake a crease out of the skirt. 'It's not really my thing. You know, dresses and hats. Still – proves I scrub up OK.'

'Ben's not here?'

'Yes – he's waiting in the car until the press go. See him?'

Sally looked across the graves and the cypress trees and saw a dark-blue Audi pulled up in the patchy sunlight. Ben was inside it, wearing sunglasses. 'He's staring at us. He doesn't look happy.'

'Ignore him. He reckoned we shouldn't have come to the funeral. Thinks we're nuts.'

Behind Ben, Nial and Peter's Glastonbury vans were parked. Peter had got into his and now Nial was unlocking the side door of his and pulling it back to let in some cooler air. In the days since the inquest Nial had painted yellow flowers and skulls on it. He'd stencilled a line around the middle, a Plimsoll line in pale blue, with the words 'Projected Glasto mud level 2011'.

'They're going to Glastonbury tonight,' Steve told Zoë. 'Sleeping in the van for three days. Nice.'

'The Pilton mudbath? Oh, Christ, I feel so jealous. You're happy to let her go? After everything?'

Sally watched Millie lean into the cab of Nial's camper and attach something – a charm or a ribbon – to the mirror. She saw Nial loosen his tie – he still had a brownish mark on the side of his face where he'd scraped it in the tumble down the cliff. Both of them looked awkward and wrong in their formal outfits – a white blouse and black skirt for Millie, bare legs in black pumps, which looked vulnerable and out of place, Nial in a suit that was a little short in the legs, his hands dangling out of the sleeves. He

539

was growing into himself, just as Sally had known he would eventually. There'd been story after story about him in the papers. Nial – little Nial, suddenly pushed into the shoes of the hero – leading Kelvin to Pollock's Farm away from Millie, whom he'd hidden in the camper-van. The tarot had been wrong that Millie was going to die. A warning, of Kelvin and what was to come, but not a warning of death. 'I'm not worried.' Sally smiled. 'She'll be all right with Nial.'

'He's totally in love with her,' Steve said.

Zoë laughed. 'He might be in love with her, but what about Millie? Has it worked? He's a hero now – is she in love with him?'

'No.' Sally sighed. 'Of course not. Poor Nial.'

'No?'

'It's Peter. It's always been Peter.'

Zoë narrowed her eyes at Peter, who was sitting in his van fastening his seatbelt. 'That waste of space? I never liked him, not from the moment I set eyes on him – he's too full of himself.'

'I know. He's split up from Sophie now, though, so you never know.' She shook her head. 'One day Millie'll look back and see what she missed in Nial. I just hope it's not too late.'

Sally meant it. She was sure Nial was the right one for Millie. It wasn't just the heroics of the night, it was something that had happened the day Nial was released from the hospital. He and Millie had come to Sally with serious faces and told her a different version of the events at Pollock's Farm. Even now she was still turning this new version round and round in her head, trying to decide where to put it, what to think of it, whether she should be angry with them. They had told her that, coming home from school the previous night, Millie had been terrified about what Sally might be doing and whether she was going to confront Kelvin. They both knew what he was capable of, so Nial had taken the situation in hand.

Kelvin hadn't followed Millie out to Pollock's Farm at all. In fact, quite the opposite. He'd been lured there by Nial, who had decided, as part of his heroic fantasy, that he was going to take Kelvin on. Fight him face to face like a man. Millie hadn't known anything about it, Nial insisted valiantly, until at the very last minute. All she knew was that twenty minutes after they'd got home Nial had stepped outside to make a private call. Minutes later he'd come hurrying back inside, telling her to hide quickly in the Glasto van. Of course he hadn't foreseen the awful outcome, the long, clumsy chase that had taken them over the edge of the cliff. He'd only done it because, above everything, he and Millie had wanted to protect her, Sally.

She'd smiled quizzically at him when he said that, flattered, but puzzled. She wondered why anyone would ever want to protect her. She felt like a lion. She didn't think she'd ever need protecting again. She thought life was very wild, and weird, and wonderful.

'Zoë,' she said now, 'do you think it's OK to do the wrong thing for the right reason?'

Her sister put her head back and roared with laughter. 'Good God! What do you think I think?'

'But what about the pattern?'

Zoë smiled and let her eyes wander over to Ben's car. 'The pattern?' she said softly. 'Oh, that always works itself out in the end.'

Sally smiled at that, and blushed, and looked down at Steve's hands, linked across her lap. She thought about the three of them, she and Zoë and Millie, locked for ever to one person by a secret. For Zoë it was Ben and for her it was Steve. And that was OK. They were the people they wanted to be locked to. But for Millie . . . ?

Well, for Millie it would happen eventually. One day she'd look at Nial and know she'd met the one.

3

As soon as Zoë got into the car she saw that Sally had been right: Ben really was in a mood. His expression was solemn. Guarded.

'What?' She buckled the seat-belt and glared at him. 'Because I went to his funeral? Well, I know why now. We wanted to show strength, not cowardice, like he did. Is that a sin?'

He took off the sunglasses and started the car. 'It's not that.' He checked the rear-view mirror and pulled out of the parking space. 'Not that at all.'

'Then what? For Christ's sake.'

'We've got to talk. About all of this.' He waved a hand behind him to indicate the church. 'Something's gone seriously awry.'

Zoë stared at him. She could feel a pulse ticking in her temple. 'Awry?' she said carefully. 'What does "awry" mean?'

'I've been going through the stuff from Kelvin's place. We weren't just looking for things to connect him to Lorne, we were looking to see if he had anything to do with David Goldrab's disappearance.'

'I know.'

'It would be such a lovely tick in the box on our clear-up rates.'

'Did you find anything?'

'Not what we expected. We found something that turned everything around.'

'What? What have you found? Something I left? My phone?'

'Not a trace of you. No, we found something that . . .' he moved his jaw from side to side, grinding his teeth '. . . something that just doesn't make sense. However I look at it.'

4

Sally stood next to the window in the utility room at Peppercorn Cottage, washing a lace blouse in the sink, her eyes raised to the perfect blue sky, criss-crossed with vapour trails. The awful silences that had gathered around Peppercorn after David's death had gone and now it felt like a proper home. Steve was in the garage, hammering back some weather-boarding that had come loose. Next to the garage Nial and Millie were swarming around the VW camper-van, piling things into it. A cooler that Nial had adapted to run from the cigarette-lighter socket was stuffed with beer – no food or anything of any nutritional value as far as Sally could tell. There were rolls of bedding and Millie's dresses arranged on hangers in the windows. She was already frantic – Nial had accidentally dropped her mobile phone into the washing-up bowl: it now lay in pieces on the dashboard, drying off in the sun with two of her blouses, a pair of denim shorts and some underwear that hadn't come out of the wash in time.

'You just don't get it, Mum. If we don't get there

like *radically* early we're so stuffed. The best pitches go in the first ten minutes – even in the camper-van fields. Honestly, we should have packed before the funeral. Peter and his brother's mates will already be there.'

Sally gently wrung out the blouse and hung it up in the window, where it would catch the rest of the day's heat. Outside, the yellow smudges of kerria and forsythia had long gone, and now the thick, heady summer blooms were beginning, delphiniums and poppies, bees swarming around them. Millie passed the window on the way to the van, arms full of clothes, and stuck her tongue out at her mother. Sally smiled. How incredible, when all along she thought she was the one protecting them, that *they*'d been protecting *her*. Nial put some music on the van's sound system – Florence and the Machine – making the van shake. Not kids any more. No – they were adults.

She straightened the cuffs on the blouse. She'd wear it tonight and let Steve take it off her. They were going out to dinner. They would talk for hours. They'd get silly drunk. She'd tell him about the job she'd been offered by the hippies who'd bought her tarot cards – chief designer for a whole new product line they were launching. He'd tell her he loved her, and, maybe for the hundredth time, he'd make her a promise she didn't want to accept. He'd say that if anything about David Goldrab ever came out, he was going to take the blame. He kept saying over and over again that he'd made the decision and that, if it came to it, Sally's name was never going to be mentioned.

5

Ben drove Zoë home in silence. He wouldn't say any more until he had her in the living room and had closed the doors. She half expected him to close the curtains too, he was in such a sombre, secretive mood.

'What did you find? Something to do with Goldrab?'

'Sit down.'

Shit, she thought. Sally had been right. Kelvin *had* taken photos of her that night.

'Ben – just tell me. What have you found? Is it Goldrab?'

'There was a contract out on Goldrab – you knew that. The SIB have taken Mooney in. He's not talking.'

'And?'

'We found Goldrab's teeth – buried in Kelvin's back garden.'

She let her breath out. 'OK,' she said cautiously. 'So it was Kelvin, then, who killed Goldrab?'

'Looks like it. But that's not what's worrying me.

It's something else. What happened was that while we were searching we found a bunch of paperwork. I've been going through it all this week. And now . . .'

'Now what?'

'I've decided he didn't kill Lorne.'

She gaped at him. 'Didn't *kill* her?'

'Or rape her.'

'Jesus. What the hell did you find?'

'OK, OK. Listen. He did what he did to you and, Zoë, that was the worst thing I could imagine happening. Ever. I still don't know how I'm supposed to be about it – and I still don't know what it's doing to you. Not exactly. But I've got to look past all that. Because none of it means he raped Lorne too.'

'Hang on – what about all the things you found at his house? Her fleece. Her mobile phone.'

'That was what really got me thinking. He'd gone to a lot of trouble hiding any evidence that you'd been there – there wasn't a trace of you. So why didn't he get rid of Lorne's phone too? The lipstick?'

Zoë shook her head, mystified.

'I'll tell you why. It's simple. He didn't hide it because *he didn't know it was there . . .*'

'*What?*'

'Look. After he got caught up with the accident those bomb-disposal guys had in Basra, the work they had to do to put him back together again was awesome. He spent three months in the Selly Oak military hospital in Birmingham while they stabilized him, then another two months recovering from a cranioplasty. They put a titanium plate in his skull, but it was causing him trouble. On the seventh of May he was having a scan to see what was wrong.'

Zoë frowned. She wasn't getting it.

'Lorne was killed while he was in hospital. I've checked. I've seen the admission records, I've spoken to the staff who were on duty. It's solid, Zoë, solid. Kelvin Burford was in the hospital all of the seventh and on to the eighth. Under sedation. He could not have killed Lorne Wood.'

She sat down abruptly. Her head was buzzing. 'But . . .' she began. 'But . . .'

'I know. It was easy to jump to conclusions.'

Easy to jump to conclusions . . . At those words something dark and nasty skittered across Zoë's head. Something that had been waiting there since the day Kelvin had attacked her, something she'd avoided all along. She remembered lying on the bed at Kelvin's. Remembered saying, 'Just do it. I want you to.' All those years ago when Kelvin had watched her from the shadows at the back of the club, she'd known what he'd wanted. And lying on the bed that day, she'd told him he could. If she was totally clear-eyed about it, totally honest and rational, he'd only done what she'd asked him to do. He'd battered her. Brutalized her. But the rest? Was it rape? Technically?

'No,' she murmured, almost inaudibly, 'he killed Lorne. He had to have.'

Ben held her eyes solemnly. 'I know you think all I do is go around looking for miscarriages of justice. But, Zoë, rapist and all-round shit though Kelvin was, I think he was set up. I've got something to show you. Wait there.'

He went into the kitchen. Started opening cupboards. She stared numbly at the open doorway, letting it all filter through her. Kelvin in hospital the night of the rape? Someone else in the frame?

Ben reappeared in the doorway, holding a bundle of papers in a blue plastic wallet. 'The analysis of Lorne's phone. And some photos.'

He sat next to her and began to pull out the sheets – page after page of request forms and data-protection forms from the Intelligence Bureau to the phone company. He got to a separate folder. Hesitated. 'Not nice, this part.'

'Fuck off, Ben, I'm a police officer too.'

He shrugged and pulled out the photos. Four of them. They showed Lorne splayed out on the ground in the nettles. In the first she was alive, her eyes on the person taking the photo. She was holding out her hand, a universal pleading gesture. Tears ran down the sides of her face and her nose was thick and crusted with blood. In the second picture she was still alive, but the silver gaffer tape holding the ball in her mouth was there, and her expression had changed utterly. In this one she knew she was dying.

'These were taken on her own phone. He didn't even bother to hide them. But . . .' Ben shuffled the papers '. . . something *was* hidden on the phone. You've heard of data-recovery software? The boys in High Tech use it to find all the kiddie-porn the perverts think they've got rid of by hitting *Delete*. We used it on the phone. Didn't find much that had been hidden. Except three texts that had been deleted the morning after she died.'

He held out the paper to Zoë, pointed to the places that had been highlighted in pink. She read: Hi L. Good 2 cu 2day. U looked hot. Spk soon

Then, lower down: don't u fucking bother to acknowledge ur mates any more? I'm not a rapist u know - grin - not going to lay a hand on u. U looked lovely. i think u r lovely i love u. 4 true

And on the last page: This is pain like I never knew you give me pain babe. Don't ever think it isn't true

'These were deleted?'

'Yes. Nothing exactly incriminating in them, is there? Apart from the fact they were deleted. Which kind of puts a red light over them.'

Zoë couldn't drag her eyes away from the photo of Lorne looking into the camera. Her expression looked as if she still wasn't sure whether this was a joke or not. As if she was thinking, *He's not serious. He's going to stop it and let me go.*

'You think this person – the text person—'

'He set Kelvin up. Planted the fleece, the phone and the earring at his house. Probably cannot believe his luck that Kelvin's dead – that he's not around to deny it all.'

'Is there a name?' She shuffled through the pages. 'He doesn't sign the texts. Is there a name?'

'A number – look here.' He put a finger on a number that had been highlighted in green. 'But no name. The computer geeks think the address list was copied over – nothing they can do to recover it.'

Zoë pushed the papers aside. She put her hands to her temples, thinking hard. The words Kelvin had said when he found her in his house came back: *Don't think you'll get away with this again.* As if he'd known someone had broken into his house before her. Damn it all to hell, why hadn't she thought of all this before? Someone else out there? Someone who had done this unspeakable thing to Lorne? And Kelvin just set up? Kelvin just the lout, the one capable of assault and battery, maybe, of doing what he'd done to her, but not capable of killing a teenage girl?

'OK,' she said, after a while. 'We dial it.'

Ben smiled. 'I love you. Here's the phone.'

She took it from him, set it to speaker, tapped in *67 to block her phone from registering on caller ID, then dialled the number. She gazed out of the window as the call connected. There was a line of puffy clouds moving across the horizon above Bath. A pigeon sat on the window-ledge, watching her beadily. The phone rang and rang in the silence. They were just starting to expect an answerphone message when the phone clicked and a voice said, 'Hello?'

Ben held a finger to his lips, but Zoë cancelled the call and sat back, dropping the phone on the table with a clatter. She was cold. So cold she was shaking. She'd been wrong. All along she had been wrong and Debbie and Ben had been right.

'Why did you do that?' Ben said, standing up.

'Why the hell did you hang up? He might never answer again.'

'We don't need to call again. I know whose voice that was.'

6

Sally was helping Millie sort out the containers of juice and crisps and the hopeful bags of fruit she'd insisted on putting in. They got the picnic hamper half into the camper, then found it wouldn't go any further. Sally looked to the front of the van for Nial to help. He was at the offside wheel, prodding the tyre with his foot, his phone up to his ear.

'Hello?' He went to the driver's seat and leaned inside to turn off the music. 'Hello?' he said into the phone.

'Who is it?' called Millie. 'Peter?'

'I don't know.' Nial gave the screen a look. He switched the phone off and put it in the back pocket of his jeans.

'Nial?' Sally said. 'Any chance you could help us back here . . . ?'

He came round to them, took the hamper and gave it a good shove inside. Then the three of them piled all the sleeping bags and cagoules on top of it. Nial slammed the door and smiled. 'I suppose that's us, then.'

'Wait.' Sally fished in the pocket of her cardigan

and pulled out a pack of cards. 'Since you're going to be hippies for the whole weekend, I thought you might like these.'

Millie swooped on them. 'Your *tarots*? Mum – you can't. They took ages.'

'It's OK. My new company have copies of them. In fact, next year you might even see them on the stalls at Glasto. Please.' She pushed them at her. 'I want you to have them. Enjoy them.'

'Oh, *Mum*. Mum!' Millie jumped up and down like a three-year-old. She tipped them out of the box and began shuffling through them, holding them out for Nial to see. 'Do you remember these? Look – there's me. The Princess of Wands.'

'What happened to it?' Nial frowned at the card. 'Her face is ruined.'

Sally smiled, thinking of how scared that image had made her when she'd first seen it. She'd painted a new card for the printers, but she hadn't got rid of the original. It had no power over her now. 'I don't know. It's nothing. There are others of her.'

'The Magus and the Priestess.' Millie was still happily flicking through the cards. 'And – oh, my God, that's Dad, isn't it? Dad, and – *bleck* – Melissa. And Sophie, and Pete. And look – here's you, Nial.'

Nial took the card from her and studied it.

'Do you like it?' Sally asked.

'It's great.' He turned the card to the light and inspected it, looked at the places the pegs had left a mark where it had been hung up to dry. 'The Prince of Swords. What does it mean?'

'It means clever,' said Millie.

'And intelligent,' Sally added.

'Except,' Millie said, 'if you turn it upside down it means treacherous and untrustworthy. The trickster.' She laughed the open-mouthed little-kid's laugh she still hadn't ironed out, no matter how cool she tried to be. 'See? Mum, you always had Nial sussed. The trickster.'

'That's me,' Nial said, handing back the two cards. 'The trickster.'

Millie pushed all the cards back into their box and put them on the dashboard. In the house the phone was ringing.

'Aren't you going to get that?' Nial said. 'Cos we've got to go. Got to get that space. The ravers, they are a-coming.'

'I'll get it later – they can leave a message.'

Nial got into the van and put the key in the ignition. Millie clambered into the passenger seat next to him. She'd found a ridiculous Stetson somewhere and now she opened the window and waved it out. 'Yee-hah, Mum. Yee-hah.'

Sally shook her head, half smiling. She stood next to the window, looking at Nial. He was wearing one of his faded seventies band T-shirts. Baggy shorts. His legs were already tanned. She could smell the freshly cleaned clothes, and the not-so-fresh sleeping bags all tumbled into the back. She could smell the sandwiches they'd packed for lunch and she could smell their skin. She felt jealous. Just for a moment.

'You know something, Mrs Cassidy?' he said.

'No.' She smiled. 'What?'

'I don't know if I'll ever let you get away with it.'

Sally's smiled faded. The words had cut her dead. And there was something ugly in Nial's face. 'I beg your pardon?'

'I said,' he spoke slowly, enunciating every word as if she was stupid, 'I'll never let you get away with making it so difficult. For me to take Millie to Glasto.'

There was a long, uncomfortable pause. They stood, eyes locked. Then, like the sun breaking through the clouds, he smiled. Laughed. 'I mean, I really won't. I never thought you'd let me.'

Sally hesitated. She looked at Millie, who had stopped waving the hat and was sitting scowling at her hands. Feeling a little stupid, a little confused, Sally forced a laugh. 'Well, you'll have to promise to take some photos of her.'

'I will.' Nial put his hand on hers. 'I'll send them to you on the phone. They'll be the best you've ever seen.' He leaned over and kissed her cheek.

This time Sally smiled for real. She held his face as he pulled away. 'Thank you,' she said warmly. 'Look after her.'

'I will.'

Sally walked around the front of the camper-van as Nial started it up. She leaned in the window and kissed Millie on the cheek.

'Yeah, OK, Mum,' Millie said, rolling her eyes. 'Respect the makeup.' She pulled down the sun visor. Checked the mirror and rubbed the place she'd been kissed. Then, in a sudden rush, she leaned out of the window and threw her arms round Sally's neck. 'I love you, Mum. I love you.'

'I love you too. You're going to have the best time. The time of your life. Never forget it.'

Nial revved the van. Sally stepped back. A plume of smoke came out of the exhaust pipe. Steve came out of the garage and stood, his arm around Sally, to wave the teenagers goodbye. The van jolted once, then the tyres bit and off it went, out of the driveway, past the hedgerow where the first tea roses were coming out. Millie stuck her arm out of the window. It was long and slender. By the time she got back from Glastonbury it would be burned to a crisp, Sally thought, folding her arms. That suntan lotion would stay in the rucksack.

Steve put his arm round her. 'See?' he said. 'Didn't I say it would all work itself out in the end?' He kissed the top of her head, and murmured into her hair, 'I told you there'd be no punishment.'

The van turned left. Not right, the way she would have gone. 'You'll never get to Glastonbury that way,' she wanted to shout. And then she caught herself: trying to interfere. She had to smile. Leave them alone, she thought, dropping her head against Steve's chest as the van disappeared over the hill, going in completely the wrong direction, the strains of Florence and the Machine fading until there was nothing but birdsong left in the garden. You just can't go on worrying about your children for ever.

Acknowledgements

Years ago Transworld Publishers went to great lengths to assure me they were a happy, committed company, faithful to their authors and readers – with the love of reading firmly rooted in their ethos. At the time, if I am honest, I suspected it was a lot of puff to impress me, and I didn't believe a word of it. Over the years they have proved me wrong – one hundred per cent wrong – and for that I'd like to thank everyone there: Selina, Larry, Alison, Claire, Katrina, Diana, Janine, Nick, Elspeth, Sarah, Martin (the list goes on).

Jane Gregory is my agent and my rock and how can you express your gratitude to someone who is always there when the world threatens to crumble (which it does frequently, believe me)? The same goes for everyone in her team – Claire, Stephanie, Terry and Virginia.

The following allowed me glimpses into their worlds and without those glimpses I couldn't have done justice to some of the scenes: Alex 'Billy'

Hamilton talked me through a lot of the super-sleuthy telephony stuff and Colonel Len Wassell, Deputy Provost Marshal, RMP, gave me huge insight into the workings of the Special Investigations Branch. Others who helped were Corporal Kirsten Gunn (Signals Regiment), Dr Hugh White (HM pathologist) and Jeremy White. A little thank you to the Green and Black's gang, especially Sarah and Michael for letting me borrow Peppercorn Cottage as a name, and Marc Birch for gleefully painting all those lurid gamekeeper stories. Also Hazel Orme and Steve Bennett – two people who never ask for or expect thanks and praise, but absolutely deserve it.

A big apology goes to the City of Bath for playing merry havoc with your geography – intertwining Hanging Hill and Freezing Hill. Bath, you are old and wise, and I believe you will forgive me.

Above all, a little whisper of gratitude and affection to my family, my amazing, patient friends and, last but certainly not least, Bob Randall for his continuing help, support and miraculous, inexplicable faith in me.